STARSHIP STANDOFF

"Procyon ship, this is Captain Rieka Degahv of the C.F.S. *Venture*. You have been identified as the *Vendikon*. You do not have clearance to enter Commonwealth space. Turn back immediately. I repeat, leave this star system immediately or I will be forced to take military action. This is my final warning."

"No change in course or speed, Captain," the helmsman said.

Thoroughly annoyed with the situation, Rieka rapped her fist on the arm of her command chair and looked at her executive officer. "Then I think it's about time for a bit of nonverbal communicating. Power up the main antimatter battery."

CUTTING EDGE SCI-FI NOVELS

JAN CLARK

PRODIGY

A ROC BOOK

ROC
Published by the Penguin Group
Penguin Books USA Inc., 375 Hudson Street,
New York, New York 10014, U.S.A.
Penguin Books Ltd, 27 Wrights Lane,
London W8 5TZ, England
Penguin Books Australia Ltd, Ringwood,
Victoria, Australia
Penguin Books Canada Ltd, 10 Alcorn Avenue,
Toronto, Ontario, Canada M4V 3B2
Penguin Books (N.Z.) Ltd, 182–190 Wairau Road,
Auckland 10, New Zealand

Penguin Books Ltd, Registered Offices:
Harmondsworth, Middlesex, England

First published by Roc, an imprint of Dutton Signet,
a division of Penguin Books USA Inc.

First Printing, September, 1997
10 9 8 7 6 5 4 3 2 1

I would like to thank the following people for their help and support. Without you, this book would still reside only in my slightly warped and extremely vivid imagination. I hope I can one day return the favor.

Bunnie Bessel, C. J. Brown, Jan Christensen, John Clark, Mark Noe, and Jonathan Shipley.

One

"Thirty thousand kilometers and closing."

Captain Rieka Degahv shifted uncomfortably in her seat, her attention fixed on the yellow blip representing the invading vessel. The Dimensional Graphics Imager provided her with a stunning three-dimensional enhanced picture of space, but the ship was still too far to see.

The dot moved again. Her jaw muscles tightened.

They'd tracked the unwelcome blip for almost half an hour. She sensed the tension in her crew and knew they were waiting for her to make an error in judgment. To slip. To fail.

She glanced to her left at the communications officer. "Warn them off again."

"Right away." Plemik looked at her, his pale pink Aurian eyes openly questioning her ability to cope with the intruders, then repeated the signal.

"Still coming," the helmsman reported. "Now twenty thousand to the line."

The line he referred to was the ten-AU radius from the nearest Commonwealth star, Eta Cass. They'd been delivering a shipment to the colony on Groot when she'd received news of the Procyon's approach. From that moment to this, Rieka silently prayed the unmanned station's warning signal had been nothing more than an elaborate joke.

She could endure playing the fool. She had before. But playing at politics made her uneasy, as if she had to lie to get what she wanted. Rieka refused to admit she and the *Venture* could not cope with their increasingly difficult assignments. Until now, she had managed to meet her schedule with few delays. In the last several months, however, her orders had often put her in a position to err, or to face situations a captain had no business facing.

And now, this.

Her stomach churned. She folded an arm over it and continued to concentrate on the visual display. "What are they doing?" she wondered aloud.

Plemik, an Aurian who couldn't control the color of his bibbets to save his life, looked at her again. The row of raised bumps just below his hairline had darkened from pink to rose, almost matching the shade of his eyes.

Rieka pretended to ignore his silent affront, hoping he wouldn't notice her own angry blush. She didn't need this infantile behavior from her junior officers. Especially now. No one had crossed paths with a Procyon vessel in almost five years.

It didn't help that Admiral Bittin, chief of Internal Affairs, had dispatched that curious communiqué notifying her to expect Procyon contact at Eta Cass. He'd actually told her to destroy them.

Clearly, there must have been some prior discussion between him and the Procyons. Aside from that, the absence of any reason for the order created yet another problem. His instructions directly opposed the ethics inherent in the Command Oath, forcing her to choose one over the other.

Herring, the fair-haired Centauri navigator, manually adjusted the DGI's magnification. The blip disappeared. The Procyons had come close enough for a long-range visual.

That rankled, too. Standard procedure called for a detailed examination of the ship's interior by three separate systems. Unfortunately, most of the *Venture*'s sensory equipment had been off-line since yesterday.

Her tech-pros had not yet determined what caused the fire. The DGI image was all they had.

Rieka leaned her forehead into her hand and massaged her brow. At the moment, they had no way of determining the number of Procyons aboard, if the ship carried weapons, or if, due to some technical reason, they were unable to respond.

There was no point in contacting headquarters, either. The swiftest reply would come days from now. The situation called for a Human's intuition. She wasn't sure if she dared rely on hers.

"On the line," Herring announced.

She slid a glance to her executive officer, Midrin Tohab, the Indran-born Centauri seated to her immediate left. The blond woman's expression seemed almost enrapt as she followed the alien ship's path. Rieka watched Tohab and felt the knot twist in the pit of her stomach. Centauris, especially those from the planet Indra, took great pride in remaining professionally detached. Right now, Midrin looked anything but. She'd begun to fidget in her seat, clearly excited about this unwelcome turn of events.

Rieka dismissed the odd reaction and concentrated on the current problem. Her executive officer's opinion and friendship were things she valued. Tohab had never tried to discredit her or usurp her authority. "We've gone by the book so far, Midrin," she said softly.

Tohab's tight-lipped nod was slight. She lost the glassy-eyed stare as she pulled her attention from the DGI. "Not much on the record with regard to etiquette in this situation, Captain."

For some reason the reply irritated Rieka. It wasn't like Tohab to be so ambiguous. "Reestablish audio-video, Plemik."

"As we speak," he replied.

Rieka straightened her shoulders. She glanced at the three silver bands running down the sleeve of her blue-and-rust uniform, wondering if the Procyons recognized her authority. She waited for her armrest console to illuminate in the proper quadrant, then looked directly into the holographic camera above the DGI's display.

"Procyon ship, this is Captain Degahv of the C.F.S. *Venture*. You have been identified as the *Vendikon*. You do not have clearance to enter Commonwealth space. Turn back immediately. I repeat, leave this system immediately, or I will be forced to take military action. This is my final warning."

"No change in course or speed, Captain," the helmsman said.

Thoroughly annoyed with the situation, Rieka rapped her fist on the arm of her chair and again looked at her EO. "Then I think it's about time for a bit of non-verbal communicating. Do you agree?"

Tohab nodded.

"Power up the main antimatter battery," Rieka ordered, glancing to her right. The broad back of Lieutenant Berk, in charge of weapons and security, tensed as he followed her command. He was the only other Human on the bridge, the only one who could empathize with the difficulty of her decision.

"Power up the insulation and repulsion screens, too, Berk," she added.

He swiveled to look her in the eye, then nodded. "System's ready, Captain."

She treated him to a small smile. "Their position, Herring?"

"Eighteen thousand kilometers over the line, Captain."

Rieka inhaled, exhaled, and tried not to think about what could go wrong. In her entire career, the only shots she'd ever fired had been during simulations. She found it strange that, at this moment, she felt completely detached from the commands she'd ordered, as if this reality was just another fabricated exercise.

The knot in her gut suggested otherwise. It seemed Admiral Bittin might get what he wanted. "A warning shot off their bow. One sphere."

"As we speak," answered Berk.

She watched the antimatter sphere sail past the *Vendikon*. The ship's trajectory and speed did not change.

"Line up two more and close the margin," she said, relieved that the decision was no longer before her. She preferred to be committed to an action rather than bogged down by the tedium of thinking it through. Triscoe Marteen had once teased her about it, telling her Humans preferred deed to thought.

"Fire when ready, Berk," she said.

"They're away, Captain."

Still, the mysterious ship continued.

Rieka sighed. She could not allow Procyons to enter the Eta Cass system. The member world, Medoura, and the colony world, Groot, paid for the Fleet's protection. There had to be some way to force them to return to unclaimed space. She gnawed on the inside of her lip. If only Admiral Bittin hadn't insisted she destroy the ship, this would not be the complicated mess it had become.

But he had, damn him. And he'd sent the message knowing there wouldn't be time to contact Admiral Nason. That fact alone made her resist the order. Instead of destroying them at their approach, she had followed procedure. It should have worked. But the Procyons had now breached both treaty and territorial space, forcing her to act.

Although obligated to follow a direct order, Rieka knew she could not arbitrarily take a life. She found some comfort in the fact that Admiral Bittin's department was Internal Affairs. By issuing an order directly to her, he'd undercut Admiral Nason's authority. Since the intruders were now within the ETA Cass system's recognized space, she decided to accept Bittin's wrath and follow Nason's standing orders.

Sitting straight, Rieka glanced at her EO. "We can't destroy them. They've given us no cause for such—"

"They are in the system, Captain," Tohab countered. "That is considered a hostile act."

"We've fired at them, not the other way around, Commander."

"True. But did you not tell me that Admiral Bittin—"

"The admiral is overstepping his jurisdiction," Rieka snapped, and immediately regretted allowing her emotions to show. She took a breath and tried again. "We take orders from Nason. This isn't some kind of test of loyalty, Midrin. Lives are involved."

"Yes. Ours—and those of the colonists on Groot—and the people on Medoura."

Rieka shook her head. She wanted to argue the point, but not in front of the crew. Never that. "I disagree," she said simply. "And, fortunately, my decision stands. We're still a good distance from Groot. There's more than a chance we can sort this out without killing anyone."

She noticed Berk trying not to smile. "A single sphere, minimum charge," she told him. "Aim for the propulsion reactors. Maybe we can just put it out of commission."

He nodded and turned to his console to relay her orders.

"Fire when ready."

"Sphere's away, Captain."

The bridge crew watched, transfixed, as the bright red dot of shimmering energy sped toward the *Vendikon*. The shell made contact with the propulsion drive, touching off the tiny amount of antimatter contained within the magnetic sphere. The consequent explosion sent arcs of light across the little ship. For a moment, it looked as though it were cringing. The running lights on its wedge-shaped hull flickered, then went out.

"Hail them again, Plemik."

"No response, Captain."

"Fine," she muttered. Though the trip would take years, their present trajectory sent them well into the

Eta Cass system. Tohab had been right about one thing: the Procyons could not remain in the Commonwealth.

But the *Venture* wasn't equipped to move objects in space—at least not something that big. Still, she knew there had to be some way to get the *Vendikon* out of her jurisdiction. Creativity being her strong suit, Rieka considered a solution, then looked at her helmsman. "Herring, let's give them a tug in the right direction, shall we?"

"Captain?"

"Put us close enough to the *Vendikon* so that it's directly below and equidistant to our gravity well. Once they're caught, swing around 180 degrees. We'll pull the Procyons out of the system and into a twenty-AU orbit of Eta Cass, then break off quickly so that we lose all gravitational influence. That should solve the problem for now." She turned to her EO. "Do you agree?"

Tohab shrugged a shoulder. "As long as it puts them past the line."

"Do it, Lieutenant."

Herring nodded, grinning. "Yes, ma'am." The sound of his voice rang with approval. He seemed surprised at her ingenuity.

"Clever," Tohab admitted.

Rieka said nothing. She would not allow herself to. The only thing a Human could do that was worse than making a mistake was to gloat over an achievement. Besides, she couldn't take credit for the novel solution to their problem. That posthumous honor went to her father. Trying to explain the unseen force a magnet produced, he'd put one on a table and used it to lead a paper clip around in a circle. Rieka smiled at the recollection and watched as Herring performed the maneuver, effectively turning the Procyon ship around and taking it out of the system.

This way, she would not be condemning them to the vast emptiness of interstellar space, simply a huge orbit that could be tracked. When she reported the incident to Fleet Headquarters, someone else would be assigned to deal with them. Admiral Bittin would not be happy, but even if he brought charges of insubordination, Rieka knew Admiral Nason would support and, if need be, defend her.

She gave the thought of Bittin's ire another moment of serious consideration, then dismissed it. Worrying wouldn't help. She eased back into her chair and let her mind wander as she watched the DGI.

I've got to tell Triscoe about this, she thought, trying to predict the big Centaurian's response. She imagined that contagious laugh of his—at the way she'd got the ship turned around—and realized she was smiling.

The expression left her face when the *Vendikon,* now at the fringe of visual range, erupted into a ball of immense energy and disappeared.

Triscoe hurried through the door to his quarters and sat at his desk computer. He switched it on and watched it change from black to green. "Request communiqué from Robet DeVark."

"Identify, please," the computer replied.

"C.F.S. *Providence* captain, Triscoe Marteen."

A panel above the screen lit and passed a bead of light across his face. It swept over oak-colored skin, wide cheekbones, and a pair of deep brown eyes. He forced himself not to blink as it penetrated his pupils to scan the schemonic nerves. "Identity confirmed," the synthetic voice replied.

A moment passed as the message decoded and Triscoe took the time to wonder why Robet had gone to such lengths to send him the latest gossip. He'd sent it Code Three, forcing Triscoe to leave the bridge in order to watch it. Robet had a flair for the dramatic, as most Aurians did, that would someday get him into trouble. As an Indran-born Centauri, Triscoe felt both confident and thankful he'd never have that problem.

"Tris!" The square-faced captain's likeness sprang from the flat graphics screen and appeared in three dimensions. Fiery red hair was swept back from the row of bibbets on his forehead. The pale complexion looked flushed. Something profound had taken place, and Robet had probably compromised several security regulations just to be the first to tell him.

"It's Rieka," Robet continued, his pale eyes opening wide. "She's under arrest! For treason!"

Triscoe sat straighter at the outrageous statement. "That's impossible," he said softly, then watched DeVark's image seem to stumble over what else he had to say. How could Robet believe such foolishness? Worse, why would he risk fines or demerits by communicating such tripe over restricted channels?

"I'm having trouble accepting it. But it's true. Believe me," the Aurian managed, finally. His expression was intense, and Triscoe recognized the seriousness in his voice.

"She was at Eta Cass—making a scheduled delivery at Groot—when a Procyon ship called the *Vendikon* entered the system," DeVark explained, his jaw flexing from side to side as it did when he was agitated. "Her orders, as far as I've been able to dig up from Nason and the news channels, were to rendezvous with the ship and escort it to Council Headquarters at Yadra. There was supposed to be a special envoy aboard who was bringing a document of some kind to the president."

Triscoe absorbed the information and watched, fascinated, as DeVark pressed his lips together for a moment, then said, "She used her antimatter battery to destroy the ship, Tris. One sphere, and she signed her own death warrant."

When Robet allowed his bibbets to color, Triscoe felt a cold shiver pass through him. Robet's concern could not be questioned. This wasn't gossip. It was fact. Dumbfounded, Triscoe let the recording continue, hoping Robet would provide him with some clue as to how they could help her.

"I'm on Yadra right now," he continued. "The

Prospectus had been fitted with some test equipment that Nason wanted to have a look at, himself, before we start a field analysis." He shrugged. "I know how you feel about these calls, Triscoe, but it's all over the planetary news. I figured I'd better tell you before the grapevine did. It's the worst thing I've ever seen."

He stopped and seemed to collect himself. The bibbets faded to a pale pink. "They won't let anyone near her—I don't know what to do. I'm shipping out in five days. You're not far, so I'm going to expect some kind of reply." His face split into an innocent-looking grin. "If you happen to drop by Yadra for any reason, page me. That's about it. DeVark out."

The image of his face froze for several seconds before it dissolved. Triscoe stared at the blank screen. He felt detached from his body, as if his mind refused to accept what he'd heard.

"Not Rieka," he whispered. "Not my Rieka."

He leaned back with a sigh. It wasn't hard to understand why Robet had lost control of his bibbets. The three of them shared a unique multirace friendship, and knew one another too well to accept such news at face value. Yet, was there anything either of them could do?

Pacing always helped him think, as if the increased CO_2 flow in his circulatory system caused his brain to work harder. He walked from his sitting room to his bedroom and back, his long legs taking him the distance in only six strides, and considered the excuses he might use to get the *Providence* to Yadra as soon as possible.

On the second lap, Triscoe glanced at the small geode Rieka had given him. It was a piece of Earth, she'd said, like her. She had called the gift, "a remembrance," and he kept it on his bedside table—remembering her often.

He sat on the mattress and picked up the rock. It looked ordinary on the outside, but the cut-away half revealed an inner surface of jutting lavender crystals. How like her, he thought, not for the first time. With an exterior both smooth and rough, but something quite unexpected inside—though not so irrational as to destroy a Procyon ship, in or outside a Commonwealth system.

For over two centuries, various members of Rieka's family had dedicated themselves to the preservation of Earth and the Commonwealth. Her great-great-grandfather had been among the first Humans contacted by the Centauris after the deadly asteroid had struck the Humans' planet. Though the restoration was nearly complete, Earth had been home to only a few natives in all that time.

She would never do anything to taint her name.

He had often tried to understand that one quirk in her character. That sense of Human persecution. Rieka often claimed that because Humans did not live on their own world, the Commonwealth devalued them to something less than equals. The Commonwealth was based on trade. Goods and services. Supply and demand. Humans produced as much as any other race—certainly more than the Lomii, Bourns, and Medourans. Those species were so alien that even physical contact was difficult.

Sweeping his hand through his short-cropped blond hair, Triscoe brought himself back to focus on the problem. Rieka had destroyed a Procyon ship. The idea seemed outrageous. But for her to engage a Procyon vessel when no one had seen them in almost five years meant—what? That she'd been chosen? Set up somehow? Suddenly, Robet's message took on a more sinister feel.

Triscoe set the geode down and twitched the muscles of his left cheek. The tiny instrument in his ear switched on with a click. "Marteen to Aarkmin," he said.

"Aarkmin here, sir," his executive officer's disembodied voice replied. She was Indran, a second-daughter, and had fled the homeworld's matriarchal system to build a base of power on her own. Triscoe found it almost laughable that she had chosen the Fleet, where females were considered equal to males.

"Have V'don send a message to Captain Robet DeVark on Yadra. Tell him I'll page him in twelve hours."

"Yes, sir," she said. "Any particular reason?"

"Of course. And send a second communiqué to Admiral Nason. Tell him we've developed a flux in the ion propulsion curve and Memta is concerned. The base at Dani is too far, at that moment. He'll understand."

"Acknowledged, Captain. Shall I make the necessary course changes?"

"Please. I'll be up in a few minutes. Then, we'll talk."

"I'll look forward to it," she said, and cut the comlink.

Triscoe smiled at her abrasive tone. Being Indran, too, he understood her desire for all the facts, but she would simply have to learn to be slightly less enthusiastic about her job. Nipping at his heels in her zeal for a command of her own was something he wouldn't allow. Triscoe saw a younger version of himself in her and wondered, not for the first time, how he'd ever gotten promoted.

He left that thought, went back to the desk, switched on the computer, and called up as many news stories as he could find. Sure enough, Rieka had become a celebrity of sorts. One report had dubbed her "The Pzekii of the Fleet," another, "Human Hypocrite." He sighed at the slurs, especially the one directed at all Humans, and switched it off.

There was nothing he could do to help her until he reached Yadra.

Two

For what seemed like the thousandth time, Rieka's eyes scanned the cell's grim interior. They'd charged her with treason, and she still couldn't understand why. Sure that she'd done nothing wrong, Rieka couldn't see how the prosecutor thought she could bring the case to trial. But the woman's confident attitude told Rieka she'd not only be placed in front of the tribunal, she'd be found guilty as well.

Had there actually been an emissary aboard, as the woman said? Were the Procyons genuinely offering to communicate for the first time since the ten-week border war five years ago? Or had the ship been rigged to blow and cause an incident? Was the whole thing done purposely to set her up?

Recalling the Aurian prosecutor's stern face, Rieka considered the other aliens she knew. Most were not friends. The *Venture*'s junior officers certainly weren't. They'd corroborated her story, but only to a point. Midrin had known Admiral Bittin sent a communiqué, but she hadn't seen it herself. All any of them knew for sure was that they'd fired on an enemy vessel.

Rieka sat, trying to unravel the puzzle, aware of little more than the hard chair and the camera in the ceiling, when the door opened with a slight whoosh. She heard someone step into the room.

A quick glance told her everything she needed to know. The young Centauri man who had entered wore the blue-and-rust Fleet colors arranged in a businesslike uniform. He carried a datapad. Obviously yet another member of the legal profession.

She pulled herself upright in the chair. "Go away," she ordered. "I've had enough of you people. Your questions, your accusations—and your patronizing looks."

The man simply nodded and crossed the room to put his computer on the table. Ignoring her remark, he smiled and offered his right hand in a typically Human gesture. "I'm your new counsel, Captain Degahv. David Chen."

The hand hung there. "Human?" she asked, looking past it to his face. The eyes were dark, but he had no Oriental features. His skin was incredibly pale and his hair nearly white. The ashen Centauri look had recently become popular with many Humans, she knew. Despite the fact she'd never pay to lighten her skin or hair, Rieka could understand why others did it. Why look Human if you could get more respect looking Centauri? What she couldn't understand was why he'd kept the name.

"Human to the core," Chen replied.

He looked to be in his mid-twenties, more than a recent graduate but far from seasoned. "And you expect me to drag your thus far obviously dismal career—to what, the absolute bottom?"

He treated her to a toothy grin. "Actually, I was hoping to start off my career with a bang."

She stared at him. What she had considered impossible circumstances received new definition. "You've lost already, Chen. Do you know that? You're committing suicide letting them do this to you." Frustrated, she slid the chair back and slapped the table because there was no one else to slap. Poor Chen was just as innocent as she.

"I'm afraid I don't understand, Captain." The hand fell to his side while the confused expression only fueled her anger.

Rieka raked her fingers through her dark hair and

gestured up at the camera. "They're *using* you, Chen. Don't you see that? I'm somebody's scapegoat. I could have been born yesterday, and they'd still try to convict me—and probably succeed. I bet none of the other more experienced people in Legal would even touch this case." She got up and paced between the chair and the table, clenching her fists while trying to smother the need to hit something.

"Captain Degahv, I assure you, every other attorney in Legal is committed."

"To laughing at you," she finished. "Or, more correctly, both of us." She stopped to look into his dark Human eyes. "Look, Chen, I've had three other people from Legal Defense in here. They weren't assigned to me. They were interviewing me—to see whether I was worth it to them to take the case. The Commonwealth Fleet vs. Rieka Degahv, *Human*." She gestured at him. "Since you're here, it's obvious no one wanted me. And let's not even bother bringing up ethics." She leaned over the table. "Is this sinking in at all? You've been had."

To his credit, Chen didn't smile. "Whatever," he said. "I realize you're distraught over what's happened and—"

"Distraught!" Rieka laughed at the look of confusion on his face. "Distraught? Gods, Chen, are you completely naive? Did that surgery wipe your memory, too? Have you no idea what it's like?"

He frowned. "I was simply—"

"To do the best, the absolute *best* you can—and rarely, if ever, be recognized for it?" She jabbed an accusatory finger at him. "And then have it thrown back into your face? To be falsely blamed and have no one believe you? To have all your friends and colleagues turn their backs, when you need them most, and believe filthy *lies*?"

She fought to control herself as she glared at him. He still seemed to be looking at her in that slightly patronizing way, as if, damn him, he'd expected as much.

"If you're through, Captain," he said finally, "might we sit down and talk this out?"

The frown stayed rooted to her face. "Why bother?"

This time he did smile. "Despite the way I look, I know what it's like to be Human, Captain," he offered quietly. "I've gone over your file—the one provided by Admiral Nason—not just the one covering this case. I think you're innocent, and I'd like the chance to prove it."

Stunned, Rieka found herself blinking at the notion. He'd already spoken to Nason? Perhaps David Chen wasn't quite as innocent as he looked. "Fine," she said. The sarcasm was intended for them both. "It's your neck."

"No, Captain," he corrected, "it's yours." Chen held out his hand again, and she took it. The grip was warm and sturdy. He gestured to her chair.

She watched while he sat and picked up his datapad. If he really understood the covert bigotry Humanity suffered, then why had he changed his coloring? To blend in and fight them on their own turf? A grain of hope welled up in Rieka. Maybe she wasn't as alone as she felt.

She shook her head and almost smiled. "You're wrong, Chen. This has to do with a lot more than me."

His attention left the device to look her in the eye. "A lot more," he agreed.

Deciding that there was also a lot more to David Chen than she'd first imagined, Rieka pulled up her chair and sat.

They spent the next hour together, going over the statements she'd already made. Chen tapped additional notations in his datapad and finally excused himself, telling her he would return later. She found it odd that she missed him. His was the only friendly face she'd seen in days.

Rieka was gnawing on her thumb, trying to piece together how, exactly, she'd been framed when the door opened again. "Back so soon? I hadn't—" As she turned and saw him, her tongue switched gears. "I hadn't expected to see you at all, Paden."

Her brother's sickly smile was his only response. He walked around the table, looking her up and down. "You've really done it to yourself this time, Rieka."

She leaned back in her chair and crossed her arms over her chest. The gaudy white-and-gold cape did nothing for his slim shoulders, though it did accentuate his dark skin. She watched as he straightened a large ring over his knuckle. He glanced around the cell and sniffed.

"All right, Paden, what the hell are you doing here?"

"Offering my support," he said seriously.

Rieka knew it was all an act for the camera. "I don't need you, or your kind of support. Please leave."

His expression switched to a grin. He sat down in the other chair and leaned across the table. "I'm not going anywhere, Sis. You've got yourself into real trouble, this time, and it's going to take a lot of favors to get you out of it."

"Quit acting so sincere. You'll make me sick." Unable to sit at the table with him, Rieka got up and leaned against the wall.

"But my baby sister's up on charges of treason," he replied in a sweet voice.

"I've been set up, you worthless excuse for a Human." When he didn't react to the slur, she threw up her hands. "So help me, Paden, if I find out—"

"No." His lips drew taut over his teeth, and Rieka knew the act was over. "You listen, Rieka." Paden stood and moved close enough for her to see the flecks of amber in his green eyes. He put his hands on her shoulders and squeezed. "You've taken this xeno-phobia thing too far, this time. Humans are *not* treated like dirt."

"You have absolutely no idea—"

"Maybe in the Fleet it's a little different," he admitted. "But out in the Commonwealth, in reality, we're just as good as everyone else."

"That's what you want to believe, Paden. So you do."
He shook her. "That's how it *is*!"

She shrugged him off. "You've lived a different life
from me," she reminded him with a sneer. A dozen
years her senior, he'd had every advantage politics
could bring. "Mother *wanted* you."

"You still believe that?" He laughed. "If she hadn't
wanted you, you'd have never been born."

"Father wanted me."

"Oh, yes," he agreed, not even trying to hide his
grin. "The great Herald, Stephen Degahv—the man
who devoted his short life to restoring Earth from the
Great Cataclysm of the twenty-second century. The
one who taught you the basics of paranoia."

She wanted to slap him. To slap that mocking sneer
off his face. Her palm itched with the notion, but Rieka
wouldn't let herself sink to his level. "As assistant to
the Earth Herald, Mother held a seat of power, too,"
she countered. "But she wanted more. After the
divorce, she must have been very angry—angry
enough to turn you against him. Against what he
believed. What he taught me to believe."

He watched her for a long moment. "And just what
was that?"

"That we belong on our own planet. That we must do
everything possible to help it heal so Earth can support
a productive population. So that Humans can have
some meaning in the Commonwealth. So that we can
stop being treated—"

"—like dirt," he finished, the note of sarcasm
obvious. He shook his head. "Rieka, Mother *wanted*
you to stay at the Lemonne estate. Yadra has *always*
been your home. I'll never understand why you can't
see that Humans are just like everyone else."

"Because we aren't. We're all orphans—living our
lives on planets that don't belong to us. You've been
sheltered from the nastiness because of Mother, and
her money. But I lived with Father for most of my life.

I've visited Earth. Maybe it's because of that—that difference—that I can see it."

Paden shook his head. "I came here to help you, but I can see it's a useless effort."

"Help? Your only sister?" She clucked her tongue. "Paden, either you're getting soft in your old age—or there's something in it for you, probably both."

"I am here because I want to be."

"I'm sure you want—something," she replied, glaring at him. When he refused to comment, she added, "I've heard you plan to apply for Earth Herald. Uncle Alexi is retiring in what—six months?"

"So?"

"So . . . having a sister convicted of treason probably wouldn't sit well with the voters. Are you and Mother planning to pay someone off?"

He made a groaning noise, glared at her, and stormed out the door. Rieka silently wished him good riddance. Since the day her father had explained why he'd allowed Candace to divorce him, she'd blamed Paden for her sudden poverty.

Apparently, Mother wanted Paden to be the next Earth Herald—despite the fact that he'd never been to the planet. But such trivialities didn't concern Candace Pirez Degahv. Power did. She'd spent years teaching Paden the nuances of business and politics. And when he became the next Herald, she would be right there whispering in his ear.

Long minutes drifted by. She heard the door open but didn't bother to look at the intruder. Neither the Fleet prosecutor's steely face, nor the troubled expression of her attorney was on her wish list. She was looking for the strength to endure another round of questioning when her name was spoken.

Her head shot up. Her body followed and her throat tightened. "Triscoe! What are you doing here?"

"I thought you might need a friend," he said quietly. The big blond Centauri ambled into the room, the dimple she remembered so well folding into his right cheek. He stood silently, watching her.

Rieka had never been so grateful to see anyone. She felt as if she should say something, but the thoughts came tumbling so fast, none were spoken. Her hands made ineffectual gestures. She tried to smile and put on a brave front but found her face furling into a strange, twisted frown.

"Oh, Tris . . . it's all so . . ." Betraying her completely, her chin began to quiver. Embarrassed, she dropped her eyes. She had not cried in self-pity since she was a child, and she would not allow herself to begin again.

"And, perhaps a shoulder." Triscoe moved toward her, his presence filling the room. He seemed so sure of himself, so sure of her.

Before she realized what had happened, Rieka felt his arms around her. Her ear was pressed into his chest, and she could hear the muffled, steady beat of his heart.

"The last week has been like some kind of bad dream," she said softly. "Everything I've done comes right back in my face."

"I am here, now," he offered, his voice assured. "We'll sort it out."

She hung there for a long moment, absorbing the unexpected comfort. "I didn't do anything wrong, but everything I did was wrong. Except for this new Legal rep, Chen, not a single person has believed me." She tried to forget Paden's visit and squeezed Triscoe tighter for a second. "You're the first friendly face I've seen in at least thirty-six hours. I can't believe you're actually here."

She released him so she could look at his face. "What *are* you doing here? I would have expected to see Robet before you."

Triscoe nodded. "The situation warranted my presence," he said quietly. "They wouldn't grant Robet an audience. I was forced to use my mother's influence to get this far."

Rieka read the seriousness on his face. The dimple was gone, and the furrow stood out between his bushy brows. She sighed. "I had no idea. The defense attorneys have all looked grim—but I figured . . ." She gestured vaguely with her hand. It was something she hadn't really wanted to think about.

She sank back into her chair. His mother, Setana Marteen was the Indran Herald, his planet's representative to the Commonwealth. The fact that Triscoe had to resort to the use of his family's political influence did not bode well for her.

"The Procyons are very upset about the incident," he explained, taking charge of the conversation. "They've accused us of deceit, subversion, and several things I'd rather not repeat. The Commonwealth is consequently laying the blame solely upon you. The Procyons are aware of the charges of treason and are calling for a sentence of death."

Rieka stared at him for a long moment. The Commonwealth did not put people to death, not even for committing treason. But, she thought, if that's what the Procyons want, and if they whispered into the right ears . . . She looked away, trying to think of something less morbid.

Triscoe sat down at the table, and she wondered just how much had happened since her arrest. Did the public know? Had they been led to believe she was guilty? The people in Legal provided her with little information. All but Chen were non-Humans. Rieka suddenly felt blind and deaf and dumb. The air seemed too thin. She sensed that reality had changed, or at least her version of it.

"I can't defend myself, Triscoe," she said finally. There was no trace of self-pity in her voice. It was irrefutable fact. "I'm innocent, and, as strange as it sounds, I have no defense. The evidence which should prove my story is identical to that which will be used to hang me."

He reached across the table and touched her hand. She felt strength in those cool fingers and heard conviction in the timbre of his voice. "I know you, Rieka, and I believe the evidence has been fabricated," he said. "Somehow, we will find the truth of it."

He squeezed her hand, then continued. "I want you to trust me and do everything I ask. Together, with Robet's help, we may be able to unearth just exactly what has passed between the Commonwealth and the Procyons."

She straightened, suddenly hopeful her future might not be as bleak as she'd thought. It hadn't been difficult to imagine herself an unwitting pawn in the charade with the *Vendikon*. But to have Triscoe be the one to start pointing fingers amazed her. For him to assert she'd been framed gave the situation a whole new light. "You think someone has used me? Someone from within the Commonwealth? Someone with a grudge against the Procyons—or, perhaps, Humans?" she wondered aloud, airing her own suspicions.

"I don't like to speak prematurely," Triscoe replied. "I simply know you are telling the truth and am suggesting the situation is actually other than as it appears." He searched her face, then added, "I must ask a favor of you."

As a prisoner, there was little she could do to help herself. But anything, anything at all was better than sitting around waiting for others to decide her fate. "What do you want me to do?"

His warm brown eyes held hers momentarily, silently asking her not to argue with the request. "Singlemind with me. Now. I must know what you know."

It was something she hadn't expected, and it caught her off guard. He had done it with her before, connecting their minds in an unexplainable way. Knowing how she'd felt after the last time, Rieka wondered what the result of another session might be.

She hesitated for a moment, the breath catching in her throat. Fleet doctors had examined her already. According to their instruments, she was telling the truth. But Triscoe's desire to do this mind-merge made her think he doubted that truth in some way.

The determination in his face was enough to persuade her lungs to function.

"All right."

Triscoe smiled at her briefly, then closed his eyes. She knew he was preparing himself to stretch consciousness until it enfolded hers, matching her Beta pattern and effectively joining their minds.

They had performed the feat twice before, during their command training four years ago. She hadn't even known such a thing existed until he'd explained it to her. The *quantivasta*-gift was rare among Centauris, and infinitely personal. She didn't know why he'd felt the need to share this unique experience with her. And, for an equally obscure reason, she couldn't turn him down, then or now.

Agreeing with him only made her feel more apprehensive. Neither experience had been unpleasant, but after the first time he'd bridged their minds, Rieka had become aware she thought about him a great deal. After the second, she craved more than a friendly relationship with Triscoe Marteen.

The last time they parted company, her feelings of profound respect for him had evolved. She cared deeply for a man whose race devoted itself to duty and honor. Though their lives were already mapped as parallel, never to cross or unite, she was proud and grateful that he called her his friend. Whatever emotions this mysterious Singleminding evoked, Rieka had long since decided that would remain her secret. She tried to concentrate on the present problem and hoped he would not want her to think about anything else.

"Ready?"

She nodded again and extended her arms to him across the small table's polished surface. It was almost familiar now, when he grasped her wrists, kneading them. Another moment passed. His hands stilled. She stretched her fingers along his wrists and held tight. He leaned forward and lowered his head. She mirrored the movement, staring straight into his dark eyes until the angle was too great. Her lids closed. She heard him whisper.

"Relax, Rieka."

"I'm trying."

Triscoe gave her the minutes she needed to overcome her uneasiness. She could feel it when he slowly let go of his own thoughts, loosening the rein he had on his consciousness, allowing it to flow out from him and encompass her.

"Think about the *Vendikon*," he said softly.

She recalled the ship as it had appeared on her DGI. She saw her crew, heard them in her memory as they reported the position and activity of the Procyon craft. She ordered the warning shots and the final sphere to damage the *Vendikon*'s propulsion unit. Then, they maneuvered the ship into a wide orbit, and it erupted into a miniature sun.

"Now," he prompted, "go back to the message you received from Admiral Bittin."

"It was encoded," she replied. "I took it privately in my quarters."

"Show me."

She envisioned her room on the *Venture*. The graphics activated with the touch of her palm, and Admiral Bittin's starkly pale Centauri face appeared.

"We've got a situation, Captain Degahv," the admiral began. "And it's about to happen on your circuit." His face had leaned closer to the recording holocamera and practically jutted from the small screen.

"Many people on both sides of the border have opinions directly opposed to my own, I'm sure. But I can't give credit to their notions. Intelligence has reported that a Procyon ship identified as the *Vendikon* will be crossing the border in your area immediately following your receipt of this communiqué. My orders are simple and leave no room for interpretation. You are to intercept this vessel and destroy it if it enters Commonwealth space. Is that understood?"

Since it was a one-way message recorded earlier, she simply nodded.

"Upon completion of this, I want you to report to me in person at Yadra. You will receive new orders when you arrive." The screen flashed: END MESSAGE, and went blank.

Triscoe loosened his grip and lifted his head. The wrinkle appeared again between his brows. He sat up slowly and watched Rieka as she leaned back in her chair.

"You know something," she said after studying him for a moment.

He nodded.

"Well, let's have it."

"Your recollection of the event exactly matches documentation retrieved from both the *Venture* and Central Communications. They are identical with the exception of a single sentence."

"What?"

"You remember the admiral telling you to intercept and destroy the *Vendikon*. Central Communications' copy as well as the *Venture*'s record has him telling you to 'rendezvous and escort the vessel to Yadra.' "

"That's impossible."

"There is something else," Triscoe said, still watching her carefully. "I sense other things in your mind that you can't remember—or are unable to remember."

For a moment, she was speechless. Her memory was perfectly intact. "Don't tease me like that, Triscoe. There has never been a time that I cannot recall everything that's happened to me. I have an excellent memory."

He shook his head. "I am very serious, Rieka."

"No," she insisted. "You must be mistaken. You

were probably just bumping into something I was
trying not to think about."

He sighed, then looked directly at her. "I'm sorry.
It did not seem like anything you could have done
consciously."

Take the good with the bad, she told herself. At least
he hasn't found you out. "Why should that be?" she
asked, sitting forward. The quandary was quick
becoming a quagmire. How could she keep something
hidden if she wasn't conscious of it?

Triscoe shrugged slightly. "One of two reasons.
Either you are repressing the memory, yourself—
or your mnemonic abilities have been artificially
curtailed."

"You mean I might have been conditioned? Programmed? That's outrageous!"

"It *is* a possibility, Rieka."

"But," she huffed, "how? When? To think that
someone might have been . . . Could have gotten into
my mind . . . Could have made me . . ." She left the
thought unsaid as goose bumps rose on her arms.
Triscoe's expression told her it was far more than just a
possibility.

She dropped her face into her hands and wished
every one of those nameless, faceless people dead.
How could they do such a thing to her? The Commonwealth protected certain rights for everyone. Everyone—including Humans. If she ever got out of jail, she
swore she would hunt them all down.

"I'll make them pay," she vowed. "And if it's true,
how can I . . . what?" The implications of what he'd
just said began to sink in, and Rieka's eyes grew round
with the shock. "How can I be sure of—anything?"

Triscoe touched her hand, managing to gain her
attention. "Try not to worry about that."

"Try not to, yourself!" she snapped. She felt the
world turn suddenly askew. Everything she knew as
fact could now be rightly questioned. All those things

she'd said to Chen and the rest of those Legal clones,
they might have been lies. Involuntarily, she shuddered.

Triscoe squeezed her fingers. "Don't drive yourself
mad over it, Rieka," he warned. "We have to look into
the problem further before coming to a conclusion,
although I doubt the digressions are pervasive. In any
case, I can't reach such a closed-off memory. I think
the truth of your innocence is locked away there, and
we will need help to reach it."

The grip on her fingers tightened when he added,
"We both know information derived from a Singlemind is inadmissible in court. Even if we do find out
what has been blocked, and it points to your innocence,
there may be no evidence to prove it."

Rieka was caught off guard so much by the idea that
her memory had been altered, she felt as if she couldn't
think. Aside from her attorney, Triscoe was her only
lifeline to the outside. She hated putting herself in
anyone's hands, but she had no choice. The debt she
would owe both him and Chen would be sizable. She
hoped she could pay it back.

"Help me, Triscoe," she said softly. "I can't do anything from in here. They won't even let me watch the
news channels. My attorney's name is Chen. David
Chen. I think you can trust him. Tell him what you've
found out. That will put him on the right track, at least.
I'm sure he'll do his best with whatever you give him."
Putting on a brave front, she nodded.

A long moment passed, and Triscoe seemed reluctant to let go of her hand. "There is one more thing that
I must ask," he said quietly.

"Anything."

"It may come as an odd request."

She shook her head. "Doesn't matter. Whatever you
want. You've got it." She had credit enough to pay for
whatever he might need. She would never go to her
mother, but Paden, much as she disliked him, was still
her brother. If they needed him for anything, Triscoe
could probably twist his arm. A provincial administrator

had a lot of influence, though not as much as a Planetary Herald.

"I would like you to marry me."

She blinked twice before finding her tongue. "You didn't just say what I think you did, did you?"

Triscoe leaned forward, studying her. "Most seriously, I asked you to become my wife."

Suddenly suspicious but not knowing how to react, Rieka sat back against her chair and crossed her arms over her chest. "Why? Why now? What purpose could it serve to be married to someone on trial for treason?"

"There are many, many reasons." With the hint of a smile, he added, "And to be honest, I have toyed with the idea long before now. It never seemed the right time."

She bit back a laugh. "And now's perfect."

"You needn't be sarcastic, Rieka. Now is perfect. It was only a moment ago that I became aware of your feelings toward me."

Rieka was completely aghast. Not only had she allowed him to see something she'd vowed would be forever secret, he seemed to be using it as a tool to get her to agree to a ridiculous marriage.

Triscoe continued. "A Singlemind isn't wholly a joining of conscious thought. I apologize for never fully explaining the strength and complexity of the telepathic bond. It is very complex. And, if you could not tell from your end of the bridge, I hold you in a similar regard. We could not, of course, produce offspring, but I see no great difficulty there."

Rieka looked at him, speechless. A confession of love was the last thing she ever expected out of Triscoe Marteen. Now that she had it, she didn't know quite what to do. Despite their apparent feelings for each other, it seemed ridiculous to jump into a bispecies marriage, with all the complications that implied, when they were really not much more than good friends. A bonding, as the Centauris called it, was a serious thing. That comment about offspring was definitely out of place, but then so was a proposal, considering the charges she faced.

About to reprimand him for being flippant, Rieka noticed him glance at the camera in the corner of the room. Perhaps the offer was simply a device to throw whoever was watching off the track. Relieved that this wasn't a completely spur-of-the-moment thing, but part of a greater design, she smiled. She watched him look to the upper right again. There was very little to be gained—from his point of view—with regard to marrying a Human. But whatever the plan, she had nothing to lose by going along.

After a moment, she took a deep breath and nodded. She trusted this man with her life, had done it before and probably would again—if she survived the trial. "You're right, as usual, Triscoe," she replied, sounding wooden, even to herself. "And given the offer, despite the circumstances, my answer is yes. I suppose I'll leave the details to you."

"Wise decisions," he said honestly as his face blossomed into a smile. Both dimples appeared, and he seemed to deflate as if he'd been holding himself taut, waiting for her answer. "I am glad you are so reasonable. It is one of the things I like most about you."

She snorted but managed to keep from laughing out loud. "Sometimes I think you're too clever for your own good, Captain Marteen."

He stood and she followed. His voice was soft, and when he looked down at her she felt it almost as a caress. "I'll see you again, soon, Rieka." Stepping toward her, Triscoe kissed her lightly on the cheek, then turned and left.

Before the door had closed completely, she was already wondering if one of them had gone completely insane.

A soft smile eased across Triscoe's lips as he left the detention area. That incredulous look on her face when he'd proposed marriage reminded him of their first encounter, four years ago.

The border war with the Procyons had been over for almost a year. Triscoe, then in command of the *Shefflik,* stood in awe of the eight ships that had been armed and sent into combat. Having no practical experience, they'd somehow managed to drive off the Procyons.

But everyone knew they'd be back.

The months following the war brought great upheaval among the formerly peaceful Commonwealth planets, especially the way they approached interstellar commerce. Renamed the Fleet, every Transit Authority vessel carried defense weaponry, and all personnel were put through grueling months of military training. He remembered Rieka's surprise at being posted on his advanced-training team, and the set of her shoulders as she led him and Robet down a corridor off the promenade in search of privacy.

She'd turned and looked up at him, hands on her hips, eyes blazing. "They can't do this to you, Captain Marteen. How can you stand it?"

"Stand what?"

"That they've assigned me to you," she answered, waving a hand in his face. "You're being very gracious, but really, I'd feel much more comfortable with you as team leader if you'd just . . ."

"Just what, Captain?" He glanced at Robet, who seemed equally confused.

She huffed. "I don't know—look disgusted, or something. At least that way it would be out in the open. I doubt you can dispute the assignment. Even someone as influential as you probably couldn't budge the bureaucracy in this new Fleet."

"I . . . don't see any reason to dispute it, Captain." He crossed his arms over his chest, trying not to notice hers. Centauri females from either planet, Indra or Perata, did not have breasts. He shouldn't have been attracted to the mounds of flesh within her uniform, but he was. Perhaps he simply felt a latent reaction to the fad that had started some years back. There were quite a few women on both Centauri worlds walking around with synthetic implants. Funny, he'd never really noticed until now.

She sighed. Loudly. "Well . . . Look, we'll be seeing each other day in and day out for the next three months. I think it would be better if we cleared the air right now. We could accept the obstacle—and go on from there." She looked from him to Robet. "Don't you agree, Captain DeVark?"

"I might, if I knew what you were talking about," he said.

"About being teamed with a *Human*." Her blue eyes left the Aurian and settled on Triscoe, while her mouth curled into a skeptical frown.

He thought the quirky expression was one of the most delightful things he'd ever seen. Not quite understanding what she expected him to say, he said nothing.

"Or is *this* it?" she asked.

He caught the sarcasm easily enough but did not want to make her race—or any race, an issue. The trouble he faced trying to douse her outrage probably had more to do with the fact she was female rather than Human. "It . . . what?" he asked pleasantly.

He found he enjoyed the way she used her hands when she spoke. "The two of you are going to—to ignore me. To lead me around like I'm excess baggage. You'll do all the thinking—and, of course, graciously make all the decisions—not to mention take all the credit."

"Captain Degahv." He rested his hand on her shoulder and left it there even after she flinched. "I have seniority only as a Transport Authority captain. This is the Fleet now. We're all starting out from a common point." He looked from her dark blue eyes to Robet's pale ones. "As far as I'm concerned, we are a team. Equals. Is that agreeable?"

DeVark nodded.

She frowned up at him as if she didn't quite believe what she'd heard. "Even though I'm—"

"Yes! Of course. What should that matter?"

"You don't think I'm . . . inferior—a troublemaker?" It was a question, but it came across more like a statement.

Triscoe removed his hand and glanced at Robet. "You're both younger than I am," he admitted. "You have less experience. But the three of us are, from this moment, a team. If we can't accept each other for who and what we are—there isn't any point in trying to work together."

Triscoe remembered her smile, then. It lit her face slowly, like the sun emerging from behind a cloud, and he began to understand why this woman was so important. His mentor, Yillon, had told him her value to the Commonwealth was immeasurable but until that moment, he hadn't really believed it possible. Rieka's bitterness melted away, and the image she'd projected of a trapped animal dissolved as she pulled her shoulders back and lifted her chin.

"Captain DeVark?" she asked, looking at Robet.

"What?"

"Is that how you feel, too?"

Robet shrugged. "Sure."

Triscoe watched, fascinated, as she accepted them—accepting her. Finally, she nodded. "Then, in that case, you can call me Rieka."

He could smile, now, at the way she'd given him permission to use her first name. And that she'd accepted his proposal. Pleased his strategy had worked so far, Triscoe walked through the last security checkpoint ready to attack the problem at hand.

He saw Robet waiting for him in the Justice Building's main loggia. Seated on a bench in the rotunda, he scrolled aimlessly through the day's news.

At Triscoe's approach, Robet snapped off the console and jumped to his feet. "Did you see her?"

Triscoe nodded. He felt the man's bright eyes bore

into him with unasked questions and said as much as he dared in so public a place. "As I suspected, the truth lies beneath many layers of evidence."

They turned and walked down a wide gallery. "I saw you using the Net," Triscoe said quietly. "Are they letting out any new rumors? When is the arraignment?"

Robet shook his head to answer the first question. As to the second, he said, "Tomorrow afternoon."

"Then we shall have to move as quickly as possible." He picked up the pace and felt Robet watching him closely when they reached the InterMAT terminal. There were three people in line ahead of them. Triscoe frowned at the delay, though transport via the synthetic wormhole was nearly instantaneous.

DeVark nudged him. "Did you ask her?"

"Yes."

"And what did she say?"

"Yes."

The Aurian beamed. His bibbets flushed pink, and he grinned. "I knew it."

"Then why did you ask?"

"I don't like assuming things," he replied. "It can get complicated."

Another moment passed before it was their turn in the transport chamber. "We'd better start at the Indran Embassy," Triscoe said. "My mother will be able to advise us how to best handle the arrangements. I'm sure she'll be happy to give us a long list."

"List of what?" DeVark coaxed as they stepped into the cubicle. Triscoe entered the destination and stepped in beside him.

There was just enough of a delay for him to reply, "Errands."

Three

Setana Marteen watched proudly as her son signed the marriage documents. The small gathering in the meeting room at the Fleet Ministry of Justice did not impede her *quantivasta*-gift, and she was able to sense both his and his new bride's emotional states.

Rieka Degahv was frightened. More so, probably, than she ever had been in her entire lifetime. She was afraid her innocence in the current Fleet trouble would go unseen. She feared the marriage she'd committed to would never work. And, she thought Triscoe would never truly love her.

Setana found it strange that Triscoe's concerns were about those same things, from his perspective. While no one, with the exception of the Indran Oracle, could reasonably predict the outcome of today's arraignment and consequent trial, she sensed an underlying confidence in both of them. A determination to see things through, together.

She smiled and curbed the urge to speak lest he smudge his signature. Marriage, she knew, had as much to do with a union of the mind as of the body. By having previous Singlemind experiences, Triscoe and Rieka were already joined as far as she was concerned. Getting used to each other in the myriad of physical senses, she decided, would be the major hurdle.

Oddly, neither of them seemed to be concerned about that.

Triscoe turned to her. "Mother, your signature is required on the document."

"Thank you, dear." As she bent to sign the paper, she noticed Rieka had gone pale, a difficult thing to do for one with such dark skin. "Are you feeling unwell?" she asked.

"I'm . . . I'll be fine, Madame Herald," the girl stammered.

"Of course you will, my dear. We are family now, please call me Setana."

The deep olive skin that looked pale before was now shot with pink. "Are you sure, ma'am? I should think that—"

"Please," Setana insisted softly, offering an easy smile. "I shall have difficulty calling you Rieka if you do not call me Setana. Under Indran custom, you are now head of your family. We are equals in that respect."

Rieka glanced at Triscoe, then back. "I hadn't realized. If things work out for me, legally, I believe I'll have some studying to do."

"It will be most enlightening, I think." She nodded once.

"Mother, if you don't mind, I'm sure Rieka has better things to do with her time than looking up dusty old Indran customs." Triscoe showed her a tightly drawn face and painted his mind with an ugly shade of green.

"Really, dear, there's no need to get offensive. I am just stating the facts to my new daughter-in-law. My first. And a non-Indran. It's the least I can do." To his mind, she said, *Behave. Teach her about us. And treat her with respect.*

Ignoring his insulted look, she turned back to Rieka. "Did you know Triscoe has a brother and sister? Both older." When the girl shook her head, Setana continued. "Someday, we will have more time, and I shall tell you about them. My children are the joy of my life. But this one, of course," she patted Triscoe's arm, "is my special child."

"Mother."

More green, diffused with purple. She shot back a

heated orange but remained outwardly cool. "Well, of course all of this can wait for a more suitable time." She looked into those deep blue Human eyes and deftly changed the subject. "Did you know I knew your father, Rieka?"

When she shook her head, Setana offered, "I met him in his first year as Earth Herald. A remarkable man. His death was a tragedy in every sense. The position will be open for the Degahv heirs next year, as I'm sure you know. Your uncle is more than ready to retire. Have you given any thought to making a claim? Surely your people would see the advantage of electing a Fleet captain."

Rieka stiffened slightly. "I have no desire to be Herald, Setana," she replied. "Politics . . . well, let's just say that's my brother's game."

Setana allowed herself a slight frown. "Yes. Paden," she murmured, recalling the self-centered buffoon who held an administrator's spot on Yadra. "I've met him. He doesn't quite strike me as the Herald type—though I suspect Candace would be directing him at every turn."

Rieka nodded, and Setana recalled Triscoe telling her the girl held no affection for her mother, either. "And it seems to me that neither of them feel any devotion to Earth. Am I correct?"

At that, Rieka offered her a sad smile. "As far as I know. Uncle Alexi has worked as hard as my father did to make Earth habitable again. Humans should live on their homeworld—at least some of them. Let's hope another Degahv decides to make a claim."

She nodded. "Yes, let's do."

Rieka has enough to think about, Mother, Triscoe warned silently. *Don't push her.*

She'll come around, dear. Aloud, Setana said, "Actually, my presence is required in my offices in just a few moments, so I must bid you farewell."

Triscoe traced his thumb along her chin as a proper show of respect. "Thank you for everything, Mother."

"It was nothing, really. You know I will always help you if I can." She sensed that frightened yellow in

Rieka's mind, again, and turned to her. "Both of you. I hope everything turns out as expected at the arraignment. And I also hope it will not be too long before I see you again."

Rieka offered her a sad smile. "Me too. I appreciate everything you've done for me . . . and Triscoe. Thank you."

Setana reached and squeezed her arm. *He loves you,* she sent, and was pleased to see the Human captain frown as if she thought she'd heard something. Humans did not possess the psionic gift, but it was possible for Singlemind contact to stimulate certain areas of the brain. Even the simplest emotional reception would move things along immeasurably.

She turned. "Good-bye, Triscoe. Keep me informed."

"Of course, Mother."

As Setana collected her secretary and the one other retainer who had been selected to witness the wedding, she fluttered her fingers at them, then left the room. A few steps into the hall, she could not resist sending Triscoe a final message. *Good luck with Yillon.*

"I must have been out of my mind," Rieka muttered. Her stomach knotted, and she could still feel the stylus in her hand as she'd signed the official certificate. Now she paced the length of the waiting room, fingers clenching and unclenching. The arraignment was only moments away. What if the plan didn't work?

She had begun to doubt herself from the very moment Triscoe had told her about her memory. The power of her mind had been her one stronghold. Now it hung precariously, giving her cause to question everything. She was afraid to speak even one word, to think at all. Yet she had repeated the phrases and signed the documents as if the marriage had been planned for years. Doubting herself as she did, Rieka could only hope her faith in Triscoe would pay off. The thought of being manipulated, even by a man she loved, made her skin crawl.

"How could I have been so gullible?" She shook her head, not knowing whether it was the wedding or the waiting that bothered her the most.

The guard standing near the door switched on his TC and stood straighter. "Captain Degahv, they're ready for you."

Rieka looked at him, envious of the small communication device that had been stripped from her when she'd lost her freedom. Somehow, having this stranger use both her name and rank made her feel better. She pushed her shoulders back and planted her feet on the floor. She might feel like a bowl of gelatin-glot, but there was no reason to broadcast it.

She tugged her uniform and brushed a crumb of lint from the sleeve. "Of course, Lieutenant."

He treated her to a slight nod. "This way."

Rieka took a deep breath, steeling herself for what was sure to come. She stepped to the door as the guard keyed it open and allowed him to lead her down a short corridor. Two heartbeats later she stood next to her attorney, Chen, in the courtroom. Their table faced the Judicial Council's arched bench. The three distinguished and austere admirals studied their datapads, ignoring her.

Rieka looked around. Unlike civil courts, this one had only enough seats for witnesses and family to be present. Paden was there, and Triscoe, and some people she had never met. She knew her arrest had to have been newsworthy, but the horde of media people were nowhere in sight. For that, and her mother's absence, she was thankful.

The bailiff stood to her immediate left between the defense table and that of the prosecution. Prime Admiral Hursh, a huge Centauri with a hawklike jaw and sharp eyes, nodded that the proper documents had been forwarded to his screens and those of his companions. The court officer nodded back and stood in front of the small audience.

"This arraignment before the high court of the

Commonwealth Fleet of Starships is catalogued as number: 0724-331-7928. Subject in question: Captain Rieka Degahv, Human of Yadra of the Tau Ceti system, and former captain of C.F.S. *Venture*. Charges are set. Alleged acts of sabotage, disobeying a direct order, and treason committed against the Commonwealth on CD 204:46."

The bailiff took his seat between the tables.

Hursh, flanked by two dour-looking colleagues, stared directly at Rieka. "How do you plead, madam?"

The outright disgust in his tone nearly provoked her to speak up, but Chen nudged her gently, and said, "Captain Degahv pleads innocent."

Hursh sat up a bit straighter in his chair. "Does she indeed?" He tapped at his console, then looked at Chen. "Because of the serious nature of the charges, Counsel, I am directed to inquire as to what grounds."

"On the previously documented grounds of manipulation dictated by external forces."

Hursh looked pointedly at Rieka, and she knew in his mind she'd already been convicted. She gritted her teeth and stared back. Fleet chief or not, she refused to allow him to see that she was anything but a loyal officer.

The admiral frowned and directed his attention to Chen. "Have you any proof of manipulation, Counsel?"

Chen, for once, looked hopeful. He glanced down at some paper documents in his briefcase. "Negative at this time, Admiral. We have only recently recognized this as the reason for Captain Degahv's odd behavior with regard to the Procyon ship. We require time to research the matter in order to provide adequate proof."

Vice Admiral Frotii, a broad green-hided Vekyan seated on the prime admiral's right, asked, "How much time, Counsel?"

"The prosecution objects," announced the Fleet's attorney.

Rieka watched as the Aurian female rose from her chair, gloating as though victory was already hers.

Granting time to dig up the facts, if there were any to be found, was not in the prosecution's best interest.

"Admirals," she went on, "this matter is an outrage and embarrassment to every Commonwealth member world, not just the Fleet. There is no evidence to support Captain Degahv's claim of innocence. There are, however, extensive records of her committing the acts she is accused of. We need to deal with the problem now, before the Procyons grow restless. We need to put this unpleasant matter in the past."

"Eloquent, Counsel," Frotii nodded. "However, according to law, the defense must be allowed to make its case. We are not so weak that we cannot cope with . . . restless Procyons—while the whole truth of this matter is discovered." He clicked the claws of his right hand and leaned toward Admiral Hursh to confer. They were joined from their left by the hulking slate-colored Boolian, Vice Admiral Katek.

After a few moments the prime admiral nodded, and his companions sat back. "You have twenty days to gather your evidence, Defense Counsel," Hursh began. "At that time, your client will be tried for the crimes of disobeying a direct order, sabotage, and treason against the Commonwealth."

Chen looked like he was trying not to grin. "Thank you, sir." He stepped forward. "In that case, I would like to request that the captain be released on bond."

"Unacceptable," the prosecutor said.

"It is within her rights to make such a request, Counsel," Hursh reminded her. He looked at Frotii, who nodded, and Katek, who made a clicking sound with his kroi. The Prime Admiral then studied the screen before him. After a short moment, he said, "I see no point in the state maintaining custody of the defendant. This is the first blemish on Captain Degahv's record. Her mother is an affluent business-woman, and her brother holds the highly respected seat of Lemonne Province Administrator here on Yadra. I hereby remand the prisoner to her next of kin until the trial date." He and the two others on the bench pounded the table twice.

Rieka stood and looked over her shoulder at the six people who had been allowed to watch the arraignment. Paden and Triscoe both approached the defense table. They continued toward her until Paden grabbed Triscoe's arm and spoke in a tight whisper. Triscoe pulled free, and said something.

Paden's objection, "That's impossible!" was spoken loud enough to be heard across the room. The prime admiral's head snapped up from his screen.

"What is going on there?" he asked the bailiff.

"A difference of opinion, apparently, Admiral," the man replied, moving to investigate.

Quiet words passed while Rieka waited. Finally, Hursh slammed a fist onto the bench. "You there," he demanded, pointing at her brother. "What is going on?"

"She has been remanded to her next of kin, Admiral," Paden insisted. "That is me."

With an air of confidence unruffled by the scene he had created, Triscoe calmly announced, "I am Rieka's next of kin, sir. Captain Triscoe Marteen."

Hursh harrumphed. "Are you now? You will have to explain yourself, Captain."

"I am her husband."

Hursh looked as though he were about to say something, then stopped himself. He turned his steely glare back to Rieka. "Is this true, Captain?"

She knew Triscoe's entire strategy hinged on getting her released into his custody. If Hursh changed his mind, there would be no defense. She could do nothing to persuade him to keep the ruling, save telling the truth. "Actually, yes, sir. Triscoe is my husband, which in terms of interrelationships takes precedence over that of blood as stated in Article 40—"

"I am aware of what is stated," the admiral barked. His dark eyes squinted at her with irritation. He glanced out at the room's occupants, waiting a long moment before making his judgment.

"This is highly irregular," he announced. "However, owing to the fact that both Captain Marteen and his family have reputations beyond reproach among several Commonwealth planets, I see no reason to alter my decision." He fixed his attention on Triscoe. "Have you documentation of this marriage as well as personal identification?"

Triscoe drew a record from his trouser pocket and offered it to the admiral.

Hursh inserted the wafer in his computer, studied the certificate, and harrumphed again. He removed the transcript, handed it back, and murmured something. Triscoe nodded smartly. He pocketed the report, turned, and held out his hand toward Rieka.

Hursh pounded the bench top again. "This arraignment is adjourned."

Suppressing a grin that threatened the dignity of the moment, Rieka stepped forward and took the proffered hand. Avoiding Paden's wide-eyed glare, they left the courtroom with David Chen and made their way to the desk where her release would be processed. From there, Triscoe planned to transport her directly to the *Providence,* leaving Chen to face the media hounds.

Robet DeVark sauntered into Admiral Nason's outer office, delighted at any opportunity to confound his secretary. The young man sat behind a delicate-looking table that resembled a lectern more than a desk. It was always fun to gauge how long it would take the self-important facade to fall. This one, being Human, would probably either stand tall or buckle quickly like a tower of sand. Robet smiled to himself at the happy thought.

"Yes, Captain?" the voice was soft.

"I require an audience with the admiral, Lieutenant," Robet said in his command voice. He squared his ample shoulders. "The matter is extremely urgent."

The secretary consulted something on his lectern. "The admiral is busy at this moment. I have a spot open at eleven-twenty hours tomorrow."

Robet brought coppery brows down over cloudy blue eyes, purposely making the row of bibbets stand out on his forehead. Then he glared at the young Human. "Urgency implies immediate action, Lieutenant," he explained sweetly, as if to a child. "Immediate, implies now. Now is not tomorrow."

The man gripped the edge of the desk, but held his ground. "Captain—"

Robet respected this Human's need to do his job almost as much as he enjoyed testing him. Self-respect was important, but the problems at hand were pressing.

"Lieutenant, I have no intention of waiting," he snapped, silently applauding the man for keeping his cool. His bibbets, he knew, were flushing deeper pink. "I have no use for bureaucracy at the moment, or what you Humans call red tape."

He paused for effect and added, "Push the button. I'm going in."

The secretary had glanced at his forehead and apparently knew Aurian physiology. The darker the welts became, the more violent their owner's disposition. "Sir," he offered quietly. "Please," he begged. "I can't simply—"

"Announce me, Lieutenant, or look like the ineffectual plebe that you are," Robet warned, now looking as though he might explode. Concentrating on keeping his color up, he swiveled his jaw from side to side and grunted.

The lieutenant buckled at the sight of maroon on Robet's forehead. The door to the inner office slid open. "You may go in now, sir."

"Why, thank you." Robet glared at him a second longer, then strode through.

"I lose more good people that way," Nason commented when DeVark stood before him and the door had closed.

He sat behind his large ebony desk, flanked by two flat-faced comnet screens. Part of the wall on his left was a DGI, presently dormant, covered by a drawn curtain. The room had no windows. The floor and walls were decorated in deep green. Abstract prints hung strategically, lit by fixtures embedded in the ceiling. Nason glanced at one before shaking his head at his visitor and tapping the "pause" toggle on one of the screens.

"But it lets you know what they're made of, sir," the captain countered, a smile in his voice and a smirk on his face. The bibbets were once again the color of his chalky skin. Only a few individuals knew DeVark had learned to control precisely what was considered a semivoluntary pigment flow in the average Aurian.

Nason paused before he, too, smiled. "True. Now, why have you come to me? You're not due for an assignment until the *Prospectus* has completed the tests on the new Boolian equipment. That isn't until"—he glanced down to a datapad and requested the captain's schedule—"Commonwealth Date 204:53. You've got another three days of leave, DeVark."

"I know that, Admiral."

"You want to get a look at the latest report on the *Prodigy*?"

DeVark shrugged. "Well, that, too."

Nason wove his fingers together and set his elbows on the edge of his desk. With a small sigh of resignation, he forced himself to ask, "What is it, this time, Robet?"

Not known for treading delicately, even in his own personal affairs, DeVark plunged into the topic as if he were the top seed in a speed volley tournament. "Rieka Degahv, Admiral."

Nason tugged at his right ear. He had been anguishing over that fiasco for days. The facts, as presented by both the media and his Fleet sources, seemed to be all there—and yet they didn't. Knowing Degahv as he did, something did not fit. He had already launched his own investigation, hoping to find some proof of her innocence. She had never done anything remotely irresponsible, much less disloyal. Though he expected her

friends to offer their support, it was not his wish to
have them rally in her defense. They had their own
agendas to manage.

With a disgruntled sigh, he asked, "You're involved
in that mess?"

"Indirectly." DeVark helped himself to a chair and
pulled it close to the desk. "Rieka is innocent. I need
you to look the other way while some of us find the
means to prove that."

Nason swiveled his chair and sat back. Like it or not,
he had expected as much. Degahv, DeVark, and Marteen were as close as any three captains on the roster.
Sometimes, their loyalty to one another seemed stronger
than it was either to him or the Fleet.

Realizing Robet had only just come in and had
already asked him to "look the other way," Nason
knew the real request was yet to come. He could only
hope the captain wouldn't ask too much.

"I was shocked, I'll admit, when she was arrested,"
Nason said, looking evenly at his fellow Aurian. "But
I've seen the evidence. The *Venture* destroyed the
Vendikon, and she was in command."

"With all due respect, Admiral, there's a lot more to
it than that." DeVark lowered his voice. "A lot we
don't know—and a lot more we're guessing at."

"Who's we?" Nason asked, though he already knew
the answer. He also knew that a roundabout method
might gather more truth than one launched directly. If
DeVark had some means of getting to the bottom of
what had happened with the *Venture,* Nason decided it
would be worth the effort to let the man try.

Not wanting the captain to think his boss was a
pushover, however, Nason waited patiently for Robet
to plead his case.

"There are fifty-seven captains in the Fleet," DeVark
began. He tapped a forefinger on the desktop to stress
his point. "And you have personally chosen each one
of them from an enormous pool of talent. Can you

really doubt her that much? To believe fabricated evidence over her word?"

Nason was unimpressed. "Who's we?"

"We've been given twenty days to prove the case before Prime Admiral Hursh. Every minute of that time is intensely valuable."

He pretended not to notice when the captain's bibbets began to color. "Who's we, Robet?"

"Captain Marteen, myself, and Midrin Tohab, Rieka's second-in-command." He sat straighter and waited. "And her counsel, David Chen."

Nason had expected a candid request from DeVark, but this went beyond reason. He leveled his gaze at DeVark and kept his voice low, hoping his own bibbets would not betray him. "You want me to release the *Prospectus,* the *Venture,* and the *Providence* from their duty schedules for twenty days. Is that what I am hearing?"

The captain swallowed and sat back in his chair. "Yes sir," was all he said.

Reaching for his mug of *colan,* Nason took a sip and waited a long moment before responding. When DeVark's bibbets started to shift from pink to rose, he said, "Twenty days will disturb many other schedules—those of several planets, Zone bases, and rendezvous points. That does not even bring to account the personnel involved. Fleet efficiency is of great importance to the Commonwealth, Robet. We may call ourselves a Military Fleet, now, but we're still very much the sole means of transport between one planet and another. My own personal reputation stems from our adherence to the schedule. And you come in here and ask me to risk everything for one of my captains?"

DeVark frowned as if surprised that things weren't going his way. "With all due respect, Admiral Nason, you do have fifty-four other ships. Schedules can be altered. There's only one Rieka Degahv ... and the Procyons are calling for her death."

He shook his head. "The Commonwealth does not

have a death penalty—and we have dealt with Procyons before."

"Years ago," the captain replied.

"And what is that supposed to mean?"

"I don't know." DeVark shrugged. "But I can't help wondering what this is all about. Why now? Why Rieka? What's *really* going on?"

Nason smiled inside. That determined trio had already unearthed something. He found himself thankful for their loyalty, and said quietly, "What haven't you told me, Robet?"

DeVark leaned across the desk. "Triscoe Single-minded with her yesterday. Her memory of Admiral Bittin's orders differs from the record. She remembers being told to destroy the *Vendikon*. But she didn't, sir. Despite what you thought you saw in the records, she ordered the last shot to the propulsion units to cripple the Procyon ship. It did just that. Cripple it. Something, after they put it in that wide orbit, caused the ship to blow. We don't know what."

Nason considered these few facts and nodded. Single-minding was something Centauris did not take lightly. He had always wondered at the peculiar relationship of that particular pair. Silently, he wished them well. To his companion, he said, "I *had* noticed, Robet. I know the capabilities of my ships and my people. And there *was* something suspicious about the *Vendikon*'s destruction."

He sighed and shook his head. "I have misgivings about releasing you from the calendar. To whoever is behind this, three ships suddenly excused from a tight timetable will arouse curiosity. Any outside attention to this investigation of yours must be avoided. We may be in the midst of an invasion of some kind, a revolt, or even the convoluted bulwark of a vendetta designed to have Captain Degahv's reputation destroyed.

"I *am* investigating the case," he admitted. "But espionage and intelligence gathering are not my department, Robet. And I might remind you they are not yours, either."

"But Triscoe . . ."

DeVark hesitated, and Nason took the opportunity to pounce. "He what? You'd better explain yourself immediately if you expect me to grant any part of your request."

"He . . . knows someone on Perata who might be able to figure out what happened to Rieka. And I need to survey the area where the *Vendikon* was destroyed. We need evidence, sir, and we're not going to get it if we're on our regular routes."

Nason couldn't argue with DeVark's reasoning. This case was unprecedented. They would have to improvise in order to reach an acceptable verdict. And the sooner they began, the better. He could only hope it would take far less than twenty days to gather the available data.

He looked squarely into the captain's eyes, and said, "I will reinstate the *Prospectus* immediately. Your orders are to accompany the *Venture* under First Officer Tohab's command to the Jovian Cluster. There you will begin training maneuvers to benefit Tohab's experience and to field-test your new equipment."

"The Jovian Cluster is clear on the other side of the Commonwealth."

"You may be tracked to ensure your heading, Captain, but I doubt anyone will go that far to make sure you are where you're supposed to be. Probably no farther than the Dwana Nebula, do you think?" Nason wondered.

DeVark grinned. "Thank you, Admiral."

"And Robet . . ." The grin faded as he knew it would. There was really no need to state the obvious, but sometimes even the obvious was ignored. The new Boolian hardware the *Prospectus* carried was extremely sensitive. Only a few people in the Fleet knew such technology existed. Discretion would be their primary concern until Degahv's problems were sorted out.

Nason sighed and felt his own bibbets color. "Do not test the equipment."

The captain frowned, then sobered. "Of course, sir. I understand. I'll even keep it under guard."

Nason nodded and watched DeVark try not to say anything else. Apparently, he didn't want to leave without all he'd come for. "You are now thinking about the *Providence,* are you not?"

The captain shrugged. Obviously, he didn't want to push a good thing.

"I cannot justify sending Marteen on maneuvers. That would be too obvious. You and Tohab both have excuses." He paused, trying to decide what to do with the *Providence.* "I will send Marteen on a diplomatic errand. Have him let me know which planet needs to meet with him."

"Thank you, sir." DeVark beamed. "We won't let you down."

"I should hope not," Nason countered. "You are dismissed, Robet. I shall see you in twenty days."

The captain stood and saluted. "Twenty days, Admiral." He fairly marched from the room.

Nason silently wished him luck. As he watched the younger man go, he considered advising his secretary that if DeVark should, in the future, require an unscheduled audience, an appointment was not necessary—just fair warning.

Procyon High Commander K'resh-va turned his attention from the command center on his small ship, the *Novil,* and answered the blinking signal by pressing the appropriate spot on his console. "News, at last," he muttered.

A subordinate called L'gith-la appeared on his viewer. A Procyon of a lower class than he, as distinguished by the final syllable of her name, L'gith-la bore a similar, synthesized, Indran appearance. They were among an elite group that had undergone the painstaking five-year process of surgeries and chemical therapy to alter their original humanoid forms. Unlike the others who had secretly infiltrated Commonwealth space, their transformations were unique in that they resembled specific individuals. Thanks to records stolen during the last Commonwealth contact, even retinal scans could not detect the difference.

K'resh-va recalled the weeks of instruction and drills he had endured to remove all traces of Procyon vocal inflection. His mannerisms had been schooled, digestive system altered, and rate of hair growth significantly reduced. That it had taken such an elaborate scheme was of little consequence. The end result, as always, was what mattered.

"Greetings, sir," L'gith-la said. She nodded and performed the stiff-wristed Fleet salute. The recording, he noted, had taken place somewhere other than her quarters. The familiar accouterments of her room had been replaced by unadorned green-tinted walls.

"They've arraigned Captain Degahv," she began. "Her trial begins in twenty days. Nineteen days by the time you receive this."

K'resh-va frowned. He hit the pause button to think. "So long a time?" he muttered. "I should have thought they would want it over with quickly." He made a sound of disgust using the sinus cavities in his head. With a flip of the toggle, the message continued.

"The plan has carried to a point," the woman said with a nod. She brushed back a wisp of blond hair and tugged at her uniform collar. "But there are certain unexpected obstacles. As anticipated, no one in the Fleet was given access to her, with the exception of legal counsel. At the trial, they requested her release, which the prime admiral granted to her next of kin. For some reason this happens to be Captain Triscoe Marteen. I—"

"Marteen!" He pounded the switch again, and, for a moment, K'resh-va's features folded into those more common to a Procyon than an Indran. He then forced himself to frown properly, with teeth concealed, and repeated, "Marteen? What has a Centaurin to do with her?"

More curious than upset by this turn of events, he

continued the replay. L'gith-la tapped her check. "I—I was unaware of any relationship, or I would have reported it, earlier. According to our sources, the documentation is accurate. They have been married, sir. Recently. And I must admit that it is very unexpected. Very irregular.

"Because of the situation, I am wondering if I should ask to transfer to the *Providence*—as that would be the logical place to watch them both. Otherwise, I will carry on as planned." She saluted again. "I await—and will follow your orders, in the event that they reach me in time."

The image faded.

K'resh-va considered how to respond to this twist in the plan. While it would serve to have her join the *Providence,* he did not see it as worth the risk of rousing suspicions—which a sudden transfer request might do. In a few days he would be insinuating himself into the Fleet. There would be ample opportunity to watch the pair then.

He tapped the proper spots on the console to have his voice-reply recorded and sent, safe in its anonymity among the hundreds of messages sifting through Fleet channels. A month from now, security would undoubtedly be tighter. But for the moment, the Commonwealth remained blissfully unaware its economy was about to change for the worse. Their guileless sense of trust almost turned his remaining stomach.

"Commander, your report was quite interesting. But there is no need to request a transfer," K'resh-va instructed. "Remain as you are. See what happens. Plant evidence, if that is possible. Improvise. Remove her only if you perceive a threat. It is your honor to follow me as it is mine to spearhead our campaign. You may signal again if there are further developments. K'resh-va *grem pa*."

He turned and slid his magnetized boots along the floor. Practiced at this mode of locomotion, K'resh-va quickly crossed the small space between the communications console and his chair in the small triangular room's aft corner.

Allowing himself a moment of reflection, K'resh-va studied the seven Procyons before him, his crew. They bore their native exterior and worked with the quiet efficiency of the honor-bound soldiers that they were. The russet skin, beaklike forejaws, and wide, angular chins gave them a uniformity he missed. Two years after his final surgery, he still occasionally shocked himself when looking in the mirror. He knew it was the same for M'eud-va, L'gith-la, and the others. But their assigned roles were the envy of all. They were the instruments that would destroy the Commonwealth.

"Status of the reflective field, S'ntin-na?"

"One hundred percent functional at 98 percent efficiency, sir."

K'resh-va nodded, and his thin, flaxen hair bounced lightly at his shoulders. "Continue course and speed to Epsilon Indi."

"As stated, sir."

He grunted and looked down at his shell-studded uniform. It would be difficult to give up such handsome attire for its simplistic Commonwealth counterpart. But that was another necessity. And, once the assignment was over, the honors bestowed upon him would far outweigh such petty sacrifices.

Steadying his weightless form by gripping the edge of the console, he wondered, again, why Marteen was now involved with Degahv. Marteen was well-known among the Procyons as a man who missed nothing and did not sway from his objective. He was a native of Indra of the Alpha Centauri star system, a planet known for spawning intellects. Marteen as a factor disturbed him, gave him a whiff of doubt. Yet at the same time, the swelling in his heart told him the victory over such a man would be savored for a lifetime.

Four

Rieka stood behind Triscoe's captain's chair. She had watched the *Prospectus* leave orbit. Now, as Tohab dipped the *Venture*'s wide, arched canopy in salute, a great lump welled in her throat. Clenching her jaw, she nodded back. It would be a long time before she would feel completely whole without the *Venture* beneath her feet.

In a moment both ships moved beyond the DGI's range, but Rieka's gaze remained fixed on the vista of stars. She found it odd her friends had been ordered to the Jovian Cluster. Training missions were usually nearer the Commonwealth's systems. Another mystery, she decided, knowing she was purposely being kept in the dark. Though she understood the reasoning behind it, the idea grated nonetheless.

Feeling an emptiness as profound as that when her father had died, Rieka continued to watch as smaller ships moved across the DGI. Ships full of people free to make their own choices. People certain their memories were intact. Wondering if she'd ever feel that confident again, Rieka looked away from the screen to study Triscoe's perfect posture and the calculated movements of his head as he prepared for departure.

In a few moments, the *Providence* slid from a shadowed orbit into the light of Tau Ceti and past Yadra's two natural satellites. Rieka watched with silent envy as Triscoe's people worked in quiet harmony. Nothing in particular gave her the feeling of an ensemble, certainly not what they did or said. It was the way they seemed to *mesh*. No one looked at Triscoe, with or without a sneer—they simply performed the tasks at hand.

She felt a wave of resentment toward her own people because she knew she had never felt, and would never feel, as comfortable on her own bridge.

Once well clear of traffic, they slipped into a high orbit while the reactors prepared to push them near half lightspeed, at which point the transfer sequence would be activated, forming an artificial wormhole through which the ship would slide. Rieka had studied the complex process developed by the Boos, but like many other species, she didn't really understand it.

Nor did she grasp the Fleet ships' delicate-looking umbrella shape. But the Boolian technologies worked. Trips to neighboring systems that had once taken nearly a lifetime could now be accomplished in days. Rieka often wondered at the Boos' genius with antimatter and quantum mechanics. The heavy tripeds were the most "alien" of the civilizations in the Commonwealth, but they were also the most brilliant.

"Course positive eleven point two-three-six planar, fourteen point seven-seven-one port, Ohato," Triscoe ordered. "Speed at maximum when available."

"As we speak," the helmsman replied.

"We're headed for Centaurus?" she asked quietly.

Triscoe turned slightly and gave her a slow, reassuring smile, dimple included. "Rieka, I almost forgot you were there. And, yes. We have an errand." He left his chair and directed her to accompany him to the Chute. As they neared the door, he turned to his EO, and said, "Notify me of anything unexpected."

Since the moment they'd left the Justice Building, Rieka's unfounded fears began to settle on firm footing. Of course he'd married her to get custody, so they could gather the evidence to prove her innocence. But there was more to it than that. Triscoe had told her he had many reasons. And Setana had made an issue of welcoming her into the family.

Now she sensed a wall around him as though he

were distancing her despite their new relationship. His attitude seemed coolly professional compared to the easy camaraderie they'd shared before. Not knowing how to react, Rieka decided to try to be patient. Triscoe probably didn't know how to handle their marriage any better than she. He'd assigned her a suite and thus far treated her like a respected guest. There had been precious little expression of the feelings he'd talked about when he'd proposed. Rieka found herself speculating about those mysterious "other reasons" he had mentioned and none were particularly flattering.

She wanted to talk about it, now, but knew pushing him wouldn't work. She waited during the short Chute trip to the second level's passengers' quarters. He was mute. The brief stroll from there to her room was silent, too. Fighting to keep her temper and her mouth under control, Rieka realized she no longer needed to conform to the superperfect image required by a Human ship's captain. She could say what she thought without having to concern herself about biased interpretations. The idea sank in, and for a moment she felt free.

Determined to get some kind of explanation for taking her off the bridge, Rieka deliberately stopped outside her door. "Triscoe, I want to know what is going on."

His expression combined discomfort and respect. "You shall know what is necessary for you to know," he said, leading her into the salon. He sat and gestured her to a padded maroon chair.

"I don't want to sit. What I want is an explanation." Exasperated, she walked away and pulled a hand through her dark hair. "I feel like . . . I don't know. Like . . ."

"A prisoner?" He twisted in the chair to look at her. "You are, lovely Rieka. You are. My prisoner." As he spoke, his eyes searched her face.

She didn't appreciate the scrutiny. She squared her shoulders and glared back at him. "I suppose I should just escort myself to the brig, then!"

"Stop it, Rieka." He stood and looked at her. "I know you feel Humans are mistreated by the Commonwealth—and there may be some truth to that. I'm not sure."

He shook his head. "What I do know is—your people have not been judged fairly. You have not had the opportunity to live on your own self-sustaining world. But that will all change in time. The disaster is long over. Earth is being recultivated. Humans will return to a better world. Then, we shall see."

"How dare you insinuate—"

"I insinuate nothing! It is you who are always on the defensive. I know Humans are often passed over for certain positions, aren't always given the benefit of the doubt, are thought of as, perhaps, a lower species. But you are temporary inhabitants of already populated worlds. Should not those worlds look after their own first?"

Rieka huffed. "Not when we're talking about *generations* of Humans. When you're born someplace and raised there—you shouldn't have to feel like an outsider."

She looked away and put out a hand, trying to control her temper. "I'm simply saying I grew up on Yadra. It's been my home—but it's not my home-world. Can't you see that?"

She didn't wait for a reply. "I've managed to beat the odds and become a Fleet captain. Now, I'm charged with treason. If I'm found guilty, I won't be the one to suffer. It will be every Human, everywhere—even those who aren't even born yet."

"That may be—"

"It *is*, Triscoe! There are no maybes. I am innocent! And here I sit . . . waiting. No one tells me anything. Instead, I'm told what to do, where to go . . . my fate is in your hands. And you have the audacity to accuse me of being on the defensive!"

His eyes went dark above his jutting jaw. He sighed. "Must you always solicit an argument?" he asked quietly. "Have we not been over this topic before?"

"Yes. To both questions," she countered. "I *must* be found innocent, Triscoe. Not for me—but for all Humans. As it stands right now, I *can* be proven guilty. And when that happens—"

"*If* that happens," he snapped. He was at the door in three strides, apparently intending to leave her alone with her thoughts. At the last moment, he stopped, and said, "I have given my word to the prime admiral to keep you safe and return you to Yadra for your trial. I have also promised you I will find the truth of this"—he waved one hand aimlessly—"situation, and hope that it proves you innocent of all charges. I apologize if my doing that fosters your delicate sense of inequality."

She knew he'd put himself in a box almost as tight as her own, but the frustration she felt didn't leave much room for sympathy. "Then why are you—?"

"No . . . Rieka." His voice was suddenly soft. "Stop thinking of me as the enemy. Please. I believe you. What you've said. What you remember. Unfortunately, the simple fact is—I cannot allow myself to trust you."

She held her tongue when he lifted a hand in his defense. "You have undergone some kind of mental therapy. Your mnemonics have been *tampered* with. Quite simply, I have no way of knowing if you are programmed to perform another deed of someone else's bidding."

The facts hurt. He was keeping her at arm's length deliberately. It was a precaution she, herself, would take if the situation were reversed. But his confession didn't improve the way she felt. Rieka looked away, squeezing her eyes shut and breathing a ragged sigh. "I *know* that. It's just . . ." Frustrated, she left the thought unsaid.

"It won't be too much longer," he soothed. "There is someone on Perata that can help reach the memories that have been locked away by whoever did this to you. He is the one who recognized my gift and taught me the Singlemind technique. There is no other I trust to examine you. When we know what you know, then we can begin the hunt."

Rieka heard what he was saying, understood it, but could not suppress a feeling of urgency. Waiting was one of her least favorite pastimes.

"I can't stand this," she muttered. "I'm not *your* prisoner. I'm a prisoner within myself. I can't trust *me*."

"I'm sorry you are suffering so," he offered quietly. "It . . . grieves me to know you are in such torment."

He left the doorway and took a step toward her. "I'm afraid you must endure things as they are for a little while. I'll spend as much time with you as I can. It might help if you try to keep your mind busy. Use the gymnasium. Read. You have been given access to the areas of the ship equal to that of a civilian. The computer will lock you out of anything that might pose a threat to the welfare of the *Providence* or the Fleet."

"But if I'm . . . instructed, to do something, that probably won't stop me."

He nodded. "I have taken that into consideration and assigned three Vekyans from security to guard you. They're on a rotating shift."

"Guard me? Weren't we just saying—?"

"Yes." He nodded. "You may be a threat to the ship. But your presence may also cause a problem with some of the other passengers on board. A Vekyan nearby should prevent any unpleasantness. You won't go anywhere alone."

A painting of Aurian children on a picnic adorned the opposite wall. Rieka looked at it but didn't see it. Irrationally, she felt as if she wanted to jump out of her skin. Every way she turned generated a sense of manipulation. "Dear God, when will this end?"

Her answer came on a whisper. "As soon as I know all that you do, I hope." He leaned across the small space that separated them and smoothed a lock of her hair. She thought he might kiss her. But then he said, "I'll see you later."

When he was gone, Rieka felt overwhelmed by what

her life had become. Her command was gone and with it, possibly her career; maybe her very existence. She was married to Triscoe but he wouldn't allow himself to love her. Her mind had been altered mysteriously—the extent of which no one knew. The Commonwealth looked on her as a traitor. The Procyons wanted her dead.

She collapsed into a chair and forced herself to push all doubt aside. "I am innocent, dammit. I *am*."

Rieka sat for a long moment trying to focus on what she could do rather than her restrictions. The answers, she knew, would not be found in the pattern of the carpet or the pictures on the wall. Telling herself as her father had told her long ago, that knowledge was the solution to everything, she decided he was right.

Since Triscoe had told her their destination, Rieka knew the trip would take no more than another thirty-four hours. She was familiar with Indra, but had had little contact with its smaller companion, Perata. She decided it might be prudent to familiarize herself with the less populated planet in the Alpha Centauri system.

"Library computer on," she said, moving to sit at the small desk in the corner of the guest salon.

"Activated."

"Access files on the Centauri planet, Perata. I'm looking for information on an individual or individuals who have expertise in telepathic communication."

"There are 152 files within memory. To decrease the number, please be more specific."

Rieka leaned over the desktop and chewed lightly on her lip. "No," she said finally. "I think I'd better have a look at them all."

True to his word, Triscoe returned at the end of his shift. He nodded at Ensign Govidok and rang for admittance, twice. There was no answer.

"She's in there, Captain," Govidok offered. "Hasn't come out since I arrived."

Wondering why she did not respond to the chime,

Triscoe touched the access panel. The door slid open and he stepped inside. He sighed when he found her at the computer desk, chin in her right hand, the left tapping notes on a datapad.

"Rieka." She didn't hear him.

"Rieka."

She stirred. "Huh?" She turned her face from the screen. "Triscoe. Where's your horse and shiny armor?"

Since he wasn't at all sure what she meant, he said, "I have come to take your mind off your incarceration. The day shift is over. How long have you been sitting there?"

Her eyes seemed a bit glazed when she replied, "Since you left."

Triscoe shook his head and ambled to the desk. Knowing her as he did, he felt a strange sense of relief. He certainly couldn't criticize something that had kept her occupied and out of trouble for so long a time. "Save what you were doing and mark your place. You've had enough computer time today."

"But I was—"

"Rieka . . ." He moved to terminate the unit, himself.

She slapped the hand away. "Triscoe!"

"You've been sitting for almost seven hours," he reminded her with a stern look. He hardened his heart against her exasperated expression and wondered why they had recently come to argue so much. "My suggestions for physical outlets were not made lightly. You have ignored them. Now, you will suffer from lack of circulation to your lower limbs, an aching back and a stiff neck, not to mention the strain on your—"

"All right, enough." Rieka glared at him and tapped a final notation onto the datapad. She then shut down the terminal and sagged against the chair. "Happy now?"

Triscoe studied the angry curve of her lips for a moment before he spoke. "Not really. Happiness is a state of mind that does not relate to this conversation."

"Jeez, Triscoe . . ." Rieka pushed out of the seat and stretched. "I wasn't asking if you were in a state of euphoria. I simply asked if you were happy that the computer was off."

He nodded, realizing verbal barriers still existed even though everyone spoke a common language in addition to their native one. "My answer remains the same," he said, finally. "I was pleased, but not happy the computer link was terminated. Perhaps we should find another topic of discussion."

"Try me," she offered, wearing a crooked grin.

"Would you join me for dinner?"

The reply was immediate. "As long as we don't eat alone."

In the corridor, Triscoe forced himself not to smile. "Am I to assume, lady Human, that by a twist of your words I have been insulted?"

The smirk remained on her face, and he was glad, despite the turn of their conversation. It was good to have her bantering and engaging in play. The old Rieka had disappeared after her arrest. She'd been withdrawn and introspective and paranoid, as though doubting herself on a most basic level. And, with that wall in her mind, he couldn't blame her.

Triscoe found it a relief that such negative behavior appeared only temporary. If Yillon's predictions about her were to come true, she had to allow herself to reach her potential. That would not happen if she remained depressed.

When they entered the officers' dining hall, Rieka picked the table. Triscoe thought her a bit too anxious to share it with his medical superintendent, but he could find no fault with her choice of a dining companion. They selected their meals and waited for the food to be heated and brought to the table.

"And how are you handling all of this, Captain?" Dr. Twanabok asked, an expectant look on his broad, leathery, green Vekyan face.

"If I can concentrate on something other than the fix

I'm in, I'm handling it just fine." She made a small waving gesture with her hands. "A captain without a ship, though, isn't something easily forgotten."

"Understandable," the doctor replied. "If you have any free time, I have several experiments in the lab that need tending."

"Sorry. I'm working on something, myself, at the moment."

The Vekyan nodded. His thin, lavender eyes blinked acceptance of her decision. "Even so, the invitation remains. I have enough work for six more technicians."

"Please, Vort," Triscoe interrupted, "no discussions on medicine, staff, or lack thereof. We have a full ship's complement. Nason will not accept my requisition for more personnel."

"This I know," the doctor replied, switching his attention to Triscoe. "Only too well. I was simply suggesting. Since Captain Degahv will be with us for some period of time—and she is capable—the good admiral can not argue with her being put to some functional use." He rested his padded hands on the table and clicked long nail-claws on its shiny surface.

"Unacceptable, Vort. She is our guest."

"Prisoner," corrected Rieka.

Annoyed, Triscoe gave her a stern look. "That was not what I—"

She looked past him at the servebot as it rolled up to the table. He saw a gleam of devilment in her eye. "Oh, good. Here's dinner. I'm starved."

"Then eat."

Triscoe picked up her dish and handed it to her. He passed a second plate to Twanabok, and set his own bowl of *treesh* on the table. The servebot pivoted, producing beverages from a small compartment. Cups of Aurian ra-tea were served.

"Delicious," the doctor commented, chewing on a morsel he'd skewered with his tongue.

Triscoe spooned up some *treesh* and tried to sound

nonchalant as he asked, "Just what are you studying, Rieka? You seemed quite immersed."

"Nothing very interesting," she replied. She sipped her tea and casually went back to forking a piece of fish. "I'm looking into several topics. I started with telepathy. Then I deviated into mind-control techniques. I was working on Centauri customs when you arrived." She looked at Triscoe as if to remind him he'd disturbed her.

"Centauri customs?" he repeated. His curiosity was suddenly overshadowed by uneasiness. Knowing Rieka, it might already be too late to direct her away from the tender subject of his family. "Why?" he asked, trying to make himself sound offhand. "I assure you, we will not be in orbit for any longer than necessary. You'll have limited contact with inhabitants of either Indra or Perata. There is no need to—"

"Surely, you're going to introduce me to your father."

Triscoe sat straighter, almost choking on the *treesh*. The matter of his father was not, as far as he saw it, table conversation. "I would rather not discuss that."

"Why? It's customary for the son to bring home his bride at the earliest opportunity, isn't it?"

Triscoe set his spoon on the table. "That is true, but—"

"But, what?" She looked directly at him. "You're taking me to Perata to meet someone. There's a purpose in that. Your father's some kind of bigwig at a university on Indra, isn't he?"

Not quite sure what a bigwig was, he said, "He's Prefect of Art, however I—"

"Then, technically, according to custom, we're supposed to address him first. Before I'm introduced to your siblings, that is. At least that's what the Centauri files on protocol claim. First mother, then father, then sisters and brothers." She focused her attention on her plate and selected a clump of vegetables and rice.

Triscoe was silently glad to see that her appetite

wasn't a problem although his had completely disappeared. Uncertain as to how to handle her new interest in his family, he wondered if he could casually put her off the topic. "Our library files are correct. Generally. But certain formalities are not employed among all families," he explained, carefully treading the issue as if it were a narrow bridge over a crevasse. "My father would not appreciate an interruption of his work to play host to us. And don't forget, we're on an extremely limited time schedule."

"What? He doesn't eat dinner?" Twanabok asked. About to aim for another piece of seared flesh, the doctor recoiled his tongue so he could speak. "The man cannot be that busy," he said. "And I do believe that both planets are lined up enough, at the moment, that it wouldn't be but a few hours' trip from one to the other."

"Exactly!" Rieka nodded to the doctor. "I don't see why you're so opposed to an introduction, Tris. I realize this marriage of ours is all form and no substance, but it *is* legal. The least we can do is let him know we're coming and drop in to say hello. We wouldn't stay long, and I think it would be bad manners to ignore the opportunity."

"Completely," agreed Twanabok.

Triscoe pushed his bowl aside and shook his head. It was not worth continuing the conversation with the possibility he might let slip the reason for his reluctance to agree to Rieka's suggestion. The only way he had been able to keep the peace in his family was by not speaking to his father. With his mother still on Yadra, it was entirely possible that Ker Marteen wouldn't even let him in the house. Apparently, Rieka hadn't delved too deeply into the customs involving the matriarch's absence.

Perhaps, if he simply said yes to her now, he could change her mind later. He had long since decided that anything was worth keeping his private life private.

"Fine," he said. "I will notify his office when we arrive and ask him to expect us in the early evening."

"Great. I'm looking forward to it." Her brown head bobbed happily, and she returned her attention to her dinner.

While the rest of the meal passed in silence, Triscoe hoped his father would refuse the request. Without his mother's dominant presence to keep the man in line, he doubted Rieka would escape unscathed.

The InterMAT placed them on a small entry terrace. Rieka noted the rough texture on the outer walls, an aggregate of snythetic and natural materials blended to form a honey-colored coating over the entire structure. Wealth could be discerned anywhere, she realized with a smile.

While Triscoe's mother kept her lines of communication open to the Commonwealth, his father's position of Prefect of Art at the University of Bedron was a commendable accomplishment. Because of her own parents' achievements and difficult relationship, Rieka had to wonder if such a marriage had lasted because of—or in spite of—their lengthy separations.

This part of Indra was arid, the shrubs and trees scarce, but the landscape did not lack for beauty. Rieka was pleasantly surprised to find a wind-carved rock set on a raised area and surrounded by angular designs of smooth stones, pebbles, and raked sand.

"This is lovely," she said to Triscoe.

He grunted and continued to press his hand on the identification pad. "Something must be wrong with this," he muttered, as much to her as to himself.

"Why?"

"It doesn't accept my print."

Though she wanted to tease him about being locked out of his own house, Rieka said nothing. Something in his posture and the tone of his voice suggested she tread lightly. His disposition had clearly soured when, after that wicked argument in her quarters, she wouldn't change her mind. She could see no reason for his hardheaded stand on such an ordinary custom. Still, she knew Triscoe pretty well. He did nothing without a reason. The fact that he wouldn't tell her why made her determined to expose this little mystery herself.

The door finally opened. They entered the foyer of the large house as a thin, white-haired woman appeared at the far end of the hall. "Captain Triscoe," she said, beaming. "It's been such a long time. I released the door as soon as I realized it was you." She hurried toward them, eyes on the tall man, and reached out to him with her palms up.

Triscoe returned the gesture before reversing it and placing his hands lightly on hers. "It is good to see you, Nala," he said softly. Then, dropping his arms to his sides, he turned toward Rieka.

"I am pleased to introduce you to Captain Rieka Degahv. Rieka, this is our housekeeper, Nala." He stood back while Rieka repeated the gesture of welcome and friendship.

"It is most gracious of you to welcome us," Rieka replied, recalling yesterday's tutorial with the *Providence* computer.

"This home is yours," Nala said, still smiling.

"Captain Degahv is my wife."

Nala reacted as if Triscoe had tried to cut out her heart with a knife. The woman staggered back, one hand over her chest. Her eyes widened and shifted between the two of them.

"Do not tell him," she whispered.

"I must."

Rieka, both stunned and confused at the interplay, shrugged. "What is going on? I thought this was supposed to be—"

"Nala!" a voice boomed from somewhere at the back of the house. "Is that him?"

"It is, Prefect," she shouted back. "I'll bring them."

"You may bring them in," the voice sounded over her own.

Nala's smile was false this time. Rieka watched her turn and lead them farther into the house with much less vitality than she'd greeted them. Triscoe seemed stiff, almost overwhelmed by his father's voice, and she suddenly felt a shimmer of uneasiness slither down her spine. She wondered, not for the first time, what she'd gotten herself into.

The housekeeper brought them to a large room at the rear of the villa. Two central skylights served as the only windows. The walls were pale gray, emphasizing the variety of artworks that adorned them. Each piece was expertly lit from above or below.

The furnishings were large, soft, and sinuous. High-backed black chairs sat at different angles; some faced paintings on the walls—others, the room's center statue. That piece, a hologram humanoid-form obviously done by a master, was projected over a low table. Rieka was stunned by the studio's magnificence. She had never before seen anything like it in a private home.

With Nala quickly gone, Triscoe gestured for her to accompany him as he crossed the room to speak to his father.

The Prefect sat before *Reddge Entk V'lou,* an Indran painting by Olm, of a lad playing with water. Sunlight glinted off the boy-child's hair and the wet pebbles around him. It almost looked as if the water was actually moving.

"Father," Triscoe began, cleaving Rieka from her study of his picture, "I have come to introduce you to Captain Rieka Degahv of the Fleet ship *Venture.*"

While she waited for some kind of response from the elder Marteen, Rieka realized there had been no preamble of greeting or inquiry as to the man's health. Triscoe had carried on elaborately with his mother on the day of their wedding, but he'd gotten directly to the point with his father. She did not have long to wonder at the peculiar differences in his approach. Triscoe's father explained everything without having to say a word.

"Yes. Well, I suppose you have," the Prefect replied.

He swiveled his chair to glance at them, and a tan eyebrow shot up.

Rieka had long ago schooled herself to the look he gave her. She refused to allow him any satisfaction, and so took no outward notice of it, though she recognized his animosity as if it were a physical thing. This was nothing new. She could not change who or what she was, in fact had no desire to alter her appearance should the option become available. Experience had taught her to try to reveal the inner individual—a person, not a book to be judged by its cover.

"This gallery is . . . extraordinary, Prefect Marteen," she said, gesturing toward the walls. "Your collection is superb."

The man stood, and Rieka noted he was taller than Triscoe. His hair was a mixture of tan and white. He wore it short on top with the sides kept long, swept back and plaited in the traditional Indran style. He looked like an older version of his youngest son, she realized, even to the coloring of his eyes. The prefect's, though, showed no sign of compassion. Their expression mirrored his revulsion.

"Either you have good taste, Captain, or you are deft at what you probably consider a well-placed attempt at flattery," he sneered. "Unfortunately, neither matters to me."

Holding her tongue for a moment, she glanced at Triscoe. His look communicated he was not responsible for his father, and she was on her own. With a rudimentary understanding of the Indran matriarchal structure, she knew the youngest son had little to no authority to influence a parent.

Realizing the perversity of the situation, she returned her attention to the elder Marteen. "Obviously. Of course, I'm only *assuming* these are originals," she murmured.

He smiled, viciously. "They are."

Rieka waited for another caustic remark but none was forthcoming. The taller man seemed to be waiting for her to put her foot in her mouth again. She had no plans to accommodate him. "Regardless of what you might think, Prefect, we did not come here to gawk at a collection of artworks ostentatiously displayed for an audience of one—when in fact it should be shared with the masses."

The prefect puffed out his chest but she continued to speak, making her verbal attack as sweet-sounding as a new mother's coo. "Further, we have not come to disturb you or your work, arbitrarily criticize you, or in any way upset your daily routine. We are here out of Indran custom. One, I might add, that calls for reciprocation of common courtesy."

He glared at her for a long moment. When she did not melt under the scrutiny, he let out a short laugh. "Ha! If only my students had such spunk, Captain."

"Perhaps they've never been in this room," she said.

"I do not care for Humans," he began, peering down at her, "but I appreciate strength of character—in any form."

"I didn't know what to expect, sir, but I'll take what I can get."

He looked at his son. "I can see why you wished me to meet her, Triscoe," he murmured, affection absent from his voice.

"Actually, I don't think you do, Father. It was against my better judgment to bring her here. Perhaps we should sit." Triscoe gestured to the chairs around the *Reddge Entk V'lou*. He angled them away from the painting so they would face each other.

His hesitation gave Rieka a strange taste of suspense. What he hadn't said on the *Providence* was about to be unearthed. She found herself anticipating something she couldn't yet identify, and watched, fascinated, as Triscoe squirmed in his seat.

"Rieka and I—"

"Captain Degahv," the prefect interrupted, "are you not the one who destroyed the Procyon vessel?"

His eyes seared through her, and Rieka fought

valiantly not to show the uneasiness she felt. If he appreciated candid conversation, now was not a time to disappoint him. "Actually, yes, Prefect. I was arrested for treason. My trial begins in eighteen days."

"Damned nuisance, Procyons," he muttered. "Coming at us now and then . . ."

She looked at Triscoe, unsure as to how to respond.

The prefect, however, did not give her the opportunity. "So what in this wide universe are you doing here in my gallery?"

"Paying you a customary visit," she replied simply.

"Explain."

Triscoe cleared his throat, apparently ready to speak. "If you would allow me a word, Father, that's exactly what I planned to do."

The prefect sat back and crossed a leg over his knee. The ruler had apparently decided to grant his subject's request. Rieka thought this holier-than-thou business was getting old, but she recognized it now as an Indran behavior pattern. Because the matriarch was frequently absent for extended periods of time, the male parent flexed his muscle more than necessary. He had his household and children quaking at his every word—but only until his wife returned from her political duties.

"Rieka and I have been married," Triscoe finally blurted.

She had a difficult time watching both father and son. One was trying not to cower, while the other took on the appearance of a contracting star about to blow. She was ready to break the awkward silence when the prefect found his tongue.

"How could you?" he bellowed, rising from the chair. "A Human!" Ignoring Rieka, the older man focused solely on his son. "How could you even have feelings for such a creature? Perhaps the Fleet suffered a fit of *disbiksia* when they allowed a Human to become captain, but I did not expect such fault in you, Triscoe.

"Barj, Meranda, and now you . . ." he growled,

pacing the floor. "All of you . . . with not a grain of respect for my wishes. Not a care that I should have some say in the matter. Not a whit of consideration. How shall I hold my head up now? You come here with this ghastly news and expect me to accept it without argument? Without grave concerns for your sanity?"

Triscoe's response was silence.

"First, you ignore my painstaking search for career placement. Then you scorn me by accepting a Fleet commission. And now marriage to a . . . a *Human*!" He sneered, gesturing at Rieka as though she was as inanimate as one of his statues. "To say the least, I am supremely disappointed in your choice. You knew this and yet you came, bringing her with you, like sand to rub in the wound."

Rieka didn't interrupt the prefect's tirade only because she was focused on Triscoe. His demeanor had completely changed since entering the room. Eyes downcast and shoulders hunched, he seemed to be wearing a mask through which his father's ranting could not penetrate, nor could his own self-esteem. It was as though he were a child again, tolerating abuse by an overbearing parent, not a mature adult able to defend his decisions.

But when the prefect paused to catch his breath, she decided enough was enough. "I've had just about all I can take of this caterwauling," she announced, rising to her feet. She looked directly at the fuming Marteen, who seemed dumbfounded at her remark. "I thought you were a respected citizen, sir," she began, the tone of a captain's disapproval in her voice. "A gracious, educated man whose concerns were in the best interest of his fellow Indran and his family."

She glared at him, no longer caring what he thought of her. What he had done to his son was unspeakable. "I now see why Triscoe did not want to come and pay his respects to you. Why he wanted to shelter me from your prejudice and self-appointed position of power. How embarrassing to have a father not worthy of your respect. And, apparently, your other children feel the same way, too. I won't waste my breath bothering to explain it to you . . . Prefect. A pompous ass such as yourself would be too conceited to understand."

She strode to the door and turned abruptly, deciding to hit him where it actually might hurt. "By the way, I noticed that despite your dislike for my species, you managed to respect us enough to include a Human work of art in your collection. How hypocritical of you. And a V'noran shouldn't be next to a Rembrandt. It interrupts the esthetic flow of the room. Good evening to you." She glanced at Triscoe, who looked as though he'd swallowed something foul, then continued down the hall toward the front door.

He caught up to her quickly, and they passed a wide-eyed Nala, who had obviously overheard the conversation. Rieka smiled, and said pleasantly, "It was very nice to meet you, Nala. I hope our shouting didn't disturb you."

"Not at all, Captain," the housekeeper replied, her voice barely a whisper.

When they got to the front terrace, and the door had closed behind them, Rieka said, "I don't have a TC. If you want to leave, you're going to have to say something."

Triscoe took several deep breaths before he looked at her. Out of his father's domineering presence, his features softened. It seemed odd for him to jump in and out of character so quickly, but he had. A small dimple puckered on his left cheek and he shook his head as if unable to believe what he'd witnessed. "Rieka . . . no one else has *ever* done that . . . except for Mother, of course."

Her brows lifted in mild surprise, realizing his earlier gelded spirit was as much custom as habit. Fortunately, Prefect Marteen had no such power over her. "Of course."

Five

"For heaven's sake, don't you ever sleep?" Rieka groused a few hours later, covering her eyes with the back of her hand. The lights had come on with Triscoe's spoken command. "And for that matter, don't you ever knock?"

As he stood in the bedroom's open doorway, her questions remained unanswered. "We are in orbit over Perata. He is waiting for us."

Her vision adjusted to the glare of the overhead light. She looked at the wall chrono and sighed. "This had better be worth it." Swiping dark hair from eyes that felt like wet sandpaper, Rieka slid from the sleeping pallet. She wore only one garment, a maroon sleep-shift that hung midway to the knee. She glanced at Triscoe and sensed her pseudohusband's appreciation of what he saw.

As Rieka reached for her hairbrush, she offered him a patronizing smile. "Look, Tris, I need five minutes to get changed and cleaned up. Want to wait in the salon?"

"No."

She only half hoped he was joking, but being wakened from REM sleep did nothing for her disposition. The smile faded, and she pointed the brush at him as if it were a weapon. "If you don't get your carcass out of here right now, whoever the hell 'he' is can just wait until snowballs turn green."

Triscoe remained unruffled at her halfhearted threat. "Actually, on Medoura I have personally constructed a

green snowball. But I doubt that Yillon would care."
He continued to lean on the doorjamb and watch her.

Rieka felt her jaw drop and snapped it shut. "Yillon?
The Indran Oracle?"

When he nodded, she frowned. Her assumption that
Triscoe knew an accredited psiologist who would get
to the bottom of her mnemonic alteration fell flat. An
audience with the so-called Indran Oracle was dubious
at best. Still, he didn't often act on impulse. "I thought
that was just a legend," she said.

"He exists," Triscoe replied softly. "Few people
know this. Fewer have actually seen him."

Rieka nodded absently as her intellect absorbed the
information. That did not, however, stop her heart from
beating strangely, as if she was being asked to enter a
sacred shrine. "Okay. So he's real, and somehow he
knows we're coming. What's this Indran Oracle got to
do with me and my memory? I thought you were taking
me to some therapist or something." She felt a slight
chill and didn't know if it was due to her state of dress
or the conversation. Suppressing a shiver, she crossed
her arms over her chest.

"For centuries Yillon has been able to see into the
future," Triscoe began, his answer to her question evasive. "But he has many other talents. He can sift
through your thoughts and know things you don't. He
can move objects great distances. He can impress
images upon your mind and make you think you see
what is not really there."

That claim was completely ridiculous, but the look
on Triscoe's face warned her that disagreeing with him
would be taken as an insult. *He* believed in the Oracle.
And if he believed, there had to be some truth in what
he said. Wondering what she was getting herself into,
again, she stammered, "This doesn't sound . . . exactly
like—what I had in mind."

Triscoe looked directly at her, his jaw set. There was
no doubt he was serious. "The alteration of your
memory is the tip of an iceberg—to coin a phrase from

Earth. Yillon has sensed this and needs to see you, Rieka. I am charged with bringing you to him."

She huffed. "The tip of an iceberg? I thought we'd agreed this was some . . . internal Fleet—racial thing, having to do with personnel and my rank."

"I never said that, precisely. I apologize for not always speaking the truth to you, but I have not been sure exactly what to say."

She frowned at him. "And you expect me to accept that?" She laughed. "If you're trying to scare me, you'll have to do something else. I'll go so far as admit that Yillon might actually exist. And he might actually have some paranormal talents. But *you're* as normal as they come, Triscoe Marteen. There's no way you'd believe in fantasy."

He looked steadily at her for a moment, then let out a long quiet sigh. "What I believe is not central to our problem. I will grant you your five minutes of solitude." He backed up a step, and the door closed, leaving Rieka alone with her thoughts.

After splashing water on her face and giving her teeth a once-over with a sonic unit, she slipped into her uniform and went out the door to join her husband. The salon was empty. "Figures," she mumbled and, without missing a stride, left the suite.

Triscoe glanced at Rieka as she stepped into the InterMAT cubicle, her stomach rumbling. He felt suddenly guilty for waking her and only allowing enough time for her to dress. His hands hovered over the controls as he tried to come to terms with the way he'd treated her.

"An empty stomach is better than a full one," he said, thinking of his earlier visits to Yillon's subterranean installation.

"I had a few sips of poten-3," she offered. "Figured I needed something."

He nodded and finished programming the InterMAT before moving back to stand at her shoulder. In a moment they were deposited in a small white room, a cube about two meters to a side. The walls provided enough internal light to see that there were no doors or any other seams in the room's construction.

Rieka huffed. "Where in the name of Sol are we?"

Triscoe saw disbelief on her face and heard the irritation in her voice. It seemed that nothing he did today was going to be pleasant. The white room had only happened twice before. It hadn't even occurred to him that Yillon would resort to its use today. "I apologize. This is my doing," he said softly.

She cocked her head at him. "What—you misdirected the InterMAT?"

"No." Embarrassed, he was overcome by the need to look anywhere but at her. "We have arrived at Yillon's retreat. This is a preliminary place before the audience. He requires . . . I have . . . This has happened before. I am not at one with myself. He will not admit us until I have reconciled something."

"What?"

"I don't know."

She leaned her shoulder against the cushioned wall, crossing her arms. "Well, while you're deciding what *that* is, I'd like to reconcile a little something with you, myself."

He looked up and wasn't sure he liked the expression on her face. Her sapphire eyes seemed to bore into him like a drill. Certain her anger had nothing to do with Yillon's intent, Triscoe found the courage to ask, "And what is that?"

"Our relationship."

"Yes."

"We have one?"

Unsure of her accusatory tone, Triscoe fidgeted. "I thought so."

"Actually," Rieka said, correcting herself, "we have two. The one where we were good friends. Compatible. Comfortable. Honest. And the one where we're married. Cold. Distant. Grating on the nerves. Personally, I liked being friends. This marriage bit is . . . well, if I were a Boo, I'd say it factored as easily as pi."

Triscoe felt an unwelcome weight in his chest. He'd kept her beyond arm's reach for a very good reason. Unsure of how to resolve the dilemma, he hoped he could express himself to her satisfaction.

Looking her in the eye, Triscoe said, "I did not marry you with the intent of sending us into a lifelong purgatory. I knew it would be difficult when our Fleet transit schedules did not connect with any great frequency. But I also hoped we would be able to cope with that until we were no longer on touring assignments."

Confusion clouded her expression as she absorbed his reply. "I thought it was just so you could get custody of me—and get me off Yadra, so we could have this memory thing sorted out," she said quietly, the abrasiveness gone from her voice.

"I told you there were many reasons, Rieka. I meant that."

The look on her face said she wanted to believe him. She uncrossed her arms. "Truth?"

Triscoe nodded. "That is what this room is all about."

"Okay," she smiled, thankfully accepting his word. "When we first met—way back at Eridani—I remember the way you looked at me. There was this big room full of hopeful new captains. All ten planets were represented, but there were only two Humans. Xu Li and I were standing off to the side of the buffet table. You walked directly to us, but I don't think you ever saw him.

"I remember you started to do the Indran greeting, then stopped and extended your right hand. And I remember thinking, 'This guy is a Centauri, why would he want to greet the Human hopefuls?' " She shrugged. "Nobody else wanted to. But I shook your hand and introduced myself. And—"

"—and I already knew your name," Triscoe finished. "Yillon had seen you in my life," he said, admitting the one thing he had never planned to confess. "He'd written of it when I was still in school—before I'd ever considered a career in the Fleet. You and I were both children when he began my story. That book has been a painful relic," he added quietly, "until now."

The look of surprise on her face was almost immediately replaced by one of confusion. "I don't understand." She tilted her head, as if coaxing him to explain.

"You heard what my father said. He had certain plans laid for my future. When my mother learned I had the capability to Singlemind, she sent me to Perata—ostensibly to school. But in fact, Yillon had contacted her and requested my presence.

"I learned many things as his pupil, including the proper way to approach the *quantivasta*—what you call the Singlemind. Yillon had seen the course of my life and chose to direct me. My father does not know this. He simply thinks my decisions have been made to discredit him—or to spite him."

Rieka nodded. "I got the impression that he's a brilliant idiot."

Triscoe's dimple surfaced. "You have a most disarming way with words."

"Mmm. So, Yillon took you under his wing. He predicted your career and directed you to meet your destiny as a Fleet captain . . . not to mention, me." She gestured vaguely with her hands. "I don't see where this is going."

Now that he had told her some of his story, Triscoe wanted to make sure he gave her the rest of it in a way she could understand. He hesitated, pinching the knot of skin between his brows, then leaned his back against the wall. It abruptly molded into a chairlike contour.

"We must be getting somewhere," Rieka laughed. "At least the old boy's going to let us be comfortable." She pushed against the wall and sat, too.

"I did not feel obligated to greet you," he said finally. "I was *compelled* to meet you, and I have been grateful ever since that first moment when you shook my hand."

"Why? I mean, why grateful?"

"Because you are . . . magnificent. Everything Yillon had told me was accurate—but you are so much more than simple statistics. At that time, I had met few Humans. Most were rather ordinary. Some seemed bitter, probably because—as you have reminded me so often—of the second-class way they've been treated. That first time at Dani, I expected to meet a new Human captain with a chip on her shoulder. What I saw was a woman who wanted to make the Commonwealth a better place for all. How could I not grow fond of you?"

Her face showed her embarrassment, but he continued. "Our Fleet command training threw us together in highly adverse situations. None of us were used to combat—real or imaginary. I learned to trust you—so easily. It was almost alarming, yet I could not deny Yillon's truth. Our first Singlemind confirmed that truth. The second was nothing but indulgence on my part. And I felt guilty—as though I was using you. And, in a way, I was. Yet you stuck by me, invited my friendship . . ." He looked at her. "How could I resist?"

"Tris, are you trying to tell me I've been manipulated since the moment I met you?"

"No. Rieka . . . don't ever think that. I would have cared for you even if I'd never met Yillon. You have acted completely on your own," he assured her. "I don't have the capacity to alter the future; no one does."

She nodded and gnawed on her bottom lip. Triscoe sensed she didn't completely believe him and searched for a way to soothe her confusion. "Which brings us to your first question—our relationship."

Knowing that once she was examined by Yillon, he would be free to trust her again, Triscoe allowed himself a margin of relaxation. He moved to sit next to her, the chair seeming to anticipate the action. Taking her hand in his, Triscoe felt an intense warmth in his chest. Her eyes were hesitant and hopeful at the same time.

"I truly wish things had been different," he began softly. "I would never have given you cause to question my feelings had it not been for—the circumstances that have brought us here. I think you must perceive my love but are unaware of its depth. When we have proven your innocence to the Commonwealth, I promise that I shall habitually make my affection for you quite obvious. Perhaps embarrassingly so."

Rieka's smile was endearing, even though she was shaking her head. "I never would have guessed that you had ulterior motives," she said. "But, I suppose I could have seen it if I wasn't so wrapped up in myself. I'm sorry if I—"

"Don't . . . apologize." Barely breathing, Triscoe lowered his lips to hers. It was nothing like the simple affectionately friendly kisses of the past. The moment he touched her, he was committed. There was no move to pull apart, no concern for propriety. They were alone and of the same mind, at last. He released her hand to slide his fingers through her hair and she wrapped her arms around his neck. As he held his wife intimately for the first time, Triscoe dismissed all doubt.

They did, as Yillon had foretold, belong together.

K'resh-va smiled his awkward Centauri smile as the ship entered the Epsilon Indi system. They cruised past the orbits of two Jovian planets, a small asteroid field, and a cold, airless world too far from its sun to be a candidate for life. He did not have to wait long for Aurie to appear before them, a small sphere glowing faintly blue. But he did not stop there. The *Novil* slipped silently and invisibly past, on course for its rendezvous on the opposite side of the star.

"How are we on the time?" he asked, fighting the desire to tap his toe. It was habit, but almost impossible to perform in magnetic boots. He wiggled them instead, and tugged at the neckline of the repulsive Fleet uniform he now wore.

"Deviations of only three millidits, Commander

K'resh-va," S'ntin-na, his second-in-command, replied. She looked up at him and showed her lower teeth in the Procyon version of a smile. "The *Shaman* has just appeared on the scope."

"Well-done," he said. "Hail them when we know Ep-Indi will distort the signal to our rear."

"At your command."

He waited impatiently until an Aurian face appeared, the man's bibbets flushing a bright pink with concern.

"Commander K'resh-va, I am honored to meet you," he said, kneeling so deeply even the top of his head momentarily left the screen. "We have been looking forward to your arrival."

K'resh-va peered at the other's image. He understood the intricacies of reading Aurian bibbets. The darker the color in combination with the thickness of the welt determined the intensity of the given emotion.

"I can see that, M'narn," he said, finally. "What has you so preoccupied? Has something altered the schedule?"

The bright welts on the Aurian's forehead all but throbbed. The smile he flashed was false, and his eyes blinked nervously. "We have suffered a small setback, Commander. Nothing that will upset our plans, I assure you."

K'resh-va pursed his lips in the now almost-habit of the alien race whose appearance he wore. "What has happened?"

The man's image shifted uneasily across the screen. "Captain Pedlam is . . . dead. There was an altercation, and the guards accidentally used excessive force. There was no hope of saving him."

K'resh-va sat back in his chair and snorted. As long as he lived, he would never understand the sentimentality of these people—even toward their enemies. "And you think I would have cared?" he jeered. "The life of one Centauri captain means extraordinarily little to me, M'narn, as does yours. Simply perform your duties, and you shall be duly compensated."

"Yes, but, Commander . . ."

"What?"

"He is dead! Someone will surely miss him. What if the Fleet should launch an investigation? It will send them directly to Aurie. Our operation would stand in jeopardy. Your plans might fail."

K'resh-va stared long and hard at the alien. From the other's point of view, such concerns might seem undeniable, he realized. It was one aspect of Commonwealth mentality he had yet to master. Fortunately, there would be little opportunity for further situations such as this to occur.

"You are mistaken if you think that the Commonwealth will have a moment to spare searching for one misplaced captain. In less time than you might imagine, their Transport Fleet will be engaged in war with the Procyon advance forces. It is a war they will not win."

"But—"

"Procyons take what they require, M'narn. And we require the resources of the Commonwealth. Nothing else matters. Our people have waited two long centuries. We will wait no longer," K'resh-va barked.

"Of course, Commander," M'narn replied, looking contrite. "I am glad that this event has proved to be of no consequence." He looked at someone to his right, then back to the camera. "We are prepared to transfer you to our ship."

"Negative. S'ntin-na will handle all transfer of personnel. Has Pedlam's ship become aware that he is missing?"

"We have received no indication of such," M'narn said. "He was instructed to tell them he would be off TC for a two-day vacation. By the time you arrive to take his place, you will have no difficulty slipping into the schedule. Of course, we removed his prints and TC before disposing of the body. You will have ample time to be fitted with those, as well."

"Very good. And O'don-la?"

"Your first officer has already assumed his role. He is presently on his way to Forty Eridani to assist in Pedlam's—that is, your—assumption of command of the *Prodigy*."

K'resh-va nodded once. He detested traitors, even those who now worked for the Procyons. This Aurian thought once the Commonwealth had been defeated, he would be well paid for his assistance and given a prominent place in the scientific community. The fool.

"Well done, Doctor," he said, thankful his contact with this man would be limited. "My second has signaled me she will be ready for transport momentarily."

"I look forward to greeting you personally, Commander," M'narn replied, his bibbets now faintly glowing pink in anticipation.

"K'resh-va out." With the signal cut, he looked at S'ntin-na. "You do realize I am unsure as to when I will be able to communicate with you."

"The *Prodigy* is scheduled for its maiden voyage in eighteen days," she said. Her head tilted at the conflicting facts.

"Do not count on it," he advised. "Delays are common with first-of-its-kind vessels. I will send word if that is so."

S'ntin-na sneered at the Commonwealth uniform on her commanding officer. He found it humorous that she did not try to hide her disgust. "I will wait."

K'resh-va-Pedlam let out a short Procyon howl and clapped her on her neck. "We shall have such a time, my friend." He smiled a lower-toothed smile. "Two hundred years has been a long time to wait, but the *Prodigy* is scheduled to spearhead the takeover of the Commonwealth. I shall ask for you, personally, when we set forth, so that you may share in the glory."

Six

A door formed in the white wall, revealing a long, dark corridor. Triscoe stood slowly, eyeing the strange passage. Rieka didn't like the look on his face. She glanced down the hallway again. It was empty.

"What's the matter? Let's go." She stepped toward the exit, but he grabbed her elbow and pulled her back. Irritated, she yanked her arm away. "Give me one good reason why we shouldn't use the door. Isn't your 'reconciliation' over with?"

Triscoe frowned, his eyes still fixed on a point somewhere far down the tunnel. "What is that Human idiom: 'Out of the frying pan, into the fire'?"

"Are you trying to scare me?" Squinting, she peered into the emptiness. "I see nothing but a corridor with a few dim lights embedded into the ceiling. The walls look like rock. This must be the way to Yillon's studio—or whatever he calls it."

"It is," Triscoe said softly. "But the labyrinth can be deadly."

Rieka bounced back from her toes to her heels and accepted the tunnel with new respect. Since there seemed to be no other way to Yillon, she arched her back and flexed her arms, took a deep breath, and exhaled. "Okay," she nodded, her body already pumping adrenaline for the waiting adventure. "I'm ready."

He took his eyes off the tunnel and focused on her. "We're not going in there."

"Of course we are."

He shook his head. "Unacceptable."

She began to wonder at his talent at finding a shortcut to her impatience. "Triscoe, there's no other way."

"If we wait long enough, Yillon will see my determination not to endanger you. He will provide us with another route."

She huffed. Despite her bridge crew's attitude, she was not used to having her decisions questioned. Centauri or not, she refused to consider Triscoe as anything other than her equal. She'd been going along with his every request for days, but enough was enough. Her answers were at the end of the tunnel, and she was going to have them.

"I'm so tired of your lame excuses, I could . . . never mind," she snapped. "But I'm not going to wait anymore. If this is the way to Yillon"—she gestured toward the doorway—"I'll take my chances. You can stay here if you like."

"I'm not about to let you enter alone."

"Then let's go!"

He looked at her for a long moment, then sighed. "All right." The set of his jaw told Rieka the decision went against his better judgment. "But we must endeavor to memorize the path in the event we need to retreat. I'll count the number of steps, you keep track of the direction we travel."

"No problem."

"Your confidence is inspiring," he replied. After one last look that almost caused her to change her mind, Triscoe took a hesitant step toward the doorway, then plowed through.

Rieka had to hustle, but she managed to keep pace with him. They entered the corridor at a respectable speed, and she hoped it wouldn't last long. But she soon found that wasn't her biggest problem. The tunnel had many forks, twists, and turns. It was nearly impossible to keep track of them all. Then, after several minutes of wondering if the fire in her calves might actually ignite, she heard a slight sound. Triscoe had managed to get a second stride ahead of her, and she was poised to argue about it when he stopped abruptly. It was all she could do not to barrel into him. She opened her mouth but choked back a retort when she saw his finger go to his lips. His anxiety pulled her attention away from both the pending argument and the task of memorization.

"What is it?" she whispered, trying to catch her breath.

"Say nothing."

He motioned her to stay put, then edged forward in the near darkness. Rieka was not thrilled to see him disappear, especially when she heard the noise again. This time, it was not far behind her, a soft, scraping noise. Cautious and curious, she turned around.

The dim passageway revealed nothing.

She very nearly called out when something touched her shoulder. Knowing instinctively that it was Triscoe, she managed only to suck in a lungful of air and peer up into his frown.

"It's in front of us," he said so softly she barely heard him.

"What?"

"A grimmut. They're scavengers of the labyrinth. Large. Carnivorous. Deadly."

She winced at the thought. "There's one behind us, too."

"That's impossible. They don't rove in packs."

"Why must you always contradict me?" she hissed, poking him in the sternum. "I'm intelligent. I'm a captain. I've proved to men better than you that I can think for myself—and yet it seems like every time I say something that doesn't happen to match your way of—"

"—shh." He clamped a hand over her mouth. She glared up at him when he whispered, "I think I did hear something from that direction."

Knowing that discretion was the better part of valor, Rieka discarded an urge to be smug while slapping his hand away. "It's a lot closer now, too. It's nearly on us."

"We must go forward." He took her by the hand and held it tightly.

"That's where you heard the first one," she reminded him.

"True, but it was much farther down. Our chances are better if we draw them closer to one another."

"How do you figure that? This way it's two against one."

"If they were close enough together, they might attack each other," he explained softly. "You've never seen a grimmut. Personally, I would prefer that you didn't."

Silently, Rieka agreed. She'd only entered the labyrinth because she hoped Yillon could uncork her repressed memories. It was supposed to be a much more clinical environment, with lots of light and no pesky grimmuts to worry about. In a reflex action, she reached for her maitu, then sighed inwardly at the weapon's absence. She still felt awkward without her TC. The lack of an instrument with which to defend herself only augmented the fact that, should she be separated from Triscoe, there was no way to call for help.

"I didn't come here to die," she whispered. "I have no intention of—"

The sound in front of them, now only meters away, motivated both her silence and Triscoe's sudden lurch to the wall. He pulled her with him, and she landed against his chest with a thud. Had he not squeezed her fingers for silence, she would have been happy to give him anything but.

The grating sound from the creature to the rear, now very close, made her dismiss the situation as adventure and look on it as a test of survival. She tried to imagine why Yillon would keep grimmuts in his labyrinth. Surely visitors were not *that* unwelcome.

She squelched a shiver down her spine when Triscoe put his mouth to her ear. He breathed once, then spoke in a tone almost softer than breathing.

"When I tell you, drop to the floor, keep to wall, and make yourself as small as possible."

The shifting, scraping sound now came from both directions. Not wanting to speak, Rieka nodded once. In a situation like this, his prior experience meant a great deal. For the moment, at least, she decided not to question his orders. They remained like a statue in the dark for another long moment. A sudden snarl made her jerk her head, but Triscoe held her tight.

The lack of light was intensely frustrating. Rieka squinted and strained her eyes through the darkness. The moment she thought she saw something move, Triscoe was pushing her down. She took this as his signal and flattened herself to the corner where the floor met the wall. Not daring to turn her head, she knew the two grimmuts had found one another. Their sounds changed from muffled grunts to higher-pitched whines and snorts. She caught a whiff of pungent stench and felt something lick across her back. She stayed like a rock until a roar filled the corridor with such a sound she thought it would shatter her heart.

A twin to the first challenge rang out, loud enough to make the floor vibrate. Then she felt the concussion of an immense thud. More horrifying noises of battle ensued, each echoing upon the other, and Rieka found her breath coming in great gulps. She managed to take hold of the hysteria she felt and was able to put it to use when Triscoe again found her hand, pulled her to her feet, and set off at a run.

One glance over her shoulder explained why he had preferred her not to see a grimmut. Almost as large as a mature polar bear of Earth, their heads were huge, possessing open-grinned mouths with several rows of needlelike teeth, many of which were broken off. At the back of the head, tubular organs not quite like tentacles whipped through the air. They had a shaggy, matted, furlike covering the color of which Rieka could only guess at in the darkness. Life-blood oozed from a shoulder wound in the closer creature. She didn't have the opportunity to see how its adversary fared, for Triscoe hauled her away so quickly the image had been absorbed in a single glance.

They hurried on for several minutes before he slowed and felt his way along the wall. Then they found an intersecting corridor, and she turned left. Rieka thought it odd when he didn't badger her as to which way they should go, but decided not to mention it. After another twenty meters, or so it seemed in the semidark, a thin shaft of brightness caught her eye. She whispered, "What's that?"

His head whipped around, and, seeing the bead of light stretching across the floor, he breathed a sigh of relief. "Our destination."

They walked toward it and found a seam in the wall, from which the light spewed.

"How can this be our destination?" she hissed. "It's just a crack."

He frowned down at her. "Pessimism is not a becoming emotional state. Do you want to see Yillon?"

"Of course."

He grabbed both her hands and held them in his. "Rieka, he knows you are here. He sees into your mind. You won't gain admittance unless you can communicate your desires and motivations. Yillon is not an oracle for just anyone who seeks advice."

"I know, I know." Irritated that he was thinking so poorly of her, Rieka bit the inside of her lip and kept her tongue. She allowed herself to focus on the light from the crack and calm her thoughts into a need to know the truth.

To her amazement, the crack slowly grew wider. The wall did not recede to allow passage, it simply disappeared as if it had only been an image in the first place. Yillon's image, she realized. In her mind.

Once the dimensions were large enough to allow them to pass, Triscoe looked down at her with such intensity she didn't know what to think. He whispered, "I knew all along it would be a simple task for you."

Not sure quite how to respond to such a cryptic remark, she removed her hands from his and turned her attention to the doorway. "Coming?" She didn't wait for an answer before putting a determined foot over the threshold.

"Yillon?" she half asked, half announced once her eyes adjusted to the light. She spoke to a small, unassuming man of indeterminate years. If it hadn't been for the sense of power she felt from him, Rieka would have guessed he was just somebody's great-great-grandfather. She smiled, and it was reflected in his face.

"Captain Degahv. Rieka. Welcome." He lifted a bony hand and beckoned her closer.

Rieka took the invitation. "I am most honored to meet you. It is an audience of great importance to me. But . . . I guess you already know that." She approached, stood a respectful distance away, and bowed her head.

"I had expected you not quite so soon," he said, his voice a magma of baritone that rolled over her. "But then, seconds are really inconsequential in the ultimate scheme."

Without an answer, she simply smiled again and nodded. She took in the man, his countenance and surroundings in a single glance. Yillon was approximately her height with parchment-pale skin and shocks of long white hair gracing his high brow. It covered his ears and trailed across his shoulders. His face was severely wrinkled, but the youth in his eyes amazed her. The combination gave the impression of agelessness.

The room was almost barren of personal belongings. She saw a cot, table, and chair along the wall to the left and a large padded chair to the right. Behind Yillon, as he stood almost in the center of the large room, was some sort of computer.

Rieka breathed a bit easier. This was more what she imagined—a well-lit chamber with at least some form of modern equipment in it.

Yillon's attention shifted. His smile emerged again as he took in Rieka's companion, and he said, "Did I not write this of you in one of my volumes? Have I ever given cause to doubt?" His tone was at once loving and chastising, like a father with a recalcitrant son.

"Yes—and no," Triscoe respectfully replied. "I am glad to see you are well."

Rieka realized he was trying to maintain his dignity—something he hadn't done with his father. The old man seemed to ignore that as he shuffled toward the only comfortable chair in the room, then sat. She couldn't help smiling. The two of them were obviously performing some kind of customary routine. Knowing what she did about them both, she felt like an intruder.

With a sigh, Yillon nodded at Triscoe, who walked past Rieka and said something to the computer terminal. The wallcovering behind the cot began to fold in on itself and Rieka saw that it masked row after row of shelves. Each was crammed with volumes of hard-covered books.

"They must be priceless," she gasped, not thinking. Books, even for Humans, were considered a thing of the past.

"Possibly," Yillon replied. "I have long since come to the realization that value is an extremely personal concept. How ironic that most of civilization as we know it uses such an abstraction as its very cornerstone. Eh?"

"I suppose that is true," she agreed. Her eyes were now on Triscoe, who had gone to a specific spot behind the table and was examining one of Yillon's many volumes.

"It is his book," the old man answered before the question had reached her lips. "I have been speaking to him for twenty-three years. A very short time. His *quantivasta*-gift is strong—though not as strong as mine. Eh?" He chuckled to himself at this small joke. "I have only a few true visitors in a year's time. It is always pleasant to see him."

"If you'd rather see more people, why don't you—"

"Be rid of the illusion of the labyrinth and grimmuts? They serve their purpose." The youthful eyes searched hers for a long moment.

"An illusion?"

"Surely. I would never allow anyone to be harmed. Did you think so? Eh?" He chuckled deeply in his throat.

"Seclusion is necessary for me, Captain Degahv. I would otherwise be inundated by those seeking a profit on tomorrow's marketline. Or spouses wishing to ascertain their partner's fidelity." He waved his hand, dismissing the statement.

"Drivel. To answer such queries is to fart into the subconscious. To create where there is no necessity is a form of pollution." He shook his head slowly, the thinning white hair catching on the nubby fabric of his tunic. "I am a keeper of meanings. Lives. Secrets. The future. You are here because of necessity—not just to you, but for everyone."

Rieka saw the truth in his eyes but could not comprehend his words. She held the truth for everyone? Could the Procyon ship have been *that* important? In a way, she didn't want to know. But it was too late to back out now.

Triscoe replaced the book in its spot and turned to them. "You were right, as always, Yillon."

The ancient man nodded and beckoned him closer. "She holds the lock. I have the key. Perhaps we should begin."

Triscoe walked toward the chair, catching Rieka by the hand as he did. He knelt them down on a cushion before the old man and closed his eyes.

"Is there some kind of preparation for this?" she asked quitely.

"The grimmuts prepared you, my dear." Yillon's smile held inner meanings. "They took your trivial concerns from you and put in their place the simple need to survive. Now, you are focused. The adrenaline in your system is still high. Close your eyes. I will discover your hidden thoughts. If Triscoe can join us, he may."

She looked once more at Yillon's broad nose and cheekbones covered with the leathery skin. That he could be a true oracle was both astounding and understandable.

She closed her eyes. "I'm ready."

Rieka felt her consciousness slide down a long dark path of restless energy before she heard his voice. "I have found your hidden time," he said softly. "Find me in your mind, and I will lead you through the door."

Rieka slowly sifted into the recent past, always with the feeling that someone else was present. She backtracked her wedding, incarceration, the trip to Medoura to deliver the shipment, the destruction of the *Vendikon*. Yillon coaxed her back farther.

She glimpsed the *Venture*'s short layover at the Vekya clearing depot and its previous stop at the Fleet shipyard at Dani, one of twelve planets orbiting Gahn, a star known to Humans as Forty Eridani.

"More," he said quietly. So intent on the task, she could not discern whether the command had been verbal or not.

Prior to the shipyard, Rieka recalled the voyage from Aurie, the planet in orbit around Epsilon Indi.

"Here." Yillon said, the words booming across both the room and her mind. "Here is where the blockade has been raised. We must find its weakness and break through."

Eyes still closed, she nodded and took a deep breath, determined to remember every detail of the layover. They had docked at the spaceport, made their delivery, and the passengers had disembarked. Twenty crewmen were granted a two-shift leave.

"What did you do on this planet?"

"Visited colleagues and an old friend," she said softly. "Socialized at the Fleet compound. Went hiking. Got into a speed volley tournament. Did a weapons inspection on the *Venture*. Wrote out a—"

"Hike," blurted Yillon. "Take me on that hike."

Rieka concentrated. She'd struck out in the early morning for a particularly picturesque area in the Krinkin Mountains of Aurie's number three quadrant. It was strange, but there seemed to be a problem when she tried to recall the entire day. She'd worn her TC but had requested a signal-block since the purpose of the hike was a few hours of solitude.

Largely unpopulated, the Krinkins were known for spectacular waterfalls. Water-creatures called *kinara*, local to the area, often grew longer and wider around than her leg, and Rieka had been told of their aquatic antics both above and below the waterline. She hoped to catch them in action, maybe take a hologram or two.

She climbed several hundred feet over reasonably smooth terrain before stopping to admire one of the less popular falls and a crystalline lake surrounded by sharp-needled trees rooted along the shallows.

The time had been early afternoon. She remembered dropping her pack to find something to eat, then deciding to wait until she was really hungry.

But her next recollection of the day found the sun close to the horizon and her position only a few feet from the edge of the lake.

"Go back, again," Yillon prompted. "Stay with that moment when the sun was against the falling water and the sky was pink and filled with high clouds."

She formed the picture in her mind a second time. Slowly, a kind of pressure seemed to build. It encased her entire being until she could feel its weight against her bones. Involuntarily, she began to tremble. She slumped forward and felt Triscoe's arms around her, but even his strength could not help.

"Stay with it," Yillon warned.

Her breath came in gasps and snorts. She moaned and whimpered, but it sounded distant, barely recognizable. She heard Triscoe speak, in her ears or her mind, she couldn't tell. He shouted to Yillon. But the old man didn't hear. He was in her head, drilling a hole through the wall around her memories.

In addition to pressure, there came pain. It wracked through her yet stayed fast in her mind. It was a searing, heat-filled wall of fire. Yillon was the cause, yet Rieka knew if she tried to push him away, they would never know the truth.

The spasms became worse. The ache intensified. She held her breath, oblivious to everything but the assault. Finally, no longer able to internalize the agony, she cried out. The sobs overtook the shrill sound as the searing pain slacked off. Yillon retreated from her mind.

When she recovered enough to be aware of her surroundings, Rieka found herself panting into Triscoe's shoulder. She wiped at her eyes and cheeks with the back of her hand and was surprised to see it smeared with blood rather than the transparent wetness of tears.

Triscoe gasped as he realized what had happened, but Yillon reacted first. "Here," he said, handing her a wad of what looked like cotton floss but felt like paper. She took the material and pinched her nose to staunch the flow of blood.

The questions in her mind were answered when the old man replied, "It was difficult. But it is done. These people are very shrewd in their ability to control memory. I did not find any other barriers to the past." He peered down at her. "I hope you are unhurt?"

"I'll live," she replied through the cotton wad. She was still breathing hard, but the earlier discomfort was completely gone. When she glanced at Triscoe and saw his concern, she knew this wasn't a normal occurrence. She also noticed the effort had taken its toll on Yillon. He looked suddenly fatigued, as if his old bones had barely been able to endure the strain.

"Can you remember, now?" he asked quietly.

Rieka sat back on her cushion. "I met someone," she said after a moment. "A blond woman. Centauri—maybe. She came running down the path. Her companion had fallen when they were exploring the cavern behind the falls. I went with her to see what I could do."

"Then what happened?"

Rieka closed her eyes to better picture the memory. "We climbed the trail to a place behind the wall of water. We found a man leaning against the side of the cave. I was about to turn off the signal-block on my TC, so I could call the ship, when he pulled a weapon on me. But it wasn't like a maitu or even a gun with a barrel. He used it to threaten me."

"Go on."

She thought for a moment. "He wasn't really hurt. The pair of them ushered me through a door behind the falls. We went down a hallway, and they took me into a room."

"Describe it."

"Nothing spectacular," she said after a moment. "Pale green walls, some equipment on one of them, some on rolling carts. A gray body pad on a pedestal in the middle. A strange light contraption in the ceiling. A couple of chairs. They put me on the body pad."

Triscoe squirmed but said nothing. Yillon ignored him. "Continue, Captain."

She dabbed at the clotted blood under her nose. "A hiss on my shoulder." She frowned. "They shot me with something. I felt like . . . like lead. I couldn't move, just breathe and look around.

"Someone else came in the room. An Aurian with dark hair. And an Oph. He carried the odor the males do when they rut. I remember his eyes were all clouded, like he'd been pounding *ciffa*. He touched my arm."

Rieka rubbed the place as she remembered the pressure of the alien's rough pads. Triscoe shifted his weight and leaned against Yillon's chair, watching her. Then he took the bloodied wad from her and got up to put it in a decomposer.

"The others were behind my head. I could only hear them. Then their voices moved away. But the Oph stayed." She grimaced. "He lifted my tunic. His paws, I remember them on my skin. I couldn't move. I couldn't even turn my head. God, I wanted to . . . I managed to make a sound that attracted the others' attention. They made him leave the room, and the woman who found me pulled my shirt down.

"They turned on the overhead light. It was bright blue. Intense. Blinding. The Aurie man with dark hair wrapped a gag over my mouth."

Triscoe reseated himself as she continued. "The room was darkened so the light was all I could see. It hurt—even with my eyes closed. Then it started flashing. It took a few minutes for them to adjust it to the exact speed they wanted. When they did, the Aurie started talking to me."

"What did he say?"

" '. . . Do as I say—or the pain will be beyond imagining. Once you're released, everything will be as before.' " She grimaced at the memory of the Aurian's words.

" '. . . An admiral will give you orders. He'll tell you to rendezvous and escort the *Vendikon*. You will not escort this vessel. You will hear him tell you to destroy her.' "

Rieka looked at Triscoe and wrapped her arms around herself. There it was. Evidence that someone had conditioned her. Goose bumps rose at the back of her neck.

"I tried to turn my head and think of something else, but then a burning—like acid—went through me. He kept telling me to destroy the *Vendikon*. And he told me not to investigate any problems with the sensor array while we were in the Medouran system.

"I don't know how long I was there. Everything after that is fuzzy. I don't remember how I got back to the lake." She looked up at the old man. "They must have sedated me because that's the next thing I can remember. It was almost dusk, and I was near the water."

Yillon nodded his head. He pursed his lips, and the wrinkles of his face formed a frown. "This is part of what I have seen, as well," he said softly. "The monstrosity I have feared is nearly upon us."

"How can you say that?" Triscoe asked. "This Aurian told Rieka to destroy a Procyon ship. I see no curiosity in that. Many Auries begrudge Humans their place in the Commonwealth."

Yillon shook his head as he looked down into Triscoe's face. "You do not see the vista, my young friend, only a corner of the woods. It is the sensors that are the key, here. Think of that."

Triscoe thought out loud. "The *Vendikon* was too small a ship to have traveled from another star system. But it could have come from a larger ship—or a mobile base that was beyond the range of the DGI." He nodded, continuing to speak as he looked at Rieka. "And you did not destroy it. You disabled it and tried to place it in orbit . . . Which means—it might have destroyed itself, or another ship could have destroyed it. Another ship that was unseen—because the *Venture*'s panoply was off-line, and the DGI was trained on the Procyons!"

"Another ship?" she wondered. "But the Eta Cass system is automated. Their unmanned station is what alerted me to the *Vendikon* in the first place. Even without my panoply on line, *it* would have told me if anyone else was out there . . ." She thought for a moment, then added, ". . . unless the station was damaged, too. Or, maybe this phantom ship had some way of hiding itself." She looked at Yillon. "I've heard the Boos are working with gravitation factors high enough to bend light."

She stopped rambling and thought a moment. "Do you think . . . the Procyons could have come across something like that? If they had such technology, and if there *was* another small ship, it could still be in Commonwealth space. And if these outlaw Aurians are working with them . . ."

The bloody nose and pain were all but forgotten. She got to her feet. "I know it's pure speculation, but we've got to do something. Warn Admiral Hursh. Go back to Aurie and arrest those people."

"Wait." Triscoe was standing now, too. "We don't know who to trust. We've got to keep this between us until we're sure of who we speak to."

About to argue with his logic, Rieka held her tongue when Yillon raised his hand. "There may be more. Replay the incident in your mind, Captain. Something,

anything, might take time to surface. It is most impor-
tant. You stand at the threshold of a divergent future.
What you do now will determine the path of the
Commonwealth."

"What?" He couldn't have meant what he just said,
she thought. Or, could he?

The old man smiled and said nothing. Then, sighing
with fatigue, Yillon gestured at Triscoe, who supported
him as he pushed up from the chair.

"I must rest," he said. "I have done all that I can, my
young friends. You read what was written in your
volume, Triscoe. Her actions have confirmed it. You
have the Indran techniques of deduction and analysis.
You have your *quantivasta*-gift. I see a future that lies
in flux."

With Triscoe's help, Yillon shuffled across the stone
floor and eased onto his cot. The old man looked at
him, and he nodded. Apparently, they were communicating without words. Rieka watched them, fascinated,
forgetting herself before coming to her senses and
thanking the ancient man for his help and offering her
future services.

"I shall have a greater debt to you," was all he would
say before closing his eyes and softly snoring.

She looked at her husband. "What now?"

"This way."

He led her to a passage which terminated at a rise of
stairs and a solid-looking door. When they climbed the
steps, the door opened to reveal an InterMAT chamber.
In a heartbeat, they were on the *Providence,* standing
shoulder to shoulder in her quarters.

Rieka was standing beside Triscoe's chair when the
navigation specialist reported contact with her ship
and the *Prospectus.* Awareness of the deception
engulfed her.

"But they were sent to the—" She bit off the last
of the remark and looked pointedly at her host.

"Protecting me from myself, again, I see," she observed acidly.

Triscoe cringed at the inflection. "This was decided on the day of your hearing. A great deal has changed since then," was all he said.

"The *Prospectus* is hailing us, Captain," the communications officer announced.

"Acknowledge it, Briz."

Robet's robust face appeared immediately, and he flashed the bridge crew a disarming smile. "We're here," he announced, his bibbets glowing a light pink.

"I see that," Triscoe replied. "And by the looks of you, you've found something."

Robet looked disconcerted for a moment and ran a hand over his forehead, lightly brushing his bibbets. "I suppose I'll have to take some additional conditioning therapy." The bibbets got paler. "But I have got news." He paused. "Permission to come aboard?"

Triscoe nodded. "InterMAT directly to my quarters."

"On my way," Robet replied. He terminated the signal and Rieka followed Triscoe off the bridge. They hadn't been in his room for more than a few seconds when Robet arrived with a small popping sound.

"The *Venture* did not destroy the *Vendikon*," he announced.

"You're sure?"

"Absolutely. I've got sensor documentation. We went to the area in question and started replaying the events before the attack. With Midrin's help, it became obvious Rieka's sensors weren't trained on anything but the incoming ship."

Rieka was amazed at Triscoe's self-control. He nodded thoughtfully, as if this were news. "How is that, exactly?" he asked.

"Midrin reminded me that certain portions of the sensory panoply were under repair at the time. There had been a fire the day before. The primary array was completely out, and the reconstruction crew had part of the secondary unit off-line as well. Effectively, the *Venture* had a huge blind side."

"And somebody knew it," Rieka murmured. "Somebody planned it."

"Go on, Robet," Triscoe urged, swiping a glance at her.

"The record shows Rieka fired three warning shots that didn't make contact and one minimally charged shell that hit the ship's propulsion reactors. We know the ship stayed in one piece long enough to be hauled out to an orbit beyond the Eta Cass system's border."

"Yes. So?" Rieka demanded, hungry for solid evidence to support their theories.

"You say you were told to destroy it. And I say somebody wanted it destroyed badly enough to wait around and watch you do it."

Robet looked directly at Rieka. "Didn't your report on that fire include the word: suspicious?"

"Yes, it did. But at the time—"

"Well, there you go!" he told her, his red hair flying as he gestured. "They'd planned to watch and somehow made sure you couldn't see them watching. When the *Vendikon* didn't blow up from that last shell, our invisible someone did the job themselves. They used some kind of a remote maser-based weapon. There's still residual radiation all over the area that nails it like a thumbprint. It's imprinted all over the debris."

Rieka looked up into Triscoe's face. "The Procyons use masers."

"Interesting, isn't it?" Robet smiled cynically. "And the mystery ship's trajectory can be traced by a path of ion particles." He paused then let go a sigh of disgust. "It looks like they were headed for Aurie."

"We learned a few things on Perata, too," Rieka offered.

"Really?" Robet's expression was openly curious.

"Yes. And I'm sorry to tell you that Aurie seems to be our common denominator."

Seven

Triscoe sat in a small conference room on the *Prospectus,* following the fringe of the discussion. His attention, he had to admit, focused on two of his companions. Tohab sat straight in her chair and wouldn't look at Robet unless she spoke to him, and then with only a fleeting glance. She seemed almost fearful. Triscoe wanted to laugh. Afraid of Robet? Ridiculous.

Nevertheless, he decided, something strange was going on between them. Rieka, who had thus far remained quiet, was watching them, too. And the look on her face said she agreed with him.

Robet had a look in his eye Triscoe had seen before. He found Tohab attractive. He'd touched her arm several times since they'd sat down. She'd pushed him away twice. Was she truly keeping him at arm's distance, or was this only a facade for the sake of appearance? Perhaps she simply didn't want to seem unprofessional in the company of superior officers.

Triscoe found he didn't much care for the affair, either way, but that was their business. Still, either because of them or something else, there was an electricity in the air that gave him a feeling of someone pricking his forearms. He didn't like it.

"So what you're saying is that we've stumbled upon a very real conspiracy," he said softly, forcing himself to concentrate on the reason for the meeting.

"Absolutely," Robet replied. He leaned forward to punctuate his remark with a tap on the table. "It's elementary." He grinned. "We've got the corpse, the smoking gun, and a trail of blood. All we need now is the murderer and the motive." Sitting back, he smiled at Rieka. "We could have your case dismissed in less than a week."

She shrugged. "Don't hold it against me, but I won't start celebrating until after Admiral Hursh tells me himself."

Triscoe sighed. Robet had been a fan of murder mysteries since before he'd joined the Fleet. He had an intensely annoying habit of creating analogies where they weren't appreciated. "Please, can we keep your hobbies out of this and stick to the literal facts?"

"Just trying to make things look a little less nauseating," he replied. "Got all this evidence, and, at the moment, we can't do anything with it."

Triscoe understood his frustration. Rieka's encounter with the *Vendikon* now appeared to be part of a larger plan that had something to do with Aurie. To bring forth evidence that would clear her, now, would also alert whoever was in control of that plan.

"Are we in agreement that there is more here than just the destruction of an enemy ship?" he asked, looking first at Robet, then Rieka.

"Yes. Definitely," Robet said. For once, his voice was completely serious. "Rieka's got to have been a pawn in this—scenario. She was probably picked because she's Human, true, but it could have been either of us, Tris. Or any other captain. Whatever is happening, we can't let it go."

Triscoe agreed. He had no idea what was going on, but more importantly, he wanted to know why. What was the objective? The takeover of the Fleet? That would supply a person or group extreme power and wealth. Without controlled-cost rapid transport of people and goods, many private companies would have to rely on old-style space transport. A round-trip to certain planets through physical space rather than quantum foamducts would take a lifetime.

And, while a takeover was plausible, another

possibility could not be dismissed. The Procyons could be preparing to invade the Commonwealth again. If that happened, this time the Fleet would be ready for war. An enterprising individual aware of the plan could take advantage of that knowledge. And there were plenty in the Commonwealth who would do anything for money. But how would framing a Fleet captain initiate the plan?

As he sat watching Rieka, Robet, and Tohab, Triscoe felt the idea stick in his throat. Since the Procyons' last attempt to take a Commonwealth system, almost five years had passed. The Transport fleet had been upgraded; weapons added. Every planetary system now had unmanned tracking stations in their outer orbits, and the Boos had designed a Uni-class vessel packing firepower more than twice that of anything presently in space.

That ship, the *Prodigy* was now only days away from commission. Even so, the opportunity for a last-second attack on the Commonwealth definitely existed. Triscoe decided it was worth the time to run the numbers through the computer to check the odds for that theory. One thing he knew for sure: the Procyons took what they wanted.

He nodded to himself and cleared his throat. "You're *sure* about the evidence in the Eta Cass system? We don't want to go snooping in a *vrill* pond, you know," he offered, speaking of the innocent-looking waterworms that could kill by touch.

Robet looked at Tohab and put his hand over hers. She tensed, glared at him, and pulled away. He pretended not to notice. "We're sure. Antimatter spheres don't leave wreckage, Tris, we all know that. And we found enough flotsam floating around to discredit anyone believing the *Vendikon* was destroyed by a sphere. The *Venture* could not have destroyed it, period."

He glanced again at Tohab, then back to Triscoe. "And then there's the maser trace. Procyons use masers—at least they did five years ago, but it doesn't make any sense that they would destroy their own ship."

"I agree," Tohab said, keeping her hands folded and away from Robet. "It makes more sense to conclude that someone wanted to conceal their identity by using masers instead of a more traditional weapon—to point a finger at the Procyons—should the plot be unraveled."

"That's true enough," Rieka agreed. "But the question is: who?"

Triscoe nodded. Yillon hinted they were overlooking something significant involving the *Venture*'s sensors. He had to have meant the identity of the ship that had actually destroyed the *Vendikon*. Was it Aurian? Procyon? Or someone else?

He studied Tohab as she tried not to watch Robet. A first officer wasn't always privy to her captian's every intent. But then, the reverse held true, too. He sat straighter in his chair and leaned across the table. "We still have sixteen days to make our case to the admirals. You have sent documentation of what we've found to your attorney, haven't you?" he asked, looking at Rieka.

She nodded. "As soon as we got back from Perata."

"Then he should have it soon. Right now, I suggest we take the obvious step and follow the trail to Aurie."

Robet nodded. "All of us?"

"I don't see why not," Triscoe replied. "Do you, Commander Tohab?"

"There is no reason to separate," she agreed quietly, glancing at Rieka. "We still don't know who is involved in this . . . conspiracy. And we must find evidence to prove Captain Degahv was conditioned to do something against her will. Logic would dictate that we are only safe in trusting each other."

"Well, if there is an Aurian connection to this, I'd be the first one to admit my disgust." Robet frowned and allowed his bibbets to color. "I've spent my life working toward a better, safer Commonwealth. This whole thing really turns my third *ribah*."

Triscoe smiled crookedly at the sentiment. His own digestive tract had not been functioning smoothly, either.

"It will be more efficient if we power up and take the foamduct in formation." He tapped the datapad in front of him. "I make it about thirty-four hours total travel time. That will give us just over fourteen days to get back to Yadra." He looked at Robet. "When we get to Aurie, I'll contact our offices there for a search-request. We should have legal documentation to inspect this place in the Krinkins."

"Absolutely," Robet agreed.

"If you require anything, you know where to find me." Triscoe stood, collected the datapad, and walked toward the door. Rieka joined him.

"The *Venture* is waiting for your swift return, Captain," Tohab blurted.

"Thanks, Midrin," Rieka said. "I appreciate your confidence."

"Think nothing of it."

Rieka's fingers tapped at the controls of InterMAT Station Four. The *Providence* had been in orbit over Aurie for less than ten minutes. She knew serious repercussions would come as a result of this, but she couldn't stop herself. She *had* to go. Using Triscoe's personal identification code, she programmed the device for her destination.

She gnawed her lip when she couldn't recall the exact coordinates. "Don't do this," she muttered, either at herself or the machine, she wasn't sure.

It didn't matter anyway, she decided. She was going whether she wanted to or not. And she wasn't about to tell anyone, either.

An odd thought crossed her mind. Yillon had warned her to try to remember that still-blank time before she woke up near the lake. Had something else happened? What?

Her hand hovering over the touchpads, she whispered to herself, "What do I do?"

A voice in her head said, *Return. You must return.*

Completing the transport request, Rieka stepped back and into the InterMAT chamber, then waited for it to power up. In a moment, the foamduct sucked her away.

The Krinkin Mountains loomed in front of her, their snowy caps contrasting directly with the purplish sky, craggy rocks, and dark tangle of vegetation that hugged the range's lower elevations. Far enough away from the taller peaks to distinguish the western slope, she was thankful the InterMAT had placed her where she could get her bearings almost immediately.

She judged herself to be a few kilometers from the pond she now vividly remembered from the session with Yillon. Near it would be the path leading both down to the park's offices and up behind the waterfall. Her destination was the latter of the two.

Eyeing the late-morning position of Epsilon Indi, or Aura for the natives, Rieka started across the meadow.

"I know it's there," she muttered, trying to justify leaving the ship while wading through the silvery, wet grass. "It's got to be."

As she entered the first copse of tall, angular stalks, Rieka recalled every one of her arguments regarding this self-appointed mission. She knew trying to infiltrate the base alone was a stupid idea. But the others would not understand the pain, embarrassment, and frustration she'd undergone at the hands of these people. She had to do this, alone. She *had* to return.

Still wrestling with herself, Rieka slowed her pace. "Triscoe is going to lock me away," she muttered, and kept walking.

She knew it increased the odds against her that she didn't have a weapon, but Triscoe's orders had restricted her to civilian areas. She told herself no one would be waiting for her here—a second time.

When she finally reached the hiking trail, Rieka struggled with another wave of uncertainty. If she went to the secret installation unarmed and without a TC, a gross act of stupidity, she would either find it occupied or not. And she would either gain entry or not—though probably not undetected. The result, most likely, would be her capture, again.

"I can't do this," she told herself.

You must return.

If she went down the trail toward the park buildings and contacted the *Providence,* she would face Triscoe's wrath, but he might send a squad to help her make an assault on the Krinkin outpost. More likely, though, he'd have her transported back to the *Providence* before she could finish her first sentence.

While she fought her desire to go up the trail in direct contrast to the logic that told her to descend it, she heard a soft popping sound. The InterMAT.

"It is difficult to believe that my commanding officer can behave with complete disregard for every rule she's ever been taught."

Rieka turned, startled, but smiling. "Midrin! How did you find me?"

"I know you well enough," Tohab replied. She stood only a few feet away, shaking her head. "And *I* realized the benefit of a TC and maitu. You Humans have no respect for logic at all."

Suddenly aware how much she needed company, Rieka laughed. "And Centauris do? They why are you here?"

Tohab seemed to consider the question. "Loyalty," she said finally.

"Well, then, let's go." Rieka pointed the way up the path. "The outpost is not very large, as far as I can recall. At least we'll have the advantage of surprise."

She took the lead, with Midrin a step behind. They skirted the water in silence and made their way up the steep path. The waterfall was loud enough to be heard through the needled trees long before it was visible. Rieka stopped to check her bearings and point to the spot where the path appeared to end but actually continued behind the water. Then she and Midrin hurried through the cloud of mist generated by the tumbling narrow falls.

Looking at the place where the man had threatened her with the strange weapon, Rieka resisted a shudder. That the event had been completely erased from her ability to recall it made it doubly eerie. Searching her thoughts now, she couldn't remember seeing any security men or equipment. Apparently whoever built the place relied totally on its concealed location.

"There's a door," Tohab said, pointing to a break in the rock wall. When she walked to it, it slid open. She took a step back. The door slid closed.

"Not very discriminating, are they?" Rieka wondered aloud. She couldn't recall the circumstances of its opening before. It didn't seem likely that the door would open for just anyone.

"Perhaps they are just sure of their concealment," Tohab suggested. "Or, maybe we're expected."

"The only important thing is that it opens." Rieka moved close enough to make it slide, again. Tohab responded with a tighter grip on her maitu, and they stepped through.

The corridor extended a short distance into the mountain, with only a few doors leading off it. At least her memory appeared to be accurate. The installation was not large.

Tohab looked at her. "Do we have a plan?" she said softly.

Rieka nodded. "We try the doors one by one until we surprise someone. This place is pretty small. There can't be but a few people, if any, here at the moment."

"The lights are on," Tohab observed. "The air's fresh. My guess is it's occupied."

Rieka went to the first door on the right. She warmed

the access panel with her hand, hoping it needed no special print.

The door opened, revealing a small room. The walls were lined with boxes. A variety of tools sat scattered around the floor, mostly computer hardware and robotic pieces. Rieka retreated and tried the opposite door while Tohab stood at the ready with her maitu in hand.

The second room had the appearance of a live-in office. There were a pair of desks and beds on opposite walls. Between them stood a row of shelves full of objects ranging from anatomical models of Commmonwealth species to musical instruments, power cells, datapads, and food packets. The floor was cluttered with clothing and refuse. Rieka decided the inhabitants, traitors or not, were slobs.

They backed out of that room and Tohab looked at her expectantly when they stood before the third door. Rieka saw her squeeze the cylindrical weapon in her hand, resting her thumb lightly on the discharge button.

When the door opened, Rieka was overcome by a shiver down her spine. This was the room where she had been conditioned. She recognized the equipment, consoles, the strobe embedded in the ceiling, the examination table. But, like the others, this room had no occupant. She tightened her jaw and turned around. Tohab stepped back, and they went to the fourth door.

"This is the halfway mark," the Centauri whispered. "We should find someone soon."

The faint hum of machinery changed to a roar as the acoustic door slid aside. Rieka stepped past the jamb and looked around. The largest room so far, it measured roughly four meters across, two high, and eight deep. She recognized a hydroelectric generator at the end and understood why the power had remained on even though the installation was apparently unoccupied. Leaving Midrin near the door, Rieka took a quick survey of the room. With that task done, she returned to the hallway.

It was empty. She was alone.

She pivoted, hoping that Midrin had followed her. But canvassing the room a second time proved fruitless. Nervously, Rieka clenched her teeth and went back to the hallway. Not knowing what else to do, she tried the next door.

Relief flowed through her when she saw Tohab seated at a table in what appeared to be a dining room. She released a tense sigh.

"I thought we were going to do this together," she said, with a disapproving tone.

"Sorry, but I had other plans."

Rieka whirled, half-crouching, immediately recognizing both the face and voice of the Aurian from her restored memory. He was holding an alien weapon twin to that which had threatened her on her earlier visit. He did not seem surprised at her presence.

"Captain Degahv, how pleasant to see you again. I admit you aren't scheduled for a second session, but since we're not busy at the moment, I see no reason why we should ignore the opportunity." He flashed her a false smile.

Rieka squared her shoulders and looked him in the eye, remembering Midrin had a working TC. "I assure you, the commander has already summoned the rest of our party. You are not in any position to order—"

"She has been told to do nothing—or I will kill *you*. This is not an idle threat, Captain," the Aurian said. He moved away from the wall with his weapon trained on her. "Likewise, I will kill her if you choose not to cooperate."

Rieka stood perfectly still, watching him as he eased left to get a better angle for his weapon. Her mouth was going dry but she managed, "No one's going to cooperate."

"Well, there you are wrong." Again, the man flashed his smile.

The sound of someone coming down the corridor divided her attention. When the person cleared the open doorway, her eyes instinctively slid in that direction. It was the Oph, the one who had touched her. She recognized the marks on his floppy ears and the odor of *ciffa* dust. But this time, his interest was not Rieka. He ambled past her without so much as a glance, grabbed Midrin by the arm, and pulled her, struggling, out the door.

"Take your paws off me," Tohab warned as she wrestled with his grip.

Rieka tensed, wanting to help but knowing it would be hopeless. The Oph was easily twice as strong as both of them.

"Now, Captain," the Aurian said softly, turning her attention back to him. "Do not think I disregard your concern for your officer. I assure you, Rimbua has been instructed to wait before he seeks whatever gratification he might garner from a Centauri. Only a few more weeks and he'll be his old self again." He smiled too widely. "But then, I think you've already met Rimbua, haven't you? I believe that was the day he'd started pounding his third block of *ciffa*. Nasty habit, of course. Smells awful. But it does help relieve the urge—when no Oph females are available."

Rieka said nothing.

The Aurian's tone sobered. "If you do as you're told, he will leave your Centauri officer alone. If you choose not to cooperate . . ." He left the thought unspoken. "Have I made myself clear?"

"Crystal."

"Excellent. I believe you know which room awaits."

Still brandishing the weapon, he ushered her across the hallway and gestured her onto the table. She moved slowly, looking for a moment when he lowered his aim or his attention was diverted, but it did not come. Seated on the table, she stared into cold ice-blue Aurian eyes that seemed to have some great purpose hidden behind them.

"Why? Why are you doing this?"

"It is my destiny," he replied cryptically. With the weapon still in hand, he lifted it to her forehead and pushed her back onto the body pad with her head below the strobe.

"I'll resist." Trying to look braver then she felt, Rieka glared at him.

"No one can resist," he said. "Your presence is all the evidence I need."

There was a hiss at her neck. She winced and felt the relaxant release her control of her arms and legs. Knowing her mind was the only thing that would keep her from accepting the treatment, Rieka closed her eyes.

Ignore him, she told herself. Don't listen. Think of something, anything. But pretend to go along. Somehow, we'll get out of this.

Thinking of Tohab made her realize something else. Indrans and Peratans both had excellent hearing. That last room had been noisy, but Midrin had stood near the door. How could she have been caught?

The light came on and, in a moment, began to pulse with a frequency she remembered. With it came a strange kind of pain that involved the memory of Yillon recovering her past. She heard the voice of the Aurian. "Now, Captain Degahv, I have only one instruction for you, today. There is no way to fight it, and I will not even gag you as before. You may accomplish this task in any way that is available.

"You must kill Captain Triscoe Marteen."

Eight

Triscoe stepped onto his bridge and studied the DGI. Aurie's Quadrant One was visible. Its deep pink atmosphere tinted a small block of continent and the immense ocean dominating that section of the planet with shades of lavender.

The communications officer glanced at him, then did a double take.

Triscoe's thick brows lifted at the odd reaction. "Is something wrong, V'don?"

"No, sir," the Aurian replied. "I didn't know you were back."

He frowned. "Back? From my conference with Memta and Demki in engineering?"

"No, Captain," the lieutenant replied. "From Aurie."

He straightened. "I haven't yet been to the planet, Lieutenant. I'm waiting for documentation for the search-request. What makes you think—?" His mind raced. Rieka knew his InterMAT code. Damn her, he wanted to shout. What could she have been thinking?

"Search the ship for Captain Degahv," Triscoe ordered. He went to his chair and tapped in the signal for Aarkmin to assume the bridge immediately. Then, looking up at V'don, he said, "When you don't find her, I want the exact coordinates used with my code sent to Station One. Assemble a squad for a search party and be sure to include three armed security personnel. Have them meet me at the station."

"As we speak."

Triscoe left the bridge and stepped into a Chute. As

he traveled across the center level of the *Providence,* he activated his TC. "Link to the *Prospectus.* Marteen to DeVark."

A moment later he heard the familiar voice. "What can I do for you, Tris?"

"Robet, we have a situation. Rieka has gone to Aurie herself. Without a TC or weapon. My search-request has not arrived yet. That is moot, now. We can't wait."

"Understood. I'll assemble a team and join you," the disembodied voice replied. "Where are we transporting?"

"I will let you know as soon as I find out myself."

Robet's tone barely contained his concern. "Why would she do such a stupid—?"

"I have no idea," Triscoe replied. Exiting the Chute, he strode to Station One. "Rieka can be most unreasonable at times." He read off the latitude, longitude, and elevation coordinates to Robet and waited while his security people arrived. They assembled in the chamber and he gave the order to transport.

Once on the planet, Triscoe frowned at the landscape. It was an immense area. Rugged. Barren. "Jarah," he said softly, trying not to allow his concern to show, "begin scanning as soon as you're calibrated. Set it to detect any kind of electrical activity. We are looking for an installation located behind a waterfall."

"Understood, Captain." Lieutenant Jarah tapped at the settings on her device and stepped away to relay the orders to the rest of the squad. The three-man team fanned out quickly, covering as much high ground as possible.

When Robet appeared, accompanied by four of his crew, he was scowling. "Midrin's not on the *Venture.* She left over half an hour ago." His bibbets pulsed a bright pink.

Triscoe noted his concern. "Have you been able to reach her via TC?"

Robet shook his head.

Triscoe's hand slid to his maitu. Both of them could

be in serious trouble. Anxious, with nothing to do but wait until the scanners had picked up their quarry, he decided to air his opinion. "You've been spending a lot of time with her, Robet."

The Aurian grinned, as if embarrassed to be caught. "More than professionally necessary," he admitted.

Triscoe looked disapprovingly at him but said nothing. Robet's conquests were his own business. Despite the wide range of physical differences between Commonwealth species, this Aurian seemed to find a plane of satisfaction. "Do you think that it is wise under the circum—"

"Captain," Jarah shouted from a short distance away. She pointed toward the smaller of the mountains to the east. "We've located a source of hydroelectric power at fourteen point zero-one-one degrees elevation at four kilometers distance. It's through the scrub brush to the southwest."

"Too far," commented Robet.

Triscoe mentally judged the time it would take to traverse the terrain. "I agree." He activated his TC with a twitch, and V'don's voice instantly responded in his ear. "Get an InterMAT engineer to reset the controls, Lieutenant," he said without preamble. "Have our entire party transported to the coordinates Jarah provides."

"Working on it now, Captain," V'dorn replied.

Less than a minute later, they were in a large, noisy room containing a hydroelectric generator. He took in the surroundings, then nodded to Robet.

"Weapons," he ordered over the hum. Three of his crew stepped forward, the small steel gray cylinders of their maitus in their hands. "Injury and loss of life are not on my agenda," Triscoe advised. "Any individual found here is to be taken into custody with as little force as possible."

"Understood, Captain," replied Killiam, the security squad's team leader.

Triscoe looked at Jarah and gestured to her scanner. "Are you getting any activity within the area?"

She nodded, her eyes on the instrument. "There are chambers to our left, all read cold, unoccupied. Across the central corridor—outside this door—there are two hot spots, and a lot of power is being used. Nothing to the right for at least six meters on either side of the corridor. Then I read three more hot spots. No extraneous power associated with them."

He looked at Robet. "You take the right. We'll go across the hall." The Aurian nodded, and Triscoe pressed the door release. The Fleet officers spilled into the hallway and hurried toward their destinations.

Triscoe was first to the door. Not particularly caring whether the lock worked or not, he pressed his palm against the flat surface. If it didn't open, he would force it or have himself InterMATted in. He didn't take the time to show his surprise when the heavy bulkhead slid away, revealing a dark room filled with sophisticated equipment, pulsing light, and an Aurian wearing a visor. And Rieka.

"Move," he said softly to his people, unable to take his eyes off the prone figure of his wife.

His crew entered and fanned out. Lieutenant Killiam pushed the Aurian away from the table, threatening him with a maitu, while the other two checked for any hidden weapons or alarms. Triscoe was confident they would complete their tasks without his supervision.

At the table, he bent over her. Although the flashing light distorted his vision, he could tell she was in pain. "Rieka, I'm here. You'll be all right." He tore his attention from her to face the startled Aurian.

"Turn off the light."

The visored man shrugged slightly. Tipping his head to examine the stripes running the length of Triscoe's sleeve, he said, "Really, Captain. You are interrupting scientific research."

Triscoe's expression remained cold and determined. He wanted Rieka off the table. But the mental shock of removing her, physically, without this man's help, might do more harm than leaving her there. Quietly and with complete control, he lifted a hand and grabbed the man's tunic. "Turn off that strobe, or you will suffer far more than incarceration, Aurian."

The man buckled faster than Triscoe expected. "The first console, yellow button, next to the keyhole," he croaked.

Triscoe released him and hit the switch. The overhead light stopped flashing and dimmed. He twitched his TC on and spoke again to V'don. "Have Twanabok transported to me as soon as possible."

Jarah touched his arm. "We've swept everything, Captain. Found only one weapon. I will need to analyze its components for an accurate report."

"Very good," he replied with a nod. "Can you get any information out of the computers? Perhaps a tutorial on the equipment—or some history of the staff?"

"Right away, sir," the lieutenant said. She pocketed the weapon and turned back toward the console.

Returning his attention to Rieka's captor, Triscoe cocked his head. "Now," he wondered aloud, "what to do with you?"

The prisoner removed his visor with a shaky hand, but put up a brave front while smoothing his tunic. "Please, I have done nothing wrong, Captain," he insisted, his bibbets glowing bright with worry. "I am a scientist. I have not harmed anyone."

"Not directly, perhaps," Triscoe agreed softly. He had to force himself to keep his back toward Rieka in order to concentrate fully on the man. "But you are responsible for ruining Captain Degahv's life."

Lieutenant Jarah, sitting at a computer console on the opposite wall, looked over her shoulder. "He is Dr. Grie M'narn, sir," she reported. "The computer has no information on the benefactors of this research facility. But he is the director. There is a staff of seven; two others are presently on-site."

"Good work, Lieutenant." M'narn receded to the

wall as Triscoe stalked him. "Have you anything to say for yourself, Doctor?"

"Such as?" he asked in a strong voice, though the color of his bibbets gave away his fright.

"A confession of treason to the Commonwealth would be an excellent start. Then you can divulge your employer."

The Aurian's bibbets flushed deeper maroon. "I . . . would be killed."

Triscoe's sandy eyebrows rose on his forehead in mock surprise. "Really? How awful for you." He glanced at the prone figure of his wife. "I suppose I could allow you to change places with Captain Degahv. At least that alternative might prove interesting."

M'narn was vigorously shaking his head when Dr. Twanabok appeared via InterMAT, with a small pop, and moved immediately to Rieka's side.

"Killiam, he's yours for the moment," Triscoe ordered, indicating M'narn.

When the Oph lieutenant took his place, Triscoe gave his full attention to Twanabok. "This is some sort of mental manipulator, Vort," he said. "We need to find out what she's been told to do—and undo it."

He looked at the knotted brow over Rieka's closed eyes and noticed her breathing was labored, agitated. Without thinking, he covered her hand with his. Instantly, her eyes opened.

"Rieka, are you conscious?"

The eyes seemed to focus on him but that was all. They closed immediately, and, for a moment, Triscoe thought he'd only imagined them open. Twanabok elbowed him out of the way, grumbled to himself, and punched some controls near the head of the table.

"Fortunately," the Vekyan remarked, "this is a standard issue exam pallet." He scrutinized the display panel. "She's been sedated and given a strong muscle relaxant. Otherwise, there is no chemical alteration to her general health."

He looked at Rieka, felt the pulse in her neck with

his pads, nodded to himself and shifted his attention to Triscoe. "Captain, I've had some limited experience with this type of technique for treating psychosis, not the alteration of memory. The pulsing overhead light duplicates electrical frequencies of the brain. That, in conjunction with suggestion and medication, I suppose, can change the way a person recalls something. Mostly, it's done to change undesirable behavior."

Triscoe didn't bother to tell Twanabok how close he'd come to the truth. "Can we get her to tell us what's happened?" he asked.

"No!" gasped M'narn.

Triscoe turned. "You are under arrest for treason, Doctor," he said carefully. "Anything you say or do will be held against you as you will be held accountable for your actions. Should you wish to make any comments, please direct yourself to the nearest data-pad. Make another sound, and Killiam"—he gestured to the tall Oph—"will be happy to render you unconscious. Am I understood?"

"Completely."

To his physician, he said, "Well? Is there anything we can do?"

"We can try." Twanabok turned to the banks of instruments beyond the head of the exam table. "But I will not guarantee anything."

"This is the control for the overhead light," Triscoe offered, pointing to the yellow pad. "It was flashing when we entered."

Twanabok nodded and touched the button. The light warmed, glowing with mild intensity. A few seconds later it began to flash. "Clear the room," he said.

Triscoe signaled his crew to leave. "Place Dr. M'narn in transport stasis and have everyone wait outside," he instructed Killiam, taking the Aurian's visor from him. "Contact Captain DeVark and see if he requires assistance. If not, wait for me in the corridor."

"Yes, Captain," Killiam replied. He waited for Jarah

and the others to leave, then with a paw around M'narn's arm, stepped out the door.

Triscoe put the visor on and was relieved that the strobe effect all but vanished. "There's a visor on the top of that console if the light bothers you, Vort," he said.

The doctor shook his head. He slid a chair up to the console and sat. While he tested the controls, grumbled to himself, and tapped notes on the datapad that resided in the pocket of his overjacket, Triscoe stood vigil at Rieka's side. He kneaded her shoulder with his left hand and kept the other on her cool fingers.

Some minutes went by before Twanabok finally harrumphed to himself and swiveled the chair. "The equipment doesn't seem to have been customized." He checked the display on the table. "The levels of both chemicals have reduced slightly. She'll be gaining some voluntary muscle control soon."

Triscoe nodded. His grip tightened on her hand and he watched the doctor's broad back. "Rieka, can you hear me?"

"Of course she can hear you, Triscoe, she isn't deaf," Twanabok said. "While she's still under, I'll need to access and eliminate whatever instructions the Aurian gave her." He checked the level of muscle relaxant in her blood and poked the point of a claw against her upper lip. She twitched. "Should be able to speak in a moment."

He went back to the console and increased the strobe's intensity. "Captain Degahv, what are your instructions?"

She sucked in air as she attempted to make a sound. A frown molded her face, as if she'd eaten something horribly sour. She groaned.

"Take your time," eased Triscoe.

"What are your instructions, Captain?" insisted Twanabok, his bumpy green face only a few inches from hers.

She heaved a great breath, gasping more air with each sound. "K . . . ki . . . kill. Kill. Kill!"

Triscoe leaned over her, trying to force her eyes open with his fingertips. "Kill who?

"Kill. Kill. Kill myself . . . kill myself . . . kill my—"

"The Aurian told you to kill yourself?"

"No. No!" Her head rocked from side to side, the grimace still firmly intact.

Twanabok looked at Triscoe. "She isn't making any sense. Maybe we should intensify the light a bit."

"No!" she pleaded. "No. Hurts." Her legs began to tremble.

"Perhaps we're simply not asking the right questions," Triscoe observed. "Rieka, who are you supposed to kill?"

"C . . . C . . . Captain Marteen. Kill Captain Marteen. No! Kill . . . myself." Silent sobs wracked her body. Her hand slipped from Triscoe's. "Myself."

Triscoe's eyes met the doctor's. Twanabok pulled himself upright and shrugged in the Vekyan manner, heaving his chest out and back. "Humans," he grumbled as he checked the readout at the head of the table.

Triscoe ignored him for a moment and soothed Rieka to a semicalm state. "I can't imagine how she's got around the suggestion," he said, "unless she concentrated so intently on herself that she wasn't consciously able to listen to him."

"Possible. Possible," the doctor agreed. "But now to stop her from the act." He left the console and moved to stand on the side of the table opposite Triscoe.

"Captain Degahv, can you identify the voices you've been hearing?"

"Yes," she replied, eyes still closed. Her expression relaxed slightly. Apparently, speaking on a general subject did not cause any great discomfort.

"Identify them."

"Vort Twanabok, chief medical superintendent on the *Providence*. Triscoe Marteen, *Providence* captain. My hu—husband." She heaved a sigh.

"Good. Very good, Captain," Twanabok said, patting her arm. "Now, you have been told to kill Captain Marteen but you will not do that. Is this correct?"

"Correct."

"You will kill someone else, instead?"

"Myself."

"Why?"

"I will not murder. I will not do a thing *they* want. I won't kill him." She winced.

Watching her, Triscoe decided there was some kind of distress associated with disobeying the suggestion.

"You will not," the doctor agreed. "You will not do anything to harm him. This is your new instruction. Will you comply?"

"Yes." Her face relaxed a bit.

"You are instructed not to harm him—Captain Marteen. And because of that, it follows you will not harm yourself. Do you understand?"

"Yes."

"Is this agreeable?"

"I will not harm him," she replied. "Or . . . myself."

Twanabok nodded and shuffled around the table to the display screen. "The drug levels have almost completely dropped off the scale. Should have muscular control quite soon," he muttered, turning toward the console.

"Do you think that's it? She's—released from that thing?"

"Triscoe," Twanabok began quietly, "the original instructions were painful to her. I gave her a command she could live with—something from her own nature. You can see for yourself, she completely accepts the new information." He tapped the yellow button and the overhead fixture switched off.

Triscoe removed the visor. His hand went to her face, the skin still warm from the light's intensity. "Rieka. It's Triscoe. Look at me. The light is off. Open your eyes."

She did as she was told, squinting at first, then

relaxing her lids. She groaned as she raised herself from the pallet. "Forgive me, Tris. I never should have . . ."

He pulled her to his chest and held her while her body twitched as the remains of the drug wore off. "It's all right now. You're free of this place. Don't concern yourself with what should have been." The look he shared with the doctor, however, said the incident would not be forgotten.

Twanabok nodded in agreement and turned to shut down the rest of the equipment.

"Midrin!" she gasped, her hands suddenly like a pair of vises on his shoulders. "Is she all right? What did he do to her? Have you seen her? The Oph—he's still here. He took her—"

Instantly, Triscoe switched on his TC, quieting her with a raised finger. "Robet, we're all clear in the lab. What's your status?"

There was a smile in the voice in Triscoe's ear. "We found Midrin in a holding room. She's okay. The two with her have been taken into custody. Unless you want us to stick around, I'm going to regroup on the *Prospectus*."

"I will speak with you later," Triscoe replied. His smile answered the question in his wife's eyes. "She's fine, Rieka. No harm was done to her."

"Thank God." She sighed. "Triscoe, I'm so sorry. Can you ever forgive me? I couldn't wait . . . I felt compelled to come here. Like a voice telling me to return. No matter what argument I used, I found myself needing to be here. I don't know why."

"It may have been suggested," Twanabok offered as he approached them. "I couldn't think of a better reason to do what obviously goes against one's own sensibilities. What better way for these people to maintain their control?"

"But I wouldn't let him," Rieka replied, slipping from the table onto her feet. She sagged and Triscoe supported her. "I refused to listen."

"And that was fortunate for this young man," the doctor said. "That Aurian should be charged with attempted murder, in addition to treason." He flicked his tongue and glanced around the room. "Now that everything is secure, here, I suggest we retire to the *Providence,* where I can get a good look at you."

She groaned, but Twanabok played the part of the deaf physician.

Triscoe touched her cheek. "Go. I'll have a look around and meet with Robet. Vort will take care of you. I'll see you later." Wanting to do much more than stroke her chin, he forced himself to leave the room and went to find Lieutenant Jarah.

Robet stood grimly beside Triscoe and Tohab in a private exam room aboard the *Prospectus.* His medical superintendent, an Oph named Illma, was working over the prostrate form of M'narn.

Tohab whispered, "Do you think he'll be able to get anything?"

"Absolutely," Robet replied. "I've seen Illma pull the truth from a stone." When Triscoe glanced at him, he amended, "Figuratively speaking, of course."

"Of course."

The doctor turned his attention from the patient. "I think he's ready, Captains. Which of you wishes to question him?"

"I'll do the honors, Illma," Triscoe said, stepping forward.

Robet prudently restrained himself and hoped his Centauri friend would not lose sight of their objective. He glanced at Tohab and noticed a similar look of apprehension on her face. There was something else there, too, though he could not quite place the expression. Somehow, it seemed as though she were gravely concerned, perhaps even fearful. But why?

The Oph guard hadn't touched her. Robet had made sure of that as soon as the security team had him in custody. For once, his curiosity had nothing to do with how she might perform sexually. Did she know something? Had Rieka confided in her? Robet wondered if, using the obvious ploy of a pass, he could get her to talk. He decided to plan a way they might have a discreet chat.

"Your name?" Triscoe asked the prone prisoner.

"Grie M'narn."

"Your occupation?"

"I am an Aurian psychiatrist specializing in memory retention in the erect bipedal species of the Commonwealth."

"Have you been in contact with the Procyons?" Triscoe demanded, throwing a quick glance at Robet.

"Yes."

"Who, exactly?"

"K'din-va, a high commander."

"Anyone else?"

"I have spoken to officers named O'don-la and K'resh-va."

"Is that all? You haven't been in contact with any more?"

"Yes. That is all."

Anxious, Robet sighed audibly. "Push him a little, Tris," he suggested.

"Were these individuals within the boundaries of Commonwealth systems when you had contact with them?"

"Yes."

"How did they manage that?"

"Their ships can't be seen by panoply sensors. They can go where they want to," M'narn said.

The information hit Robet like a physical blow. "Then why haven't they invaded already?" he blurted.

Illma lifted a paw. "Please Captain, only one inquisitor. The patient will falter if too many voices interact with him."

Robet nodded and gestured at Triscoe to ask the question.

"Why haven't the Procyons invaded, then, if their ships can't be detected?"

The prisoner sighed and shook his head. "Too great a power consumption," he replied. "They can only use the system on very small ships that have minimal weapons."

"Makes sense," Robet said softly. "Don't you think?" He looked at Midrin. She was concentrating so intently on M'narn, she hadn't heard him speak at all.

"Is that how the *Vendikon* was destroyed?" asked Triscoe.

"I do not know," M'narn said. "But not long after that, they came to Aurie."

"Who?"

"K'resh-va."

"Was he the one that hired you to alter the mind of Captain Degahv?"

"No. It was K'din-va who hired me and provided funds for our outpost."

Robet wondered how Procyons could pay people in Commonwealth credit, then decided he didn't really want to think about it. It was just too hard to believe they had been in the Commonwealth long enough, and were prosperous enough to afford such an undertaking.

He glanced again at Midrin, whose face had become unreadable. It seemed as if M'narn had not said what she'd expected him to. He felt somehow disappointed.

M'narn shifted and tried to lift his head.

"He is coming out of the sedation now," Illma advised them. "That is all he'd be able to answer with absolute truth." The physician looked at Triscoe, then Robet. "He will not be able to undergo the treatment again for another thirty-six hours, Captain. I hope you got what you wanted."

Robet shifted his jaw from side to side. "Well, at least it looks like we've got a culprit for the *Vendikon*'s destruction."

"A Procyon. Probably the one named K'resh-va,"

Triscoe agreed, nodding. "But there are a lot more unanswered questions."

"True. Unfortunately, I doubt that M'narn had much contact with the entire operation. The Procyons are clever. Probably only a few of them know the whole of what's going on."

Triscoe remained silent.

Robet stared at M'narn. He felt a *ribah* flip in the lower part of his chest, telling him to eat, soon. "What I'd really like to know is why they wanted to pin the destruction of a ship on Rieka," he mused. "There's got to be more to it than simply whipping up an anti-Human frenzy." He shrugged. "The Commonwealth's been going through phases of that on its own for almost two hundred years."

"It might coincide with something," Tohab offered. "Or maybe this K'din-va seeks to glorify himself by throwing the member worlds into some kind of hysteria against both Humans and Procyons."

As much as he liked her, Robet thought that had to be the stupidest thing she'd ever said. He floundered for a suitable comment, but Triscoe beat him to it.

"Possibly," the big Centauri agreed, watching her. "But the two species cannot be compared except by the most rudimentary criteria. Both can be violent, true, but Humans have a great respect for life of any kind, even nonsentient. If the Procyons occupied a planet that underwent a catastrophe like that of Earth, they'd abandon it—not exhaust every resource trying to save it."

She shrugged. "It was a thought. I am just suggesting theories, Captain. Right now, we don't have much of anything but."

"I agree." Robet smiled. "But at least we've got a witness. We knew Rieka didn't destroy the *Vendikon*. And now, we've got solid evidence for the 'outside influence' defense."

Nine

With Twanabok watching her intently, Rieka knew better than to fight the clamps holding her head and arms immobile as she sat in the surgical chair. But the small suction device had slid out of place and saliva had begun to build up in the back of her throat. She was either going to choke or drool, neither of which was a pleasant option.

She swallowed.

"Stop that!" Twanabok warned. He pointed a claw at her to punctuate the order before moving out of her line of sight.

Sure, she thought. When was the last time *you* had a TC installed. She sighed through her nose. Lumpy green dictator. At least he hadn't started up that one-sided discussion, again.

Having a TC after being without one for so long made Rieka feel like a newly assigned ensign. She had a future again. And it might not be as bad as she'd thought. That Triscoe had overlooked regulation in favor of her safety said even more.

The urge to swallow returned.

"Almost over," Twanabok said. "These new TeleComms are even trickier than the old ones. Extra connections ... makes them more fragile, I say. We had no power-consumption problems in the 330 series. The cells didn't have to be replaced for years. Don't see why they want it hooked into the nervous system, too."

He'd gone through this litany before. Twice. While

the instruments at the end of the robot arm worked their magic in her ear, she realized Twanabok enjoyed carrying on a monologue for an audience of one, and a captive audience at that. Rieka wondered how she'd come to be typecast in such an unpleasant role.

"Done," he announced finally. The robot arm eased back into its recess in the wall, and the sterile field switched off. He loosened the catch at her jaw. "Hurt much?"

The ear tingled, and she felt a residual warmth from the light. "Not right now," she replied. The other clamps were removed, but she stayed put in the chair.

Twanabok looked her over carefully, his lavender eyes missing nothing. He issued a long sigh from his thin nostrils and clicked his claws together. "I'll put you on the call board," the doctor said, finally. "Come in at any time and the attendant will treat you for pain. Right now, I'll give you a timed-released dose." He removed a slip of plastic from a drawer and scraped his foreclaw across it once. Then, positioning her head with his other hand, Twanabok jabbed the small bump of cartilage just in front of her ear. The contact did not break the skin.

"Now, you're to relax for a while. No sports. Nothing strenuous."

"Understood," she said. Carefully avoiding his wide hips, Rieka slipped out of the chair.

"Give your system some time to get used to that TC before you use it. Next thing you know, you'll be back in here for repairs."

"You must have me confused with some Vekyan captain," she teased.

Twanabok ignored her. "And you're to come back within thirty hours, young woman." He turned and pointed as she escaped the surgery area. He pursued, keeping the claw aimed at her. "I'll want a full scan on you then. It is impossible to predict consequences of today's ordeal. Human memory is a complex electrochemical scheme. And I will check the status of that TC."

"No problem." She smiled, scooting through the outer door before he could say anything else. Once in the long, sloping corridor, Rieka sighed. "Let's hope that's the last escape for the day," she murmured.

Because Fleet ships were identical, Rieka could almost convince herself she was aboard the *Venture*. Wishful thinking, she knew. But she belonged there, not on the *Providence* as a guest/prisoner.

Near the engineering lab, she ran into Lieutenant Roddik, one of the Boos who kept the gravitation in place on the *Providence*. She suddenly missed Tyrinne, her own chief engineer on the *Venture*. Tyrinne had been patient beyond belief when coaching Rieka on the intricacies of the Boolian language.

"Coming down to Varannah?" the large being asked after a short drag on his chlorine tube. The voice translation, emanating from a small box sutured to his chest, was like a combination of a Human male's gravelly tone, and listening to something through water.

Looking up into his broad rough-textured blue face, Rieka shook her head. He was probably headed for the gravity pod. "Too much for me, Roddik," she replied. "You know that."

Wide black eyes opened beneath a double set of perpendicular lids. He leaned down until his head was almost even with hers and clicked his kroi together. The vibration of the leathery folds deep in his chest represented emotional release. Rieka could recognize almost thirty tonal variations of kroi, covering the scale from gentle humor to violent rage.

Roddik's kroi sounded light. He seemed to leer at her with his huge, smooth, multifaceted eyes. "Human bones do not factor well. Unable to equate the heat." The leathery lips of his oral cavity moved, but had Rieka been deaf, she knew she would never have been able to read them. The only sounds she understood came from the box.

It took a moment, but she recognized the "heat" reference and smiled. "Not my kind of kitchen, I'm afraid. My Varannah's in the sky." She pointed to the deck. "This is as much gravity as I can take."

"Not so," Roddik replied leaning even farther. Quietly, he added, "Commonwealth business holds much gravity—different—absent of physical nature."

As she smiled, Rieka had the feeling he could see directly through her skin. "You're right, of course. But with luck, they'll find me innocent."

The Boo pulled himself erect and touched his dappled blue chest with a star-shaped hand. "Roddik is never wrong. Luck is nothing to the root of it. *Eurympa* in your cup. By the ninth."

She bowed slightly to his superior intellect, marveling that they could communicate at all. His language intimidated her with its complex numerical pathways and culturally important events. It took a long time for any Boo to grasp the Commonwealth standard language well enough for the translator to work. It was a given that no other race could really begin to comprehend theirs.

"Later on the morn," he said, taking another draught on his atmosphere compensator. He ambled to a Chute on his trio of stout legs. His great blue body, clad only in a drape of clinging material the colors of the Fleet, traversed the threshold with remarkable grace. She had to remind herself his natural habitat possessed a gravitational force close to that of the gravity pod. Exposure to that many Gs would plaster her to the floor.

Roddik stuck one arm past the opening, palm toward her, and undulated the many rows of cuplike structures along its surface. She waved in return. The kroi sounded again and the bulkhead closed. Above the Chute door, a light flashed. He was gone.

Rieka looked at the door a moment longer, recalling the only time she'd ever been in a gravity chamber. It was on the *Andromeda,* just before the ship had been commissioned. She had only a vague idea of the mathematics that had been required to create such a chamber. The Boos were a thousand years ahead of the other planets in the field of quantum physics. Without them, the Commonwealth would have no Fleet, no gravity chambers, and no InterMAT system. They were indispensable.

Silently, Rieka envied them.

While she considered the Boos, the other non-humanoid races of the Commonwealth flitted across her mind. They couldn't serve aboard Fleet ships because the standard biped environment was either unsuitable or hostile to them. The Boos, of course, had their tanks of chlorine to compensate, but Bournes were nocturnal, and their *burrow-skiffs* could simply not navigate the curved corridors. The Lomii were just too fragile.

Her TC clicked on. "Captain Marteen," the tiny automated voice said within her head. It startled her for a moment before she remembered the new model had been integrated with her nervous system. Twanabok warned her that it would be different than her old one. She just hadn't expected the voice to seem so intimate.

"Captain Degahv," she said softly. Another click, and she heard a voice again, this time with intonations she immediately associated with Triscoe.

"Am I the first to test your TC?" he asked, though he obviously knew the answer.

"Of course. Twanabok wanted nothing to do with it."

"Ah." His voice smiled. "And how is it?"

"Different," she answered, shrugging to herself. "Hard to explain, exactly. I don't hear you in my ear, but rather in my head. And it isn't your voice—though it is a close approximation. Am I coming through clearly?"

"Same as ever," he replied. "I need to talk to you, Rieka. In person."

She took this to mean he had something to discuss with her about the Aurian situation and did not want to risk the chance of someone picking up the conversation. "Certainly. Where?"

"My quarters as soon as is convenient."

"I'm on my way." The unit clicked again. *Off,* reverberated across her mind. Rieka decided it would take a while to get used to the new TC.

She took the nearest Chute and ordered the destination. It slid quickly across the curved face of the ship, dropped one floor, and continued to glide on the horizontal. Silently, it stopped and opened, depositing her at the command and guest accommodation section.

"Hello," he said, greeting her the moment she reached his door. "Come in."

Rieka smiled at him, then glanced around the room. Instantly, she felt homesick for her own quarters on the *Venture.* "I've always loved this view," she said softly, moving past him. In truth, there was no view. The captain's quarters merely had a DGI that covered the top half of one wall and a meter of the ceiling. The effect was that of a terrace from which one could see any programmable vista. Triscoe's DGI displayed a particularly dramatic view of the Crab Nebula as seen from Indra.

"One of the reasons I wanted to be captain," he quipped.

She laughed, but it came out more like a snort through her nose. "I didn't realize Centauris appreciated the finer subtleties of," she grappled for a word that wasn't too insulting, "telling a whopper."

"Hyperbole," he corrected, a smile in his voice.

Silence filled the room for a long moment. He was watching her. She could feel it. It made her nervous.

"What are you thinking?"

Rieka turned from the electronic vista. "Is it that obvious?" She didn't wait for a reply. "I miss the *Venture.* I miss my schedule, deadlines . . . my people." She looked at her fingers, aware that she'd clamped them together. "I want to go back to my life. But that's impossible . . ." She sighed. "A few days off is one thing. But now everything's changed." She pursed her lips as if trying to keep herself from speaking it would stop her from feeling it.

"Then let's think of something else."

Watching the relaxed line of his posture, Rieka couldn't help but go along. "I'm game," she said. "Do you have something specific in mind?" When he unfolded his arms and ambled past her toward the next room, she followed muttering, "I don't even know why I bothered to ask."

She stopped at the doorway of his sleeping room. Triscoe had opened the refrigeration unit at the base of his bedside table, and removed a bottle. Standing straight, he gathered up two goblets from the table and turned to her, smiling. He collected a gold scarf from the dresser top and met her in the open door.

"Come, Rieka."

She followed him back to the couch. He gestured her to sit beside him. She did, slowly, watching his steady hands as he opened the bottle and began to pour the silvery liquid. "Is the *Boggi*?"

He nodded.

Rieka felt her heart flip and then take up residence somewhere in her throat. She rubbed her fingers across the palms of her hands and tried to relax. *Boggi* she knew, from her extensive study of Centauri—specifically Indran—culture, was an aged fermented beverage served only at the nuptials of a wedded pair. Of course, they had been married for quite a few days already, but this was serious. The *Boggi* symbolized permanence.

She glanced down at the scarf he'd picked up in the bedroom and made the association of its significance. It had to be a *wruath,* the swath of truth. Eyeing the silky material, Rieka wondered if she respected his culture enough for it to force her not to lie. One look at his face told her she did.

Triscoe handed her a delicate goblet containing little more than a swallow of *Boggi*. Picking up the length of gold fabric, he circled it first around her shoulders, then his. He took up his own goblet and her free hand.

Rieka watched his eyes as he began the ritual. There was no sign of hesitancy or doubt. He had truly committed himself to their union. Rieka knew he expected her to do the same.

"I know that you are uncertain of your future," he began softly. "I admit that the evidence may not be enough to clear you if the judges have been influenced. But so much can happen between then and now . . . do not concern yourself."

She wet her suddenly dry lips and swallowed. His eyes held hers, mesmerized.

"Rieka, from now until my death you shall have my love, trust, and deepest respect. I pledge to care for and keep you the best way I know how, from this moment on." He put the rim of the cup to his lips and swallowed the silvery liquid.

Rieka knew she should speak the ritual back to him. She opened her mouth, but nothing came out.

He frowned at her uneasiness. "What is wrong?"

She bit her lip, stopping short of cutting the skin. "I can't. I'm not Indran," she explained hastily. "Those words have great meaning to you—beyond the literal intent. I would be lying if I repeated them—just to complete the circle." She glanced at the *wruath*, still around her shoulders.

His expression softened, accepting her resolve to do the proper thing. "Then say your Human words," Triscoe whispered, kneading her palm with his thumb. "I know you do not have a specific ritual—but there are certain customs, are there not?"

She sniffed. "Okay." She paused, giving herself time to think. "All right. I can do that." Taking a deep breath, Rieka began. "Triscoe, I've known you a long time. You've been my friend. You've saved my life. You've saved my spirit. I owe you so much more than words can express. I think I loved you for a long time and didn't know it. Now, I feel as if you have somehow become a part of me.

"I want to promise you so many things—but I can't."

She watched him frown and quickly explained herself.
"If I complete the pledge, you'll be bound until your
death, and I want you to be happy, no matter how long
I live. It pains me to think that you might carry on,
alone, because of this." She shrugged, indicating the
wruath and *Boggi*. "I'm not Indran, perhaps it can be
taken as a technicality," she wondered with a hopeful
smile. "But I do love you, Triscoe, and I commit
myself to you for as long as I live."

His slight nod gave her the courage to swallow
the bitter *Boggi*. She was glad to have it gone in one
gulp. She reached to put the goblet on the table, then
touched his face with her hand. "Human marriage is
often completed with a kiss," she said, easing him
toward her. He had no trouble accepting that part of her
custom. When she finally leaned back, she noticed the
wruath had slid from her shoulder. "How long does
this have to stay on?"

"Its function is over," Triscoe replied, his voice
gravelly. He collected and folded the shimmering
cloth. "We will use it in the future when the complete
truth is required. Sitting this close, it is difficult to lie."

The term brought a smile to Rieka's face. "Isn't that
what we're supposed to do next?"

"What?"

"Lie together."

He looked suddenly self-conscious. "That is . . .
Indran . . . custom," he mumbled.

"So?"

He averted his eyes. "I have done research on
Human customs. There is a great deal of importance set
on romance and emotional intimacy." He refolded the
wruath. "Indrans perceive intercourse solely as a
means of procreation. *We* already know children are
not a possible result from such an act between our two
species. There is no reason to assume that you would
be required . . ."

She let a moment of silence go by. The conversation

was ridiculous. "Are you telling me Indrans don't enjoy intimacy?"

"Probably not the way Humans do," he admitted with a shrug. "We believe it is the creation of new life. Psychologically, there is a third party involved."

Rieka cherished his uneasiness as she watched him fidget. "You never know, it might be interesting without the excess baggage of a third party. Just tell me the minute you aren't enjoying yourself. Is that a deal?"

His dimple appeared. "Absolutely."

After a moment's thought, she went to his desk and tapped on his computer. "Environmental," she said softly, touching the proper spots and numerical pads, "we'll reduce the present illumination." The lights dimmed considerably. "And increase cabin temperature." A rush of warm air came from the ventilation system.

Rieka looked up, noticing Triscoe's questioning look. "Aesthetic," she continued, her attention back to the computer, "let's have the sound of a distant shoreline and soft music. Um, Corbeen's eighth Trikata at twelve decibels."

Rieka waited while her orders were carried out. She watched her husband take in the changes to his quarters. He seemed transfixed. "DGI," she continued, figuring she might as well make the fantasy complete. "View from a terrace at, oh . . . twenty meters up, on a hillside overlooking a tropical lagoon on Earth. Zero-two-hundred hours."

The holographic screen complied. The essence of the room changed subtly as the view of the nebula faded and the requested image took its place. The audio synchronized with the DGI so that the waves actually seemed to be lapping against the creamy sand. Moonlight caressed the calm sea, shimmering and glinting across the gentle rollers in the lagoon, glowing softly through the palms arching up from the sand along the beach. Rieka could pick out only a few Earthconstellations in the dark sky, but the depth of the heavens in the DGI image made her feel their unimaginable distance.

Almost forgetting Triscoe, she stood straight and walked to her imitation balcony. Caught up in the remarkable view, she had to remind herself they were on a spaceship rather than that small, blue planet over eleven light-years away.

"Breathtaking," Triscoe remarked at her shoulder. "You've completely redesigned the environment. My quarters have taken on an intangible quality."

"Do you want it back the way it was?"

"No."

She turned to him. "This is romance, Triscoe," she said. "Making something real out of—nothing more than an idea, a feeling. I don't think it's beyond you."

His eyes took on a black cast in the darkness. "Perhaps you are right. But I will need to study it. Extensively."

"And now, you're positively flirting with me, Indran," she teased.

He stood straighter, apparently pleased with himself. "I like it."

She laughed and watched as he enjoyed her amusement. "Now, shall we get you out of this stuffy uniform?" She reached for the collar clasp, but he stilled her hand.

"There are physical differences, too, Rieka," he warned softly, his fingers tense. "They will not be easy to overlook. Perhaps you will change your mind when . . ."

His smooth Centauri skin was pale against hers. She smiled. There were Humans with skin as light as his. Rieka wondered if he realized that only since joining the Commonwealth had the people of Earth learned to overcome differences of their own races.

"I've seen medical files on Centauris, love. What you've got won't come as a shock. We Humans aren't the same, but we're similar. I'm sure we'll find some way to give each other pleasure."

He took a long breath through his nostrils when she completed the task of undoing the clasp. The fabric parted between her fingers, and, in a moment, he slid his arms free from the tunic.

"Nothing new here," she smiled, tapping her fingers across his chest. A bit wider than a Human's, it was smooth. Adorned by neither hair nor nipples, Triscoe's equivalent of a rib cage was, at least, contoured with the appropriate muscular bulges.

"But not so, for you."

She dropped her arms and allowed him to release her tunic. His breath caught when she slid out of it and turned to toss it across the back of the chair.

"Yup, there they are," she grinned, doubting that Triscoe had ever seen Human breasts before. She undid the clasp of her bra and gave him his first view, albeit dim, of what he'd committed to.

"Amazing," he breathed, lifting one hand to touch her. "And so soft, no musculature at all. And ... heavy." His eyes glittered up to her own. "Rieka, you are remarkable."

Her face seemed stuck in a grin. One in a few *billion,* she thought. But she managed to accept the compliment gracefully. "I was hoping you'd say something like that."

"It is difficult to comprehend why you would have evolved with such an important glandular system unprotected," he began quietly, referring to the fact that Centauri women carried the glands used to suckle infants within their chest cavity. "Even the males of your species—the important organs of their reproductive systems are virtually external. It is a wonder you survived at all."

"The evolutionary process simply picked what worked," she answered, thinking back to those files she'd scanned on male Centauri anatomy being nearly all internal until required for the process of fertilization. "But we're losing our sense of romance," she chided.

"We're slipping into the scientific." She watched a pulse point in the center of his chest as it throbbed.

"I don't think so," he whispered, eyes still on her breasts. He touched her, again.

Rieka drew in a sharp breath. "You're right. Maybe we can combine the two," she finally managed.

"Excellent choice of words, my wife. Will it infringe upon your dignity if I carry you to my bed?"

"No."

Almost before she spoke, Triscoe easily lifted her. He seemed mesmerized by the mobility of her breasts. "You are incredible, Rieka," he whispered.

She touched his dimple as he set her on the gel-core mattress. The sudden power she had over him felt like a drug. Her hand slid down his chest. "Good, maybe. Incredible? We'll see."

After dinner, Rieka decided to move her things from the guest suite to the captain's quarters. She was returning with some clothes over her arm when Triscoe looked up from his datapad.

"I have discovered a lead, I think," he said. "Come and sit."

She draped the clothes over the back of a chair and eased onto the edge of the cushion. "A lead? I thought we had this problem resolved as far as—"

He kissed her, then shook his head. "Is your TC off?"

"Yes." Intrigued, she waited for him to continue.

"I did some searching in Admiral Nason's files."

She frowned. "I don't understand. How did you get access to them?"

"I asked for the data before we left Yadra."

"And he just gave you his files?" she asked, incredulous. The idea of the admiral's doling out such information didn't seem likely.

Triscoe shook his head. "I requested select transport data. He sent me the files via InterMAT, and I've had one of my personal computers sifting through them ever since."

"Looking for what?" She was confused. They had solved her case, hadn't they?

He shrugged. "That was the problem. I thought there might be something in the transport files that would be a clue as to why you were being set up. And yes, I was even looking for evidence of a conspiracy against Humans," he offered, answering her unasked question.

He touched a series of controls on the datapad, then reached for a screen magnifier on a nearby cushion. He angled it so they could both see the image.

"Once I went through the files confiscated on Aurie, I began to see a connection," he said softly, as if the information had been in his possession days rather than hours. "M'narn kept accurate records but used no names—as a precaution, I suppose.

"But look, here." He tapped a few more commands, and the screen split. "By feeding the information into my datapad and correlating it with Admiral Nason's files, a pattern begins to form."

Rieka examined both sides of the screen. Names and dates appeared on the official Fleet record, dates only on M'narn's. "Okay, so some Fleet personnel traveled on the same dates that Dr. M'narn used his—machine. What does that prove? Our people move around a lot."

Triscoe's eyes glinted, but he said nothing.

She smiled at the expression expectantly. "What?"

"Now, watch while the computer makes a comparison of the two separate files." He tapped one final command and the small screen reconfigured.

Rieka watched as the new data appeared. Her jaw went slack for a moment. "No. That's impossible! It can't be." Her eyes slid to Triscoe's face, and she felt the hair on the back of her neck prickle.

"I've done the correlation at least a dozen times," he said. "This is much more than what I would have guessed."

"You're trying to tell me that all of these people went

to Aurie and have been influenced by M'narn's machine?" she asked, almost choking on the words. The screen clearly showed Admiral Nason's documented date and travel destinations of Fleet ships as well as their crew and passenger manifests, compared with the Aurian doctor's ministrations. A total of forty-nine individuals had gone to Aurie, been there during the time the machine was used, and left shortly thereafter. "This is unbelievable."

"You have to consider that, in your case, quite a few of your crew took shore leave on Aurie but, apparently, only you were treated."

Rieka huffed. "That's a pretty big assumption, Tris. You can't be sure—"

"True," he replied, gently interrupting. "But you must admit weeks have passed since you had the *Venture* in orbit over Aurie. No one else in your crew has done anything remotely out of character. And because of the nature of this list, I'm also guessing the three other ships didn't have their shore crew influenced, either." His expression was a mixture of concern and pride. "Nevertheless, it gives us a pretty good picture of who's been under that light."

Rieka nodded, overwhelmed. The probable list included Admiral Bittin, Captain Din of Aurie Base, herself, Captains Tairie, Pedlam, and S'trie, Vice Admiral Dirkin, Governor Lim of Boo, the CEO of Centauri Exports, an Aurian ambassador, her brother Paden, and a number of junior personnel.

"Paden! Admiral Bittin!" She looked at Triscoe, feeling as if he'd turned her universe on its side. Then, collecting herself, she said, "On the one hand, some of these could be nothing more than coincidence. But, on the other hand, there could be several of these machines—anywhere. We only know about this one." She shook her head, feeling the weight of what they'd discovered. "We still don't know who to trust."

"I know," he said softly.

She exhaled, catching her lip between her teeth. There

were goose bumps on her arms. "Those are important people, Tris. Fleet and government officials. To think of even some of them being controlled . . . After what happened to me, I'm scared."

"We all are, Rieka. I spoke with Robet while you were out. He is beside himself."

"Do you think Admiral Nason is . . . in on it?"

Triscoe shook his head. "No way to tell for sure. But I doubt he would have released his records to me—or spoken as candidly as he did to Robet—if he were under mental suggestion. And he isn't on the list. Then again, who knows?"

She squeezed his hand while reaching with the other to turn off the small computer. "Where will this end?" she wondered aloud. "What's the point? Why was I told to destroy a Procyon ship? It couldn't be to incriminate me as a fallible Human." She pointed to the dark screen. "There are four Commonwealth races on that list."

"Precisely. The next task is to determine the motive and perhaps backtrack to define the objectives."

Sighing, she closed her eyes and rubbed her forehead. "Do we have to do that right now? I think I need time to digest this."

He returned the datapad to his desk. "Of course. Actually, I wanted to celebrate."

Her eyes snapped open. "What? Your newly discovered sleuthing ability?"

His dimple appeared as he crossed his arms over his chest. "No. Far from it."

Rieka immediately recognized the intent of the smoky smile, but she played innocent. "Then what are you talking about?"

"Us."

Ten

K'resh-va took refuge in his rooms aboard the Commonwealth ship, *Yelga*, away from the inferiors that surrounded him. The suite belonged to the Centauri, Captain Pedlam, who was now dead. That this crew had accepted him as the original said a great deal about their attention to detail. He'd caught himself growling, twice.

The ship had emerged from its foamduct an hour ago and the breakdown-speed sequence was underway. As expected, incoming messages flooded the communications port, and he had done his best to seem casual when collecting the ones addressed to Pedlam. Now, with the door locked, no one would interrupt his privacy.

Even in his urgency, K'resh-va stood transfixed for a moment, absorbed by the magic of the DGI on the far wall. Though the technology was truly amazing, in a private room the thing seemed a waste of technology. No wonder the Procyons were having such an easy time encroaching on the Commonwealth. Fleet officers were too busy enjoying themselves.

The image, a direct feed from the bridge, looked rather ordinary. The unremarkable starfield centered on Forty Eridani, still many AUs away. Somewhere in its orbit, the *Prodigy* waited. For him.

He examined the small communiqué squares, trying to decide which one contained the message he wanted to hear. All were tagged as official documents, even missives from his cronies. Purposefully, K'resh-va rechecked the locked door and began to insert the wafers of plastic into a slot in his datapad.

The fourth one produced an image of E'bid-va.

"Greetings, Captain," he began, using the proper title under the circumstances. "Although I shall be seeing you soon, I decided to take this opportunity to let you know our plans are carrying through smoothly. Everyone anticipates your command of the new ship. There is some strangeness in the particulars, however. Our pawn is no longer contained and other factors are now involved. Admiral Nason is looking into this situation without help from my department. It is difficult to deter him, and I am sure he may eventually question you. His thoroughness is inspiring.

"As always, my service is to our cause. I realize time is short, but if you require anything of me, you have only to ask. I will speak to you next in person."

The datapad slid the chit out of the slot. K'resh-va switched it off and took the wafer to the recycler.

"So, Nason is *thoroughly* investigating Degahv's trouble," he grumbled. He had deduced as much once Marteen had become involved. Only the admiral could have authorized that.

He sat down to think. He had not heard from L'gith-la for some time, but he trusted her instincts. She already knew the schedule—as did everyone in the Fleet. The *Prodigy* would be commissioned for its first tour of duty in fifteen days.

He had tried to keep track of the *Venture*'s whereabouts and found it erratic beyond the logical. Supposedly, it had gone with the *Prospectus* to the Jovian Cluster of planets orbiting Alkalurops. That would have taken L'gith-la far from the quarry. The *Venture* then appeared in Aurian orbit, suspiciously close to the time he'd left the planet himself. M'narn had said nothing about expecting them. K'resh-va could only hope, if the machine should be found, that the doctor kept no documentation of his treatments. He was a fool if he did.

Sniffing through Centauri-shaped oval nostrils, K'resh-va paced the floor of his quarters. He could not deny an unwelcome sense of frustration. The plan called for tight control of the variables, and they had begun to slip from his grasp the moment that Indran, Marteen, had gotten involved. He'd married the Human! The concept was completely alien, its implications revolting. No Procyon would ever consider life-bonding with an outsider. Purity and continuation of the species were paramount, especially since planets were conquered quickly, often within a lifetime.

The real problem had to do with the team of Degahv and Marteen. They might uncover his plot, possibly thwart it—or at least disrupt the schedule. The idea rankled. He did not want to remain looking like a Centauri for a moment longer than necessary. Prolonging the agony was thoroughly unacceptable, though he would do anything to attain the ultimate goal.

In light of that, taking orders from E'bid-va grated, too. The old man would not deviate from a timetable if his life depended on it. K'resh-va could not help wondering if there would be a problem with E'bid-va's decisions in the future. He wondered, too, how E'bid-va would react in a crisis.

At that moment, his TC switched on. "Captain Pedlam?"

"Pedlam. Yes. Who is speaking?" he replied, wondering if he could ever get used to the Fleet's communication system.

"Evak of engineering," the Boolian voice gargled, followed by a strange clicking sound. "We are at a point to power on final speed sequence. You requested our applause."

"Applause?" K'resh-va shook his head, confused. He wondered if anything could assist his comprehension of the Boos. Applause? The intricacies and inflections of the language were lost on him.

"The factor of notification to the first."

"Yes, yes. So I did. I will be there directly. Pedlam out."

He heard the device click off in his ear and wanted to tear it from his head. Clamping his teeth together,

K'resh-va stomped out of his quarters, telling himself things would be better, soon.

Through the thickness of sleep, Triscoe barely yawned in response to his TC. He tried to roll onto his back but found something blocking the way. It was warm. Soft. He turned his head. Rieka. A hazy smile crossed his face. There was no question now. The Human in his bed, his wife, had shown him love, humor, and adaptability in the face of their bispecies relationship. She *was* incredible.

The device in his ear clicked again. This time he rolled his face toward his pillow. "Marteen."

"Did I wake you?"

He stifled a sigh, hoping to give Rieka a few more moments of peace. "Robet, you're awake painfully early today."

"But you're always up by now." There was a pause. "Oh—" the Aurian's voice sounded uncharacteristically contrite—"I didn't realize you might still be . . . with Rieka?" Another pause. The tone changed. "Then I guess I should offer my congratulations!"

"Mmm." He rubbed his eyes. "What do you want?"

"I just thought you'd appreciate me telling you I'm leaving."

Triscoe pulled himself up against the pillow. "You're what?"

Robet's voice seemed to whine slightly with over-stated purpose. "One of us needs to check back with Admiral Nason," he said softly. "You know I can't explain more on a TC channel."

"But wouldn't it make more sense for the *Providence* to go?"

"Everyone knows Rieka is with you. I don't think it's a good idea for her to go back to Yadra until we show up in court with enough evidence to have the charges dropped."

Triscoe had to agree. "You've got all the documentation for the admiral?"

"Got it."

"And the *Venture*?"

"It'll stay here. But I think you should both pull out of Aurie orbit. The presence of two ships might be taken wrong by the Council."

Triscoe knew when to take the advice of a native. "What would you suggest?"

"Something discreet, say—five AUs from Indi. They'll know you're out there, but nobody's going to complain."

"Sounds like you've done a lot of thinking," Triscoe said softly. He noticed Rieka's breathing had changed. Her eyes opened, and he watched her yawn herself awake.

"Absolutely. I'll let you know something as soon as I can. If you don't hear from me in four days, you know what to do."

"Understood. Good luck, Robet. Marteen out."

Rieka rolled onto her back to look at him, all but exposing her breasts through the thin sheet. His pulse jumped in response. "Good morning, wife."

"What did he want now?" she asked lazily.

"He's going back to Yadra to meet with Nason." He spoke softly, as if the words meant something else. Her olive skin, the quality a bit rougher than an Indran's, called to him to be touched. And there was so much of it available at the moment.

She stretched. "Still keeping things from me for my own good, are you?"

Triscoe nuzzle her neck. "Never again." He slid his hand across one of the irresistible lobes over her rib cage.

"I thought you were all business during the day," she said. Her lopsided smile was not lost in the subdued lighting.

Triscoe pretended not to have noticed. "My day hasn't started yet," he murmured.

She wiggled closer and slid a hand over his chest, glancing past him at the wall chrono. "By the looks of things, you'd better get busy and finish off the night. Your alarm will sound in about ten minutes."

He checked the time and turned back to her. Hazy gray eyes glinted at him above lips still curved in that peculiar smile. He watched the rise of her rib cage as she inhaled and realized it was impossible to comprehend what her breasts did to his libido. When they were encased within her uniform, he accepted them as he did any other Human's. But revealed, as only Rieka could reveal them, Triscoe was surprised at his near obsession with the exotic structures.

"I wonder what other interesting secrets you Humans have kept from us," he murmured, almost to himself.

"What are you talking about?"

"Sex with no other purpose than recreation." He shook his head in wonder. "It's an extraordinary concept."

Three hours later, Rieka was still having a hard time concentrating. As she sat at Triscoe's desk, images of him kept swimming through her head. She'd had serious concerns about intimacy with a Centauri though she'd never have admitted that to Triscoe, had hardly admitted it to herself. Thankfully none of them mattered. Once she'd become accustomed to their differences, she'd enjoyed herself immensely.

Looking at a screen filled with only three lines, Rieka chided herself for letting her mind wander, and purposefully began to write. Her documentation of the machine and Dr. M'narn provided her attorney a solid argument for getting the case dismissed. It would be impossible now for the court to deny the facts. She hoped.

She'd only written another page when her TC clicked.

"What now?" She'd sent Chen preliminary correspondence several times, but this report required painstaking detail. Saving what she'd written so far, she stretched the kinks from her back. "Degahv."

"Tohab, Captain," Midrin's voice soothed within her head. "I had heard you'd received a TC. Congratulations."

She smiled. Recalling the many times Midrin had stood by her, Rieka hoped things could be put to rights.

Taking into account what had happened on Aurie, she was suddenly aware of her extraordinary bad manners.

"Never mind about me," she replied. "How are you feeling? I apologize for not getting back with you, yesterday. Things just seemed to—"

"No harm done, Captain," Tohab answered. "The Oph simply took me to a holding area. The Aurie doctor used him as a means to make you cooperate." Her tone gave the impression the subject was closed.

Rieka accepted the fact that her concern had been recognized. "Is there something I can do for you?"

"Actually, yes. That is the reason for this communication. This is Lieutenant Gorah's Advancement day. The ceremony will commence in three hours." She paused. "I am acting captain and therefore expected to conduct the rite. However, since your presence would lend distinction, I thought you might be persuaded to do it."

Rieka noted a touch of anxiety in her first officer's voice. Midrin was not fond of pomp, nor did she feel particularly comfortable in front of a group. Though she was an excellent statistician and able leader, Rieka knew that such deficiencies of character, minor though they were, might keep her from a command of her own.

"I would love to, of course," she said. The Oph traditions for a female who reached the breeding age carried great weight with the species. That certain members of the race were unable to return home for Advancement had initially caused great uproar among native Ophs. Since that time, years before Rieka was born, ships' captains carried out the *Gringihad* ceremony as authentically as possible. Admiral Nason saw to it that the Advanced were given leave as quickly as the Fleet's schedules would permit, allowing them to return home and choose a mate.

"I'll have to speak to Captain Marteen, though," Rieka amended. "Shall I invite him as well? I would think Gorah would be pleased with the distinction of two captains in attendance." She smiled at the thought of her stoic electronics chief flattered into a preseasonal shedding by Triscoe's presence.

Tohab's voice was solicitous in her head. "I don't think so, Captain. Gorah is nervous enough. She has already started shedding."

Giving a little sigh at the thought of the Oph engineer truly losing handfuls of her lovely cream-colored coat, Rieka said, "Not a problem. I'll tell him it's ladies only. I'm sure he won't mind. We're half a billion miles from the nearest planet. Aside from the *Venture*, where could I go?"

"Thank you, Captain."

"I'll let you know for certain once I speak to him. Degahv out."

Her TC shut down and Rieka looked at the report still glowing on her console's screen. She tapped out orders for a copy of it to be sent to Yadra with the day's other communiqués. Chen would receive it in about thirty hours, and she could expect a reply in sixty-four. With luck, she wouldn't even have to return to court.

"Never count on luck, Rieka," she murmured, repeating her father's often overused maxim, "—it might just turn out bad." Then, she shut down the computer link and went to find Triscoe, deciding a request to leave the ship should be made in person, not via TC.

Two hours later she surveyed the assembly hall on the *Venture*. The room was filled with several dozen members of her crew, all female, who had been invited by Gorah to witness her Advancement. The audience chairs had been assembled in a circle that left a large clear space for the ceremony. Rieka stood on the perimeter. The Oph was dead center.

Gorah knelt and placed her furry hands out in front of her. Slowly, she dropped them to the floor. She threw back her head and let out a piercing wail that eventually shifted to low and rumbly tones. She looked at Rieka.

"Why should this woman be Advanced?" Rieka asked the crowd.

PRODIGY   159

In the front row, directly opposite, four crew members stood. One after another, they answered the question with words anchored in antiquity. "She is strong. She is brave. She knows herself. She is ready."

"Are you these things, Gorah? Do your comrades speak the truth?"

The Oph nodded. She stood slowly, bringing her head up last. Rieka watched her eyes. Dark now, they would soon open enough for the halo to be seen around the edge. Gorah widened her stance and did a complicated movement with her arms and padlike digits. She turned and repeated the movement to the three other points of the audience, each point representing a child that she might bear.

"I am strong. I am ready," she said in the low, gravelly voice of her kind.

Rieka allowed herself a small smile. She bowed formally in the way of Ophs, knees slightly bent first, then a straight back tipped forward, followed by the head dipping until the chin was on the chest. When she pulled herself up to her full height, Gorah returned the gesture.

Rieka held out her right hand. Tohab, seated just behind her, handed her the *mimga,* the Oph symbol of strength. Rieka took the long thin ceremonial artifact. It looked like a heavy belt without a buckle, but was much more. She adjusted her stance to account for its incredible weight. It amazed her that any Oph had the physical power needed for an Advancement.

She held the *mimga* before her, arms straining, and glanced at the ornate blue markings along its length. "Show me your strength."

Gorah stepped forward to take the flexible ornamented strap of metal. She lifted it easily out of Rieka's hands and held it over her head. Behind her, the four who had spoken before began to play replicas of ceremonial instruments, similar to Human drums, castanets, cymbals, and blocks.

With the beat established, Gorah began to dance. Carrying the *mimga,* lifting it, swinging it—using it as both prop and partner—she danced. The grace in her lithe form was remarkable, considering that the strap of metal was about 20 percent of her body weight. After a short time, the music changed, growing more energetic. Gorah kept up, her two-inch golden fur echoing her movements like animate fringe. Her eyes opened to the point where the irises were ringed in yellow. The *mimga* was tossed into the air, caught, and tossed again. She never lost control of the dance or the artifact. Rieka could hear her breath becoming labored as she moved, but her steps never faltered.

After long, exhausting minutes, when it became tiring even to watch Gorah in her rapturous dance, the music subsided. She performed the ceremonial lessons representing old age, slowing her movements in sync with the halting beat. The tempo continued to wind down until she performed her own symbolic death, flinging the *mimga* before her as she dropped to the floor. It slid to just beyond the reach of her hand-paws.

Rieka straightened her shoulders and walked forward in the reverent silence to put a booted toe on the strap. She searched the audience, her expression expectant. "Does anyone challenge this woman's right to Advancement?"

While she waited for a response, Rieka looked down at her electronics chief. Gorah was panting from the ordeal but recovering quickly. Her coat was matted in spots from the exertion, her head down in the event of a challenge. There was none.

Rieka stepped across the *mimga* and touched the top of Gorah's golden head. "By the power I possess as your superior officer, I Advance you, Gorah," she said. "Rise."

As the Oph got to her feet, Lieutenant Rldn, one of the advocates who had spoken earlier, came forward. She held an instrument that looked like a castanet. Rieka took it and clamped it over Gorah's floppy left ear. Gorah did not so much as flinch during the procedure. When a light on the hinge end of the instrument flashed, Rieka removed the object and handed it back to Rldn. A gleaming piece of metal, ornately adorned with bits of glittering stone, had been fused into the Oph's flesh.

Gorah was Advanced.

Pride glimmered in her eyes as Rieka smiled. She lifted her right arm and flexed back her hand. Gorah mirrored the movement, and they touched palm to pad. "Congratulations, my friend," Rieka said softly. "We will miss you while you are gone."

"As we have missed you," the Oph replied.

Rieka was startled by the unexpected honor. She took a deep breath, then smiled at the sentiment. "I'll be back."

"As will I."

The captain turned toward the audience. "This woman is Advanced," she declared. "It is the time for celebration."

The party lasted until the early evening. Rieka was surprised to find that her crew had felt her absence as much as she'd felt theirs. Some, like Plemik, who would never trust any Human, felt no loyalty to her. But nearly everyone, even those on duty, took a moment to stop and pay their respects.

"Herring," she said, offering the Centauri navigator her open palms, "how have you been?"

"Fine, Captain." He completed the greeting and sat beside her. "We've been following your case. I . . . have been concerned."

She couldn't help smiling. "Me too. Seriously, though, I think it'll be dismissed. You could be taking orders from me again, very soon."

Herring nodded. He glanced at Tohab, standing a few feet away, then looked at Rieka. "That would be . . . desirable. Your presence on the bridge is missed."

At that, she had to laugh. "Not by all, I'm afraid."

"You refer to Plemik." Herring nodded. "And you are correct. But Aurians are not always understood.

And they are emotional. Even without you in command, he has spoken out of place."

While Herring said good-bye and moved off into the crowd, Rieka wondered how Tohab handled Plemik. Aurians, she thought. They're almost as bad as Boos to figure out.

After greeting most of the crew, she found herself yawning behind her hand. Triscoe checked in on her TC and she told him she'd be getting back to the *Providence* soon.

Someone touched her shoulder and Rieka braced herself for yet another brief conversation. But as she turned, Tohab gave her a curious look. "Come, Captain," she said.

Rieka followed her first officer into the corridor and to a Chute. In seconds, they were standing at the entrance to her old quarters.

"What's this—?"

"I thought you looked tired," Tohab said. She led the way into the suite.

"But, really, I've told Captain Marteen I'd be returning . . ." She stepped across the threshold and felt her heart skip. It was like going home, yet knowing you couldn't stay. Walking aimlessly about, Rieka touched things that felt like cherished old friends. The timepiece she'd found on Vekya. The weathered statuette from Medoura. The fossil from Earth.

Her eyes swept to the DGI. It held a view of Earth and the moon. She felt a swelling in her throat. Only a million or so were permitted residence there at present, all involved in the restoration. She hoped that, within her lifetime, the Earth could be slowly repopulated and, perhaps, earn a modicum of respect from the rest of the Commonwealth.

"Here," Tohab said, offering her a cup of something and sitting on the small blue divan.

Rieka accepted it and sat. She sipped the *colan*. "I hadn't realized until now, how . . . homesick I've been," she said.

Tohab watched her. "I prefer being an executive

officer, Captain. I have no desire to take your place. If the court rules in your favor and Admiral Nason remains behind you with his trust, I see no reason for you not to return."

She took another sip of the drink. "I can't speak for anyone other than myself, Midrin. My innocence in this is certain. My future, however, is a bit gray. It scares me I might not command again."

"They would be fools to demote you."

Rieka chuckled. "Bigger fools have changed history for less than this." She waved her hand to indicate the ship. She yawned. "Sorry. It's been a long day. I thought the *colan* would pick me up."

Tohab nodded.

"Do you think they'll offer you the *Venture* if I'm dismissed?"

"I've heard nothing, but I would not accept command."

"Out of deference to me? Really, Midrin. Is that what this conversation is all about? I can't imagine . . ." She blinked and took a deep breath. "I can't imagine you doing such a dumb thing." The tumbler began to slip through her fingers, but she caught it. Her body, even her mind, felt numb. A strange wave of terror crept over her but she was unable to form it into coherent thought.

"Of course . . . of course, if something happens to me, you should command the *Venture*," she mumbled. Her lids felt too heavy to lift. "Sorry," she slurred, "I'm feeling rather . . ."

Unconscious, Rieka sank back onto the divan. Her eyes rolled up beneath her lids. Her jaw fell open.

L'gith-la stood and collected the cup to dispose of it. Her smile was decidedly Procyon in nature. Standing near the door, she turned to survey the anesthetized body of Captain Degahv. It was safest here, for the moment. No one would come to these quarters. They were vacant now that the captain was in Marteen's custody. Marteen would miss her, of course, but by then it would be too late.

Eleven

Triscoe glanced impatiently at the clock in his quarters. He had spoken to Rieka less than an hour ago. The celebration was still going strong and she'd told him she would return to the *Providence* soon. Soon? What, exactly, did that mean?

Knowing how easily she could be offended, Triscoe didn't want to use his TC again. It had taken too long to reach their tenuous acceptance of each other to risk a setback now. He decided instead, to diplomatically make a formal inquiry as to the *Venture*'s status. Contacting Midrin Tohab would keep him from pestering Rieka.

On the bridge, all was quiet. Because of their wide orbit around Epi Indi, all but two of the positions were unmanned during the evening hours. His day-shift communications officer, V'don, had been replaced by Lt. Avery Ortega, a Human from Aurie. Lieutenant Lisk, an Oph, maintained the helm.

"Ortega," he said conversationally, "open communications with the *Venture*."

Triscoe sat in his chair and glanced at the first few screens on his readout. He looked at the DGI image of the *Venture* before turning to Ortega. "Is there a problem, Lieutenant?"

The Human gave him an ambiguous nod, frowned, and reset his console. "This is not . . ." He touched the board in front of him, again.

"Lieutenant?"

Ortega shrugged. "They're not responding, sir. I've

double-checked the equipment. I'm sure they're receiving. It's just that, well, nobody's answering."

Triscoe felt an unwelcome sense of urgency. Forgetting protocol, he clicked on his TC. "Link to the *Venture*. Marteen to Captain Degahv." He waited impatiently while the TC unit linked the signal. It should not have taken half a second.

"Rieka, acknowledge please."

Nothing.

He touched the access pad to InterMAT Station One. The immediate response from the intercom doused his anxiety. "Station One, Kyliss."

"This is the captain. Link into Captain Degahv's TC signal and prepare to transport her to the *Providence*."

"Understood, Captain," Kyliss replied. A few seconds later, he added, "Signal coming in clearly."

"Well-done. You may—"

"Captain! The *Venture*!"

Triscoe's attention snapped to the DGI. Nothing seemed wrong. "What, Lisk?"

The Oph tensed as he worked his console. "I am reading multiple life-forms appearing outside the hull."

"The crew?"

"Apparently, sir."

Triscoe directed himself to the InterMAT chief. "Kyliss, alert your stations. Scan the area within InterMAT radius of the *Venture*. Commence immediate transport of all TC signatures."

"From space, sir?"

"Don't ask, just do it." He tapped another pad on his console. "Medical. Vort are you there? We've got incoming casualties. Probably plenty. Alert your staff. All InterMAT stations are bringing in casualties."

"From where?" Twanabok's voice sounded confused and thick with sleep.

"The *Venture*."

"I'm dispatching people now."

Triscoe left the channel open and heard the muted voice of his InterMAT chief give the orders to the remaining three stations. He waited anxiously while all chambers were programmed and began pulling in the *Venture*'s crew. Hopefully, most of them would realize what was happening and remember their space-exposure training, giving him the chance to rescue them, uninjured. At the very least, they needed to keep their eyes closed and their mouths shut.

Lisk tensed again. "Captain, she's powering up her antimatter spheres."

Not now, he thought, realizing the trap they'd fallen into. How could this have happened? Who was in command on the *Venture*? He tapped his intercom again. "Crew of the *Providence*, this is Captain Marteen. Condition red. All hands to your stations. We are under attack. This is not a drill. All hands to your stations."

His fingers clenched the arms of his chair. Simulations and training were one thing, but there had been no attack on a Commonwealth vessel since the last Procyon skirmish, years ago. Now, he was about to be forced into firing not only on a sister ship, but Rieka as well.

The *Venture* continued to eject its crew into space. Lisk adjusted the panoply sensors to survey the eerie scene. There was just enough light to see tiny figures appearing outside the hull. At least a hundred of them, so far.

On whose authority? Triscoe wondered frantically. Rieka's? Or someone else? There wasn't time to speculate. He watched the crewmen disappear as they were picked up by his InterMAT. While it was in use, he couldn't protect the *Providence* from attack. His duty had become a double-edged sword.

He had to think of something soon, or his ship and both crews would be annihilated. The IRB system on his command board caught his eye. He tapped the indicator to bring the system on line.

Wondering if the tactic would work, Triscoe transferred controls from the presently unmanned defense console to his own. Becker would be along in a minute, but he couldn't wait. If the *Venture* attacked them, they'd have to respond immediately. The only option was to try to predetonate the incoming spheres. It would be tricky, but it might work. He hoped.

"Captain, insulation screens?" asked Lisk.

"Not until the InterMAT stations have reported," he replied. The synthetic wormholes could not be controlled properly through an intact repulsion screen. He wondered if Becker could come up with some way of getting around that, in the event the IRB didn't work. He checked the board to refamiliarize himself with it, and set it to track incoming spheres.

"She's firing," Lisk said, sounding as if he didn't believe himself. They watched a single bright spot leave the *Venture* from just above the pod and speed toward them.

Triscoe tapped out additional commands for the IRB, but the continuous beam was not designed to hit anything traveling at high speeds. It could not maintain contact long enough to crack the sphere. In his peripheral vision, Triscoe noticed Becker take his position at the weapons console. Maybe he would have better luck.

"Evasive maneuvers," Triscoe snapped. "Keep us in InterMAT range, Lisk." The ship pivoted while he continued to fire. The shell erupted less than two kilometers away.

There was a jolt. "Concussion, Captain," Lisk reported. "The explosion just scraped us. The panoply's been damaged, slightly. DGI still operational."

Becker turned in his seat. "Shall I switch over and return like fire, sir?" he asked.

Triscoe shook his head. "It's bad enough we've got to pull those people through a battle zone. As long as they're being jettisoned, we can only try to defend ourselves."

He tapped his screen and glanced up at Becker. "Command of weapons is now on your board. Try to pick off incoming spheres with the IRB. Lisk, back us away from the *Venture* as far as you can. We need more room."

"She's firing again, Captain," Lisk reported.

They watched as the DGI showed a sphere heading for them, aimed at the gravity pod far below the thin upper hull. "Becker—?"

The lieutenant was shaking his head. "The IRB can't track a sphere. It's just not fast enough. Wait. I think I've . . ."

Triscoe saw what was happening and quickly called up a screen fragment on his own console. He adjusted its position between the incoming sphere and his ship. Under Becker's control, the IRB cut through the magnetic shell. The ensuing blast flared from the DGI, momentarily blinding them.

This time the jolt was severe. The ship shuddered. Without the protection of a full screen, the gravity pod had taken a severe blow.

Lisk groaned. "DGI's been damaged."

"All hands prepare for zero G," Triscoe barked at the intercom. He and the rest of the bridge crew pulled on their waist straps. He snapped his head around to Ortega. The communications board looking as though it had reached capacity, and then some. "What's happening in the pod?"

"Commander Memta is occupied with his equipment. Lieutenant Roddik is reporting casualties, Captain. Gravitation is off-line. They're evacuating now."

Triscoe nodded. "Becker, power up our spheres and prepare to engage the entire screen. Kyliss must have almost all of them by now."

With the intercom still on, the InterMAT chief spoke up. "We'll need at least another full minute, sir. The *Venture*'s still spitting her crew, but taking her time about it. And it's difficult to clear the chambers with so many." His voice was tense, Triscoe noted. Setting the InterMAT controls and fighting zero G at the same time couldn't be easy.

"Incoming sphere," Lisk reported. "Impact in twenty seconds."

"Ready the insulation screen," Triscoe ordered.

"Lisk, maneuver us in an arc thirty degrees to port, positive one thousand meters. When the sphere tracks us there, wobble back to starboard, negative fifteen hundred. If we can make the thing chase us, maybe we can buy some time for Kyliss. Becker, hold off on the IRB this time."

"Understood, sir." Lisk programmed the helm and the now-blurry image on the DGI began to shift. The *Venture* and starfield behind it drifted off the lower right side. A few seconds later, the picture returned and slid away in the opposite direction. The incoming sphere seemed to pick up speed as it both followed the zigzag path and closed the distance.

"Got, 'em, Captain!" Kyliss reported.

"Go."

The screen formed and almost immediately repelled the magnetic sphere containing the antimatter charge. Becker launched return fire, but by then there was nothing to hit.

"She's moving away at maximum acceleration," Lisk reported. "I'd say she's powering up for a quantum-slide."

"After her, best available speed," Triscoe said. "We may not catch her, but I want to know where she's going."

"Understood." Lisk programmed the new heading, and the *Providence* took off in pursuit.

Triscoe deactivated the DGI when the image became too fuzzy. He would not switch it on again until the panoply was repaired. Fighting the urge that told him it might be better not to know, he spoke into the intercom. "Kyliss, report."

The voice of his Centauri InterMAT chief was still intense. "The four stations successfully transported 211 individuals, Captain."

"Go on."

Twanabok's voice replaced that of the Centaurian. "Those that made it here are well, Triscoe. They were taken from their beds, mostly. Casualties are being routed to the medical ward. All minor. I've got three scheduled for pressure chambers. Some minor surgery, eardrums, mostly. But that's about it. The InterMAT accounts for 211 souls. With an original compliment of 236, that leaves a remainder crew of 25 still aboard."

"Twenty-six," Triscoe corrected.

"I've subtracted wrong?" inquired the doctor, sounding insulted.

"No, Vort. Rieka was aboard. There was an Advancement ceremony. She was late in returning from the festivities."

"Sir," Kyliss's voice sounded contrite. "We prioritized when the emergency occurred. Captain Degahv remained on the *Venture*."

"Of course she did," he said softly. "Vort, please see to the accommodations for our additional crew. Kyliss, secure your stations. Commendations for your people will be forthcoming. Well-done."

"Thank you, Captain."

Triscoe tried to lean back in his chair, but the lack of gravity made it awkward. While his officers performed their duties, he fidgeted. He could not imagine this to be Rieka's doing. Why hadn't she responded? Was it because she wouldn't or couldn't reply? Who was in command on that ship? He cast an inquiring glance at Lisk.

"*Venture*'s still accelerating," he reported. "General direction is for Tau Ceti. My guess is she'll foamduct for Yadra in another five hours or so."

Triscoe nodded. "Continue pursuit, Lieutenant. When she does slide, maintain course and speed. We'll have to wait for repairs before we can go anywhere, but I want the trip to be as short as possible."

"Understood."

He released the strap that held him to his chair and found the designated handholds to the Chute door. It took a bit longer than usual to return to his quarters, but all Fleet personnel trained in zero G, and it was simply more time-consuming than inconvenient. Regulations required him to report to Admiral Nason promptly, but Triscoe needed a few minutes of solitude in order to sound coherent when he sent the communiqué.

As she woke, Rieka wondered if she'd been transferred to Boo. Gravity seemed to pin her down. Her arms and legs felt leaden, her mouth dry, eyes swollen. But a glance around the room told her she was still in her quarters aboard the *Venture*. Propelling herself off the sofa with a firm push, she went to the lav and splashed water on her face. It helped, slightly. Glancing numbly at the chrono, she grimaced. Triscoe would be furious. She was way overdue.

Rieka clicked on her TC. "Link to the *Providence*. Degahv to Marteen."

Nothing. "Probably too angry," she muttered. Still feeling groggy, she dismissed Triscoe's silence and decided to take a shower. She then found a clean uniform in one of her drawers, donned it, and tried to contact the *Providence* medical section to apologize for not returning as Twanabok had requested.

No response. Even from Twanabok, that seemed strange.

Bracing for a lecture, she signaled Triscoe again. Nothing. He wasn't just giving her the cold shoulder. He wasn't there. Neither was Twanabok. Her mind still felt fuzzy but not so much so that she did not sense trouble.

She reset the TC to request access to the *Venture*'s computer.

"Query?" the mechanical tones sounded in her head.

"What's going on?"

"Specify."

She sighed. "Why can't I communicate with the *Providence*?"

"Ships in real space cannot be reached while phasing in foamduct."

She didn't like the sound of that, at all. "Who is phasing?"

"The *Venture* is currently in foamduct," it said.

"Where are we going?"

"Yadra."

"Damn," she muttered. It was sounding worse all the time. "Give last known location of the *Providence*."

The synthesized voice responded, "Approximately forty-seven AUs from planet Aurie, 115,000 kilometers aft of this vessel. Spacial coordinates: 116—"

"Never mind coordinates." They had been about five AUs from Aurie during Gorah's Advancement. Forty-seven was a long way out. And, considering it was aft of the *Venture,* something didn't sound right. "Was the *Providence* in pursuit?"

"Unknown."

"Why did it not slide with this vessel?"

"Estimated cause for inability, damage to sensor panoply and engineering."

Rieka rubbed her temples. "I don't understand. What caused the damage?"

"Antimatter spheres released from this vessel."

"No!" She groaned and her hands balled into fists as she clicked off the TC. Her head ached. She realized she'd probably been drugged. But by whom? When? At the party? She couldn't recall much of what happened after the ceremony. Her eyes scanned the room as if she should remember something that happened here. After a moment of concentration that produced nothing more than a sense of uneasiness, she decided to look elsewhere for some answers.

The door slid open, but before she could move through it, a hulking body stepped in her path. Searching the lavender eyes of the Vekyan security officer, she frowned. "I didn't expect to find you here, Elindok."

"That is not my concern," he said briefly.

"But guarding me is?"

"True."

"Okay." She thought about that for a moment. "Are you keeping me safe, or keeping me prisoner?"

"Prisoner."

"Why?"

"I will not substantiate that query with an answer, traitor."

She did not like his tone in the slightest. Not only was he being insubordinate, the lieutenant was downright insulting. A few senior officers of her bridge crew notwithstanding, the crew of the *Venture* had been loyal. Judging from their attitudes at yesterday's Advancement celebration, they also liked her. Elindok included.

Rieka bit back a retort. Vekyans were quite literal. If she wanted information, her questions needed to be direct. "Traitor to whom?" she asked.

He looked at her squarely, the venom in his raspy voice clear. "Traitor to the Commonwealth, the Fleet, to your spouse, and to your crew."

Aghast at the insult, her jaw dropped and she snapped it shut. Taking a deep breath, she said, "I am no traitor, Lieutenant. Something is wrong, and I'm going fix it. Right now." She tried to shoulder her way past him but he sidled in front of her, his tongue snaking out a silent warning.

"You will return to the confined—"

"It's quite obvious that you're mistaken, Elindok," Rieka insisted, ignoring the blue tongue that flicked only inches from her face. "I intend to speak to Commander Tohab immediately and have this confusion sorted out."

He raised his maitu. "It is you who are mistaken. Step back."

"Elindok." She stopped trying to wrestle her way past him. "I'm your captain."

"You are my prisoner," he corrected. "You will remain here until we reach Yadra."

She smiled and nodded, trying to confuse him. "Sorry, I can't accommodate you. I've got to get to the bridge. Why don't you come with me?"

He shrugged that odd way the Vekyans did, with his chest heaving in and out. "You may not leave the confines—"

With a final shove, she cleared his bulk and squeezed into the corridor. Elindok was a good and faithful security officer. She doubted he would shoot her. Before she could make it to a Chute, however, the maitu jolt made her back feel as if it were on fire. She gave a little cry as she fell, the image of the floor melting into blackness.

Rieka's body felt limp as Elindok roused her with the butt end of his weapon. He said nothing. Her vision was blurred, an aftereffect of the stun, and she took her time getting to her feet. He led her out of her room and to InterMAT Station One. She was shoved into the chamber, still at gunpoint, and a moment later found herself in a place immediately recognizable. It was an area just off the entrance hall of her brother's consulate in Lemonne. Had Midrin been ordered to bring her back to Yadra? By who? Being transferred to Paden's custody also concerned her. He was, after all, on the list of people that might have been influenced by the machine on Aurie.

Keeping her expression stony, she eyed the Oph lieutenant who stood at the exit of the transfer chamber. "This way, Captain," he said stiffly, his weapon in hand but unaimed.

"Of course," she replied, stepping through the doorway. Not knowing why she was an object of his hatred, Rieka decided a few gentle questions, in addition to absolute cooperation, were called for. "Is it possible for you to tell me what any of this is about?" she inquired as they turned down a wide corridor she recognized as the administrator's wing.

"No discussion is permitted, Captain," he replied curtly. "In here." He fingered a control on his belt that opened a door, then gestured her through. He stepped back, and the opening was sealed.

"Friendly chap," she muttered. The residual effects of the maitu were still causing her vision to blur slightly. That, coupled with the earlier drug plus lack of food, put her in a foul mood. She blinked until the edges of things no longer looked fuzzy and turned to scrutinize the room. An oval table flanked by six chairs stood on a bare floor, a sideboard console with a tray of beverages sat against the wall nearest the door. There was an ornate lighting fixture hanging from the ceiling, undoubtedly concealing a monitoring device, and no windows. The beige walls were paneled, each section resembling a molded door. The room looked as though it had been designed to suit Paden's paranoia. She imagined armed guards storming through the door panels at any moment.

With nothing else to do, Rieka helped herself to a tumbler of juice. Sitting at the table and wishing for something to eat, she consumed half her drink before looking directly at the chandelier. "Paden, my patience with you is about to run out," she snapped. "I'm here for a reason. Let's get on with it."

A moment later a section of the wall opened, and her brother stepped through. He was in a tailored tunic-suit in a warm brown that complimented his complexion, nearly as dark as her own. The outfit, along with ear clip, three gaudy rings, and a cufflet, would cost a Fleet captain half a year's pay. He eyed her carefully, poured a drink for himself, then sauntered to the table, staring at her with open disgust.

"What, no guards?" she teased. "Oh, I forgot, they're behind the walls. One false move, and I'm pet food, right?"

"I am completely baffled by your attitude, Rieka," he said finally, then pulled out the chair opposite her and sat.

"Really? How's that?"

"You kill almost all of your crew, attack the *Providence*, then come dancing in here like you haven't a care." He lifted his hand to gesture utter futility but stopped when he saw her expression.

Rieka felt suddenly faint. "My crew?" she gasped. The hair on her arms prickled, and it seemed that her lungs had ceased to function. "What's happened to my crew?"

"As if you didn't know," he murmured, looking down his regal nose.

Her jaw was tight as she glared at him. "Paden, if you don't answer my question, I'm going to leap over this table so fast your people won't know what to think. And when they start shooting, it will just as likely be you they hit."

Her tone was apparently deadly enough to get his attention. He stopped gloating and frowned. "You don't know?"

"Dammit, Paden." She put both palms on the table and was pushing out of the chair before he gestured her to sit.

"All right. Relax." He looked her in the eye. "You had them ejected."

She frowned. That had to be the dumbest thing she'd ever heard. "Ejected? Where?"

"Space."

"Space!" Her hand went to her throat. She gritted her teeth to fight a wave of queasiness. The room spun slightly, but she would not succumb to it. Instead, Rieka gripped the edge of the table and took a shuddering breath.

"How many?" she managed.

"Two-hundred eleven."

"Good God!" She looked away, stricken by the number before glancing back at him. "Who told you this?"

"Your first officer, Midrin Tohab."

She frowned in disbelief but said nothing.

"It was confirmed by Captain Marteen when he reported the attack on the *Providence*," Paden continued.

She sat back and rubbed her temples. Her first thought was of the Aurian machine—that that M'narn fellow had somehow managed to program her again. But Twanabok had assured her he'd reversed the suggestion. And Yillon had told her nothing had been left of the first session. But there had been that suggestion she didn't remember—to return to the installation, alone. Had M'narn given her more? She just didn't know.

She had no recollection of anything after the Advancement celebration, save her confrontations with Elindok. Finding Paden's news impossible to digest, she turned to his secondary topic. "And who attacked the *Providence*?"

"You did, Rieka, while in command of the *Venture*."

"That's completely absurd."

"You deny it?"

She sighed and looked at him. Sympathy seemed to be beyond reach at the moment, but anything at all was better than nothing. "Of course I deny it. I haven't been in command of anything since my arrest. This has something to do with—" She stopped, checked herself, then said, "the initial black mark on my record. I can't figure how, but whoever wanted me court-martialed before must be running scared I'll be acquitted."

She watched Paden consider her remark, belch silently behind his hand, and set his glass on the table. "And you expect me to believe that?"

She ignored his sneer. "Bring in your consulate physician. I'll submit to a regressive mnemonic analysis to prove I didn't order my crew's death—or attack Captain Marteen." She leaned across the smooth surface of the table. "I've got just as much—no, more—moral integrity than you, brother. And in the end, I'll prove it."

A muscle twitched in his cheek. "What are you implying, baby sister?"

She was about to start up the old argument again, but stopped herself and switched tactics. "Paden, we don't get along. I admit that. But until all of this started, I've never been called a liar—because I'm not. And I've certainly never lied to you." She leaned back in the chair, waiting for some kind of acceptance of that fact. There was none, and Rieka wondered if he lied so much that he assumed everyone else did, too.

"Whatever you think, I've uncovered proof of my innocence. It's been documented. Triscoe Marteen,

Robet DeVark, and my attorney, Chen, are in possession of all the facts. I'll be acquitted. You can count on
that "

He sniffed through his nose and looked thoughtfully
down it at her. "That has nothing to do with this new
trouble," he scoffed, crossing his arms and leaning
back against the chair. "But I suppose you've got an
answer for that, too."

"Actually, I don't. But I think you ought to be made
aware of something. We found an installation on Aurie.
In it there's a machine that has the capability to program a person's mind. I was put under that machine and
told to destroy the Procyon ship."

His expression did not change. "Go on."

"I was also told to forget that I'd ever been there."

He sighed impatiently. "Where is this leading,
Rieka?"

She spoke slowly, carefully, her eyes never leaving
his face. Surely, even if he wouldn't admit it, she could
read what she needed in his expression. "You've been
on Aurie recently, haven't you?"

"I was there just about a month ago for a conference.
It's hardly a secret."

She nodded. "Fine. But can you recall every waking
moment of your visit? Or are you missing a few hours
out of a day? That's all they need, you know. Just a few
hours—and your life is no longer your own."

Paden frowned but she couldn't tell if he was identi-
fying with the information, or had simply become
annoyed with her. "I have other appointments," he
said, rising. "I'm sure I will see you again before your
trial. I've taken the liberty of notifying your counsel.
He'll come by later to see you."

Chen would probably be having a fit over the latest
trouble. Bad as it was, she tried not to think about it.
"Thank you, that was very considerate."

He rubbed a finger under his nose. "You *are* my
sister."

She treated him to a smile. "One other thing."

"What's that?"

"Today's date?"

"One-forty-five."

Two days had gone by. She'd lost all that time.

Paden sniffed. "So, you see, you're way beyond the thirty-six-hour cutoff for that regressive memory analysis you volunteered for. How convenient." His smile was false. "You've got ten days to prepare your case. Cases now, I suppose."

Paden left immediately, and the guard reappeared. He escorted her to a large guest room and promptly locked her in. She clicked on her TC hoping to reach the central comnet. She needed to speak to Admiral Nason, Chen, or even Setana Marteen. But the TC refused to function.

Reviewing the afflictions her body had been put through in the last several days, she decided the new model couldn't handle a maitu stun. Perhaps the doctor had been right. Tying it into the central nervous system wasn't really such a good idea after all.

A cursory inspection of the room revealed no communication terminal, so she went to the single, unopenable window and watched water splash in the courtyard fountain. Her eyes took in the manicured garden, but her mind raced, trying to piece together this new twist to the puzzle. Nothing seemed to fit. It was like a particularly testy cryptogram. Just when she'd thought she might eventually understand everything, someone had changed the code. Whoever was out to get her was both motivated and capable.

She knew something had happened after the party. Something to do with her quarters. She had to remember!

Twelve

Robet sat in Admiral Nason's quiet office, wondering what had gone wrong.

Things had been moving along nicely. The admiral seemed convinced of both Rieka's innocence and the possible infiltration of Procyon agents. His people were looking for traces of questionable communications, seemingly chance meetings, odd acquaintances.

And then the *Venture* attacked the *Providence*.

Robet hadn't even bothered to look smug when Nason's secretary waved him through without a word. He was too preoccupied with both apprehension and relief that the admiral had sent for him. Triscoe had sent a second message. Robet sat swiveling his jaw with nervous energy while he waited for it to be decoded.

The admiral entered, strode to his desk, and sat down. He looked haggard. The stress of not knowing who to trust was wearing on them all.

"Care for some *colan*, Robet?" the older man asked.

"Thanks, no, sir. That stuff doesn't get along with my system. *Ribah* trouble."

Nason nodded and sipped from a cup that had been on his desk. "As you may have guessed, I am apprehensive about conferring with my peers on this particular matter. And, those who might have believed in Captain Degahv's innocence before—are hardly convinced now."

"Has the *Venture* made orbit?"

"Yes, some minutes ago."

"Where is she—Captain Degahv, now? Still on board?"

"No." Nason settled back in his chair. "She has been placed where she should have been—was originally ordered to go, I believe. Lemonne Province. On her brother's estate."

Robet let his bibbets flush pink. *"Fez,"* he muttered, and ran a hand across his jaw.

Nason's bibbets colored faintly. "Is there something wrong?"

He looked at the admiral and willed his stomach to stay calm. "Recall, if you will, sir, that the name Paden Degahv was on the list of persons who might have been 'externally influenced' by that machine on Aurie." He leaned forward and rested a forearm across the desk. "We may just have played right into their hands. Giving her back to them—like some kind of sacrificial offering."

The admiral thought it over, his brow wrinkling below his now pale bibbets. "Possible," he said quietly. "At this point, I would believe anything is possible."

An aide entered carrying a small flat box. "Captain Marteen's report, sir," she said. She laid it on his desk and left.

Robet licked his lips while Nason opened the lid, removed a small square of plastic, and slipped in into a slot on his console. Together, they turned and looked at the large DGI screen on the opposite wall.

Triscoe's face was tense, the furrow apparent between his brows, his jaw tight. Behind him was the image on the DGI in his quarters. He had not taken the chance of recording this report with others present.

"Admiral," he said with a slight nod. "I have received your request for an 'unofficial' update and will do my best to review the occurrences of the last twenty-eight hours. In sequence, they are . . ." He went on for some minutes, describing the circumstances leading up to the attack on his ship, finishing with, "Since Memta is anticipating a thirty-hour delay, I estimate that we will be en route to you by the time you hear this report."

When Triscoe paused to consider something, Robet

drummed his fingers on the admiral's desk. "He hasn't said anything—about anything. What about—?"

"Admiral," Triscoe went on, his face now curling into a curious frown, "I have no evidence to support what I am about to say, but I must report any assumptions I can make. I have come to the conclusion that the attack was ordered by Captain Degahv, or by Commander Tohab. Only someone of command rank would have had access to computer functions to control both the InterMAT and weapons under such bizarre conditions.

"Rieka, I believe, is no longer under the influence of the Aurian machine. I lean toward the conclusion that Midrin Tohab gave the orders. Tohab, you may recall, was also on Aurie during the last visit made by the *Venture*. It was an oversight not to have considered her suspect."

He took a breath and continued. "The next question is: why? I have postulated an answer. In the light of the near death of so many crewmen, I feel the Procyons are somehow responsible. Robet must have told you by now, the information we got from Dr. M'narn." He stopped, rubbed his face with a hand, and sighed.

"I have no ETA at this time but will report to you at the soonest available moment. Marteen, out."

The screen went blank. Nason removed the message from his console, then leaned across his desk to dispose of it. "Well, that's a mouthful. Though I can't say I'm surprised."

Robet accepted the admiral's assessment, though he didn't like the part about Midrin. He found it difficult to believe she could have attacked the *Providence* and ejected the *Venture*'s crew. Of course, he found it equally ridiculous that Rieka could have done it, either. And if Rieka could be programmed, so could Midrin. "You mean about the Procyons?"

"No." The admiral sighed. "About what Triscoe *wouldn't* say."

"Sir?"

"What they're after."

Robet felt himself clenching his jaw. He was too close to the problem, had lost his sense of perspective. Silently glad he wasn't in the admiral's chair, he sat up a bit straighter. "What *are* they after, sir?"

"The *Prodigy*, of course. We've created the ultimate defense vessel—designed to destroy anything an outside force might use against us. But in the enemy's hands, the *Prodigy* could carve up the Commonwealth planet by plant—all the while picking off Fleet ships like inconsequential insects."

Robet nodded. With a prototype like that in their hands, the Procyons would annihilate the Commonwealth in a matter of weeks. The problems involving Rieka must have been a decoy designed to keep the Fleet's attention off the true threat. Concerned as he was about his friend's welfare, Robet knew his responsibility to Admiral Nason and the Fleet came first. "I suppose I know what you're going to say, next."

Nason looked at him quizzically. "Really? And what might that be?"

"Don't get on old Finot's bad side." Robet knew the huge Boo in charge of the yard at Dani. He'd been a fixture there for nearly a century. He wondered if Finot could be convinced that Procyons might be after his newest ship. And, because the *Prodigy*'s commander, Captain Pedlam, was on Triscoe's list of possible traitors, would there be some way to pull him off the job? At the very least they'd need to have him examined by someone who could detect whether or not he'd been "influenced."

"Good advice," the admiral said, smiling. He sobered quickly, adding, "I'll alert Captain Finot myself. He should be able to accommodate you by the time you get there. Stop this thing before it gets out of hand, Robet. But be discreet." He stared down at his desk, bibbets coloring slightly, and rubbed a finger along the lip of his cup.

Robet had seen him tense, before, but not like this. He was really worried, and rightly so. If the Procyons were after the *Prodigy,* they only needed a little more slack.

"I'm convinced of an attempt to disable the Fleet," Nason said softly as he looked at Robet. "And, without that mortar, the Commonwealth falls into chaos. Eight races scattered on ten worlds—unable to travel or conduct business. It's a nightmare." The pink of his bibbets went a shade darker, but he quickly brought himself under control. "I will send the *Providence* along to help you once I'm assured it's adequately repaired. And I will try to do what I can from this position," he finished, indicating his desk.

"Understood, sir." Robet nodded. "The *Prospectus* will leave as soon as possible." He got up to go, but before he reached the door, the admiral's voice stopped him.

"Robet."

He turned. "Sir."

"Use as much discretion as possible. Without proof, we can't make any arrests. We can't even make accusations. These people need to think we have no idea what they're up to. That may be our only advantage. But time is our enemy."

Nason tapped on his computer and glanced at the screen. "The *Prodigy* will be commissioned in ten days. I'll be there in a week to attend the gala and give a speech. That gives you precious little time."

Robet gave him a quick nod. "Yes, sir. I'll do my best." He excused himself and left the room.

Awareness arrived in bits and pieces. Pain. A draft of cold air. Darkness. Rieka woke with the bitter knowledge she'd been abused, again. She opened her eyes only enough to peer through her lashes.

Alone.

She rolled to her side and sat up, then waited while a wave of nausea passed. The dirt floor was warm where she'd lain. Obviously, she'd been there for some time.

"Just great," she grumbled. "Now where am I?"

Able to see little more than shadows in the room's dusty corners, Rieka studied the source of the limited light. An open window, chest high, too small to crawl through, and barred. She rose slowly, so as not to invite another attack of nausea, and walked numbly to it.

"Think, think, you idiot," she mumbled, knowing she could probably identify the planet if she concentrated on details. She rubbed at a sore place in the small of her back. Gravity and temperature registered easily. She shortened the list of possible planets without much trouble.

"Yadra, Earth, Indra, or Aurie?" Resting her arms on the gritty sill, Rieka inhaled deeply, trying to both detect any familiar odor and get more oxygen to her brain.

The sky was hidden by high clouds, obscuring her view of the stars. In a few moments she realized dawn was approaching. She watched with purpose, noting the colors of the sky, the crescent shape of a distant moon, the hue and size of the sun's radiance.

Rieka recognized the ball of gas as Tau Ceti and the planet under her feet as Yadra. The answer to her question did nothing but form a chain of many more. At the top of the list was, Where, *exactly*, am I?

The area outside the window looked like virgin forest. She picked up a delicate but familiar fragrance. Still slightly groggy, she knew she could identify that odor.

Concentrating and sniffing herself almost into hyperventilation, Rieka put the pieces together. Lemonitte trees grew only in one small area of Lemonne Province.

Paden, being an administrator, had plenty of land. He'd relocated her to one of his outlying properties. The next questions tumbled helplessly in her mind. Did he know the land was being used in such a way? Was he, too, a victim of their mind manipulation? Or worse, had he accepted a bribe, unaware he was dealing with Procyons?

Rieka shuddered. Had she not accepted Triscoe's proposal, Paden would have been her warden from the

start. In that case, she'd probably be dead by now, with
no one the wiser.

Feeling a bit better now that she was on her feet,
Rieka used the increasing light to survey her cell. A
filthy cot lay overturned in the corner. Beside it sat a
chamber pot. The walls and floor were an aggregate
mix of mud and small stone that provided the foundation for various insect nests and webs. The ceiling, too
high to reach even while standing on the cot, was made
of an unidentifiable metal. Though unpleasantly cold,
she made use of the pot and tossed its contents out the
open window. That action gave rise to the beginnings
of an escape plan.

Testing its strength by pushing on it with all her
weight, Rieka found the metal pot both strong and
light. It made a unique but fitting weapon. Now, she
needed a victim.

First, she checked the overturned cot. Musty and
covered with webs that connected it to the floor, she
dusted it off and positioned it so that it faced the wall.
Then she removed her boots and placed them carefully
at the foot of the cot. She went back to the door twice
to check the angle. On the third trip, she was satisfied it
looked as though she'd been on the cot when it
tipped—and hadn't moved since.

Light from Tau Ceti spilled through the bars of the
window, now, almost blinding in its intensity. She
paced nervously, warming her muscles for the fight
she knew would come, when she heard a noise beyond
the door. She leapt to the corner and breathed a small
sigh of anticipation when it opened.

Rieka tightened her grip on the pot's handle and
stepped silently from her cover. The male was taller
than she, with unruly hair on his head and arms. An
Oph, although it didn't matter much, now. As he stood
squinting at her boots, Rieka swung.

When he went down only as far as his knees, she
clouted him again, then kicked the maitu from his paw.
He reeled in pain while she scrambled for the weapon,

then leapt upon her, driving the air from her lungs. Rieka heard another guard at the door and knew there would be no second chance. Her fingers wrapped around the cold metal while the Oph grabbed her by the throat.

She twisted her wrist and fired, feeling the maitu's jolt as it shocked his muscles. Instantly, she realized the thing was set to kill.

Gritting her teeth, Rieka pushed him off her as the second guard fired. She rolled, barely in time, aimed and fired again. He was dead before he hit the floor.

Rieka waited for reinforcements, cursing herself for not resetting the maitu. The Ophs might have meant to kill her, but she had no such intent. When no other sounds followed, she got up, retrieved her boots, and stepped over the bodies, wondering, among other things, how long she'd been sequestered in that small room.

The empty passage was short, maybe three meters. It ended at a room about four meters square. In it, she found a table, two cots, food rations, and some small entertainment devices: a video receiver tuned to one of Yadra's public channels, and three handheld games. She checked the door and found it locked with a simple mechanical bolt. Opening it, Rieka understood why. The small building sat in the middle of nowhere. Aside from a cleared area about thirty meters in diameter, she saw only dense undergrowth and tall trees.

Thankful no other guards were present, Rieka backtracked down the corridor and found a door twin to that of her former cell. Hefting the maitu, she threw the bolt and peered inside. The room mirrored her own, with the exception of a pair of high windows and one other significant thing.

The cot was occupied.

Cautiously, she stepped toward it. The individual wore a Fleet uniform. Rieka held her breath and went closer. The garment was too large. Perhaps it didn't even belong to the prisoner. Then, she recognized the rank on the sleeve and ring on the first finger of an emaciated hand. Rieka's jaw dropped, and her heart felt as though it were on fire.

"Midrin," she whispered in disbelief. "My God! Midrin?"

The body stirred. The pale hand lifted. "No . . ." she moaned. "No, don't."

Rieka smoothed the hair from her first officer's face and cupped the cheek. "Midrin, it's Rieka. You're safe."

Unable to say anything more, she made a sound in the back of her throat. The woman before her had been starved, possibly tortured. The image of the Midrin Tohab on her ship suddenly brought everything that had happened into fine focus. Yes, of course. An impostor. To set her up, both times. The Procyons not only had the ability to influence individuals, they could replace them as well.

Silently, she vowed that someone would pay. And she knew the exact amount.

"Rieka?" It seemed an effort, but Midrin opened her eyes. She gasped once. "I'm dying. I'm dreaming," she whispered.

"No. It's me, really. You aren't dreaming," Rieka offered, her throat still tight. "Can you sit up?"

With help, Midrin managed. Now fully awake, she lifted bony hands and held Rieka's face. "Captain . . . Rieka . . . how did you get here?"

Tears fell as she held the gaunt form of her comrade and friend. She felt a removed sense of helplessness. "How long has it been since you've had solid food?"

"How long? The days have passed slowly. How long have I been here?"

"I don't know." Sniffing, Rieka wiped her eyes, then Midrin's, and carefully lifted her from the cot. So light, she thought as she took her to the table in the guards' area and searched the rations for something suitable.

"Liquid first," she decided, producing a blended fruit juice from a cooler unit and watering it down by half.

Midrin took it, swallowed timidly, then drained the contents of the mug.

"Do you know how many guards there are? The rotation?"

Midrin nodded. "They change every three days. The new ones got here last night. They'll be expected to check in tomorrow morning."

Rieka gnawed her lip. They would have to get out of here, soon. "Does your TC work?"

"No. They disconnected it right away. Yours?"

"Dead." She looked at the comm unit on the table, deciding she could probably find a frequency of someone who might help them, but didn't know who she could trust. "We'll be fine, Midrin, don't worry." She placed another mug in front of her, then sat down at the opposite side of the table and frowned in deep thought. Something didn't add up right.

"What is it, Captain?"

"There's an ache in my chest that they could do this to you, and I didn't even know. When was the last time you saw me?"

Midrin sighed tiredly, as if even thinking was a burden to her frailty. "On Aurie. We'd just gotten to the surface, and you wanted to go hiking."

"But you'd heard about the shopping center at Derng and couldn't resist."

Midrin smiled and nodded. "It was fun. I spent two weeks' pay."

"And then what?"

"I—I remember stopping for something to eat. I wanted to try the Aurian *vedaka*. There was a café at the end of the market-street. I ate there. The *vedaka* was good. Then"—she closed her eyes in an effort to remember—"nothing. I woke up in the cell. Many days ago, I'm sure."

Rieka bit her lip and shook her head. "Weeks." She saw the look of shock on Midrin's face but continued. "It's been at least twenty-eight days since I took the

Venture out of Aurian orbit. A *lot* has happened since then."

"Such as?"

Rieka got up to fetch herself something to drink, then returned to the table to tell Midrin everything that had occurred in the last four weeks. At each significant turn of events, her eyes seemed to grow wider.

"I had no idea she wasn't you," Rieka admitted finally, frowning into the dregs of her cup. "Granted, I thought you seemed preoccupied, you weren't wearing your ring, and I hadn't seen that much of you at all since I was arrested but . . . I feel . . ."

Midrin pushed her matted hair behind her ears and nodded. "I understand," she said softly. "We learned years ago the Procyons have no shred of decency when it comes to taking what they want. When days began to pass, I realized the possibility that no one was searching, but I didn't have any idea I'd been . . . replaced. I did try to take the guard's weapon, when I still had some strength, but it wasn't enough." She stopped and pressed her pale fingers over her eyes. "They're so strong, you know, especially when they rut. But I was helpless against the two of them. I . . . I'm just grateful Oph sperm are incompatible with Centauri."

She sighed. "I'm glad you killed them, Rieka. I'm very glad."

It was noon before Rieka put solid food in front of her first officer. Midrin only nibbled, but she had begun to breathe steadily, and the light was returning to her eyes. Rieka joined her for a meal at dusk and announced her plans when they'd cleaned their plates.

"If you're up to it, we're leaving tomorrow. We can't chance being here when the guards are expected to check in. Someone will probably come looking for them right away."

Midrin nodded. "I know what you're saying, but I'll slow you down. Couldn't you send someone for me once you report to Admiral Nason?"

"I'd be happy to, if I knew exactly who would come for you. We can't trust anyone, Midrin. I'm not even certain Admiral Nason is who I think he is. We have to stay together."

"Agreed." After a moment's thought, she added, "Let me digest this lump in my belly and see how I feel in the morning, then."

Rieka smiled and watched Midrin lift herself from the bench and plop in one of the guards' cots. Centauris had an amazing metabolism. She knew they'd be able to make decent progress tomorrow. They had to.

Midrin had already fallen into a deep slumber when Rieka decided to take the bodies outside. Investigating the disappearance of four individuals would take a lot longer than that of two. The Oph guards were heavy, but she managed to lug their stiff forms out of the small building to an area of high grass.

That done, Rieka felt much like her old self. Purposefully looking away from the corpses, she squinted through the trees. There was enough light left to take a short tour of the area. She'd gone about ten meters into the undergrowth when a squawk cut through the quiet murmurings of the forest. It was followed by another.

"Damn," she muttered. Peering up into the dark sky, she recognized a huge form as it sailed past. A third screech sent her running back to the building. The Oph guards would be little more than bones by morning. Cheerlessly, she knew bolwins would be her fate as well as Midrin's—if they weren't very, very careful.

"You told me twenty-four hours, Memta," Triscoe said, annoyed, as the huge Boo casually stepped off the Chute that had brought him up from the pod. All engineering functions were accessible here in the engineering suite, with the exception of those governing the pod many hundreds of meters below. There, the Boos had exclusive control of two crucial ship functions: gravitation and foamduct travel.

Irritably, Triscoe wondered if Memta had stayed

down there on purpose, to avoid him. His suspicion solidified when the Boo turned and spoke to a crewman before giving his attention to his captain.

"It is true we swim again in gravity," Triscoe offered with a nod, stepping as close to Memta as he could without craning his neck. "Our DGI sees like a *bling*. We're nearing point five lightspeed. I am as the sun arrives at Varannah."

The chief looked down at him and blinked his double-lidded eyes. The voice box warbled, "Good!"

"Yes! But we *must* slide," Triscoe insisted. "Are you ready to power up the foamduct, or do we remain here like a minnow in a pond waiting to be swallowed by a bigger fish?"

The color of steely storm clouds, Memta sucked on his chlorine tube. He peered down at his commander, exposing a row of stubby teeth that translated as a smile. His kroi clicked pleasantly. A patch of flesh flicked up and down over one eye, and he said, "Funny captain."

"Depends on your point of view," Triscoe replied, not knowing whether the comment was about him, or what he'd said.

"Minnow waiting to be swallowed," the Boo repeated. "Large joke. Who would want to swallow us? Ship taste bad. Exotic matter too tart. Like throwing up to Varannah." His kroi clicked together rapidly, and his head bobbed atop his nonexistent neck.

"Your humor eludes me, Memta," Triscoe replied, knowing his engineer often enjoyed the advantages his appearance had in intimidating other species. "And right now, I've no time for it. Do we slide or don't we?" Despite his irritation, he had no intention of picking a fight with his engineering chief, and he knew nothing he could say would change Memta's mind. The physical universe could only be altered so much. Even the miracles of quantum mechanics required a certain amount of time.

The discussion really wasn't about space travel, Triscoe conceded, and both of them knew it. It was more a matter of Centauri anxiety. He desperately needed to get to Yadra.

"Equipment repair 95 percent complete," Memta replied, undulating digits that could not quite pass as fingers. "Tests on travel feasibility follow. Then we power up." He looked down to meet Triscoe's eye. "I'll take another hour, hour and thirty. Don't worry. No big fish close. We get our catch."

Triscoe nodded and watched silently as Memta shuffled away. Try as he might, he could barely pronounce the proper sounds, much less make himself appear intelligent to a Boo. Strangely, however, he sensed this Boo's understanding and sympathy.

"Hour and thirty, Captain," Memta called from his console.

On his way back to the bridge, Triscoe went over the battle again. Although his suspicions still centered around Tohab, he could not help but wonder if Rieka had somehow caused the attack. Had it been a ruse, to spirit her away?

With the Singlemind link firmly established now, Triscoe knew he would be able to find her, anywhere. If Yillon's predictions were to come true, she had to stay alive until he could rescue her.

But what about Tohab? A traitor? He'd accessed her file when the idea had first come to him. Her record was impeccable. She was Rieka's right hand, as Humans said. Trustworthy. Brilliant. Able to command but not yet the diplomat required of a captain. To consider Tohab as a cutthroat or a mercenary at the heart of a coup pushed Triscoe's imagination to the limit. But what else could he think? Robet had often misquoted the old Earth idiom: "When you rule out the possible, you're left with the impossible."

The door opened and his EO, Aarkmin, acknowledged his arrival with her customary nod. Triscoe returned it, as was his habit, and a thought struck him. Rieka's first interaction with the Procyons displayed a typical Human trait. She'd done the *un*expected. She merely fired on the *Vendikon* when she'd actually been given orders to destroy it.

That it was destroyed didn't alter the facts. She had been ordered to do something and did not do it. Rieka never disobeyed an order, yet she'd sided with the Command Oath and her moral code over Admiral Bittin's apparent whim. The decision must have been difficult, but she'd ultimately chosen not to kill. If Triscoe's assumptions were correct, then his faceless attacker had to have been Midrin Tohab.

"Ohato, plot a foamduct back to Yadra and be ready to implement it the moment Memta gives us the word the system is ready."

"Right away, Captain," the Vekyan helmsman replied. "Travel time will be twenty-one point one-three standard hours."

Triscoe nodded. In that amount of time, almost anything could happen. Even though he could get to Yadra by simply asking for transport from another Fleet ship, he needed the *Providence* and her crew to see the job done properly. He forced himself to acknowledge his good fortune that both the foamduct system and his engineer had not been more severely damaged. Travel via secondary systems would have taken them years.

The women began their trek shortly after dawn. Rieka packed a small duffel she'd found with the essentials: food, a water conditioner, and cups. She appropriated two blankets from the guards' cots and rolled them tightly. They fit in the sack, after much rearranging, and Midrin helped her hoist the thing onto her back.

"It looks heavy," she said.

"It'll keep us alive." Rieka looked at Midrin, glad to see a healthier color than yesterday, and nodded. "This handicap of mine ought to give you a good chance of keeping up. We'll need to travel as fast as possible."

Midrin glanced at the maitu stuck to Rieka's hip, and she followed her train of thought. "We only use the weapons as a last resort."

"Yes, Captain."

Rieka bit her tongue. Of course Midrin knew that whoever investigated their disappearance would carry equipment that could identify the energy discharge of a maitu. It would be like sending out a signal to them. She had no idea why someone hadn't been sent to check out the two blasts she'd fired at the guards, but decided not to question her good fortune.

They set off on a northerly course through the densely overgrown woods, hoping to run into one of the old transport roads that might lead them to a town. They both carried knives, thanks again to the guards, and hacked through trailing vines as they made their way toward salvation.

While she carved the way ahead, Rieka considered the implications of her discovery. With the real Tohab only a meter behind her, the woman who'd been her first officer for the last month was—what? A person who'd been altered to look exactly like Midrin Tohab and coached to take her place. Okay, she thought, if an Aurie like M'narn could be bought by the Procyons, probably anybody could, Centauri and Human included. But why go to all the trouble of duplicating people? Wasn't it easier to manipulate them—as they'd done to her? Knowing Paden and his deviant ways, she couldn't say for sure.

But she could draw two conclusions. She hadn't ejected her crew. And she hadn't fired at Triscoe, damaging his ship. The other Tohab must have done that, since only she had the authority to issue those kind of orders.

Rieka shook her head, trying to see things in this new light. Was there a way one could tell if a person had been either programmed or replaced? ID scans obviously didn't work. Other than an audience with Yillon, how could anyone know for certain?

By noon, with Tau Ceti almost directly overhead, Rieka began to feel hot and tired. She glanced behind her, as she'd done many times before, and saw that Midrin was laboring to keep up.

"Time for a break," she announced, breathing heavily. The pack slid off her shoulders and hit the ground with a solid thump. She stretched sore muscles before digging into it for lunch.

Midrin took the water conditioner and brushed back some debris in order to set it on a firm foundation. Then she caught some tender vines with one hand and hacked them free with her knife. "Think this is enough?"

Rieka looked up from the food packets and shrugged. "I've never done it with vegetation, before. I've got no idea."

Midrin shrugged and stuffed the leaves and stem of one cutting into the conditioner's receptacle. She closed the door and switched it on. A few seconds later, she poured pure water into the cup Rieka gave her.

"Not much."

Rieka peered into the container that now held about two ounces of water. She looked at Midrin. "Keep at it. We can't risk getting dehydrated. We can stop if we find water later, too." She smiled and was pleased when her companion mirrored the expression.

They ate their lunch and trudged onward.

Long before the sun began to approach the horizon, Rieka stopped every so often, searching the huge trees. How they would camp would be a toss-up. If they slept in the branches, they might avoid the ground-dwelling nocturnals but not the bolwins. On the ground, they could be set upon by both, but she felt much safer with something solid under her feet. Rieka was thankful the weather was warm enough not to require a heat source. It would be tricky to light a fire without using a weapon.

When dusk had settled, Rieka stopped and pointed. "How about that one, Midrin?"

Her companion looked at the huge tree in question and nodded. Rieka realized she was too tired to speak.

"You should have said something sooner," she chided. "You're exhausted. I'd have stopped." She dropped the backpack and stepped toward the broad trunk.

"I would have, but this is the first suitable tree we've come across, Captain. Centauris learn as children not to complain about things that cannot be changed."

Rieka planted a foot on a large root. "Wish they could teach that to Humans. So, do we go up or stay here?"

"Up is safer."

"True. But there's no place to run if we get in trouble."

Midrin nodded. The nocturnal sounds of the forest had begun and she glanced around. "I'd just rather face one obstacle at a time."

Rieka didn't need to ask what that meant. "Okay." She hauled herself up the great tree, using the horizontal ridges in the trunk for finger- and footholds, and made it to the first branch with little difficulty. It was wide enough to seem flat where it joined the trunk. She leaned over and looked down. "It's a lot like climbing a ladder. You need any help?"

"Maybe," Midrin said. She carefully climbed the bark until Rieka was able to grasp an outstretched hand. In another minute they were both seated on the limb.

Rieka looked around in the darkness, trying to size up the neighborhood. "You know, I think the trees seem father apart now, without so much growing between them."

"You're right," Midrin agreed.

"A good sign."

"I think I hear running water."

Holding her breath, Rieka was able to ignore the chorus of insects and the wind in the canopy to make out the sound of a creek or stream of some kind. "I'll check it out," she said. When she'd climbed back to the ground, she took the blankets from the pack and threw them up to Midrin. After ferreting out the water conditioner and cups, she threw the duffel up as well. "I'll be back in time for dinner," she called.

The creek was wider than she'd expected and, she guessed, reasonably deep. She rinsed out the cups, filled them, and headed back to camp. When the chore of conditioning the water had been completed, she climbed partway and placed the cups in Midrin's out-stretched hands.

Midrin had set the blankets out and selected meal packets for them. With her cup nestled between her thighs, Rieka leaned back against the trunk and dug into her dinner.

"What's the creek like?" Tohab asked after wolfing down most of her food.

"Decent," Rieka said. "We can take a dip in the morning, if you like. Neither of us smells any too good at the moment."

"I wasn't thinking about that, Captain." Midrin folded her empty packet and put it in the duffel.

"About what, then?"

"About—bolwins."

It took a moment for Rieka to fathom her reasoning, but a swooping shadow jogged her memory. Bolwins would have nothing to do with running water. A second shadow followed the first and she was glad for the bulk of the huge tree behind her. "The creek it is," she whispered. "But it's fast, and I think there's some white water downstream. I suggest neither of us panic and run."

"Absolutely," Midrin agreed quietly.

They were silent for a long time. Rieka pulled the second blanket over them. She dozed, more than vaguely aware of the discomforting sounds of the night. After several hours, a thump jerked her to attention. Her eyes opened and swept about the darkness.

The light of two moons, though neither in a full phase, was enough for her to make out the hulking shape of something perched on a limb about six meters to the right. Another thud. The second one had arrived.

Midrin nudged her silently to let her know she was awake. Rieka returned the tacit communication. While sharing an immense tree with two bolwins was not an automatic death sentence, neither could it be taken lightly. Motionless, they waited and watched the roosting carnivores.

Thirteen

As the minutes passed, Rieka's anxiety grew. What were they waiting for? Bolwins were known for stalking their prey. They hunted in pairs. One would get the prey's attention, while the other sneaked up from behind.

She held her breath when one of them flapped and settled on a closer branch, but seemed to pay no attention. Clenching her jaw, she counted herself lucky that bolwins traveled in pairs, not packs, and that the huge tree at her back provided a decent defense.

She felt Midrin tense when the creature began to walk along the branch rather than flitting from one to the other. She could not see it clearly in the moonlight but knew that the things were huge, about thirty pounds of muscle, with an eight-foot leathery wingspan. Their heavy, beaklike mouths were sharp, and strong enough to crack Human bone with little difficulty. They were black with a patch of red at the base of the throat and huge, yellow-ringed eyes. Eyes, Rieka knew, that were trained on her and Midrin. They could see in the dark three times better than a Human.

Rieka's gaze slid to the second creature. It, too, had changed positions. Now, closer to the trunk, it sought to find a place to get at them from behind.

When the bolwin to the rear disappeared from her line of sight, Rieka began to wrap the blanket around one of her arms. "Give me a knife," she whispered as softly as she could. "When they try for us, I want you to jump down and run for the creek."

"But—"

"I'll be as close behind as I can."

"Understood." Midrin put the hilt of one of the knives in Rieka's hand after rummaging in the duffel.

They did not have long to wait. The bolwin to the rear came at them from Rieka's side. There was a mad rush of air and the tree thrummed from the impact. She felt the scratch of a talon on her upper arm but the tree blocked most of the charge. She dodged the snapping beak and at the same time yelled, "Go!"

Midrin slid down and away, and Rieka scooted across the thick limb, avoiding the creature's continuing attack. In the blackness, she slashed blindly with the knife, coming in contact with something solid once, before the weapon was wrenched from her grasp. She backed up against the main trunk and grabbed the duffel by one of its straps. She smashed the heavy bag against the creature's head, relieved to hear it whine and back off. The other swooped closer and began hopping toward her. It hissed, and Rieka flinched at the grating sound.

She stood and balanced on the branch, willing herself not to fall. When the bolwin got within striking range, Rieka swung the bag again. It connected with a solid thump, throwing her off-balance. She teetered precariously for a moment before steadying herself. With the bolwin slightly dazed, she tossed the blanket over its head, hoping sudden blindness could buy her some time.

The first one, now on a branch over her left shoulder, screeched, setting off a corresponding sound of panic from the small creatures inhabiting the surrounding woods. It was closing for the kill when Rieka clambered down the tree, dropping to the grass after only a few feet. The woods had erupted in a flurry of noise. She hoped it would distract them enough to forget about her as she ran for the creek.

Midrin was waiting at the water's edge. As they jumped in, a bolwin shrieked overhead.

The cold current tugged at her clothing, pulling her slowly downstream. Rieka looked for Midrin and found a pale blond head bobbing a few meters in front of her and to the left.

"Are you all right?" she called, still breathing hard.

"A few scrapes. I'll live."

Rieka paddled closer and brushed the water from her eyes. "I think I hear rapids ahead, Midrin. Maybe we should get out while we're still in one piece."

Another screech from above made the decision for them.

The creek narrowed as it swept them along, and began to churn. Rieka's legs were pounded by submerged rocks while she tried to catch herself and push off the visible ones. She saw Midrin slam into a huge boulder, but immediately lift her hand, signaling she was all right. When they reached calmer water, Rieka waited to see if the bolwins had followed. They were still screeching, but the noise had grown distant.

She caught up to Midrin. "You hurt?"

Exhausted, Midrin could only nod. Rieka caught hold of her and pointed to the shore. They paddled toward it and pulled themselves out. Rieka wrapped her arms around her knees and heaved a sigh.

Midrin groaned. "My shoulder hit that last boulder pretty hard."

"Dislocated?"

She lifted the arm carefully. "I don't think so, just bruised."

"We lost everything, I'm afraid."

"We're still alive," Midrin observed, rubbing her shoulder. "And we're free. That's better than the day before yesterday."

"I'm getting cold," Rieka offered. "How about you?"

"Cold," she agreed, then stood, and Rieka followed her example. "I think we'd better keep moving, Captain. At least it will keep us warm."

"Are you up to it?"

"I'll be fine," Midrin told her.

They walked on in the darkness, keeping close to the creek. It seemed to be flowing in a northerly direction and provided them with sanctuary from the bolwins. They kept up their pace until Tau Ceti began to illuminate the sky.

"We'll stop as soon as it's full light," Rieka said. "The bolwins will be roosting by then, and we can get a few hours' sleep."

K'resh-va marched smartly from the InterMAT to Captain Finot's office. That a Boo was in charge of the Fleet's shipyard gave credence to the idiocy of the Commonwealth in general. This being was a triped with whom communication was almost impossible. To give such an alien creature so much power was foolhardy. Any Procyon child could recognize that. He decided to deal with Finot as remotely as possible.

The secretary in the outer office announced him and gestured to the door. Once inside, he gave himself a moment to become accustomed to the being's great size. This one was immense, and the stark blue of its skin was unsettling, as were the black pupil-less eyes.

"Finot," he said.

"Captain Pedlam, welcome to the Little One in the Light."

"The what?"

"The Little One. This moon." Finot gurgled the words and waved a strangely shaped paw.

"Yes," K'resh-va replied, nodding. "Of course. Thank you. I'm here to assume my responsibilities for the *Prodigy*."

"As the smiling Vehs of the square of the third day."

K'resh-va stared at the creature, completely dumbfounded by the comment, but refused to allow himself to look foolish. "Correct."

"Ah. So it is with us," Finot said, then sucked on his chlorine tube. "Sit. Please, Captain. We have details of the equations to be figured before us."

"I wasn't aware of any—"

"Sit, Captain."

K'resh-va sat in the proffered chair. "What equations?" he asked, then heard that strange clicking sound all Boos made and watched as the thing blinked at him strangely.

"The ship requires work before the light of Varannah," Finot said. "Many crews are laboring the equation through all shifts. It will be done by gala-time."

K'resh-va frowned. "What time?"

"Gala. The dedication of our new dawn on the horizon. The departure of our deciding factor."

"Of course. Yes. The dedication ceremonies. I know all about that," he said, leaning back and crossing his arms. Apparently, Finot's people had slid behind schedule and were working extra shifts in order to meet their deadline. Perhaps this wouldn't be as difficult a conversation as he'd first imagined.

"The equation seeks its balance then," Finot went on. "The factor of X leads the way for all variables."

K'resh-va nodded absently. He could not fathom what the thing was talking about, now, despite the fact that it was speaking much more clearly than other ones he'd met. "Is something required of me, then?"

"Hostly duties. Captain duties. All are in the basket with no name."

"Wonderful." He smiled with his Centauri face, but behind that mask, scowled at the diversity of the Commonwealth, the Boos especially.

Finot nodded. "I knew you would see it thus." The creature exposed some teeth and wriggled the flesh over its eyes. "The matter is pi, then, Captain."

"Certainly." He could only hope he sounded intelligent to the thing. He saw no point in arousing suspicion, so he added, "It has been a long time since I've had a real conversation with anyone of your race. I hope I don't sound—"

"—like a cloud over the heart of Mohb? Not." Finot

repeated the clicking noise and sucked on the tube again. "Definitely, not . . . Captain."

The odor of chlorine overwhelmed him. Not wanting to sniff, since that would make matters worse, K'resh-va blinked, trying not to let the tears trail down his cheeks. "Will that be all, Finot?"

"Only so that you agree. The ship is yours once my people are done with the preliminary functions."

He rubbed at his burning eyes. "What preliminary functions?"

"Gravity. Final engineering. Final electrical and panoply systems. This is acceptable?"

K'resh-va nodded and stood, ready to agree to anything so long as he could leave the room. Backing toward the door, he swiped at his eyes again. "Acceptable," he announced. "I must attend to something now. I will check back with you, later."

"Feel free to visit the ship any time in Varannah."

"Yes."

He turned and fled to the outer office, catching Finot's last word, "Pzekii," and wondering what it meant.

Rieka woke with a start. She was lying on the ground, her back pushed firmly up against Midrin. The sun was high in the sky. At least they'd gotten a few hours' sleep.

A moment later, Midrin eased away and sat up. Rieka yawned, rubbing her eyes with dirty fingers. "I guess Centauris really do recover from physical trauma," she mumbled. "I'm so stiff, I don't think my legs remember what it's like to bend." She looked up and saw from her expression that Midrin was not interested in banter. Her attention was off on the horizon.

"Captain, am I hallucinating, or does that look like an artificial cut in the trees?"

"Where?" Forgetting her bruises, Rieka scrambled to her feet.

Midrin took her by the shoulders, turned her, and pointed. "There."

Rieka shaded her eyes. A low hill to the east sported an unnatural gray stripe. "You're right as usual, Midrin." She smiled. "It must be the old road to Creyunne. And it can't be more than a kilometer away."

Half an hour later, they came upon a ribbon of pavement.

"Milner Creek Road," Rieka explained, at Midrin's confused frown. "This was the main transport highway before Creyunne got an InterMAT terminal. The parish can't be too far from here. I remember visiting it when I was a kid."

They walked the rest of the day, keeping the road in sight at all times. When dusk approached, Midrin noticed artificial light ahead, and Rieka breathed a sigh of relief.

The road ended at a small park. Beyond it they glimpsed the town, a rambling agricultural village that encompassed just nine blocks of small commercial buildings before spreading out in modest residential housing.

"The InterMAT station is in the building nearest the park," Rieka said.

Midrin nodded. "Hotel Redjahan." She read the sign aloud. "Why would they need a hotel with an InterMAT in town?"

"Doing business with people in these little agro towns often means getting to know them. You're wondering why anyone would want to live way out here, when there are beautiful cities like Rhonique—and a quick way to get there and back?" She gave Midrin a minute to think, then answered the question, herself. "Because the city is crowded. It's full of activity day and night. Some folks need peace and quiet. So they live in a small parish. And if you're a Fleet supplier, you'd better get to know them before you write up a contract. If I remember right, the hotel has historic significance. I know I've slept there."

They waited until the streets were deserted. Then Rieka asked, "Do you want to come?"

"Absolutely. I may be your only defense."

She grinned. In her condition, Midrin couldn't fend off a curious pet, much less an able attacker.

Both the building and terminal were unoccupied, as she'd guessed, and Rieka stepped to the console. Tired, hungry, and not thinking straight, she looked down at the familiar touchpads and command keys. A sense of closeness passed through her.

"What's the matter?" Tohab asked quietly.

She dismissed the strange feeling and said, "My access code will probably set off alarms—not to mention shut down the system."

"So use mine. No one should be tracing that."

"Fine. But where do we go? We need information as to what's happened in the last three or four days. I'll have to contact someone I can trust without—"

"How about Admiral Nason?"

"No. We talk to no one in the Fleet, yet. Without knowing who's in orbit, that leaves us with the entire surface of Yadra to choose from. Triscoe's mother's embassy residence is in Flah, but even if she's there, I'd rather not involve her in this mess. My mother's estate is outside of Kilpani, but I'd rather die than—"

"Your mother is alive?"

"Yes, as far as I know."

"But you've never spoken of her." Midrin frowned. "I thought she was dead and the memory too painful to speak of."

Rieka sniffed. "There's a lot of pain associated with my mother, but none of it is posthumous. I know this will sound strange to you, but we choose not to speak. Period."

"That is odd, even for Humans, isn't it?"

Rieka knew Midrin would have a hard time conceiving such a mother-child relationship. Indrans had a different way of looking at things. "Yes," she admitted, finally. "My mother was never a nurturing person. She bore my father two children, then left him when it became clear, to her, that Paden was the obvious heir to the Degahv legacy. Since Candace couldn't be Herald herself, she figured she'd mold Paden into the Herald she wanted to be."

"How awful for you."

Rieka accepted the compassion in Midrin's eyes. "I turned out fine, living with my father. But I won't go to her for help—even now."

"Well . . ." Midrin shrugged. "We can't stay here."

Rieka's eyes scanned the console while she considered her options. She shook her head, trying to get rid of that odd sensation.

"Is something wrong?"

"No. I just . . . I feel like someone's here. No, not here." She shrugged. "It's as if there's a presence."

"Of course," Midrin said, her face splitting into a smile. "Captain Marteen."

"What?"

"He is here. He's found you."

"Midrin, I think you need to lie down. I told you the *Providence* was damaged. Remember?"

"Of course. But that was days ago."

"Memta *is* the best engineer in the fleet," Rieka agreed. "And Triscoe would have pushed him to the wall to get the ship fixed. He would want to get to Yadra as soon as possible since he is—"

"—your mate. You have been married for twelve days." She smiled, and when Rieka gave her a curious look, said, "Surely, by now you understand the depth of our rituals."

"What rituals?"

"Those of the marriage ceremony."

Rieka frowned. "You mean drinking the *Boggi*?"

Midrin paused before continuing. "Indrans do not take this subject lightly, Captain. It is obvious you have been through the *quantivasta,* or as the Commonwealth calls it, the Singlemind. You have both been Impressed by the other. He would search for you. He would begin here, in Creyunne."

Rieka pulled her eyes from those of her companion and examined the console more closely. She thought of the hotel. Did she feel something from there, too?

"We should start at the hotel first," Midrin said, echoing her thought. "But we can't simply walk in there and ask to see the register." She gestured at their tattered clothing. "If we happened across anyone, it would be obvious our uniforms do not meet regulation standards."

Rieka nodded. "There's probably a back door."

"True, but I would suggest a safer means."

She shook her head. "Like what?"

"If he can locate you, what would happen if you tried to find him?"

Rieka put her hands on her hips. "I'm afraid I have no idea of what you're talking about."

Midrin leaned against the console. "When an Indran mates, it's a different concept than Human matrimony, which can be separated . . . uh, undone—reversed. Do you see what I mean?"

It was late. She was bone tired, ravenously hungry, and clearly confused. It didn't help matters that Midrin was rambling and making little sense. "No," she answered irritably, rubbing her eyes. "I don't see at all."

"Indrans promise marriage to the death—of both parties. And we mean it. We don't part company as Humans do—or Aurians—or any other species. It isn't done. It is beyond us to comprehend the transient state you aliens embrace."

"Where is this leading?"

"We have the *quantivasta*, the Singlemind, which is performed at the marriage ceremony to weld the two individuals into a kind of—cleaved whole. In effect, you are bound. You have a sense of the other whether in their company or not. To divorce them is to divorce yourself. When they die, it is inconceivable to have another take their place."

"Fine," Rieka mumbled, "but what has this got to do with—"

"You performed a Singlemind at the nuptials, did you not?"

"No," she replied softly, "we didn't. It was a fast, civil ceremony. In jail."

Midrin tilted her head, confused. "This does not follow," she said. "For Captain Marteen to have found you, it would be necessary to have been joined with a Singlemind at the—"

"We have," Rieka interrupted. "Just not at the ceremony."

"When?"

"Years ago. Yillon told Triscoe I was part of his future. He somehow arranged to be in my military training class." Her eyes lost focus as she recalled the sequence of events. "We were teamed up on the same squad—with Robet DeVark. We worked well together. Once, an attack simulation got out of hand and Triscoe saved me from getting seriously burned. Soon after that, he made up some lame excuse and asked if I would Singlemind. I didn't really know what it was. I thought he was trying to impress me. I liked him, so I said yes. We've done it a couple of times since then. I didn't see anything particularly momentous in it. But it's . . . an experience I won't forget."

Midrin's face took on a glassy look. "Yillon? You said Yillon."

"Yes."

"He foretold this?"

She nodded. "He's foretold a lot, as I understand it."

"And Captain Marteen knew of the prophecy before he met you?"

"Didn't I just say that?"

"Then in the heart and mind of the captain, you were united at that first Singlemind. I was not aware he had the *quantivasta*-gift, himself. Usually, a third party must oversee the joining."

Rieka nodded slowly. Things from the past were beginning to lose their soft focus. She wasn't happy to find she'd been lied to, but on the other hand, she was flattered, sort of. "I understand the ability is rare."

"Quite," Midrin replied. "But we have digressed. The union of the Singlemind allows the pair to . . . for the want of a better term, *sense*—the other. If one of the individuals has the gift, this sense is stronger. If both have it, they can speak to one another with their minds."

"Well, that lets me out."

Midrin shook her head. "Not necessarily. The Human brain contains many untapped areas. No one has yet determined its total potential."

"Well, it hasn't happened to me yet, so I doubt it's going to." Not wanting to think about anything more than the present dilemma, Rieka said, "So you think he should be able to find me in a town the size of Creyunne?"

"No. You are limiting your perceptions of this trait," Midrin replied. "He has come from light-years away. And he has come here. The problem is, our needs are immediate and at this late hour, Captain Marteen is probably asleep. But I think if you can get close enough to him, he may respond."

Triscoe sat up suddenly, breathing hard. He had not been dreaming of Rieka, yet he could think of nothing else. Disoriented for a moment, he didn't recognize the strange room, but the where and why of the place came to him quickly, and he made a conscious effort to calm down. The bedclothes were pulled from the corners of the pallet and tangled around his legs. He righted the sheet and stood. The room seemed unusually close. He couldn't tell if it had anything to do with his sleeping on a planet for the first time in months, or not. Whatever it was, he felt compelled to leave. To find Rieka.

He dressed quickly and packed the small bag he'd brought from the *Providence*. He'd known finding Rieka would be faster if he were in closer proximity to her and hoped the strange compulsion he now felt had something to do with it.

He could almost feel her presence, now that he was concentrating, but that was ridiculous. She did not know how to project herself across a distance. And it was extremely doubtful that the process would come to her instinctively, as it might an Indran. Still, Rieka was nothing if not full of surprises.

"You'll find her," he whispered, then frowned. Talking to oneself was a symptom of emotional trauma. He had never done it before. A glance in the mirror reminded him that despite what he was feeling, there was still a need to act the part of a Fleet captain. He took a deep breath to steady himself, then left the room quietly and checked out at the automated night teller in the lobby.

Outside, Triscoe's heart began to hammer. The wild notion of Rieka's being nearby filled his mind. He told himself she could not know how to reach him, but since he'd been searching for her with his gift, she might have become sensitive to it. That thought lifted his spirit, and the idea of actually finding her urged him forward.

He walked down the empty street and rounded the corner, then stopped. A column of dark space filled the alley between the bank and a small civic center on the next block. Something, he wasn't quite sure what, made him pause and study the darkness.

The street had been moderately lit in this hour before dawn, and it took Triscoe a moment before his eyes were able to adjust. Near the service door to what he judged to be the hotel, he made out a large dark form. As he stepped closer, it became apparent there were two individuals leaning heavily on one another and the hotel's rear wall. Before realizing what he'd done, he dropped his bag and went to them.

"Rieka," he murmured. It was a statement, not a question. When she tipped her face from the wall, he pulled her to his chest and held tight.

She collapsed against him, and he felt immensely proud of her. He had no idea how she'd managed to call him, nor did he care. He promised himself never to let her out of his sight.

"And who . . . Tohab?" He pushed Rieka behind him and struck a defensive stand, wondering how Tohab could be in two places at once. When Tohab shrank back, he looked closer. Judging by her physical condition, it was impossible that she could be the same person who, just days ago, spoke to him via DGI. He looked from one to the other. Neither seemed eager to speak.

He squeezed Rieka's shoulder in the darkness. "Tell me what happened," he insisted softly.

Quickly, she recounted the circumstances that brought both her and Midrin to Creyunne. She concluded with, "We need to be where no one knows we are, Tris. And Midrin needs medical attention and something to eat."

"You both do. With most of the crew on the *Providence* working double shifts to make repairs, no one will bother us there." He activated his TC. "This is Marteen. InterMAT this signal. Three individuals to my quarters." He grabbed up his small case, stood between the women, and added, "Initiate sequence now."

When transport was complete, Tohab sagged onto a chair and Rieka went to her. Triscoe clicked on his TC again and roused Twanabok. He ordered two meals to be brought from the dining room via servebot, and a few minutes later watched silently as the women gulped their food.

When the doctor arrived and recognized the occupants of the room, he grumbled at Triscoe, but went to work immediately.

"How's that new TC?" he asked.

Rieka pursed her lips while she chewed. "Doesn't work," she said. "I think when Elindok used his maitu to keep me from leaving my room, the discharge must have—"

"Exactly what I thought would happen," Twanabok said. "These engineers always trying to one-up themselves ... they've got to fall over their claws sometime."

Triscoe had been alternately pacing the floor and staring at Tohab. The ability to program people was one thing, but actually replacing them was quite something else. The implications were immense.

"There is to be no record of either of these officers on the *Providence,* Vort."

"Of course," Twanabok replied. He pulled himself erect. "I suggest you keep Tohab here to reduce the chance of discovery."

Triscoe nodded. "I had that in mind."

Tohab stood and swayed against the physician. "I'm suddenly tired," she admitted wistfully.

"After what I've given you, you'll sleep for a good long time, Commander." Twanabok clicked his talons and gestured her to the sofa. Less than a minute later, Midrin was asleep. The doctor helped Rieka tuck a blanket around her, then left.

"And that leaves you," Triscoe said, casting a worried look at her.

"I found out about what happened," she offered quietly, following him as he went to the sleeping room. "Paden told me how you were attacked by the *Venture* and how my crew was ... ejected. I actually believed I was responsible for a while. But then—then I found Midrin. And I knew that the other one had been trying to frame me since before we contacted the *Vendikon.*"

Triscoe sat on his bed, reached for her hand, and drew her to sit beside him. He stroked her palm and said softly, "We cannot change what has happened."

"But my people ..." Her jaw clenched, and he saw the unshed tears.

"Rieka, I am sorry for those we were unable to retrieve and those that were injured, but the rest are here on the *Providence*. Temporarily. Admiral Nason has already begun to reassign them."

"What? You mean they're alive?"

The change in her expression was remarkable, he thought. Humans had the most intriguing faces. A moment ago hers had been wrung with grief. With a single movement, the emotion had been not only erased, but replaced.

"Your brother told you they were dead?"

She nodded, unable to say anything. He liked the way she looked at him, her eyes shining. This Human, his wife, did not even need to speak, and he was content. He squeezed her hand and shook his head.

"But how can that be?" she insisted. "They were ejected, weren't they?"

Triscoe shrugged. "They remained in space for seconds only. Kyliss is an excellent InterMAT chief."

"They're all here?"

"All except those that Tohab—the other Tohab—required to run the ship. Twenty-five. Your entire Boolian complement and a few officers. They may be suffering a worse fate, I'm afraid."

"We'll have to find them," she said.

"I can't promise anything, but—"

"No." She shook her head, and Triscoe saw the determination in her eye. "No. They're my people. My responsibility. I may need your help, but *I* am going to find them."

Judging from the set of her jaw, he knew better than to argue. She had managed the impossible before—he didn't doubt she would do it again. He smiled and dipped his head.

"At your service, Captain."

Her laughter was nothing less than musical.

Fourteen

"Docking complete," the *Prospectus*'s helmsman announced.

"Didn't even feel the lock-up." Robet smiled, complimenting her. Then, directing himself to the comnet officer, he continued, "Have passes filed for all off-duty personnel. I need an interview with Captain Finot as soon as possible. And have Mister Rolian pull all the actuarial reports on our test equipment."

"Yes, sir."

A moment later Captain Finot's blue face appeared on the DGI. "DeVark, I hadn't expected such a low pass of Morado for another twenty days." Big black eyes slowly double-blinked at him. "The degree of the angle has increased the square of the fold."

"Can't say I'm happy about it," Robet replied, not even trying to decipher or imitate the Boo. "Admiral Nason insisted the new stuff be checked out, and my people trained specifically on its function and repair."

"How goes the test placement to settle?"

He smiled. "I'd say everything's gone well, so far. Testing proved satisfactory, well within the given parameters. We haven't pulled off a lengthy term, as yet. Just a few minutes at a time."

"Well it goes then in the vacuum," Finot said, nodding. His kroi clicked a positive cadence. "Here, you will sing with the Kinniki to Varannah. I have three to act the teacher. Two speak well as I in the morning."

Again, Robet suffered his best guess. "I'll be waiting." He paused, then asked, "How's the *Prodigy*?"

"The sum of the vectors has been held to the nth. The equation slides to Varannah on the dew," Finot replied, his kroi sounding proud. "Early peek you wish?"

"Sure, I'd love a tour."

The great gray-blue head bobbed. "Eighteen hundred, sure. At my place on the Little One in the Light. We shall see the new Varannah."

"I'll be there," he said, smiling. "DeVark out."

Settling back in his chair, Robet could not have been more pleased. In just over two hours, he'd be given a tour by old Finot himself. He'd caught a glimpse of the *Prodigy* when they'd swung into orbit. Other than its size, it looked identical to the *Prospectus,* but its primary purpose had nothing to do with transport. Built for research and defense, its firepower nearly tripled anything in space.

They could not let the Procyons get their hands on it.

Rieka paced the length of Triscoe's sitting area, but it didn't help. He'd reminded her not to leave or initiate communications with anyone, and she wanted to slap him for it. She glanced at Midrin.

"How can you stand it?"

"What?" she asked, looking up from the computer screen.

"Waiting. Doesn't it bother you?"

"Waiting is a waste of time, Captain," Midrin explained. "I try to keep myself productive."

Rieka couldn't find fault in that. "What are you reading?"

"The Aurian stock report."

Rieka huffed and rolled her eyes. She went back to walking the floor. Paden, or whoever controlled him, must have come to the conclusion by now that she and Midrin had escaped. Fortunately, there was no trail to follow.

Triscoe had gone back to Creyunne twice, as if still looking for her. He'd spoken to Paden, whose concern seemed genuine. But her brother was a cagey politician. He might have thought both she and Midrin had become bolwin fodder—or not. It was impossible to tell.

Now, Triscoe had been in conference with Nason for almost two hours. Acquainted with such meetings, she knew they were never trivial. What really rankled was that she hadn't been included.

"Come on," she muttered, still pacing. "This time, I'm going to demand to have a say in what happens." She glanced at Midrin, who had stopped reading to watch her. "I just need an idea. A good one."

"An idea about what, Captain?"

"We need to outsmart the Procyons."

Midrin said nothing.

Trying to unravel her jumbled thoughts, Rieka started walking, again. She had fought for every scrap of respect and dignity she had. She was trained and, more importantly, ready to fight. And she had a definite grudge against the Procyons. She could not be dismissed simply because Triscoe didn't approve.

She flexed her hands and balled them into fists. They had to let her do something! She wouldn't sit back while Triscoe and Robet dealt with a coup. She had earned high marks on military training missions. Nason couldn't ignore *that*.

Only the small matter of regaining her command stood in the way, she thought. Somehow, she'd have to get to Nason and do some fast talking.

"If I could just get . . ."

She heard a footfall at the door. Midrin was already moving, and they dashed into the bedroom. They heard the door open, then close.

"It's me," Triscoe said.

Midrin nodded and went back to the desk. Rieka followed, noting his sober expression, but her own frustration prompted her to say, "We've been good, so far. Midrin's been reading, and I've been exercising."

Triscoe was all business. His shoulders were stiff,

brows pinched. "Fine. Stand here. Both of you." He indicated a spot beside him.

"Why?"

"Your presence is required elsewhere." He frowned, and she read the expression as distaste for what he was about to do.

"On Yadra?"

"No," he said tersely. "On the ship."

"I thought—?"

He wouldn't look at her. "So did I. But the decisions are no longer in my hands."

Rieka took the words as a bad omen. Triscoe was being forced to do something. She accepted the seriousness of this excursion and closed the small distance between them. Midrin followed her example.

He twitched on his TC. "InterMAT this signal to conference room one."

Rieka raised an eyebrow but that was all she had time for before the transport effect began. When she could focus again, the second brow joined the first. Seated at the conference table were Dr. Twanabok, Admiral Nason, and Triscoe's first officer, Aarkmin. A bit more white accented Nason's high Aurian brow, but the steely look in his pale blue eyes was the same. His bibbets, held under tight control, were a cream color Rieka didn't particularly like.

"Admiral," she said, offering him the Fleet salute, a gesture first to the head, then the heart.

He nodded. "Captain Degahv, it is good to see that you are still in one piece."

She had to smile, just a little. "Thank you, sir. I had hoped my next audience with you would have been under more pleasant circumstances."

"Undoubtedly."

Midrin had saluted, too. He returned it and nodded. "Dr. Twanabok tells me you're recovering well, Commander. I hope so. I may need your services, soon."

She nodded. "Yes, sir. Thank you."

"Sit." He gestured for them to take the seats across

from him at the dark, highly polished table. She glanced quickly at Triscoe, wondering why he considered Nason an enemy.

When they were settled, the admiral tapped his stubby fingers on the table. "Allow me to begin by explaining that this meeting never took place. My datapad will, however, document the discussion should certain facts be needed in the future."

Rieka nodded along with the others, agreeing to his request for secrecy.

"I will begin with the obvious," he continued, "the indictments against Captain Degahv." He paused for a moment and sat forward in his chair. "From the documentation I have received, it is obvious any court would throw out the case. You were kidnapped, assaulted, and your mind was raped. Because your crew was not privy to your orders, they simply corroborate the prosecution's case that you fired on the *Vendikon,* and a few minutes later, it exploded."

He gestured vaguely with his hands, as if to say that was to be expected. "Counsel Chen has informed me that, in the light of what you've uncovered, the prosecution has no case against you."

Rieka said a silent prayer for the admiral's faith in her and thanked whatever gods there were that Chen had confided in him. She nodded.

"Unfortunately, that may not matter to the Judicial Council—as it stands now." The admiral shook his head slightly and sighed. "Yesterday, I received an interesting communication from Lom Dilva, commander of our training facilities on Vekya." He leaned across the table toward them and knotted his fingers. "A scrap of clothing had been found in a shuttle. A sleeve off an admiral's uniform. Curious, he had the base physician do an analysis of the fabric and anything that might have been sticking to it. Apparently, it had once belonged to Admiral Bittin."

"No." She groaned, then found herself inhaling as if she couldn't stop.

Triscoe shook his head, the frown firmly implanted on his face. "Are they sure? The admiral might have—"

"The sleeve was found a week ago," Nason continued, glancing at all of them one at a time. "The admiral's behavior has been erratic since just after your arraignment. He did some traveling, too. Went to Indra, Earth, and Cronis. I have to consider the possibility that, like Tohab, he has been replaced."

"I see," she said softly.

"That is why I have doubts that your case will be dismissed, Captain. The Procyons are counting on your trial as a smoke screen. With one of their own in a position to bend the ear of both the Judicial Council and the media, it will be a small matter to create a circus out of what should realistically be thrown out of court. Further," he continued, "I believe *this* Bittin has the power to generate what the Humans once called a witch-hunt, equivalent to an Aurian *minda*. And in the midst of the ensuing chaos and the legal disposal of Captain Degahv, I believe they will make their move."

"To do what, sir?" Triscoe asked.

"To do exactly what you have surmised, Captain. To attempt a coup. To steal the *Prodigy,* systematically destroy the Fleet, and pick off the unprotected Commonwealth worlds like pearls on a string."

"How?" Tohab wondered aloud. "There are fifty-seven ships in our fleet. We're scattered over twenty cubic parsecs of space. Even though there are only ten member worlds, there are dozens of colonized moons and secondary planets. I don't see how—"

"And that is exactly it, Commander," the admiral blurted, his finger aimed at her. "No one can see how we could be taken apart piecemeal. No Commonwealth citizen would consider it a rational possibility. But it *is* possible. Computer projections have accomplished the scenario dozens of times. Our entire culture is based on fast and efficient transport of goods and people. With the *Prodigy* in their control, the Procyons need not bother to wait until they have an adequate number of personnel infiltrating the Fleet—or storming into our solar system. They can do it now, by picking off our ships one by one."

Rieka sat back and sighed. She, Triscoe, and Midrin had had a similar discussion. Based only upon what had happened to her, the idea seemed unreasonable. But the admiral's announcement substantiated everything. She understood why Triscoe was so upset. The fact that the admiral had included her in this briefing meant she would be involved. She found herself grinning, ready to dole out some of what had been done to her. With pleasure.

"What do we do, sir?"

"We *appear* to do nothing," he said, returning her smile. "We appear as if all is well and they are completely undetected."

"Give them enough rope to hang themselves, you mean?" she asked.

"Exactly. We have only two advantages. The first is—we are aware of the situation, and the surprise is now reversed."

"And the second?" Triscoe asked.

"The second is, quite simply, Captain Degahv." The admiral looked at her evenly while Triscoe shook his head.

"Unacceptable, sir. Rieka has been taken by them three times. It is foolhardy to consider the possibility—"

"Captain, your opinion has been noted," Nason replied, his tone ending further discussion. "Captain Degahv is dead as far as they are concerned. Paden's people have apparently called off their search this morning. No bodies were recovered. Neither Rieka nor Commander Tohab surfaced in the only inhabited spot within reasonable walking distance, which is the village of Creyunne."

He looked pointedly at Triscoe. "You wisely made it look as if you hadn't found them. And there is no record of them here on the *Providence*. Our enemies must think both women died sometime after their escape—probably attacked and consumed by bolwins.

As far as the Commonwealth and the Fleet are concerned, officially, Rieka is still in Paden's custody for the transgressions against her crew and the attack on the *Providence*. And Tohab is in charge of the *Venture*.

"The Procyon faction cannot announce their deaths. That would ruin their plans for the upcoming trial. But they can't go to court without her. So they are stuck." His bibbets colored slightly and he smiled. "And we have the captain and the commander."

"Where is the *Venture*?"

Nason looked at Rieka and rubbed a finger across his bibbets. "I was informed by Admiral Bittin that Internal Affairs required the use of the *Venture*," he explained. "I tried, but he wouldn't give me the particulars. I think, however, that the false Tohab was in too deep, and they required her to be out of the way for a while. There's still a chance we can recover what's left of your crew, especially if they realize she's an impostor and are game enough to mutiny."

At that, she had to smile.

Midrin cleared her throat, and Rieka glanced at her. "What about Midrin?"

Nason nodded. "You will need rehabilitation before you can be of any use to this cause, Commander. You'll return to Yadra with me and, if you have recuperated satisfactorily by the time I leave for Dani, you will accompany me there."

"Understood, sir," she said.

Rieka caught her eye and smiled. Midrin had as much reason as she did to want some form of retribution. More, probably.

Triscoe interrupted her short reverie. "You said, 'And we have the captain,' Admiral. What, exactly, does that mean, sir?"

Nason glanced at him once before settling his gaze on Rieka. "You will have your appearance altered, be given a new identity, and be assigned to Dani. You'll receive orders to do a systems check on the *Prodigy* panoply and DGI screens. While on board, you'll reprogram the weapons system's telemetry and attempt to identify the Procyons. This information, you'll forward on to me. We control what happens to the *Prodigy* while it is still in the dock. We can't afford to waste any time."

"Rieka has had enough contact with Procyons and their pawns," Triscoe announced. "I volunteer for the mission."

Rieka knew his protective instincts were crossing the line. She looked at him out of the corner of her eye and kicked him under the table.

"Unacceptable," Nason replied. "As a Centauri captain with an excellent reputation, you are quite visible. It would appear more than coincidence if you suddenly took leave of your ship and a person of similar physique showed up anywhere near Dani. Captain Degahv is the best choice."

Rieka nodded. She willed herself not to be smug in the face of Triscoe's displeasure, even as he bent to rub his shin. "I agree," she said. "And as long as this disguise isn't permanent, I have no trouble with the plan."

The admiral angled his head. "Twanabok, you can arrange something?"

The physician nodded. "Centauri would be best, I think. No use in complicating things with artificial bibbets."

"I agree." The admiral turned back to Rieka. "You will not be on your own, Captain. The *Providence* will arrive at Dani as soon as possible and remain there for complete repairs to the gravitation system. The *Prospectus* should already be there by now. Captain Finot will be made aware of my plans. If there is any trouble, consider him a safe haven."

Triscoe leaned forward, asking pointedly, "Why bring more individuals in on your plot, Admiral? I thought the fewer to know the true situation, the safer we are."

Irritated that he was doing it again, Rieka whacked his thigh with her knee. He glanced at her, and she shot him a look meant to warn him off. He ignored it and returned his attention to the admiral.

Nason nodded once. "Correct," he replied. "But I have analyzed Procyon activity to a greater extent than you. They avoid Boos, and I believe I know why. As far as we know, Procyons seek *only* to dominate and violate. They take what they want and move on."

He smiled gamely and it seemed to Rieka it was the first change of expression in the man she'd seen in an eternity. "The Boos go against the grain. Their planet possesses a gravity beyond that which humanoids can comfortably tolerate, so it is not a candidate for colonization. And the species is so *alien*—even those who seek to comprehend them have trouble. The Procyons have avoided Boolian contact. It is my guess that they are counting on the Boos in each ship's complement to keep those vessels going once the Fleet has been assimilated. And, in a way, they may be right. Boos have never displayed a sense of loyalty."

Midrin said softly, "But they've never been given a choice such as this."

"True," the admiral agreed.

Rieka felt her breath catch. Midrin was right, their choice could make all the difference.

"That may be another disguised advantage," Nason continued. "Unfortunately, only time will tell." He looked at Rieka and she saw both commitment and concern in his eyes. "Use whatever tools and talents you possess to get the job done. I shall continue to press the counterfeit Bittin for continuances and postponements of the trial.

"I expect a daily report from you, Triscoe. Rieka, you will use the roundabout means of reporting to me by employing this address code." He reached into a satchel and produced a datapad with an eight-digit number glowing on its face. "Do not code your messages, as this might raise suspicion. A member of my staff will receive the documents each day and send a reply. I suggest you place any information within the body of your chat. Sign off using your first name only—the name you will be given, that is. If you refer to your addressee, her name is to be Dramie, a lieutenant who works in the scheduling department. Is that understood?"

"Yes, sir." Rieka passed the pad back across the table and added the name Dramie to the memorized address code.

"If you miss one day, a search will be conducted. You will not be considered expendable unless the most undesirable situation takes place."

"And what might that be?" she asked.

"If you are on board and they actually take the *Prodigy*."

She nodded. Nason would then order it destroyed by an means possible. Tacitly, this meant to sabotage it herself, if she could.

"All precautions are being taken," he said evenly. "Remember, by any standards, the Procyons are ruthless. They care little for life other than that of their own kind. Ethics and morality are meaningless concepts to them. They take. And they will continue to take until what's left is of no value. I will not allow that to happen. What our forebears have built out of nothing will not be destroyed by a single species of marauders who care little for civilization as we know it.

"Are there any questions?"

Rieka nodded. "How do we know who's been influenced?"

"We don't," he answered succinctly. "Even those citizens staunchly supportive of our cause may have been 'treated' for some specific purpose. But it is my believe that everything is hinging upon the takeover of the ship. Quite simply, be on your guard. All of you."

Rieka saw the white-knuckled grip Triscoe had on his chair. He wasn't happy with the admiral's plan, but she wasn't arguing about it, either. She slid her hand over his and said, "I think that's one variable that we can count on, sir."

* * *

Rieka and Midrin had been in Triscoe's quarters, discussing the plan and wondering what Midrin's part in it might be, when Twanabok arrived. An autobot table followed him in and, after the furniture had been pushed to the walls, was set up in the center of the room. The doctor hooked up the power couplings and activated the warmer surface. "Time to strip, Captain," he said, turning his broad greenish face in her direction.

She nodded and complied unenthusiastically. Hiking herself up onto the table a moment later, she was thankful the surface wasn't icy cold. Twanabok positioned her, faceup, and began his ministrations of her epidermis with a small flat-faced device that left a trail of altered pigment along her skin. It was the color of pale oak, she noted, much lighter than what she was used to, but nothing as alien as the chartreuse of a Vekyan or a Bourne's three shades of coffee black. She peered down at him while he worked slowly, as if to taunt her, and said, "Won't this just wear off?"

Holding the device daintily between his claws, the doctor shrugged with a typically Vekyan, chest-in-and-out movement. "Not exactly. Well, yes it does, on Humans. But I'll be giving you a pigment-altering treatment as well. That will take care of the long-term difference of hue. This, what I'm doing now, is no more complex than an expensive cosmetic tan." He pulled himself straight and added, "In reverse, of course." Then bent over her, again.

"How long is 'long-term'?" she inquired skeptically.

Twanabok replied without shifting his attention from his task. "Long-term is defined, in this case, as forever. With the supplemental treatment, you'll be able to pass yourself off as a Centauri for the rest of your life, if you like."

"And if I don't?"

"Find someone to change you back," he replied indifferently.

Rieka frowned. "And my hair?"

"I'll take care of that, too. It is another process whereby we alter the pigment in the existing hair and dose you up with a subsidiary chemical treatment. No one will guess you're not Centauri."

"No more complaints about Human-bashing." Midrin laughed. "I hope the admiral assigns me to you."

The doctor pulled himself erect and looked at her. "No one is able to predict the future," he said. "Not even the Oracle of Indra is completely accurate in this realm. The easiest thing to do is make yourself inconspicuous."

While she considered his strange comment, he had her lift her knees to stretch the skin. "And the fact that Centauris don't have breasts?"

Twanabok glanced at her once but continued working on her leg. "Not a problem, I should think. They're not associated with a vital organ system. I'll remove them."

Rieka jerked up on her elbows. "Oh, no you won't!"

Twanabok was unruffled. "You've married an Indran, Captain, you won't produce any young to suckle. I don't see why you're so disagreeable."

"I'm keeping them," she said, not about to tell him that no matter what she thought of her breasts, Triscoe found them fascinating. That reason alone was enough to pick a fight.

"As you wish, Captain," he murmured.

"Fine." Unfortunately, the discussion hadn't resolved the problem. "But we have to do something. I'll be crew, Doctor, not command. Living in shared quarters. Surely, someone will catch on if I require total privacy to dress and bathe."

"Bind them?" Midrin offered.

At that, Twanabok stopped and thought. He reached a clawed finger and poked at the petite glands on her chest. "That will work under a uniform. I'll give you hairline scars, too," he decided. "Anyone gives you trouble, you tell them they're artificial. Your boyfriend or some such folderol."

She had to give him credit for quick thinking. "If it works," she said, smiling.

"Certainly it will work. Centauri females do completely stupid things to attract mates. Have done for years. The Human breast obsession started when I began medical school. Just don't get into any situations where someone will discover you've got nothing but recently implanted synthetic hair on your abdomen. It could create a problem."

"I'll try to keep that in mind," she said.

When he set to work on her torso, Twanabok added, "And I'll need to give you a new TC. An old one, actually. Knew the damn things were too delicate. We'll do a postmortem on the one you still have. No doubt that maitu butchered the circuitry."

"No doubt."

"I'll do that just before we arrive at Dani."

Rieka's mood soured at the thought of sitting motionless but awake for another hour. "Of course," she said.

The door opened then, and First Officer Aarkmin entered. "Doctor. Captain," she said formally from just inside the closed door. "I have brought the dossier on the identity you are to assume, Captain." Hesitantly, she circled Twanabok and moved to Rieka's head.

Rieka gave her a halfhearted smile. She wasn't uncomfortable about her nudity with this woman any more than she was with the doctor, but she sensed an unease from Aarkmin and knew that Centauris valued their privacy. "Am I supposed to memorize it now?" she asked in as conversational tone as she could muster. "Or is it something I should study on my own?"

Aarkmin's eyes remained fixed on the floor. "I have no idea, Captain, since I have not been given access to this file." She held the datapad for Rieka to see.

"Put it on the desk, please. I'll get to it as soon as the doctor is done."

Aarkmin complied and turned to Midrin. "Admiral Nason requires you at Headquarters now, Commander. We shall transport together on my signal."

Midrin went to Rieka's head, standing opposite Twanabok at the table. "I think this is good-bye for the moment. Good luck, Captain."

"Thanks. Get well fast, Midrin. I'll need you." She lifted her hand so that Midrin could touch her palm.

The women left, and, for a while, both she and Twanabok said nothing. Then she felt a subtle change within the ship. "We're moving," she observed.

"Don't know how you Humans can tell," he muttered. "But you're probably right. Admiral's orders— we're to get to Dani as soon as possible. We spent over a day at Yadra. The crew from the *Venture* have all been assigned. I should think we're patched up enough for a quick trip, by now."

She nodded. He was working on her midsection. Her skin had begun to tingle, but Rieka wasn't sure whether it was from his instrument, the new hue, or the fact they were headed toward a confrontation with the Procyons.

Fifteen

That his people had located Setana Marteen in the Arts District didn't surprise Nason. He knew her for a vocal supporter of all cultural expression. To have a husband who was a Prefect of Art seemed only natural. No wonder Ker'd had a fit when Triscoe joined the Transit Authority.

Nason walked purposefully along the minicity's manicured paths, just east of Fleet headquarters. The finest creative minds had somehow managed to work in tandem to build an assembly of structures that spoke of harmony in the face of diversity. It had an esthetic quality unsurpassed by anything else in the Commonwealth.

As he strode past a theatre, the Symphonic Consortium's hulking blue edifice greeted him with gleaming glass and native stone brought from the Omicron Eridani system. As he approached, the ornate portcullis shimmered and disappeared, allowing him entrance. Stepping over the threshold, he shivered and wrinkled his nose against the cold, pungent smell of ozone.

Nodding to a pair of tall, frail-looking Lomii working behind the clear walls of their frosty, climate-controlled box office, Nason walked across the empty lobby and entered the concert hall's lower level. If he knew Setana as well as he thought, she'd be there rather than a balcony. He continued down the main aisle while a single musician on the stage played an unrecognizable piece.

The work lights on, he easily located Setana seated

well back from the judges. "Herald Marteen," Nason
crooned softly, "what a fortunate coincidence that I
should run into you." He slid into the plush blue seat
next to hers as she glanced at him. The expression he
received told him she knew he was lying. But the Marteen matriarch only lifted her palm and nodded a silent
"hello."

When the soloist completed her short performance
and the air around them was hushed, the Herald gave
him her attention. "Admiral Nason, I sincerely doubt
that auditions for the Symphonic Consortium have ever
piqued your interest," she said quietly. On stage, the
young Aurian departed with her *yikka,* and a cellist
entered from the wings.

"They do if that is where I can bump into you
socially."

"I have a grandnephew in the running for a third seat
bienda," she explained. "Actually, he's already played.
But I do love the cello for its rich, full tone. It's one of
the few Human inventions to blend perfectly into our
multicultural orchestra. Don't you think?"

Nason nodded and turned to watch the young Human
holding the instrument between his knees. Though the
single voice cried for accompaniment, it tapped feelings that Nason would rather not have recognized. A
quality of sadness, loneliness, and apprehension per-
meated the vibrant tone. He found himself hoping it
would be over soon.

When the music faded, Setana touched his arm. "If
we want to talk, we'd best to do it elsewhere."

"I agree." Wary of almost everyone around him,
Nason somehow knew he could trust Setana. The odds
of her being kidnapped and programmed were relatively nil, since she never went anywhere alone. As
they walked back up the aisle, a Centauri woman rose
from a chair and followed at a discreet distance, the
bodyguard proving his point.

Setana led him outside and to a courtyard nestled
between the Symphonic and Theatrical Consortiums.

The bodyguard remained near the symphony building. They sat on a bench overlooking a small yellow pond on which ebony, wingless *gikfowl* floated and dived. The breeze rippled the trees, and Nason felt certain they were alone enough for the conversation he had in mind.

"Begin at the beginning," she advised in her uncanny way of making him feel understood and suspicious at the same time.

"It has to do with Triscoe, Herald," he replied, purposely using her title. "He is in danger—as are we all."

"And Rieka?"

He sat straighter, watching her curiously.

At his unspoken question, she nodded. "My daughter-in-law is not unknown to me, Merik. I attended the marriage ceremony. There is an investment there that I would like to see pay off."

Nason nodded. Of course she would have known about it. But did she know everything? "If you'll pardon the inconvenience," he said abruptly, "I'd like to use this." He pulled a small flat device from his pocket and set it on the bench. When she nodded, he touched the flat upper surface and the disk issued a nearly inaudible thrumming sound that would render any listening device useless.

"The beginning," she prompted again.

"Your son, his new wife, and Captain DeVark have stumbled across a plan to take control of the Commonwealth. Through deduction, we have reasoned the Procyons are behind this coup but, as of right now, have limited solid evidence to support the theory."

She nodded as if this were not news. Although it surprised him, Nason didn't bother to waste any energy trying to decipher how she knew. "Right now, DeVark is at Dani and Captains Degahv and Marteen are en route," he finished, trying to ignore the fact that the sun was becoming uncomfortably warm on his shoulders.

"The *Prodigy*," she said with a slight frown, tilting

her regal head with concern. "I suppose it should have been foreseen."

"Was it?" he asked bluntly, cutting quickly to the hunch that had prompted him to seek her out.

She pivoted slightly, angling her ramrod posture even straighter. Her brown eyes, so much like those of her son, bore into him with total clarity. "What do you know?"

He shrugged slightly. "Nothing for sure. It's mostly conjecture. But I must ask." He paused for only a moment. "Is there a Yillon, and does he know anything about this?"

Her eyes left his and looked out over the water. "Yillon exists," she said softly. "I am of his line, though this was told to me only after my mother died. He knows . . . much of what is to come."

Nason leaned forward and rubbed his hands on his knees. "Setana, I've know you a long time—since before Triscoe joined the Fleet. I consider you more than an acquaintance," he admitted, smiling. "I hate to ask, but I must. I have to coordinate almost sixty ships against an unknown force. Can Yillon give me a clue as to where the Procyons will strike first? If not, I'll have to spread the Fleet thin, covering every planet and colony."

He shook his head and wondered if his anxiety was some kind of signal that he'd gotten too old for his job. "We've never been stronger, but the Commonwealth will be in serious trouble should the *Prodigy* fall into Procyon hands. They'll drown us like a cresting tide."

Setana nodded solemnly. "This type of vision is most difficult, Merik," she advised. "Yillon has told me the overall future is difficult to see and even more difficult to divulge. He has already spoken to me of impending upheaval, but it did not seem to be on such a grand scale as you fear. I am one of three Centauri dignitaries scheduled to be present at the *Prodigy*'s dedication. We leave in three days. I shall try to have an answer for you by then."

Nason felt as if a weight had been lifted from him. He set his back against the bench and inhaled the sweet-smelling air. "Thank you, Setana," he said softly. "But I must warn you—the Procyons have managed to disguise themselves as Commonwealth citizens and, in some instances, have actually taken their place. Beware of whom you trust."

"Your concern is flattering." The scarf across her shoulder became displaced by the breeze. She righted it, then smiled. "I am blessed with a touch of Yillon's gift, my friend. This sense allows me to see beyond the three-dimensional. This is how I knew of Rieka's innocence."

"I wondered why you allowed Triscoe to form an attachment to an enemy of the Commonwealth."

Setana made a small gesture with her right arm and wrist. "The attachment was out of my hands," she admitted, glancing out at the pond. "It had been arranged years ago by the Oracle. If I had been against it—it would have been like arguing with a planet to change orbit."

Nason smiled at the simile. "But they are good for each other."

She nodded. "Of course they are."

As Robet ambled along the *Prodigy*'s main corridor at what might be construed as Finot's shoulder, the Boo clicked his kroi strangely. "With me, it is the cube of Perindon at the Falls," he said cheerlessly.

Robet, awed by the ship's size, was nudged back to reality by Finot's tone, even if he didn't understand what he'd said. "I should think Pedlam would be thrilled with the assignment," he said.

"Not unlike the snap of a jaw, my friend," Finot replied. "Ugly in terms of etiquette, is this man. Unwilling. Unfriendly." The base captain stopped and studied Robet, taking the time to blink in that complex double-lidded way. The kroi clicked again. "Not Centauri," his translator gurgled softly.

Robet returned the gaze. "Thank you for the observation, Captain. I am sure it will . . . come in handy—as the Humans say."

Finot turned again and continued down the gracefully arched corridor. "Nason had brought my eyes into the light before Mohb. Humanoids are as the wind through whistling rock. The formula is clear, the equation yet unsolved. I understand. The . . . gravity."

Chuckling, Robet punched the other's arm lightly. It felt like stone. "Lighten up, Finot," he said. "Your ship is safe."

"Above the variables," came the abject reply, insinuating that once the *Prodigy* left port, that would no longer be true. But Finot left the subject closed as they made their way into a Chute to tour the second level.

Robet was impressed with the big ship's advanced weapon system as well as the space dedicated to scientific research. Finot had explained that, with 80 percent of the ship's peripheral edge acting as an enormous gun barrel, it was all but impossible for it to be surrounded. Antimatter-sphere production had been redesigned and streamlined, thus making it feasible to produce them at a fantastic rate. With shielding efficiency up almost 35 percent, the *Prodigy* was also almost impervious to attack. Robet felt his stomach flip. This vessel, when fully operational, would be all but invincible.

Military aspects notwithstanding, the science research lab was immense. The isolation fields and procedures were well beyond anything he'd thus far seen in space. Obviously, the *Prodigy* would eventually be given exploratory missions. The Commonwealth, with its planets and peoples interconnected as they were by the Boos' genius, still needed outside input. He was convinced, as they passed through research areas marked physics, quantum, zoology, botany, space/time, and dimensional, that this ship was a solid investment in the future. Recalling Finot's earlier remark, Robet reminded himself that the future he imagined required an absence of Procyon intervention.

An increased work space also meant a larger crew. The area designated for housing, midway up the canopy, occupied the same proportions as any other ship. Because of the *Prodigy*'s size, however, the crew still only required 15 percent of the total space.

Robet wondered how many of them were Procyons.

"Are all the systems and conduits compatible?"

Finot waved a starfish hand. "Similarities are clear as the sky at Varannah. Negating the additional labs and alternate storage space, with eyes closed only the linear steps counted differs."

Robet nodded. Despite the fact Finot hadn't mentioned the huge areas used strictly for defense, the places he might need to access would be where he could find them, even if he had to use a datapad. He hoped Admiral Nason's orders would not need to be carried out, and that they would not be forced to destroy the Fleet's first true warship.

"Environmental section, Captain," the Boo explained, ushering him into yet another entryway. He collected a pair of goggles on the wall and handed them to Robet. "Sterilization-room requirement," he explained, then walked into the next chamber and closed both pair of eyelids.

Robet followed, goggles in place, not bothering to remind Finot that he had an environmental suite on the *Prospectus*. When surface sterilization was complete and the inner door slid open, they stepped into the lab proper. He hung the eyewear next to several others on the wall.

This section, along with areas in both the electrical and recreation departments, spanned the main hull's full three stories. Surrounded by balconies and catwalks, the huge water-recovery and atmospheric-refining tanks dwarfed the crew that worked around them. Circulators located at all three levels connected the system like the heart in a physical body. He was considering the thought when Finot tapped him on the shoulder and pointed.

"There he sits like Pzekii on the new day," the Boo muttered.

At that moment, Pedlam looked up from his spot on a lower catwalk, a strange, puzzled frown on his face. "What now, Finot?" he shouted. "I can't be bothered with another one of your—"

Finot made a discontented sound with his kroi and said, "We come with honor, Pzekii Pedlam." He lurched down the catwalk.

Robet tried valiantly not to laugh aloud as he followed. Pedlam had just been insulted and, judging by the look on his face, he had no idea. To anyone familiar with Boos, as certainly a Fleet captain should be, the significance of being called Pzekki would be obvious. Five hundred years ago, Pzekki had tried to restrict information accessibility. The name was synonymous with traitor.

They descended to Pedlam's level. "An errant with the reserve?" Finot asked.

"The thing is pushing too much oxygen," Pedlam groused. "And your tech-pro cannot correct the problem."

"The premix is fine, sir," and Aurian lieutenant said. "I can't figure what's happening." He offered his datapad for Finot's inspection.

Finot took it, glanced at the markings and handed it back. "Reset the baffle number six," he said. "The new bacteria are efficient to the flow." Then turning to Pedlam, Finot blinked twice. "Brought you a visitor to the gates of Vigoon."

Pedlam looked at Robet and extended his hands in the Centauri manner of greeting. "Captain DeVark," he said casually. "Nice to see you again."

"Same here," Robet replied, unable to detect any deviation from the Pedlam he'd met one or two times in the past. "The captain's been showing me the

Prodigy," he continued casually. "You've got yourself one sleek ship."

"Oh, she'll do the job," Pedlam said.

"No doubt."

"I regret that I cannot be more hospitable at this time," Pedlam continued. "We're running under a tight schedule, and little things like this do not help." He gestured toward the lieutenant. "Perhaps we can have dinner later."

"Sure," Robet agreed, smiling. "I'll look forward to it."

The lieutenant studying the datapad tapped it twice and looked up at Finot. "That's done it, sir. We've reduced the rate 15 percent. It's in the margins, now."

"A ride to Varannah with the factors of the dew," the Boo replied cryptically. He turned and retraced his earlier steps on the heavily supported catwalk. Robet followed.

"Deck one, section forty-six B. Nineteen-hundred," Pedlam called.

Robet turned and nodded. "I'll be there." As he followed Finot out of environmental, he wondered why this Pedlam was being so friendly.

The Boo answered the unspoken question. "Pzekii has designs," he remarked softly. "Like the deterioration of an antimatter shell."

"Dammit, Triscoe—"

Rieka stopped herself before she said something she'd regret. She clamped her jaw shut and breathed out of her nose. Arguing didn't accomplish anything, but it was all he seemed to want to do. She left her uneaten dinner on the small table in front of the sofa and stomped to the DGI.

"Earth," she spit, still keeping a tight rein on what she said. The unit responded immediately, and she was appeased slightly by the small planet whose atmosphere and seas were once again a healthy blue. She watched the computer-driven jet streams and felt her pulse slowing. The planet of her ancestors gave her a sense of continuity, of strength, of peace. She folded pale arms over her flat chest and wondered at the cruel joke God had played on Humanity.

Triscoe left his chair to stand a short distance behind her. "I am afraid for you," he said softly. It was a statement, not an apology. "You're putting yourself in a cage with a bolwin. I have every right to—"

"Shut up. Shut up. Shut . . . up." She stepped away, clearly out of reach. "I don't want to hear how you're afraid. How *you* feel." She waited a moment and found the courage to say, "I count on you to be strong, Tris. I always have. When I feel like—I don't know—not myself, anyway, I think of you being strong, and it helps. Don't turn to mush and put my well-being before the Commonwealth's. Not now." She looked at him crookedly. It was a dare, an accusation, and a request rolled into one.

Earth's image was not geosynchronous. Africa had slipped into view. A moment later she could make out the blackened area that had taken the meteor hit—just beyond what was left of the Mediterranean's new outline. Rieka wondered how many centuries would pass before the ugly scar of impact would fade from orbital perception. Triscoe's voice brought her back to the present.

"I am simply—and failing badly at it—trying to protect you," he said. "Your orders are difficult for me to accept. I want you to be safe. So much has happened in the past few weeks that I—"

"Keep me safe!" She tried, but couldn't curtail her anger. "Oh, just keep your noble intentions to yourself," she muttered, not bothering to hold back the spite from her voice. "If you love me, you should understand that I have to do this—for my people—for *our* people. I would have volunteered if Nason had not ordered me!" She turned and looked at him, eyes blazing with the frustrations of a lifetime lodged in her craw. "The admiral understood. Why can't you?"

"I don't want to see you hurt, again," he said finally.

Rieka sighed. She could not bring herself to look him in the face. Their argument was about two different things. But she wouldn't, couldn't back down.

"I hurt," she said poking a finger at her chest, "and there's nothing you can do about it. Nothing you could ever do—nothing you could ever have done. From the moment I was four years old and an Aurian child pointed at me and called me Human in a way that made me wish I could seep into the floor—I hurt. And I will go on hurting. The pain is what gets me through times like this . . . when I must walk away from you to do something that could save us all—and perhaps soften the way people think of Humankind."

Rieka turned to watch the DGI. "I have been belittled all my life," she said softly, her voice cracking. Suddenly, she couldn't look at the Earth anymore. Feeling as though she had disappointed that world in some inexplicable way, she sighed. "I've done nothing to scar my reputation, but they've accused me of treason. I'll never be valued as a true equal to you or Robet or Midrin—or anyone who isn't Human." She touched her bleached skin. "I might not look like one now, but I still am."

"Rieka, don't do this to yourself."

"I have *done* nothing!" She squared off to him, glaring into his pale face. "I was born. That was enough. A Human is treated like something secondhand. Like a collective possession. A Human is a Commonwealth citizen with the rights and privileges given to all—but unjustly assigned the social status of a menial. And don't give me that innocent look, Triscoe Marteen. You've done a fine job of manipulating me, yourself. You and your Singlemind."

She snapped her jaw shut at the incredulous look on his face and wished she could take back her words. She never planned to tell him she now knew the significance of their first Singlemind—that he had bound himself to her without her knowledge.

"I'm sorry," she said quickly. "I know you've never

meant to . . ." Her throat tightened, and she couldn't speak. She'd just broken her promise to herself never to sink to "their level." She couldn't seem to control the angry, hurried rhythm of her rib cage or the burning in her eyes.

She heard Triscoe sigh, then tensed when he put his hands on her shoulders. "Come to me," he murmured as his fingers pulled her forward. She resisted. "I am ready to tell you everything, Rieka. I have no wish to argue anymore."

When she moved into the wall of his chest, the strong Centauri arms encircled her and held tight. It felt like going home—to be held like this. But she said nothing, and kept her arms at her sides, refusing to give him any slack.

"When Yillon first told me you were the one," he began softly, "I had a hard time convincing myself that a Human could be so important. One Human. It seemed outrageous. Unbelievable. I have tried to overcome that momentary lapse. I still wonder what could have made me react with such blatant prejudice. I try to tell myself it was something born of outside influences, not my heart speaking. But I can't be sure."

He said nothing for a long moment. Rieka stayed in his embrace, trying to calm her uneven breathing. She nestled closer when he caressed her short-cropped, recently blond hair.

"Humans are intimidating, Rieka. I think the rest of us have formed some kind of unspoken conspiracy to keep you under control," he said finally. "No matter the calamity, you refuse to back down or accept it. You take up the challenge. And win. This is astounding to us. Look at your planet. Look at you. The blows you have been dealt would have crushed the spirit of any Lomii—even an Aurian or Vekyan. I have doubts about the reactions of my own people. Yet you stand here arguing with me about responsibility and commitment."

He lifted her face and looked down at her. "Truthfully, I did not think you could endure the things that have happened—without help. But you have proved stronger than I ever imagined. Even in our Singleminds, I did not sense such strength. Maybe . . . I did not look for it."

Rieka allowed her jaw to tighten. "And are you going to be honest about the Singlemind, too?"

"I never meant to deceive you—well, not for personal gain." He shook his head. "No, that doesn't sound right."

She waited as he took a breath and started again. "Of course I knew what I was doing. Mother and I both have the gift. We can converse freely in thought. I've done the same with Yillon. It was he who, as I said, pronounced your significance. The first experience I had other than communicating with him and Mother, was with you. I thought I could be closer to you, watch out for you, if we touched minds.

"I had hoped," he said softly, brushing her temple with a finger, "that you would have a touch of the gift—that perhaps we could communicate via thoughts as well. I sense something of you all the time. And it has become more pronounced since you found me in Creyunne. Have you begun to sense me, too?"

She frowned, thinking, then shrugged. Nothing in the last few days came close to what happened during a Singlemind. "I've had a headache. Twice. That's it."

He nodded as if that might be meaningful. "It could prove to be extremely convenient . . . shall I continue to try?"

Rieka took a breath and blew it out. "You're asking me to go along with what you've already been doing for four years. I'm—" she searched for the proper word—"insulted. I can follow your reasoning, but that doesn't change how I feel, Triscoe."

She crossed her arms over her flattened chest and took a step back so as not to have to keep craning her neck to look at him. Determination slowly replaced the anger she felt. There was no time to argue over what-ifs and might-have-beens. They had a job to do, and teamwork might very well be the only way to get it done.

"I am willing to overlook the past—on the condition that we start with the whole truth and keep it that way. I accepted you for life," she admitted, "but I'd rather shoot myself than have to live with a closet full of old problems."

Relief blossomed on his face. "How can I not love such tenacity? Even if she no longer looks Human? And I agree. We will start over. You have deserved better."

Rieka tried to glare up at that irascible face. How could he tease her and be serious at the same time? It was both infuriating and endearing. The brown eyes softened. The dimple appeared. She gritted her teeth to keep from smiling.

"And yet, how could I resist wanting to keep you safe with me?"

She rolled her eyes.

"I am teasing you, wife."

"I know." The chuckle finally escaped. "It feels very strange coming from a Centauri."

"I have decided to acquaint myself with more Human things," he murmured.

"Good. I suppose I should be flattered, especially now, since I look like—"

Apparently, he was through bantering. When Triscoe touched his lips to hers, Rieka resisted at first. Even though he'd admitted to his obsession with her safety, she wanted to strangle him for it. But after a moment, when he hadn't given up, she capitulated. She could not ignore the fact that Centauri lips were more articulate than Human. And Triscoe was a talented kisser.

"I apologize," he said finally. "I have used you. But it was not for personal gain. And it certainly wasn't to show you your place as a Human."

"I know." She could see it in his face now. All the things he had explained, some things she'd figured out on her own—it was all there. "But since the day I met you, I've had a personal guardian, and, up until this moment, I've resented it. Now, I see it's just been a team effort. Too bad no one bothered to tell me I was on the team."

"You are the star player."

"Then there's nothing you can do. I've got to play. Otherwise, we have no chance of winning."

Triscoe remained quiet for a long moment, and his smile slowly faded. His gaze moved over her face as if he were memorizing it. His eyes were dark and suddenly intense, the expression similar to the times he had touched his mind to hers. Rieka felt an electricity in the air and waited, uncertain as to what he was going to say, or do.

"As long as you play with me first, love." He took her hand and she let him lead her through the open doorway. She much preferred a quiet mattress match to a raucous round of speed volley—or whatever the game was they were playing with the Procyons.

Rieka gave in to her baser needs when he called for twilight illumination. She began to disrobe, thankful to be rid of the binding, and the way Triscoe looked when her breasts were finally free. The unbroken plane of his lower abdomen no longer surprised her, nor did the thicket of shaggy hair that grew in an oval pattern just below the small X-shaped navel.

Rieka found herself offering assistance as he tugged at the remainder of her clothing and let it fall in a heap beside his. Barely aware of their previous argument, she rolled with him onto the mattress and teased the taut flap of skin that protected his strange, Centauri sex. She welcomed the heady sensation of being cherished when he murmured Indran words and rendered pleasure with his hands and with his mouth. She ignored the obstacles of the universe as she held him tightly, marveling at his ability to combine their alien separateness into a single entity, even if only for a moment.

And later, when he dozed in a restful sleep, she wondered just what he'd meant about Yillon's prediction of the awesome importance of one Human being.

Sixteen

As his kroi clicked, Rieka nodded at Finot and made more notations on her datapad. The routine, he'd told her, would be relatively simple. Prior experience with all the equipment helped, as well as a refresher course en route from Yadra. The trick would be in convincing everyone else she was just another tech-pro.

"Such a small weapon in the Eye of Mohn," Finot stated from behind the large podium that served as his desk.

"The Humans say, 'Never judge a book by its cover,' " Rieka recited, and was pleased to see the huge blue being angle his head and blink twice.

"I will venture to meet more Humans in the lines of the dawn," he replied. "The language speaks colorfully to my mind."

Seated in one of two large chairs in his office, Rieka willed herself not to smile at his delighted reaction. It was probably the only way the Boo would recognize her seriousness and dedication to the task at hand.

He'd already told her about Captain Pedlam. Finot's advice about not being alone with him made her chest feel tight. The "book cover" quote, she now saw, could be viewed on many levels.

"Not all Humans speak the same tongue, I'm afraid, sir."

"It is not a care to Varannah, Captain Degahv who is no longer." He clicked his kroi and blinked. "The roster speaks of a new reciprocal. Lieutenant Dra Mogin of Perata-Centauri. To the crest of the wave with you, it speaks. Impressive percentages. Panoply and DGI technician. Coincidental is it not?" Finot looked down at her.

She watched him, and it occurred to her that of all the races in the Commonwealth, only the Boos did not discriminate. They could certainly make life uncomfortable for someone on an individual basis, but never, as far as she knew, on a general one. Finot knew she was Human. Nason had made the arrangements before the *Providence* slid into its berthing dock.

"Coincidental?" she asked.

"A ship does not function well if it is blind. Even one with sharp teeth."

Rieka nodded. "Absolutely. This is my part for our ride back to Varannah."

He lifted one appendage and clicked his kroi in approval. "My new lieutenant is linear. My ears shall remain open." Finot inhaled from the chlorine tube. "I shall board you here, on the Little One in the Light, if you wish. Nason spoke not of this. I should not be calm on the river if you did not keep some axial time away from the *Prodigy*."

Rieka nodded. He was not only aware of the pending danger concerning the ship, he also felt responsible for her safety. While she wanted to spend as much time as possible taking the *Prodigy* and her crew apart, she realized sleeping in their midst could be asking for more trouble than was already afoot.

"I would like to stay with you here, on the Little One, Captain," she replied in the best way she knew how, "but I must have access to the ship as Dani has with her children. It would look . . . like an eclipse on the horizon—if I did not."

Finot considered her words and bowed. "Clear as the sky over Varannah, Captain. Unlimited access to all factors is granted."

"Who knows what is happening here at the Falls?" she asked.

"I. Your husband-captain, his first, and Twanabok. Only these."

"What of Captain DeVark?"

"His trajectory has eluded me of late. Nason has imparted orders to him. I shall equate this to his mind when next we meet."

She stood. "If there's nothing else then, sir, I'll be getting on with it."

"Negative. Stay," he said, the gravelly voice stopping her with a strange foreboding before she could move.

"What is it?" she asked.

"The *Prodigy* is not the only factor of the slide of the Procyon intent. Merely the catalyst. Is this not correct?"

"No one has said anything, but I've wondered that, myself."

"The quanta speaks to me," he rumbled.

Rieka felt her throat tighten. "What . . . does it say?"

Finot paused long enough for the constriction to work its way down to her ribs. Kroi clicked slowly. "Your elimination of the *Vendikon* undulates the facts. I have seen rough schematics of the vessel. It did not slide for long terms."

"No," she agreed. "I didn't think it did, myself. It was quite an enigma when I found it beyond the Eta Cass system."

"And now, the percentages of Procyons among us gives you no alarm?"

She shook her head and shrugged lightly. "Of course they do."

"A ship that cannot efficiently cheat time from space with quantum foam slides—does *not* travel faster than half lightspeed in real-space transit."

She nodded. That was given, unarguable fact. "—and their last-known homeworld is about forty light-years from Tau Ceti. I know. It's a huge amount of space to cross. Even at half-light it would have taken over eighty years. That just leaves a lot of questions, Captain."

"Negative." He made an odd gesture with his hand,

then clicked his kroi strangely. "More than one small ship has played on the Commonwealth."

"How do you know that?"

"Tyrinne, your chief of the *Venture* has imparted this to me."

Rieka slowly sat until she was perched at the edge of her chair. "When?"

"Under the command of the Tohab—who does not follow the equation. The *Venture* sat in orbit of Aurie some clicks ago. There were traces of particles in the wake of a ship."

"I'm not following you, Finot," Ricka admitted, frowning. "Tyrinne sent you a communiqué about particles she picked up in space somewhere near Aurie. So?"

"Specific particles," Finot explained. He blinked and angled his massive head at her. "New equipment on the *Prospectus* emits similar particles. I am unable to speak of this further."

"I'm afraid you've lost me." Rieka shook her head. "Can we get back to what I did understand? The *Vendikon*—"

"—did not come from a Procyon planet. And there are more in its sisterhood. The equation points to a facility."

"A base?" She allowed herself a moment to digest that fact, and a lot of things suddenly made sense. "Have you talked to Nason about this?"

"On his arrival will I. His mind functions are excessive at present. The *Venture* is now gone—added to the other side of the equation. And like the bridge from Whinn, after your intrusions, the Procyons will be allowed to take the faulty *Prodigy*. Two ships will not damage the Fleet's equilibrium. Many ships will."

"I still don't understand why Nason has elected to let it get that far. Why even give them the opportunity to take it at all?"

Finot made a sound with his kroi. "To the horizon this is exact," he replied. "But we see not the hidden valleys. When once the Procyons feel they can slide to

Varannah, all will be visible. Then we will know the Pzekii among us."

Rieka nodded. It *would* be much easier if the Procyon spies were known. And if they were facing a fleet of ships ready to be dispatched from a base that could be hidden just about anywhere, snatching the *Prodigy* wasn't just a last-minute attempt at overthrowing the Commonwealth, as previously thought. Capturing the big ship was either insurance that the offensive would work, or else it was another diversion. The Fleet's attention would be on the *Prodigy* while the Procyons executed their takeover. Either way, the future didn't look pleasant.

Rieka raked her too-short blond bangs from her forehead and let them fall where they might. She heaved a sigh and got to her feet. "I guess I'd better get started."

Finot remained silent as she walked to the door, then he said, "Warn you that I have felt something like the wind in the sail at Odran."

She stopped and turned, not wanting to hear more. His last insight would be giving her nightmares for a month.

He blinked. "I have sent positive word to our Nason, and it is most delicate." He paused and clicked his kroi once. "Like this Pzekii Pedlam, those on the ship that are not what they are . . ."

"Yes?"

"Are Centauri, not."

Rieka saw the room's skewed reflection in his gleaming black eyes and at the same time found herself lost in them.

"You mean the Procyons are disguising themselves exclusively as Centauris—not Humans or Aurians?"

"To my eyes."

She considered his observation and thought for a moment about the invaders' complex plan. How ironic that they'd chosen to hide themselves among the most sophisticated race in the Commonwealth. When one looked at it that way, considering the Procyon egocentric nature, it shouldn't be too hard to figure out the impostors.

She grinned. "The sediment below the Driel has more imagination than the Procyons."

While alien kroi clicked at the joke, Finot waved eloquently. "Humor is one way to reach Varannah, Captain. I shall be vigilant on the InterMAT."

Her smile faded at the sobering thought of having him pluck her from danger, but she pulled herself erect and saluted. "This Human thanks you."

On the way to the equipment lockers, Rieka felt a wave of something she could not quite recognize. Pride? Hypocrisy? Individuals of every race were looking her in the eye and nodding as she passed. Two ensigns actually saluted.

No one ever saluted me when I was Lieutenant Degahv, she thought perversely. Not unless it was a formal situation, and they had to.

She'd begun to accept the attention when she stepped into a Chute. Another passenger got in behind her. Rieka turned to face the door, routinely expecting him to move around her. Instead, they stood there for a moment, looking at each other until she realized the Aurian commander expected her to give way. Embarrassed, she took a large step back.

"Excuse me, sir. I—didn't know you were there."

He nodded at her and said nothing. Thankfully, the ride was short.

Trying not to look as awkward as she felt, Rieka located her assigned equipment locker, all the while watching for anyone over the rank of lieutenant.

The InterMAT chief at the port deposited her on the *Prodigy*'s platform, and she stepped from the chamber, wondering if someone was going to meet her. Because the ship was not yet spaceworthy, only a few TC channels functioned. She went to the console and manually activated the comnet.

"Communications, Lieutenant Blenda," a singsong voice replied.

"Lieutenant Mogin reporting for duty," Rieka stammered, trying to recall how junior officers conversed with their own. "I'm in Station Three. Have you got any idea where I'm supposed to report?"

A long moment of silence passed, and Rieka had to warn herself not to snap at Blenda's inefficiency. "Found you, Mogin," the voice said. "Kona ought to be there for you anytime now. We're running a little behind schedule today. Welcome aboard."

Silently, she wondered how the ship could be appropriated by Procyons or anyone else with a crew as haphazard as this. Or, maybe, that sloppiness was just what they were counting on.

Ensign Kona arrived, a tall, thin Human of African descent. Her welcoming smile seemed to cover her entire face, even touching her dark, almond-shaped eyes with a tacit sense of humor and grace. Rieka returned the brief salute and followed her into the corridor.

"I'm supposed to take you on a short tour, Lieutenant," Kona said, her voice bright and cheerful. "I hope you didn't want to get to work right away."

"Well, actually I did, Kona. Is there some purpose for the tour?"

The woman stopped when they reached a Chute door. "The *Prodigy* is huge, sir," she said. "We're all supposed to familiarize ourselves with not only where things are but how long it takes to get there."

Rieka nodded. It sounded reasonable. The door opened and she gestured to the ensign. "Lead on, then. I am all ears, you might say."

Kona relaxed quickly. She began chattering on about the research labs and recreation areas. They walked through holographic gardens and woods, had a brief peek at an ocean beach and a longer look at the immense gymnasium.

"This is almost the best thing about being assigned here," Kona said, grinning. "With such a large number of individuals confined in such a limited space—on

long research voyages, the psych experts insisted the
facilities were essential."

"It sure beats any other ship I've seen," Rieka
agreed.

They walked through the medical section, followed
by the maneuvering and defense center, and Rieka
began to get a realistic view of the *Prodigy*'s size.
There were forty thrusters and sixteen cannon along
the outer rim. It took them nearly ninety minutes to
walk the circuit.

As the Chute slid them back toward the main axis,
Kona said, "If you'd gotten here last week, I could
have taken you down to the gravity and antimatter
chambers—before they were activated. It's too bad.
That reactor is really something to see."

Rieka smiled grimly at the thought. Last week she
and Midrin were escaping from her own brother's
clutches. "Couldn't be helped, I'm afraid."

The Chute arrived at level two, quad four, section B,
and the energetic ensign led the way into the corridor. "Before you spend the next shift working the
panoply, how about some lunch, Lieutenant?" she asked.

"Okay." Kona had been an admirable tour guide. As
much as she itched to get her hands on the equipment,
Rieka took the opportunity to let a fellow Human know
she'd done a good job. The panoply could wait, and the
dining room wasn't crowded.

Time well spent, she thought to herself later, linking
up her equipment with the DGI net. She'd seen eight
Centauris at lunch whose behavior didn't follow proper
Centauri patterns. Two had growled at each other in
some kind of argument, and three had actually used
their fingers when eating. The others just seemed—out
of place. Using that base for her estimate, she figured
there were probably about thirty to forty Procyons in
disguise aboard. A lot more than she'd originally
guessed. If they were trained to run the ship, a crew
that size might be able to accomplish the job. But
Pedlam needed many more if he expected to engage the

Fleet in battle. She wondered what his plans were. Take the ship, make a few scheduled stops, then depart for Procyon territory? And what of the crew? That thought brought her back to the unknown fate of her own crew and the *Venture*'s whereabouts. Triscoe had promised to help her find them. She could only hope they would have the opportunity.

A voice broke her concentration. "I see that you've gotten right to work."

She turned, startled and nearly dropped her datapad. It was Pedlam. He looked exactly like his hologram. Even though she'd known the false Tohab, Rieka was amazed at the quality of the cosmetic reproduction.

Finot's warning sounded like a Klaxon in her head. This man was a Procyon. He looked less like who he really was than she did. And they were alone. She recovered quickly from her shock and saluted. "Captain."

"Lieutenant Mogin," he said sharply. "I was not informed that the panoply required repair."

"It doesn't, sir," she replied, then launched into her prepared speech. "Each DGI system must be properly integrated from the sensory equipment via the light conduit—and into each analysis unit. Then, the individual units must be checked for discrepancies between them and their counterparts elsewhere on the ship."

"Really?"

He seemed interested in her explanation, so she nodded and continued. "Take this infrared system, for example." She turned and taped the shoulder-high cabinet. "If the signals from the panoply are not tuned exactly to the idiosyncrasies of each DGI aboard, there is a good chance that the images will be off. They won't be wrong," she continued, "but the image will not be sharp. And when you're dealing with three dimensions, accuracy of resolution is essential."

"And the same for the other units?" he asked.

"Absolutely, sir. The navigation, screening, defense

boards—everything requires accurate integration from
the panoply. That is not to say they're off, now. I'm
just checking and doing some fine-tuning."

He nodded, and Rieka saw some of the stiffness go
out of his shoulders. She itched to get back to work but
stood at ease waiting for either more questions, or for
him to leave.

"Captain Finot speaks highly of you."

"I try very hard to do a good job, sir," she replied.

"I understand you have been on leave—which
explains your late arrival for work on the *Prodigy*."

"Yes, sir."

"Perata?"

She nodded curtly. "A death in the family, sir."

"A close relative?"

"My grandmother," she lied.

"I see. And how did you manage such a speedy
return trip?"

Rieka knew Finot had been right. The death of a
Centauri matriarch should have prompted this captain
to offer consolation, and yet Pedlam glanced over it as
though it were nothing important. She felt a twang of
vengeance for that imagined grandmother, and let
Pedlam think she was still grieving.

"Captain Finot expressed some urgency," she said.
"I caught the *Dorinne* from Indra and switched over to
the *Providence* at Yadra. We arrived this morning."

He nodded. Apparently she'd answered whatever
burning questions seethed in his Procyon mind. "Very
good. Let's hope there are no more distractions. As you
were, Lieutenant."

"A pleasure to meet you, Captain."

They saluted one another. He ambled off, and Rieka
thought she understood how the Boos could see through
the disguise. He appeared Centauri, and yet, like the
crew in the dining hall, if you watched closely, he
didn't. Centauris paid strict attention to etiquette. They
didn't growl, eat with their fingers, or ignore the death

of a matriarch. She wondered if they would all be as easy to distinguish.

Pedlam stopped at the door and turned. Rieka had already given her attention back to the readout on her datapad but, sensing his continued presence, looked up. "Was there something else, Captain?"

He watched her for a long moment. "Have we met before, Lieutenant?"

She allowed her face to look surprised, as in fact, she was. "Not to my knowledge, sir," she answered, finding her tongue. "My holofile is on record. Other than that, you might have met someone who looks like me. I would have remembered meeting you, sir."

He stood silently for a bit, then said, "Perhaps. Carry on, Lieutenant."

When he finally left, Rieka let out a breath she hadn't realized she'd held. Pedlam had recognized her, even with the change of hairstyle and skin color. He must have been party to the whole ordeal surrounding her and the *Vendikon*. It was only a matter of time until he figured out who she really was. Her phony records were as realistic as any and she hoped that, and maybe Finot, would put him off the trail.

When she looked back at the datapad, a strange feeling hit her. It was a sense of apprehension—alien and intrusive—as if someone else's concern had insinuated itself into her emotions. Rieka fought down her initial reaction, panic, while she tried to decide what to do. The alien touch was familiar, she realized. It reminded her of—

"—Triscoe!" she hissed softly. "I can't do this. Stop. If you can hear me, I can't hear you. Do you understand? I'm only feeling you, not hearing you, and it's . . . it's—well just stop."

Abruptly, the sensation was gone. She breathed a sigh of relief but knew he'd keep trying until they were able to communicate freely with their thoughts as they did during a Singlemind. If he triggered some unknown talent she possessed, then she would welcome that advantage. It was just such an alien, Centauri thing. It made her feel strangely self-conscious.

She turned back to the unit and spent the next ninety minutes working on DGI circuitry. Moving to the weapons unit, Rieka heaved a sigh and told herself the sooner she started on it, the sooner it would be complete.

Of course, the unit had been properly aligned and tested during the installation process. It would take her hours, though, to reprogram all the direct-feed lines while bypassing the indicators to the bridge. She figured three degrees wasn't much, but she had to set it so no one would realize the ship's aim was off. She hoped that small margin would be enough to make the difference.

"So, you haven't had the pleasure?" Robet asked.

Triscoe sat across from him at a table in one of the base's meeting rooms. Finot stood to the side on his three stubby legs, his black eyes double-blinking while he sucked thoughtfully on his tube. Silently, Triscoe noted the variations in Robet's bibbets and the Boo's silence.

"I haven't," he admitted. The *Providence* had only been docked for eight hours. Although Triscoe wanted to do more than look at the *Prodigy,* it seemed ill-advised to impose himself on Pedlam too quickly. Their plan required the changeling captain be kept complacent until he'd fallen into the trap. Calling on him too soon could jeopardize everything.

"Patience is a gift well kept," the Boo offered. "Pzekii must slide in it if you wish the gate to open. Otherwise, the equation is erred."

Triscoe did a double take at the reference to the infamous individual out of Boolian history. "Pzekii?"

Robet grinned. "Wait until you meet him. He puts on quite a show."

He said nothing, watching them both expectantly. Finot spoke first. "It is not advised to have bodily contacts with the Pzekii. Speak to him, yes, but claims of a schedule under the weight of the Big One will relax suspicion. Cool like the moon of Darna, is this one. I will provide all pertinent information."

"Such as?"

"Schematics, personnel, timetables, preparations for the gala, whereabouts of our Karina of the Rock."

"Karina of the—?"

"Captain Degahv's reciprocal, Lieutenant Mogin."

Triscoe nodded. He studied Robet's expectant look. Apparently, they'd anticipated some argument from him on this point. But he trusted both Rieka and Finot to do their jobs. If the Boo could not guarantee her safety, then he had nothing to fall back on save his faith in Yillon. He looked up into the pair of shiny black orbs, and said, "We'll keep—Karina on the Rock and be ready to catch her, should she fall."

Kroi clicked. "It is well. And now the other factor?"

Triscoe felt himself tense. "What other?"

Robet leaned over the table. "My new equipment works. The minute Nason got the report, he ordered Finot to refit the *Providence*."

"Why wasn't I told?"

"You were en route. But you're here now, everything's ready to go, right Cap'n?" Robet looked up at the Boo.

"It has been Rige at the edge of the Falls, but we are ready, now. Just," he advised, dipping his great head slightly as a bit of skin folded over one eye.

Triscoe had been told precious little about the *Prospectus*'s special equipment, and though Nason had every right to make such a decision, it bothered him that he hadn't been consulted. He brought his brows together. Considering the tight schedule they were under, now was not the time to be making renovations. The gala preceding the *Prodigy*'s commission would begin in forty hours. The following morning, the vessel would be dedicated and begin its first outbound assignment.

"What kind of work does this involve?" he asked.

"Simplicity," Finot replied. "I shall have my people

begin immediately, in your radical. There will be a realignment of the gravitation assembly and screening apparatus. Additional factors will be installed." He looked pensive for a moment, if that could be described of Boos. "By gala time—if we start of the first breath in the hall."

"It's worth it," coaxed DeVark.

"All right. But how long will it take to retrain my people? And what is the advantage of this new gear?"

"Only a few hours to train the crew," Robet replied, his bibbets altering to a pleasant pink. "Memta should pick it up pretty fast. And I guarantee you'll be thrilled with what this stuff can do, Tris. It's absolutely amazing. I didn't believe it myself until I had proof."

"But what *does* it do?" Triscoe repeated, finding himself unpleasantly on the edge of his temper.

"It creates an alteration of gravity," Finot said.

"So?"

DeVark grinned. "It bends light—around your ship. All the way around, Tris. It'll make the *Providence* invisible."

"Commander Durak, come," K'resh-va said, receding from the door and gesturing the man to enter. He glanced into the corridor before turning to follow his guest. "Sit. We might as well partake of the customs of the people we've replaced."

The commander-in-Centauri-clothing offered his captain a brief smile. "Some customs are not so bad," he agreed, "though I don't think I will miss them much."

K'resh-va made a distinctly Procyon sound in his throat. "These creatures are *druul*, O'don-la," he said, sneering. "But they possess wealth."

"For the moment."

"True." K'resh-va sat across from his first officer. He watched his companion silently for a long moment, looking for weakness. There appeared to be none. O'don-la had been chosen and trained well for his role. It was too late now, K'resh-va realized, to worry about any faults that might have gone unnoticed.

"I have just received an installment from the other," he said, fingering the bands of silver on his sleeve. "I thought it would interest you to hear what she has to say."

"It would, Captain."

K'resh-va nodded and went to the desk to collect his datapad. He slipped the chip into the box and activated the play button as he sat on the cushion beside his officer.

L'gith-la's Centauri face appeared on the small screen. "Captain. Greetings. All is well here, as I am sure it is with you. As planned, we acknowledged contact with Medoura before departing the system on the dark side of Groot. Presently, I am at Radjie base in the process of taking on personnel."

The image shifted. She had edited an addendum to the report. He scratched absently at the pale, short-cropped hair over his left ear. "Sir, K'din-va has notified me that all is in readiness. He wishes me to request a timetable from you—to be sent directly to him, as that involves limited risk of discovery. He insists upon precise synchronization.

"I anticipate your arrival. Until then, L'gith-la."

The image stilled, and K'resh-va switched off the datapad. "Three days," he said, the light of victory in his voice, "and we shall change the course of history. Never have we undertaken an objective of such immensity. So ripe. So easy." His eyes widened, and there was an almost-hypnotic, glowing energy emanating from them as he painted his picture of the future.

"O'don-la, you and I will be renowned heroes for our people. We will give them sustenance and riches for centuries to come. We will be honored as no Acquisitors have before us."

K'resh-va let his voice harden then, and his eyes grew cold. "I count upon your ever-present assistance as Commander Durak," he warned. "You will keep the crew in line. You will maintain the ship. When the time comes, you will coordinate the transfer of the Boos on the base to the *Prodigy*. And, despite the fact that E'bid-va thinks he is in charge here, you will follow *my* orders. Is that understood?"

"Completely, sir," O'don-la said. "Everything will go according to your specifications."

"Of course." K'resh-va stood. "If it doesn't, not only will you be absent from the history books and verses, you will be absent altogether."

O'don-la got to his feet and nodded curtly. "If there is nothing else, Captain."

"Dismissed."

The man walked to the door and turned. "The Fleet has been quiet," he observed. "As I understand it, the *Venture*'s departure from Yadra carried with it some rumors, but they are fading. There is no word on the whereabouts of the missing Degahv or Tohab. Do you think they suspect?"

K'resh-va's head snapped up. "Possibly, if someone makes inquiries, but that is unlikely. E'bid-va's intensive survey of the area on Yadra turned up nothing but three bones. Oph bones are harder for bolwins to digest than Centauri or Human ones. I think they will trouble us no more. By the time Degahv is considered missing by the Fleet, we will be in control."

"Undoubtedly." O'don-la turned toward the door.

"However," K'resh-va said quickly, "it is a fool who regards anything as a sure thing. Keep an ear out when among these people. I want to know if suspicions are circulating."

The commander nodded. "As you wish."

When he left, K'resh-va slowly walked the floor, considering the possibility that they had been perceived. The prospect had to be examined even though there was no evidence of such a discovery. He considered the ridiculous Boo captain and the equal buffoon in the one called DeVark, deciding neither posed a threat. But the Centauri, Marteen, was at Dani now.

K'resh-va had wanted to match wits with him for some time. That type of confrontation, he reminded himself, would simply have to wait.

Then, taking a different tack on his dissection of Fleet personnel he had come in contact with recently, K'resh-va recalled the young lieutenant in charge of the panoply. She'd come to Dani on the *Providence*.

Again, Marteen's image flashed across his mind.

Perhaps, he decided, he could spare some time to meet the honorable captain, for one should always know as much as possible about one's enemy.

Rieka spent a restless night in her quarters. Pounding her pillow didn't begin to relieve the feeling of being caught in the middle of something beyond her control. From the moment she'd been released into Triscoe's custody, everything about her life had changed. But this was different. She had no idea of the Procyons' plans—or of Admiral Nason's. She felt lost and uneasy.

The emotion triggered frightening childhood memories of electrical storms on Yadra. What she felt now was similar to her fear then: a tightening in her chest, a sense that time had somehow slowed. Chalking it up to that indefinable trait known as Human intuition, Rieka decided something awful was about to happen.

Since Admiral Nason had insisted she report every day, Rieka followed his order religiously, using the comlink in the room Finot had given her. She had wanted to access a scramble code to avoid any risk of someone's eavesdropping or getting curious about such an important communiqué, but decided against it. To do that would simply draw attention to herself. Even so, her Aurian roommate, Tivan, hadn't been easy to elude when she made the recordings. Rieka hoped the admiral would understand the lack of privacy and be searching for any bits of pertinent information. Fortunately, nothing much happened on her first shift—save that conversation with Pedlam.

She woke early and unrefreshed. Tivan was still asleep, so she washed, trying to ignore the thicket of synthetic hair over her abdomen, and dressed quietly before escaping the tiny suite. Once in the moon base complex, Rieka relaxed. Finot had alerted his security chief, Klin, to keep an eye on her. Divorced from her companions as she was, she found some comfort in that.

After a quick breakfast, she headed for the engineering lab to collect the tools and datapad she had used the day before. Everything was exactly as she'd left it in the lightweight carry sack from yesterday. She slid one strap over her shoulder, then headed for the nearest InterMAT station. Today she required no tour and felt comfortable about finding her way around the huge ship.

Transfer complete, Rieka was surprised at the amount of activity in the InterMAT station.

"Move along, there, Lieutenant," a red-faced man dressed in civilian clothing said. "I have a strict schedule, and I am not about to deviate from it because of you."

Others, equally civilian in appearance, bustled with boxes and carts. Most appeared to be incoming. She backed off the platform and away from the control unit and found Ensign Kona overlooking the chaos from her place near the door.

"What's going on?"

"The dedication," Kona replied with an open-handed gesture while trying to coax her face to smile. "We're going to have dignitaries all over the place in the next thirty hours. This is the advance rush."

Rieka looked at the mayhem and back to Kona. "Advance . . . what?"

"Oh, they're going to use this dedication as an excuse for a lot of business deals. To put it in Human terms, these are a lot of bribes and gifts and—"

"I get the idea, Kona," Rieka said. "Insurance." She hefted the strap higher on her shoulder and sidestepped a man wielding a large crate.

"Exactly! You must have a lot of Human friends, Lieutenant."

Rieka treated her to a smile. "As a matter of fact, I'm very close to a Human or two." She gestured to the tall man who seemed to be in charge. "And the captain doesn't mind having civilians aboard?"

"No choice on that one, I'm afraid," Kona said quietly. "We'll be swamped with them until we ship out. The *Prodigy*'s extremely newsworthy right now. We're the social event of the year."

Rieka gave her a wary stare. "How many people are we talking about?"

Kona shrugged. "A lot. My list has over 150, including Heralds' staff. But it's growing every hour. Like I said, opportunity is the watchword for the next few days."

"No doubt about it." She clapped Kona lightly on the shoulder. "You're busy, and I've got to get to work."

"See you later, Lieutenant."

Rieka nodded and left. She didn't expect to see Kona very soon, not with all those people around. The statuesque ensign would be hustling until the *Prodigy* cast off her moorings and slid out into stellar space.

I certainly hope the admiral has some way to keep all the higher-ups off this ship, she thought, adjusting the strap on her shoulder again. It would be insanity to allow the false Pedlam to get anywhere near them, much less allow him to play host. Trying to recall just exactly what Nason had said during the briefing, Rieka found that he'd told them very little of his own plans.

Perhaps it was better that way. Not necessarily safer for the entire scheme, but better for the individuals and the parts they had to play. She hoped he'd let Finot in on it. Because they were so intent on knowing all the facts and maintaining a sense of equality, no one she knew had ever successfully crossed a Boo.

Rieka laughed to herself at the thought of one of those solid blue mountains being influenced by a bouquet of flowers, but not a madman with a maitu. They were quirky, to be sure, but predictably quirky.

She let that thought go, still considering the implications of so many important people on board, when she got to the second level of the electrical section. It was time to begin the day's sabotage of the *Prodigy*'s weapons system.

Seventeen

Nason had just gotten to work in his quarters aboard the C.F.S. *Purview* when the door chime sounded. He grimaced at the annoyance, then pulled himself from scrutinizing the *Prodigy*'s itinerary and shut down the datapad. "Yes?"

The door opened to reveal Setana Marteen. "May I come in, Admiral?" she asked. "I have no wish to disturb you."

He rose to greet her. "Please, Herald. Disturb me. The monotony of information processing certainly can be set aside for an audience with you."

She smiled. "I shall take that as a compliment." Entering, the Herald toured the room at a leisurely pace. "Identical to my lodgings."

Nason smiled. "Not very imaginative, our architects," he agreed. "But it does lend a sense of continuity."

"Even to the wall dressings."

"Sit down, Herald," Nason said, sweeping an arm toward a chair. "Can I offer you a beverage?"

"Thank you, not at the moment, Merik," she replied, perching delicately on a cushion.

That she had used his first name here in private explained a bit about her purpose for the visit. Nason settled into a chair across from her and waited.

"Well?"

She smiled and busied her hands with smoothing the folds of her pale blue tunic. "Not even, 'How are you,

Setana?' or 'How are things on Indra?' I do hope you have no interest in interplanetary diplomacy."

"None at all," he admitted with a grin. "No time for such foolishness, I'm afraid. I've spent too many years ordering people around. I have little patience for the art of convincing them to do what I want."

She tapped her chin twice and opened her palm. An Indran gesture involving the futility of speech. "It is often difficult to say what we mean," she admitted. "And it is so important, at other times, *not* to say what we mean." Her dark eyes glimmered beneath blond brows.

He smiled and relaxed slightly. It wasn't hard to understand how this woman had come to possess such total, yet discreet, authority. Properly chastised, he asked, "How are you, Setana?"

"I am well. I am expecting Ker to join me in three hours when we rendezvous with the *Arlich*."

"The prefect?" Aurian brows lifted toward pink bibbets. "That's a surprise."

"It isn't really, to me," she admitted, smiling faintly. "Ker is not pleased with Triscoe's matrimonial state. Livid, in fact. An affront to his dignity, you see. I expect he'll take this opportunity to plead his case to both of us."

"But certainly Triscoe wouldn't divorce Rieka. It's unheard of among Indrans." Nason leaned forward, his curiosity piqued at her unenviable position.

She shrugged. "Ker tends to be headstrong," she said softly. "Without me, he often jumps to conclusions. How fortunate, for him, that historical art is about society rather than individuals. Our housekeeper told me he said some incredibly offensive things. To Triscoe. About his wife. To her face."

Nason grimaced. He'd known the *Providence* had visited both Centauri-A planets. It hadn't occurred to him they'd seen the prefect. Familiar with both Ker's temper and Degahv's temperament, he belatedly wished he'd been present.

"So, what do you think he wants?"

"He wants to be seen on my arm at the dedication."

"No, I mean about Rieka."

"Oh. Well, quite simply, he wants to be rid of her," Setana replied. "He's said as much to me at least half a dozen times. Now, he plans to do so in person. It's as simple and as complicated as that. Can you imagine the insult? The embarrassment?" she jibed, sliding a hand to her throat with mock concern. "A Human has become a member of his extended family."

She made a tsking sound and laughed lightly. "Unfortunately for Ker, it is simply too bad that *I* am the one he seeks to influence. The man is so childish in certain things, it becomes rather funny."

Nason leaned back in his chair, satisfied she had the situation well in hand. "So, you've already played out the conversation in your head?"

"Naturally. He's brought the subject up on his last three communiqués."

"You going to ignore him, then?"

"No." Her smile, though not artificial, was just barely perceptible. Fine bones set off the slight curve of her lips but it seemed to Nason that Setana's eyes were laughing out loud. "I believe I'll tell him. Everything."

Nason straightened his spine. His felt his bibbets darken. "You mean about—?"

"My visit to your office when Triscoe hadn't yet decided to join the Fleet? I don't think so, Merik. You will not bear the brunt of one of Ker's tempers. I value your friendship too much for that. But I will tell him why I insisted our youngest son take the Fleet entry examinations. And I will tell him upon whose advice the decision was made."

Nason could only guess what she was talking about. "You don't mean—?"

"Yillon? Yes. The Oracle counseled me all those years ago—and now I believe the time is right to tell Ker. That should be sufficient to remind him of who is in charge of the family. He'll be allowed his opinion, of course. But it simply won't matter much . . . considering the scheme of things."

Nason shook his head. "Like to play with fire, do you?"

This time, she did laugh. "I am the Indran Herald, Merik. It is what I do best."

They enjoyed the joke for a moment, grinning like a pair of precocious children, before she sobered. "I have spoken to Yillon as you requested."

Nason could feel the hair prickle at the back of his neck. The Oracle was such a legendary thing that even the mention of it was staggering. It seemed too old, too hallowed to actually be a living person. "And?"

"I regret I do not possess the proper words to adequately explain his position, Merik," she apologized. He watched as, frowning slightly, the Herald concentrated on her hands. "Yillon has tried to penetrate this future you wish to know, but it is murky. Sometimes this happens. There are simply too many variables to see clearly what is transpiring on the horizon."

"But—"

She raised a palm to interrupt him. "There are specifics. Just a few. You should send reinforcements to the Cassiopeia star group. He mentioned Groot, in the Eta system."

Nason nodded. "The *Venture* was last seen in that vicinity. It's relatively close to the point where Rieka encountered the Procyon ship. This is exactly the type of information I was looking for."

"Consider the *Venture* hostile."

"No doubt," he agreed. "Midrin Tohab was replaced by a double who took every opportunity to throw blame at Degahv. After the last incident with the *Providence,* when Rieka was exiled to Creyunne Province, she found the real Tohab nearly starved to death. Fortunately, Centauris bounce back quickly. I'm bringing her with me to Dani."

He was amazed that Setana didn't find the story

shocking. She sat there listening and nodding now and then. "The Procyons probably think they've found an easy way to slip in and out of the Commonwealth."

"Medoura is a member world," she reminded him.

"But not an actively political one. The Medourans broke apart their central government half a century ago. It takes them years even to elect a Herald. With the clans running amok, it's no wonder the Procyons are coming at us from that direction. They'll be easy pickings."

"So I have brought you something you can use." It was a statement.

"Yes. Yes, you have." He frowned, thinking ahead of himself. Eta Cass had been on his mind since the *Vendikon* incident. "But can you tell me anything about the *Prodigy*?"

She sagged slightly. "I am sorry, Merik. Truly. Yillon explained that the huge number of persons involved in this—down to people like Ker—make the variables too complex to even grasp one point of clarity. He foresees a battle of some kind, in space, with ships that aren't there and blindness and confusion."

She made an ineffectual gesture with her hand. "You see how difficult it is to explain it, much less watch it unfold from a position in the past." She shook her head and repeated the gesture of tapping her chin and opening her palm. "*Brinduli ka*. Especially to one who does not even possess a *quantivasta*-gift. I'm afraid it isn't much. But it is the best he could do."

"It's plenty, Setana." Nason smiled. He leaned across the space between them and patted her hand reassuringly with his. "I'll send five ships to Eta Cass. That'll keep the Procyon reinforcements at bay. The *Providence* and *Prospectus* will remain at Dani, in the event Pedlam tries something before we're ready. And, I can bring others off their routes, if need be. We may actually be getting the upper hand, here."

"I am glad you see it that way," she said. "And now, I shall leave you to your business. I hope I can count on

you for some sort of diversion with Ker once he gets
here?"

"Of course," Nason said, following her example and
getting to his feet. "He plays Cranbonie, doesn't he?
There's nothing like an easy mark."

She shook her head. "You're insufferable, Merik. A
typical gentleman rogue."

Nason nodded, accepting the insult. "And you
wouldn't have it any other way."

Triscoe leaned against a small console in the *Providence*'s engineering suite. He rubbed his eyes, then
looked at the pair of large blue aliens who were telling
him things he didn't want to hear.

"Are you sure you have to take the gravity off-line?"

Memta sucked a breath of chlorine. "Not long to the
square of the light on the horizon."

"But we're already working under—"

"Captain," Finot said, adding a light click of his kroi,
"the gravity must go. In order to find the smile of
Varannah before the square, we make sacrifices."

"How long?"

"Six. Six-and-twenty. Not long, Captain."

Triscoe shrugged. He knew he'd been outmaneuvered. "I'll have V'don make the announcement."

"Well spoken," Finot said. He then spoke rapidly to
Memta in their native language of clicks and other odd
noises.

Triscoe left the suite. Almost immediately his TC
switched on. "Marteen."

"Welcome to Dani, Captain," a roughly familiar
voice said in his ear.

"Thank you."

"I thought you'd have insisted on a tour by now."

"Problems, Pedlam," Triscoe replied, trying to keep
his tone conversational. It was difficult, since the man
couldn't possibly be Val Pedlam. "We took an awful
beating near Aurie."

"So I heard. So I heard. What's your agenda?"

"The engineers are taking gravity off-line for the next ten hours," Triscoe replied, deciding to let the spy think repairs were costing him ten hours of gravity, not new equipment.

"That's not too bad," Pedlam's voice soothed.

"Only the beginning." Triscoe nodded to a crewman as he ambled down the sloping corridor. "We've got two weeks of hull and systems repairs ahead of us."

"Sounds like you are lucky you made it here, at all."

"You don't know how right you are," Triscoe agreed.

"Any chance, once the repair crews start working, that you'll have a minute or two to spare for an old friend?"

Triscoe paused. His old friend was probably dead. That thought passed quickly while he tried to decide how to respond. The crews had already begun their work on the hull and patched up vital systems damaged in the battle with the *Venture*. "Does this have anything to do with that tour you mentioned?"

"Absolutely," Pedlam said. "I'm off my regular shift now. Preparations for both the dedication and departure are moving along smoothly. I shouldn't be needed unless there's an emergency."

"And you'd like nothing better than to show off that new ship of yours," Triscoe muttered.

"Exactly."

"Let me check in with the bridge, and I'll let you know what time to expect me."

The voice in his ear seemed to relax a fraction. "You do that, Tris. Pedlam, out."

Rieka stepped from the Chute onto the *Prodigy*'s lower level. Studying her datapad, she passed two crewmen and took a left into a short corridor that ended in a door. She went through it, tapping the small computer's surface, and waited for the details she'd requested. She was still frowning at the device, oblivious to her surroundings, when a voice startled her.

"State your business, Lieutenant."

Her head snapped up and Rieka instantly realized she wasn't where she thought. A desk sat in front of her, security doors flanking it on both sides. Through a clear wall she saw a half dozen three-sided cubicles. Silently, Rieka wondered why the detention area needed to be powered up and manned while still in the dock. Did the Procyons think a tiny center such as this would take care of anyone who found them out? Didn't they simply kill them?

Trying not to show surprise—other than the fact that she was lost, Rieka looked blankly at the lieutenant behind the desk. "This isn't the weapons systems lab, is it?" she said, grimacing at the obvious.

He shook his head. It seemed somehow insulting.

"And here I thought I had this damn ship figured out." She ignored him and reconfigured the datapad. "Here it is. Third level. Quadrant D. A right out of the Chute and the first left." She looked at him. "That's exactly right here where I'm standing, Lieutenant." Her expression defied him to argue with the facts.

The Aurian man's bibbets flushed the palest of pink, and he seemed to be trying not to smile at her frustration. He looked neither angry nor distressed as he came around the desk and peered over her shoulder at the small map she'd called up on the screen.

"Decrease the magnification," he said.

"I don't see how—" But then, she did. There was an extra Chute exit in the engineering section she'd forgotten about. If she'd taken a left, instead of a right, she would not have ended up in the brig. "I swear this ship is out to get me," Rieka groused.

"You're not the only one, Lieutenant . . ."

"Dra Mogin," she finished.

"You're not the only one, Dra. This happens half a dozen times a shift." He smiled and looked into her eyes. "What you need to remember is to use a lesser magnification. Then the Chute doors will be more obvious."

"Thanks."

"Preshun. Lieutenant Lan Preshun."

He kept watching her and the color of his bibbets deepened. Not wanting to insult a new acquaintance, she offered a contrite smile. "Sorry to disturb you, Preshun. Thanks for the help." She turned to go but was stopped by his voice.

"Can we have dinner sometime?"

She pivoted, wondering if she could capitalize on this situation. He felt no compunction about asking a Centauri for a date. But Rieka knew with bitter certainty that if he'd met a Human Mogin, he would have said nothing more. "Dinner? I—"

"And, I could give you a tour, later. There's a holographic forest in the rec area that, well—it's very private."

"You don't say?"

His bibbets darkened. "You really shouldn't miss it."

"I suppose not."

"Just say the word."

"Thanks, Preshun," she said, having no intention of following through. "Look me up once we're under way, though. I don't have as relaxing an assignment as you. I won't be very good company until I know my system's taken care of."

"I'll look forward to it." His leer offered many silent promises.

"Oh, and you'll probably want to concentrate on your post instead of me, for the next few minutes—in case someone else walks in. Your bibbets are as dark as my boots."

Grinning to herself, Rieka escaped the brig in two strides, and felt his eyes stay on her until the door closed.

She'd just turned down the correct hallway when her name was called by a voice that sent her heart pounding.

"Lieutenant Mogin."

She stopped and looked up from the tiny computer.

"Captain." Then, noticing Triscoe in tow, she corrected herself and saluted. "Captains."

"Still working?" Pedlam asked after returning the gesture.

"I've finished the DGI system's main unit, sir," she began. "I was finding my way to the lab on this level. Captain Finot gave me a test program. It takes several hours—I thought it would be easier if I started it up now and let it run while I was off duty."

"Pragmatic as ever, Lieutenant."

"Thank you, sir," she said, biting her tongue.

"Have you met Captain Marteen?"

"On the *Providence*," she replied, looking respectfully at Triscoe. "It's nice to see you again, sir."

He nodded. "My pleasure, Lieutenant. I see you got right to work."

"Captain Finot had a long list of things to be done," she said. "I'm not going to get too many free hours before the *Prodigy* leaves Dani. I'm grateful you could get me here as soon as you did."

"I was happy to be of service."

She looked at them both. "Well, if you'll excuse me, sirs, I'd really like to get set up and see how many bugs I've got left."

"Key me a report once you get the results."

"Yes, sir." She nodded curtly at them both, saluted, and escaped into the lab. She had never thought to meet Triscoe on the *Prodigy*. It unsettled her. She wondered how he'd managed to stay so cool himself.

Taking a few deep breaths, Rieka located the appropriate console and locked her datapad into the connector. The unit took only a moment to read the information from her computer. When the square on the faceplate lit with the word: "Ready," she unsnapped the datapad and touched the indicator on the console, commanding the program to run. If anyone called up the test results in her absence, the unit would give them a false report of flying colors. Only her small computer could detect the sabotage.

While Rieka stood there watching it run, she couldn't help but wonder if they were doing the right thing by letting the Procyons have their way for another day or two, perhaps longer. Why didn't the admiral just make some kind of announcement and postpone the dedication? Knowing she'd never get an answer without confronting Nason, and perhaps not even then, Rieka checked the program status one last time, then left the lab.

K'resh-va allowed a toothy Procyon smirk to surface as he looked at himself in his mirror. He'd spent the last two hours with Marteen, and, although he found the man knowledgeable, there was no hint of suspicion. If Marteen was worried about anything other than his wife's whereabouts, K'resh-va would have sensed it.

But Marteen seemed obsessed with the search and rescue of Degahv. After they'd crossed paths with Mogin, the conversation had turned from ships, transport schedules, and cargo, to women. Marteen admitted that he'd found a conspiracy made up of Human-haters who had gone to great lengths to discredit Degahv. He seemed genuinely disturbed at her disappearance and reasonably upset that the repairs to his ship were going to take weeks instead of days. He doubted the *Venture* had been under her command when it attacked the *Providence,* but could prove nothing. Until his refit was complete, he would be forced to bide his time and try to enjoy the festivities involving the *Prodigy*'s commission.

K'resh-va chuckled at his reflection. The captain was so close to the truth and yet so far away. He imagined the expression on the Centauri's face when he found out his beloved bride had ended her days as bolwin fodder. Or, better yet, the agonies he would suffer during the Procyon invasion.

It mattered little either way to K'resh-va. Marteen was an insect to be squashed like the rest, while he himself basked in sweet victory.

Durak's earlier comments, however, made him pensive. Even if Marteen, engrossed in his ship and his wife, was not suspicious, someone else might be. Despite what E'bid-va thought, a covert investigation could be in progress. Certainly, the Fleet's Internal Affairs Department was not the only means for intelligence gathering.

K'resh-va considered what action could be taken by a Fleet officer who might have believed Degahv or Marteen. Not wanting to arouse attention, they would choose an individual able to gain access to sensitive areas without generating suspicion. Or, they could send someone whose presence would seem completely routine. He forced himself to accept that they were clever enough to use the same tactics as any decent Procyon.

K'resh-va frowned and went to the desk. He crossed an ankle over a knee and tapped at his datapad. After a few moments, he realized most everyone he'd met in recent days could not possibly be a spy. He rested his fingers on the compact computer's black surface and something seemed to click in his mind.

That lieutenant he'd run across today near the weapons lab. Mogin. She was bright and dedicated. But something about her did not seem right. He could not think what, but there was a discrepancy somewhere.

Purposefully, he requested access to the *Prodigy*'s main computer. "Give me the file on Lieutenant Mogin."

A moment later, his screen filled with the familiar information. He's seen it before. The Centauri female's hologram sat in the upper right corner, personal statistics below. She was thirty-four years old. Born on Perata and raised, from the age of ten, on the system's sister planet, Indra. She successfully completed the required courses at the academy on Yadra and had served for ten years on various ships and ports. Two years ago, Finot discovered her talents, and she transferred to the Little One.

Mogin had one brother with no interest in the Fleet.

She was single. Of above average intelligence and psychologically stable.

K'resh-va went over the details four times before he realized the anomaly, if it could be called that. The woman was bright, capable, and good at her job. She was Centauri, not Human. So why was she thirty-four years old and still a lieutenant?

He felt his arms tingle. Now was not the time to jump to conclusions. He wondered what she had done to be passed over for promotion—and how it had been covered up. Certainly, she must be unhappy with how the Fleet treated her. Judging Mogin's sentiments by her file, K'resh-va realized this woman might be bought. And he could always use an expendable tech-pro in the event the *Prodigy* required repairs after a battle.

Allowing himself a low growl, K'resh-va decided to pursue the possibility of buying the lieutenant's loyalty.

After Nason's latest communiqué, Robet could not keep himself from wondering if everything was going as smoothly as he'd been told. With the Procyons crawling all over the *Prodigy,* but no solid evidence of their plans unearthed, he felt justifiably concerned. While Robet trusted Rieka to get her job done, he had misgivings about the few facts they'd managed to collect regarding the number of Procyons on board.

Nason had asked him to work with Commander Klin, the Little One's security chief. He'd already offered himself and his crew to ensure the safety of the dignitaries attending the dedication. Nason had also empowered him to use his judgement and take whatever precautions he deemed necessary, even if it involved overruling Klin.

That order gave him reason to worry not only for the incoming political and business personalities, but for the innocent Fleet personnel that had been assigned to

the big ship. They could be used in some twisted way
to gain much more than a single vessel.

Robet decided to call on Klin again, and make plans
for other, less pleasant contingencies. Klin didn't miss
much with regard to what went on within his jurisdiction. Robet felt confident that, as far as the base was
concerned, things could be kept under control.

Klin was not in his office, as usual. The secretary, an
extremely large Vekyan, shook her head at his inquiry
as to Klin's whereabouts. "It is sixteen-hundred, Captain," she told him as if that explained it all.

"Yes, I know," he replied, smiling. "And I must
speak with Commander Klin. Where can I find him?"

Her head seemed to be on a pivot. "The commander
is never available at sixteen hundred, Captain."

Robet saw little amusement in her static monologue.
"I'll ask you one more time," he warned slowly, giving
his bibbets a chance to turn very dark. "Where is Commander Klin? This is a matter of base security."

Her lavender eyes grew wide and seemed unable to
decide whether to focus on his face or brow line. "The
nursery," she whispered, a great reluctance and huskiness in her voice. "Please do not tell him it was I who
sent you."

Confused by the secretary's response, Robet said
nothing. He turned on his heel and, wondering what on
Aurie Klin was doing in the nursery, hurried to the
nearest lift.

A few minutes later he found the Vekyan commander hovering over a table topped with a thick layer
of fine pink sand. "Klin?" he asked. "What are you
doing down here?"

Klin's head snapped up. Robet thought he had a distinctly guilty look on his leathery green face. "I am
awaiting the Emergence, Captain," he said slowly. "It
was not the intended time for the cycle, but one can do
little to fight the currents of Nature. Six are buried
there in our native sand." He reached and traced a pattern with the talons of one hand. "Of course an atten-

dant will notify me when the event occurs—so that bonding may proceed. But I visit them, regardless. It seems the reasonable thing to do."

"Of course." Robet smiled. "I didn't mean to disturb you. It's just that I've got a few questions about security aboard the *Prodigy*—for when the Heralds are aboard. Have you got that all worked out or—"

"That is not within my jurisdiction," Klin said bluntly. He raised a pair of talons and clicked them.

Robet frowned. "Who told you that?"

"Captain Pedlam. I approached him last week with a schedule and list of my people that would be augmenting his crew." The thick skin around his mouth puckered, indicating confusion. "I was told his crew had no need for additional help. The proceedings are to be held in the gymnasium. Small groups will be taken on tours following the speeches."

Robet nodded. He'd been told as much. "But none of your people are needed? Don't you think that's a bit strange?"

"Perhaps. Pedlam said his crew was large, and he had many men to spare."

"I'll bet he did." Robet mumbled to himself and patted the sand. "I'll see you later, and we'll go over the schedule. Good luck with your hatchlings, Klin."

"Thank you, Captain."

As he left the nursery, Robet realized that Finot might know about the security discrepancy. But, he might not. It was not the Base captain's job to make sure social events were properly staffed—especially if they weren't even located on the Little One.

Knowing he did not exactly have the authority to do what he had planned, Robet decided that was the beauty of it. He would be on and off the big ship in a matter of minutes, anyway. If he discovered something important, the risk was worth it. No one knew what the Procyons had in mind. Did they simply want the *Prodigy*? Would they kidnap the Heralds, too? Kill everyone? Even one clue could lead him to all the answers.

He found an InterMAT chamber, transported, and had to step back quickly to make room for an individual carrying yards and yards of blue fabric.

"Excuse me," the person said, pushing past him and hurrying down the corridor.

Cautiously, he stepped out and ambled down the *Prodigy*'s sloping corridor. With so many people coming and going, he figured no one would question why he was aboard. And if someone did, he could claim an appointment with Pedlam and ask directions as to how to find him.

He walked down the meridian, the designation defining starboard and port, and noticed two Boos in the hallway. On the aft ship one expected to see them, but it seemed odd to find two standing in the hallway. He nodded as he passed and strolled on.

Recalling Finot's detailed tour, Robet easily found the security office near the electrical section. Entering casually, he smiled at the Centauri lieutenant standing behind the counter.

"Captain," the man said, "may I help you?"

"Thank you." Robet stepped closer and leaned on the desk. "I was just talking to Commander Klin, who told me Captain Pedlam has taken charge of security for the day after tomorrow. I realize he's busy. But, I need to verify it, myself. Is that possible?"

"Certainly," the man replied. He consulted the computer console, tapping a great many more areas than Robet thought necessary before finding the file.

"Two teams of three each are scheduled for both gymnasium entrances. Three guards will be posted at each InterMAT station. All five stations, that is. The dignitaries will only be using two. And there will be one guard accompanying each tour." He looked up. "Is there anything else?"

"That sounds fine. I suppose the admiral will accept that."

"The admiral?" He glanced behind Robet to the door.

"Yes," he replied easily, wondering who the man was expecting. "Nason asked me to check on security. I'm sure you were notified."

"I had no word of such an inquiry, Captain," the lieutenant replied. He looked suddenly anxious, peered down at his console, then at the door. "The admiral is not mentioned, here. Should I have a report copied for you? For him? It is of utmost importance that I avoid any sort of error, you understand. No miscommunications, whatever."

Robet lightly slapped the counter and smiled. He could not tell if this man was a Procyon, but he was certainly acting strangely for an apparently capable officer. His suspicions had paid off. It was time for a chat with Nason. "I'm sure there's no need to worry, Lieutenant," Robet said. "Everything will turn out just fine."

"Undoubtedly," he heard a voice say. He clicked on his TC and turned quickly, but the stun from the maitu claimed his consciousness.

Eighteen

Nason looked up into Finot's black eyes, wondering if a Boo said everything he knew. "And how goes the trek to Varannah?"

Finot paused for a moment, as if trying to decide the best way to speak his mind. He double-blinked and puckered a patch of skin over one of his huge eyes. "The equation is not balanced, Admiral," he said finally.

Nason held his breath, nodded, and took the seat opposite the huge being's lecternlike desk. "How is it that we are in error?" he asked quietly. That Finot had found something disturbing enough to bring up in the first five minutes of his arrival made him momentarily forget to control his bibbets. Feeling them swell, he took a few deep breaths.

"Pzekii has been search—"

"Who?"

"Our Centauri captain who is not. The Pzekii among us," Finot explained.

Nason nodded. "I see. You've given him an infamous nickname. How charming."

"The description reaches escape velocity," the Boo said. "Your man is too large in the light to see a Boo. Too alien are we for his Procyon mind." He leaned forward. "But not so to unbalance the equation."

"How?"

"Searches he through the personnel records of Karina on the Rock. She is steady." He clicked his kroi indicating nothing was disturbed. "Then, he requests of me a discussion. Off the record."

Nason felt his bibbets color again. "What?" He had been so careful with his plans. It seemed impossible the Procyons had outsmarted him, that they could have suspected Degahv so soon. He frowned and rubbed his fingers over his warm forehead.

Finot raised a starfish hand and took a draught of chlorine. "Says to me why is she so old yet a lieutenant just?" He blinked and looked at the admiral. "I gave the same song, did I not, my friend?"

Nason frowned but said nothing. Perhaps they were only curious.

Finot continued. "Problems she, I speak to him of. Family. Discipline for insubordination. Politics. Like logarithms, one upon the next. Promotions are like mountains of Kine, not always earned, says I." He paused, sounding his kroi again. "This I speak. What he believes is unfactored."

Nason's hands gripped the arms of his chair. "But he didn't say anything about her behavior? About her work? Her attitude—anything at all?"

"Zero. Just her number of years and rank. Perhaps his theories do not equate. Why we have not seen her like the sun over Varannah? Of this, there is only linear speculation."

"Then she's doing her job well enough?"

Finot nodded. "Panoply and weapons appear unaltered. Percentages are in error." A decidedly amused sound came from his kroi.

"Well, there's that, anyway," Nason agreed. "Starting tomorrow, Pedlam will be too busy with his social obligations to concern himself with her. I sincerely doubt our Procyon has had much experience with being an amenable host."

Satisfied the situation wasn't yet out of control, Nason relaxed slightly. "Besides, her work is effectively done. Reassign her to some other ship under your care. Pedlam probably won't even remember her name by tomorrow."

"Our Mogin will find her heart cold like the stone of Sindi if you slide her now. She will see the job done."

"It *is* done." Nason found it odd for Finot to plead her case. "There's no reason for Karina to remain on the Rock."

"She will feel the inequality of your concern," the Boo advised.

Nason massaged his chin. Why would Finot defend her? He'd given her that Karina reference, too, making it sound like she was some kind of savior. The woman had value, surely, but nothing like what Finot was implying.

He shook his head. No. Her feelings could not be taken into account, not now. Both Marteens would be extremely unhappy if Degahv wasn't sent to a safe haven. For some reason, Setana's concern for Rieka went beyond the obvious. Though Nason did not relish the ire of either female, an Indran Herald could make his life more difficult than a Human captain could.

"She's been through enough, Finot, my friend," he said finally. "I want her out of harm's way."

"That is my understanding, Admiral." The Boo inclined his great head.

Nason stood, strode to the door, then turned. "This place is busier than a limis-hive, Captain. Are you sufficiently prepared for the influx of visitors?"

"Preparations have been computed and deployed."

"And *my* plans for the gala?"

"Co-ordinated," came the reply. "Details are available. The guests will encounter the new plan in one before it is scheduled."

"Good." Nason left the office and headed for the nearest InterMAT station. His intent was to drop in, unannounced, on this other Pedlam. Nothing said more about a person than being surprised by one's boss. If this Procyon could greet a Fleet admiral and conduct an inspection tour on a moment's notice, he would be an equally cool opponent in battle.

* * *

Rieka found Finot in the small conservatory on the Little One, just a few levels below his office. Stepping inside, she was impressed by the diversity of flora in the room. The perfume of blossoms and various soils greeted her. The sheer volume of potted plants thriving all around her made it difficult not to be distracted by their tenacious enjoyment of life.

"Captain," she said, greeting him near a collection of miniature Aurian *daum* trees. "You asked to see me?"

"Your duties are one hundred percent, my lieu-tenant," he said after a click of greeting from his kroi. "You are to remain on the Little One in the Light until the stream flows smoothly to Varannah."

Finot was pulling her off the *Prodigy*? Why? Rieka bit her lip to keep from snapping at him. She studied the trees' tiny blue leaves, silently wondering what had ever possessed the Aurians to cultivate them. "My mind cannot leave the equation at hand, Captain," she said, finally. "It festers there like pi. How can you ask me to forget it?"

"I must."

"But it is my life that hangs there, like Orin at the citadel. Certainly, I may have a function in my own destiny." She knew the Orin symbol was pushing it, but had no intention of backing down.

He sucked thoughtfully on his tube, kroi clicking now and then as if he were in deep thought. "It is like pi," he agreed. "I cannot gather all the places, nor the factors. But your destiny has no purpose if you are not alive to fulfill it."

She huffed at that and walked away. A pallet of variegated spider mums sat to her left. She looked at them and thought their explosion of color seemed to mirror her temper. "You know . . . you don't outrank me, you big blue monolith."

He laughed; the kroi sounded in lively staccato for a long moment. When they stopped, he said, "Nason does."

She lifted a dyed brow. "He's here?"

"Affirmative."

"They why doesn't he talk to me himself?"

"Why should an admiral seek out a lieutenant? Have we not tried to avoid suspicion? The Pzekii has made inquiries of Mogin. There was no sediment in the speech. Let us continue to look toward Varannah."

Pedlam must have recognized her. Or maybe he was just suspicious by nature. In any case, she got the idea that wasn't the only reason she was being pulled from the assignment. "You can order me. You can not *make* me—unless you have me detained."

"This is true," he countered. "Let us drop the problem. I want no part of alternative variables."

"Fine," she agreed happily. "Then, as far as you're concerned, I've gone to play a round of speed volley with Captain DeVark." Satisfied with the outcome of his on-the-surface order, Rieka sidestepped a small water garden and turned to leave. The confused sound Finot made, however, caused her to turn back.

"Is there something wrong?"

"Perhaps you cannot play with DeVark," he said.

She frowned. "Is he busy with a project?"

"There is hope of that," Finot replied. He put his tube to his mouth and shuffled away.

Rieka went directly to her quarters and looked around for her roommate, Tivan. Satisfied she was alone, she went to the desk. "Computer access," she said softly.

"Available," a tinny, Lomiian-sounding voice replied.

"Use the local grid and locate Captain DeVark, please."

A short moment passed. "The captain is not on the Little One."

Tapping her fingers on the table, Rieka frowned. "Was he on the base today?"

"Affirmative."

"When?"

"Arrival at eleven-hundred hours. Departure at sixteen-hundred zero-eight."

"Rather a long lunch date," she murmured to herself, wondering who had caught his eye this time. "Probably went back to the *Prospectus* to take a nap." She chuckled.

"The captain did not return to the *Prospectus*."

"Where did he go?"

"The *Prodigy*."

She frowned. "Computer off." The screen went blank.

"So much for that," she muttered. Then, just to be sure, she clicked on her TC. "Lieutenant Mogin to the *Prospectus*."

"Lieutenant Ril," the voice replied.

"Captain Finot is looking for Captain DeVark, Ril. Is he aboard yet?"

"Negative, Mogin. But we do have orders to report to Captain Finot as soon as Captain DeVark arrives."

"Okay. Just checking. Thanks."

Rieka switched off her TC and sat back in her chair to decipher what Robet was up to. After ten minutes, Tivan entered, wanting to chat about her day and the trials of shuffling the Heralds' belongings to their quarters. She seemed almost intoxicated with the opportunity of meeting such important people.

Tivan's excitement over the festive mayhem was contagious enough for Rieka to give Robet some slack. She allowed herself to put the problem of his whereabouts on hold, for a while. Knowing him, she should at least wait until after breakfast to formally hunt him down. To do so before then might create an embarrassing situation for him as well as his companion.

The next morning, however, after she'd checked in with the admiral using the phony communication to his agent, Dramie, Robet was still missing. Rieka recognized the uncomfortable sensation in her chest as her intuition working overtime.

She used the computer again to retrace Robet's steps

up until he left the Little One. There, the trail went cold. "What station did the captain depart from?" she asked.

"Station Four."

That one was near the nursery, she knew. But she had no idea why he would go to the nursery. "Computer, list all personnel with infants or hatchlings in the nursery."

A moment later the list appeared in yellow on the black screen. She noted with some surprise that Commander Klin's name was on the list. Smiling slightly, she wondered how he was keeping his wits about him with all the commotion involving the *Prodigy*'s send-off. Security for the Little One, she guessed, would be a nightmare.

Catching hold of a wayward thought, Rieka erased the list and addressed the computer again. "Confirm transport of Captain DeVark at sixteen-zero-eight yesterday," she said.

"Confirmed."

"Has he used his TC since then?"

"Affirmative."

"Can you tell me who he spoke to?"

"Negative. The transmission request was not completed."

That did not sound like Robet, at all. Cursing herself for not asking the right to questions earlier, Rieka said, "Request a grid link. I need to know if the captain made any additional transports from locations within the system grid between then and now."

"Grid links are available only for command personnel."

"Dammit. Computer off." Frustrated, she bounced a fist on the table. As Lieutenant Mogin, she could do nothing. She had to find someone of proper rank to help her. With Pedlam suspicious, talking to Triscoe was out of the question, as was a conversation with Finot. Who did she know that could help?

Rieka switched on her TC. "Link to the *Providence*. Mogin to Dr. Twanabok."

"I am here," he said after a moment.

"Doctor, I need you to do me a favor," she said sweetly.

"I am agreeable, depending on the request."

"I need a command clearance. The system won't do a grid link for a lieutenant."

"What do you want?"

"Can you request a search for any transport made by Robet DeVark later than sixteen zero-eight, yesterday?"

He seemed to think it over for a moment. "I suppose I could. Is there any special reason we are looking for him?"

"He went to the *Prodigy*," she said quietly, "and he hasn't been heard from, since."

Twanabok's voice sounded in her ear with conviction. "I will get on it right away. Should I contact you again, in any case?"

"Yes, Vort," she said. "Most definitely. And please, don't mention this to Triscoe."

When Triscoe entered the Little One's huge assembly lab, he found it difficult to recognize the place. The immense room had been transformed by greenery, huge lengths of draped blue material, and an army of cloth-covered tables. The center area had been cleared, obviously reserved for dancing. In one corner, a band was being set up. The expense budget for the *Prodigy*'s send-off must have been huge.

His dress uniform made him feel both honored and imprisoned. Triscoe tugged at the collar, feeling little solace in the fact that formal attire had been having the same effect on people throughout recorded history. Probably longer.

He stood inside the main entrance watching the musicians settle themselves and the impressive crowd arrive. As the influx of elegantly dressed people began to grow, Triscoe recognized several from personal

contact and others by reputation only. In addition to
Prime Admiral Hursh and two Vice Admirals, he saw
Admiral Nason amble in, deep in conversation with
several of his cronies. Captain Finot entertained the
Boolian Herald, Dzan, and his mate. Five other Planetary Heralds entered, and Triscoe wondered if his
mother had managed to squeeze in the time for a short
trip to Dani.

It wasn't until after he concluded a lengthy conversation with Wint Zevak, a Vekyan hydroponics supplier, that he noticed the back of his father's head. The
older man had bent low for a moment as he spoke to a
Fleet vendor. A pang of apprehension went through
him as his mother turned and looked suddenly in his
direction. Their eyes met across the milling crowd.
Triscoe clamped his teeth together. Obviously, Mother
had something planned. But now wasn't the time to be
facing his father after the disastrous scene of their last
meeting.

Abruptly, he turned away, consciously avoiding
another confrontation. Thinking it had been too long
since he'd seen either Robet or Rieka, he headed for
the door.

Does my son run from me?

His mind felt the words like a slap. She only spoke to
him that way when she required his full attention.
Without bothering to answer, he casually changed his
direction, making his way toward the bar. She would
know where to find him when she was ready to talk.

He considered ordering an intoxicant from the bar's
FabriMAT menu, but decided against it. With the Procyons still at large, it wasn't a good idea to indulge. He
asked for a glass of Vekyan fruit-water and sipped it
slowly.

"I am glad you decided to stay."

He turned, surprised she'd excused herself from the
crowd and come to talk privately. "I don't really
belong at this function," Triscoe replied. "Few of my
rank were invited."

His mother gave him a withering look. "I know what is going on. Merik and I have had several meetings about it."

He forced himself not to frown. "Rieka?"

Her hand touched his forearm. "That, too." She smiled as if they were talking about the weather on Indra. "I refer to the other thing, which is not so widely known."

Triscoe nodded. His mother being privy to their situation gave him a sense of relief. In all his life he could not remember one occasion she had not controlled to her satisfaction. It had to do with a kind of subliminal use of her *quantivasta*-gift and the maternal talent for getting things done her way. He smiled, allowing a dimple to surface. "Then by all means work your magic, Mother."

"I intend to, though not in ways you imagine." Her eyes left his to search the crowd. "Your father is here."

"I saw him."

"We will have a talk, later," she informed him.

"The three of us?"

"No. The four of us. Your lovely wife is expected, too." She smiled a Herald's smile, which was sweet and apparently genuine, though Triscoe could sense some inner wrath tightly leashed. "I have been led to understand she's here at Dani, somewhere. I'll be sure to give you plenty of notice so you can make the proper arrangements."

"Mother, I—"

"Triscoe, there is no point in arguing with me. You are my special child. My gifted child. But I will not let those wary brown eyes of yours sway me in this." She pursed her lips slightly in a way Triscoe knew meant her mind was made up.

"Of course," he conceded. "Have you informed Father?"

"Endless heavens, no. Do you think I've lost all six of my senses?"

The glimmer in her eye eased his concern. At this

meeting, whenever it was, she planned to set his father straight. That she hadn't forewarned Ker gave Triscoe hope that Rieka had a chance to be accepted into the family. "Of course not," he said. "My . . . wife is not available at the moment, however. She's—"

"Yes, yes, I know."

Triscoe looked at her sharply and was treated with a maternal smile. "Are you teasing me, Mother?"

She thought about it a moment. "I think I might be. Nevertheless, our little conversation can wait until whatever is going to happen—happens."

"Agreed," he said.

"There's RadiMo and his new mate, RagiMo. I had wondered if they would arrive in time for the reception."

Triscoe turned and glanced in the direction of her gaze. "The Bournese Herald?"

"Yes. They're so timid, you know, being nocturnal. But really the Bourne tribes are all likable." She sighed once and made a small tisking sound. "I had better get over there right away, before your father sees them. He doesn't mean to, but he can get awfully loud."

"He's always seemed aware of his volume to me," Triscoe advised.

"That's unfair, dear." She put her hand on his arm and leaned to allow him to stroke his thumb along her jaw in the Indran sign of filial affection. "I'll see you later."

Triscoe watched her move across the room and quietly greet the Bournese delegation. She was with them a full minute before her husband approached, clearly long enough to have the situation under control.

Smiling to himself, he turned, then stopped. Seated at a table, their backs to him, were Admiral Bittin and Captain Pedlam. Bittin's large midsection pressed against the table, and he gestured with his hands as he spoke. Pedlam nodded and smiled. Triscoe found he had to give them credit—they carried off the charade with enviable perfection. Quietly, he went back to the bar to return his empty glass.

A whiff of chlorine alerted him to a Boo nearby. "Captain Finot," he said, tilting his head to look into the black alien eyes. "Is this like a vision of Varannah?" He gestured to the assemblage, alluding to the fact that all were present to honor the *Prodigy*.

"By fractal analysis, it would seem so," the captain replied. "But it sits like pi in my mind." His kroi clicked absently.

"I know what you mean."

"There, Pzekii sits as a cold moon," Finot went on, "while we wait like an expanding star to reach the point of implosion."

"Worried?" Triscoe wondered aloud, trying not to sound astonished.

"The concept of fear eludes the Boo," the captain explained. "But they are close, and the critical point in the equation draws near. I have no desire to perform mathematics or mechanics for a race of users. The attitude and angle of the Commonwealth convinced us to share our knowledge and manipulate space for the good of all," he explained, uncharacteristically verbose. Kroi clicked for a moment. "I was a mimlet when the treaties were signed. This"—he gestured in the general direction of Bittin and Pedlam—"is sulphurous. Universally unacceptable."

Triscoe, although aware of a Boo's lengthy life span, hadn't realized Finot was over two hundred years old. That, as much as his attitude and speech, was a bit of a shock. It took a moment for him to think of something to say. "We're all doing our best to see that it doesn't happen."

"Still, it may not balance," he warned softly. "Karina has done her job, yes. But where is DeVark? Gone. Killed? Perhaps. No one knows."

Triscoe's head snapped to attention. Sharp eyes scanned the room. "He hasn't shown up?"

Finot sucked on his tube. "My tracers report he doesn't exist."

Triscoe sighed, then added a muttered Indran oath,

refusing to allow himself to believe Robet could be dead. "That means they know."

"Perhaps. Perhaps not," the blue captain replied cryptically.

"The ship won't be officially dedicated until tomorrow afternoon, but . . ." Triscoe hesitated, not wanting to state the obvious, "—but everything necessary for flight is on line now. Our time has run out. We're going to be forced to do something, and soon."

"Nason is ready. The ships are ready. Are you, my friend?"

Triscoe nodded. "But I would feel a lot better if I knew where our Karina was."

"Her TC is malfunctioning?"

He shook his head. "I tried it a few minutes ago, after I checked in with my first officer, Aarkmin. She's receiving, she just doesn't want to talk anyone. And I'd like to know why."

Nineteen

Rieka gritted her teeth against the insistent voice of her TC as she feigned a relaxed gait to the InterMAT station. Triscoe had tried to contact her some time ago and when she hadn't responded, he'd set up a tracer signal. Its beep, a high-pitched earsplitting tone, sounded in her ear every ten minutes as a stern reminder to check in. She figured it wouldn't be long before he'd come looking for her himself.

After Finot's warning, she'd decided certain precautions were necessary. The most basic one was no more TC conversations with Triscoe—at least not until she could set up a signature scrambler for her unit. TC links could be traced. Pedlam had already done something to Robet. He might suspect her, but she saw no reason to implicate Tris—or tip Pedlam off.

Clutching the dose of compressed sedative she'd gotten from Twanabok, Rieka used the InterMAT and again found herself in the *Prodigy*'s crowded station.

"Send that right up to the gym," a Vekyan said to a harried ensign poised behind a small cart. The woman waved Rieka from the chamber, then turned away to tap the communication board. She studied it for a moment. "Not acceptable. The Bournese Herald must have a skiff in the room at all times, I'm told. We must have one by zero-seven-hundred at the latest tomorrow, for the dedication ceremony."

Rieka didn't wait to hear the reply. She left quickly, heading down the corridor toward a now-familiar Chute. Making her way down the slope, she felt the first twinges of apprehension steal across her mind. She didn't know for sure that Robet was in detention, but a containment field around a cell was one of the few things that could block a TC signal. The others, including his death, she firmly pushed to the back of her mind.

The Chute door opened near her destination, and she looked up at a wall of blue. The first Boo was dark, like Finot, and had a dappled look along one side. The second was lighter, but not by much. The odor of chlorine was strong, and for a split second, she wondered why neither of them stepped back to allow her to pass. Then, she realized she was outranked.

"Commander," Rieka said, saluting. She retreated to the corner, and the Boo stumped through the doorway. The second followed, a lieutenant by the markings on its togalike uniform, and she moved to exit the car.

"Take care in your equation," the commander advised.

Rieka stopped and turned. The translator had spoken, meaning he had addressed her, not his companion. "Sir?"

"Finot speaks of the Karina to Bohm." An arm came up and the Boo tapped its chest just above the translator unit.

She nodded slowly, hoping she understood what it was trying to say. "Will you see him soon?"

"Negative. Many Boo are aboard. None will leave."

"Why not?"

Her answer was a tentative click of kroi and a slow blink. Then the door closed and she was alone.

Shrugging off the odd exchange, Rieka went down the corridor and took an immediate right turn. She'd waited until the afternoon shift because Preshun's name had been displayed on the duty roster. At the desk for over an hour, he was probably bored and ready for a diversion. Based on their earlier conversation, Rieka knew the exact angle to use to catch him off guard. She took a left into the short corridor and heaved a small sigh, bracing herself for what had to be done.

The door opened and the guard looked up. Rieka stood there, hesitating, until the frown faded as he recognized her.

"Lan," she said easily, ambling into the small reception area, "I was hoping I'd find you here."

He rose from the desk and treated her to a welcoming smile. "Well, Lieutenant Mogin, where's your datapad?"

"On the Little One. I'm finished with the *Prodigy* and I wanted to say good-bye in person."

He seemed flattered, bibbets slowly deepening in hue. Perching himself on the corner of his desk, he shrugged apologetically. "I'm still on duty."

She lifted her eyebrows. "Let no one ever accuse you of stating the obvious," she said with a small laugh. "I've only got the next two shifts off, myself. Then Finot's got me scheduled to do preliminary testing on some newly installed equipment on the *Providence*." She allowed her tone to become serious. "They really took a beating last week."

"I heard," Preshun said. "Humans. Can't figure out why the Fleet gives them any responsibility at all. Captain Degahv ought to be given a life sentence, at the very least. If this were the old days, on Aurie," he stopped himself, but only for a second, "we wouldn't have to worry about her again. Ever."

The spite in his voice told her his prejudice was getting in the way of rational thought almost as much as his patriotism. She shook her head, "You men, it does not even matter the species. It is always 'kill them and get them out of the way.' "

He looked only slightly chagrined. "Your Centauri heart is too big, Dra."

"Possibly," she agreed, glancing past him at the detection units.

His eyes slid to her flat chest. "Has it any room for me?"

She lifted her chin. "Now there is a much better topic of conversation."

The bibbets darkened slightly. "I've thought about you," he said.

"I'm flattered."

Preshun patted the desk. "Shall we . . . talk about it?"

Rieka found it easier to feign surprise than she thought. "While you're on duty?"

"Why not? There's just one occupant," he said, gesturing to a darkened cell. "He was in here when my shift started. No trouble. I'm not sure he's conscious." He looked into her eyes. "And I don't really expect anyone else to come along. Most everyone off shift went to the Little One to try and get a look at the Heralds."

She waited an appropriate second or two before seeming to make her decision and joining him at the desk. But she didn't sit on it as he'd tacitly suggested. She stood in front of him, watching his face. "So, you're saying we're alone." There was a kind of perverse satisfaction as she saw his bibbets flush.

Slowly, and with the precision that told Rieka he had done this many times before, Preshun spread his feet and reached for her, pulling her toward him. She stepped into the V of his legs and allowed his hands to rest on her upper arms. "I see you don't like to waste any time, Lan," she said.

"It's too precious to waste," he countered, nudging her closer. "Not one single second."

Rieka leaned into his embrace, allowing his lips to touch her cheek on their way to her ear, as she lifted her arms. Her hands went over his shoulders and she pulled the flat syringe from its hiding place in her sleeve. She pressed it to his neck and caught him as he relaxed. He was completely unconscious by the time she began easing him down. At the last moment, however, she let him drop. His head impacted the floor with a resounding thud.

Wiping the remains of his kiss from her face, Rieka glanced down at him and muttered, "That's for calling me a traitor. And if I were your captain, Lieutenant, you'd spend some time in disciplinary rehab for behavior unbecoming an officer." She stepped around him. "Bigot."

The desk console controlled both the outer and inner doors. Rieka keyed the access panel. She found the proper identification for the occupied cell and disengaged the screen. The lit interior told her the barrier had been terminated.

As expected, Robet was slumped across the small bunk.

She shook him. "Robet, wake up." It wasn't easy, but she managed to haul him to a sitting position. "Robet! Open your eyes. I can't get you out of here unless you're conscious. Now wake up!" Slapping him produced a groan. She looked around, noticed a tiny lav area, and poured cold water into her hands. She wiped them on his face.

"Robet!"

"Mmm."

She repeated the water treatment and slapped him again. "Robet DeVark you wake up right now. That's an order."

An eye opened. "Don't take orders from a lieutenant," he mumbled.

"You will from this one."

The tone of her voice must have gotten his attention. The other eye slid open. "What?"

She stared into his eyes, willing him to stay awake. "You've been drugged, Robet. You've been missing for hours. I've got to get you off this ship, but I can't use my TC to do it. Do you understand?"

His hand came up and he swiped his face. His bibbets had been a pasty white but were now showing signs of faint color. "Robet, don't you dare go back to sleep."

"No, no." He heaved a sigh. "I know you," he said, studying her intently like a drunk would the back of his hand. "I can't remember which name . . ."

"Mogin. Lieutenant Mogin," Rieka coached. "Can you use your TC?"

Robet took a deep breath through his nose. "Think so."

"Then do it. Go to the *Providence*. Dr. Twanabok is waiting for you."

"Got my own chief of medical—"

"Twanabok knows what is going on," she insisted. "He'll get you back on your feet."

"On my feet."

"Robet, activate your TC."

She saw him contort his face and accepted that as the best he could do. "Is it on?"

"Uh-huh."

"Good. Now, say 'DeVark to *Providence*.' "

"DeVark to *Providence*."

"Tell V'don you want transportation to the medical section. That you need to see Dr. Twanabok."

He repeated the request and Rieka stepped back, not wanting to be included in the transport signal. She watched anxiously until he disappeared with a soft pop. Glancing at the time, she left the brig and headed for the main InterMAT station. If she was lucky, she could make it back to the Little One with no one on the *Prodigy* the wiser.

A guard had been posted at the station door in an effort to control the chaos. Rieka identified her as one of the Centauri officers who acted strangely. She approached slowly, letting the other woman make her own assumptions.

"Working late?" Lieutenant Mekla smiled sympathetically.

Rieka nodded. "Finot wants everything to go smoothly."

"How can you stand him?"

"Oh, he's not so bad."

The Centauri who was not, looked closely at Rieka. "We have appreciated the work you've done, Lieutenant," she said, waving her through the door.

Rieka nodded and stepped on the platform. "Just doing my job."

* * *

". . . and not within the lifetime of many of you in this audience. The total commitment of so many species with regard to maintaining our civilization as we have constructed it, gives me great pride and certain satisfaction that I have chosen a worthy career. And, judging by the auspicious crowd in attendance for this momentous occasion, I know that we all, that is all the Commonwealth—citizens to Heralds, can share that pride and satisfaction that they have ordained the Fleet as their protector . . ."

Triscoe, seated at a table with his father, mother, and her small entourage, barely listened to the Prime Admiral. Hursh had been speaking for forty minutes, and as far as he was concerned, had said very little. Triscoe was too busy wondering where Rieka and Robet were, while surreptitiously keeping his eye on Pedlam. Worrying did him no good, so he considered possible strategies for the light-bending unit Finot had installed.

Just as it occurred to him that two ships so equipped would be a tactical nightmare, a strange sensation hit him.

Rieka was nearby. He could feel it like a source of heat, as though someone had opened an oven. Turning his head in the direction of the warmth, he realized the huge assembly door had been shrouded by blue material. Then, noticing movement to the left, he discovered a smaller door.

Shrugging a silent excuse to the Vekyan supplier seated next to him, Triscoe nodded curtly to his mother and left the table.

What has happened? she asked silently.

Rieka is close. I have to speak to her.

Setana nodded. Wondering if half the audience wouldn't like to join him in his escape, Triscoe quietly crossed the room. On the way, he kept his mind trained on Rieka. He intended to give her a firm reprimand for not contacting him.

The door was opened for him by an ensign. He

caught a glimpse of someone in the hallway beyond. Rieka? He picked up his pace and hurried forward.

"Mogin," he said in a voice loud enough to reach her as she strolled the corridor but not so loud as to echo through the door closing behind him.

She stopped and turned with a look of tight apprehension on her face. Recognizing him, and the fact that they were alone for the moment, she smiled. "Captain Marteen, what a surprise. I was just thinking about you."

The expression was contagious, and he felt his heart thumping low in his chest, but he knew it would be disastrous to jeopardize the charade. The sound of footsteps caused him to immediately drop the smile. "May I have a word with you, Lieutenant?"

"Certainly, Captain."

That challenge in your eyes, he thought irreverently, as if she could hear him, *makes me want to forget about our problems and duty and find some quiet, private spot.*

But intellect won out over libido, and he was glad she hadn't been able to pick up his thoughts. He walked toward her, acknowledging the approach of an ensign with a quick salute.

With most production and assembly areas temporarily closed, he gestured Rieka toward an equipment-storage room with nothing other than conversation in mind. But the dimly lit counter area seemed so secluded compared to the hallway, Triscoe barely had time to remind himself why he wanted to talk to her. His hands were suddenly around her waist, pulling her to him. He barely recognized himself.

Rieka didn't help matters, either. She smiled in a strange, exotically Human way, and leaned close. When he lifted himself from her kiss, the intensity flared again. He wondered if she *had* heard his mind.

"Rieka," he said softly, his eyes roving over her altered features, the difference in coloring clearly distinguishable in the low lighting.

"I was hoping I might find you at the reception," she said. "I have to talk to you."

"I'm listening." He caressed her hair.

"I thought you'd be mad about the TC business," she chided. "And while I'm thinking of it, could you stop the tracer? It's awfully annoying."

"Why didn't you respond?"

"Pedlam was getting suspicious. I didn't want to do anything that might substantiate his interest in me—like my having a series of conversations with a married captain over a TC channel."

"I see."

The skeptical look on her face told him she didn't believe he did. "More importantly, though, I had a feeling about Robet and I didn't want to—"

"Robet? He's missing according to Finot."

"Not anymore." She shook her head. "I found him. Apparently, he'd been snooping and someone caught on, probably Pedlam. He'd been drugged and put in the brig on the *Prodigy*. I knocked out the guard and sent Robet to Dr. Twanabok. It's only a matter of time before the guard is discovered—or comes to."

"And Pedlam will respond. But how?" Triscoe rubbed the side of his face, trying not to show the anxiety he felt. What would the Procyons do when they realized they'd been discovered? Run with the ship? Attack the base? Or pretend nothing had happened—because their plan required another, as yet unanticipated component?

"I did what I thought was necessary, Tris," she offered, the worry clear on her face. "But I did it without orders. Nason used Finot as a messenger to tell me to stay out of sight. I could tell Finot was concerned about Robet's disappearance. We had to have him back."

She shrugged. "I didn't know if he was in any danger, but my instinct said he was." She made a waving gesture with her hands. "I know what you Centauris think about Human instinct. But, well . . . too bad. It's saved my skin more than once, and today it saved Robet's. I suppose I should have contacted Admiral Nason, but that would have been risky—and he would have just told me to stay on the Little One. You know I couldn't leave Robet—"

"It's all right, love," he said, squinting down at her. "You have stepped up the timetable, and the admiral might be furious with you, but I doubt that getting Robet out of enemy hands is going to change history."

She relaxed. "Thanks."

Triscoe stood for a moment peering into her eyes through the darkness. "I want you to keep out of sight. I'll contact you as soon as I can."

Rieka nodded. "That's what I'd planned to do. But I'm expected on the *Prodigy* first thing in the morning. There's a final checklist, and I'm to be present while Chief Engineer Bohm goes over it."

She stopped and frowned. "It's strange . . ."

"What?"

"I met Commander Bohm today, on the *Prodigy*, just as I was heading for the detention area. He said something that didn't make sense."

"She," Triscoe corrected, then watched Rieka shrug. "She's a Boo, Rieka, are you sure you understood?"

"Female," Rieka mumbled, nodding. "It's impossible to tell. Anyway, to answer your question, yes. I understood her. It just didn't make sense. She said there were a lot of Boos aboard, and they would not leave."

"That is odd," he agreed. "Why do you think she mentioned it?"

Rieka made a face that told him she had no idea. "She knew who I was. Finot had told her. But I'm not sure what she meant. Leave what—the ship? The Commonwealth?"

"I have no idea, Rieka. But I suppose you'll figure it out, eventually." He smiled, revealing the dimple on his left cheek. "Do what's necessary, but get off the *Prodigy* as soon as possible. If anything should happen . . ." He left the remainder of the dark thought unspoken. "I'm going to tell Finot and Nason about Robet. At least that's one less concern."

"He was sedated, Triscoe," she said. "It may take Vort some time to get him on his feet."

"Robet will be fine," he assured her. "It's the safety of all those people in there that concerns me." He gestured toward the reception. "Pedlam and Bittin are probably planning to use them as hostages." He didn't bother to tell her he thought they would have no compunction about killing anyone, including Heralds.

"I think the admiral knows that, Tris. And even though he *claims* to know nothing about espionage, he can be awfully clever," she reminded him.

"Then we'll let him worry."

"Fine with me," she said airily.

Besting the war within himself, Triscoe gave her a squeeze and a quick kiss, and said, "Now go, before I forget that we're here in this dark, romantic spot—for a strictly professional reason."

When she laughed, he stood straighter. "Something is funny?"

"You didn't mean it as a joke?"

"What?"

"Calling the equipment room a romantic spot."

"But it's dark, and private and—"

"Not romantic, Triscoe."

"But—?"

She laughed lightly and patted his cheek. "Later, dear." Then, Rieka tugged her uniform shirt straight and quietly left him in the dark equipment room.

Triscoe shook his head as she left. Was it because she was Human, or simply female? She had him feeling as if he were teetering on the edge of a cliff. He hoped the coming ordeal would be over soon, and there would be enough time before their next assignments for him to explore the strange power she possessed.

He went back to the banquet and insinuated himself into the area reserved for the Boolian audience. The Prime Admiral was still speaking, now about the important of a strong military force, when Triscoe edged close enough to Finot to speak. "Our Karina found him."

"The location?"

"The big ship." The chlorine hanging in the air made his eyes water. "She freed him. I told her to disappear."

"Good. It is now best you escape to your Mohn and I will equate this to Nason. He is in need of the factors like the void needs the stars."

"Agreed." Triscoe wiped his eyes and hastily left the small group of Boos. In the hallway, still tearing profusely, he nodded at two Centauri guards posted opposite the door. "Marteen to *Providence*," he said, after activating his TC.

"Yes, Captain?"

"Transport me at once. Station One."

"As we speak, sir."

As he waited for the signal, he tried to predict what the next hours would be like.

K'resh-va sat at a table of Fleet staff, gritting his teeth against the tediousness of Prime Admiral Hursh's speech. The remains of the banquet had been removed from the table an hour ago, just before the admiral had begun. Too bad, he thought. At least the bones of the *deri* hen would have been interesting to look at.

He wondered how the Centauris got anything done if all of them were as long-winded as this particular individual. In his boredom, K'resh-va directed his attention around the room. The crowd was becoming restless. He enjoyed watching the alien faces as they tried to keep their concentration focused on the admiral.

The Heralds were the most intriguing of Commonwealth citizens. They were intelligent, well-spoken, and carried themselves with the dignity of the Crown Eglat of Kiengh, the ruler on his homeworld. They seemed to be respected not only by one another but by the Fleet officers as well. Since support for the Fleet was part of each planet's budget, he wasn't surprised to find that eight of them had seen fit to attend the dedication ceremonies. He was speculating on the Commonwealth's reaction to eight Heralds being taken hostage when a movement caught his attention. With a flash of concern, he watched the Centauri, Marteen, exit the room.

For a fleeting moment, K'resh-va wondered if the Fleet realized DeVark was missing. Then he dismissed the thought. DeVark was frequently gone for many hours at a time. His appetite for romantic adventures had inspired the strategy of locking him up.

He gritted his teeth and endured the rest of the Prime Admiral's address. There was a long round of applause. He could not tell whether it was for the speech's content or the fact that it was over. Then Admiral Bittin, or more correctly, E'bid-va, got up to introduce the first of the Heralds.

The Oph Herald, Cimpa, was speaking when a lieutenant entered the gym and made his way directly to the table. He leaned down, and said softly, "DeVark is gone."

K'resh-va's head snapped around. His furious glare sought to incinerate the bearer of such news. "How?"

"Unknown, sir. Commander Durak is waiting outside."

K'resh-va, despising the role he was forced to play, nodded. He made a whispered excuse to the others at the table, then strode toward the exit. He turned to look back at the Oph Herald and noticed E'bid-va step down from the dais.

O'don-la was pacing in the empty corridor. He turned as K'resh-va, followed by E'bid-va, emerged from the room. He saluted, spreading his hands. "DeVark is gone, sir," he said quietly. "There doesn't seem to be any explanation."

"Of course there is," K'resh-va countered, his anger barely in check. "The Fleet has somehow become aware of our intent."

"Do not jump to conclusions," E'bid-va advised. "Once we have all the facts, we will know how to proceed."

"Facts!" K'resh-va turned. E'bid-va had not only taken on the admiral's appearance, the alteration had apparently affected his mind. "Are you dazed? Can you not see they have found out?"

"How?" E'bid-va demanded, his voice hushed. "Who would have kept such vital information from me?"

K'resh-va had no idea, but the implications were not pleasant. He turned back to O'don-la. "Let's get to the holding area. I want a look at the place myself. What about the guard?"

"He was found," the commander explained as they hurriedly made their way to the InterMAT station. "He was unconscious at the time. Our physician was summoned. He may be awake by now."

"This could mean any number of things," E'bid-va said cautiously.

"Any number," K'resh-va echoed.

He said nothing more until they arrived at the *Prodigy*'s detention suite. An Aurian doctor, Draun, leaned over the partially revived guard, Lieutenant Preshun. Draun was a hireling, an inferior whose loyalty had been bought. There was no reason to worry about anything said in front of him. The Aurian lieutenant, though, was another matter.

He led the others past the doctor and went to examine the vacant cell. There was nothing amiss. The cot looked as though someone had sat on it. There were a few drops of water at the bottom of the sink. That was all.

Grunting to himself, K'resh-va returned to the outer room. Scanning it revealed nothing. There were two holographic cameras hanging in opposite corners near the ceiling, but they had not been hooked into the computer system. There was no sign of a scuffle, and, other than the fact that the guard had been found unconscious, he saw no evidence anyone had ever entered the detention area, much less freed DeVark.

"Report, Preshun," K'resh-va demanded.

The lieutenant groggily focused his eyes. He tried to say something but ended up sighing.

K'resh-va glared at the physician.

"He was heavily sedated, Captain," Draun said,

answering the unasked question. "I can only estimate the time he was rendered unconscious. His shift began three hours ago. That was the last time anyone saw him until Ensign Eilowox found him and reported the incident to Commander Durak. I have been here approximately ten minutes, myself. He's been given a stimulant but is still thickheaded. You'll have to ask direct questions."

K'resh-va absorbed the information and nodded. He looked again at the Aurie officer. "Lieutenant, did someone come into Detention?"

Preshun nodded, his eyes barely focusing on the floor in front of him.

"Someone you knew?"

Again, the same.

"This is ridiculous," E'bid-va spat out. "The man isn't even coherent. He'd agree to anything."

"You're right, Admiral," K'resh-va agreed. He looked at O'don-la. "Commander, have a technician report here immediately. I want an identification screening on the terminal. Both genetic and print, if that is possible. And I want it done immediately."

"Yes, sir." O'don-la switched on his TC and gave the necessary orders.

K'resh-va angled the admiral into a corner so they could talk privately. "This is not good, E'bid-va," he said softly. "The ship is not yet completely ours, and we are left with trying to guess what the Fleet knows."

E'bid-va gave him a withering look. "Do you not forget that I hold a significant position?" he whispered harshly. "As overseer of Internal Affairs, I have ears in many places. You are making assumptions without facts, Captain. And even if they have some idea of our intent, they cannot know who we are, our strategy, or when we plan to strike."

K'resh-va shook his head. "Do not act like an old fool, Admiral. You must consider the possibility that we might not be able to keep to our schedule. If the Fleet—"

"The Fleet is scattered. There are only a few other

ships here at Dani. And only the *Prospectus* is at full running capacity. Do you have any doubt that this ship is able to handle that?"

"Of course not."

"Then stop acting as if you've been caught in a jar. Your tactical position has not been hindered in any way—even if the Fleet suspects something is amiss. You have enough crew to man this ship. Your Boos will take your orders as they would any other captain's."

"That is true. However, in the event—"

"There are no howevers, K'resh-va," he hissed, his jaw tight.

A technician had entered and was using a handheld scanner on the console's smooth surface. K'resh-va glared at his superior officer, then strode to the unit. "Have you got anything, yet?"

"The usual," she replied. "Dust, bacteria, an entire spectrum of—"

"Has it identified the last individual to use this console?" he snapped, insistently.

"The unit's working on that, sir," the technician replied. "Picked up a few skin cells. It takes a minute or two . . . There it is. No, that can't be right. I'll have to do it again." She frowned and began tapping at the scanner.

"What did it say?"

"It was wrong, sir. Way off. Must have been a misread. This scanner hasn't been used in a while. Sometimes they—"

"What name was identified?"

She hesitated. "Captain Rieka Degahv."

K'resh-va clenched his teeth together to keep from seeming surprised. "Thank you. Dismissed."

Nodding once, the technician left quickly.

"Degahv is dead," E'bid-va growled.

"And her cells are here, on my detention console?" K'resh-va countered. "I should have known. Degahv slipped out of your hands the first time. It should have been obvious she could do it again."

"We were talking about her," Preshun mumbled.

"Who?"

"Captain De . . . Dig, Degahv. You know, the traitor."

K'resh-va kept a rein on his patience. "You were talking about her to whom?"

"Mogi," he sighed.

"Is this person a member of the crew?" K'resh-va wondered aloud. He had met all the people assigned to the *Prodigy*. The name Mogi seemed vaguely familiar, but not quite identifiable.

"No," Preshun explained. "From the Little One. A tech-pro."

"Mogi. Mogin? Do you mean Lieutenant Mogin?" The woman whose file he'd studied. The one he wanted to approach as a hireling. The one he thought he'd recognized that first time he'd seen her in the engineering lab.

Preshun nodded.

Something began to coalesce in K'resh-va's mind. "Did she come in here? Was Mogin the one who drugged you?"

The lieutenant sighed, as if trying both to comprehend the question and formulate an answer for it. "Uh, I think so."

"His mind is not clear," Draun explained. "He could be having delusions based upon the conversation he's just heard."

"Possibly," K'resh-va agreed. "But not probably." He turned to E'bid-va. "This woman was of your choosing, and she has come back to haunt us time and again. You told me Humans were the least considered race in the Commonwealth. How gullible of me to have believed you."

E'bid-va was staring at him as if his words were in some foreign tongue. K'resh-va activated his TC and spoke to the communications officer. "This ship is quarantined as of this moment, Lieutenant," he said. "Notify all decks that I want Lieutenant Mogin found and detained. Do not use the intercom system."

The bridge officer acknowledged the order and K'resh-va looked at O'don-la. "Find this woman. Mogin, Degahv, whatever she calls herself. I want her brought to me. And if she is no longer aboard, go to the Little One, discreetly, and get her."

"Yes, Captain." O'don-la nodded and left.

E'bid-va took his arm and ushered him into the corridor. "You are asking too much of my patience," he whispered. "You do not give the orders, here. And we cannot afford to alter the schedule. The entire mission is at stake."

K'resh-va shook his head and allowed himself a toothy Procyon frown. "Years have been spent in an effort to reach this moment. Thousands of our people are waiting the offensive. I will not allow your conservative attitude to interfere with it now, E'bid-va. If Degahv has not been found by the time I reach the bridge, I am personally moving the schedule up. We will leave Dani as soon as possible."

"That is madness and you know it, K'resh-va," E'bid-va hissed softly, his eyes steely with determination. "The dignitaries *must* be on board when we leave the dock—not safe on the Little One."

"The ship is what is important! Our mobility and firepower."

"No." The older man's voice shook with intensity. He took hold of K'resh-va's shoulder, gripping it tight. "The entire strategy is based upon the schedule. You must not throw all our work to the stellar winds. Unless and until we have no choice, you *must* follow the orders and adhere to the plan."

K'resh-va glared once at E'bid-va's Centauri face before he shook himself free. He then turned on his heel and strode toward the nearest awaiting Chute.

Twenty

Triscoe hurried into the medical suite's treatment area. Trying not to look too concerned, he asked, "And how are you feeling?"

Robet, his bibbets almost transparent, sat on an exam table. A cup in one hand, he rubbed his face with the other. "What kept you?"

"I ran into our Karina on the Rock," Triscoe said with a wistful smile. "She told me you were here. Otherwise, I'd still be on the Little One, listening to the Prime Admiral until my retirement."

"That bad?"

Triscoe nodded.

"We might *both* have had to suffer through it, if the admiral hadn't asked me to do a little reconnaissance." Robet shrugged. "I *thought* I was being discreet. They must really be tense."

Triscoe nodded again. "Charming place, the *Prodigy*. But I missed the tour of the brig."

"Believe me, you missed nothing," Robet offered, his chin rocking side to side.

"This is all very entertaining," Twanabok commented dryly from behind his desk, "but I have work to do. Captain DeVark needs to consume the contents of that cup. Then, if he scans within acceptable parameters, I'll release him. Since time seems to be of the essence . . ."

"I'm hurrying, Vort," Robet said. Peering into the cup, he screwed up his face. Twanabok was famous for vile concoctions.

Downing it in one gulp, Robet swallowed with effort and tossed the container into the recycler. "Satisfied?"

Triscoe chuckled to himself and stood back as Twanabok picked up a medical scanner. In a moment, the tests were complete and he clicked his claws twice.

"You'll live, Captain. You're fit for command, although I wouldn't suggest any physical effort for about forty-eight hours. That includes all horizontal or zero-G activity as well."

He looked stricken. "You're not serious?"

"I am," the doctor replied humorlessly. "Your reputation precedes you."

Robet glanced at Triscoe for support, but he raised his hands and backed up another step. "Leave me out of this. I believe I've told you once or twice about a little discretion—"

"Never mind." The Aurian's bibbets turned a dusty rose. "Let's leave it as a given I will not be partnering anytime soon—whether I feel up to it or not," he added, giving the doctor a dirty look.

"That is exactly what I am referring to, Captain," Twanabok replied evenly. "I'm just attempting to warn you of possible embarrassment."

The bibbets flushed darker before Robet could bring them back to a pale pink. "How can you stand him?"

Triscoe smiled. "It's simply a matter of staying out of his way—and on his good side."

"I think I've withstood enough of this," Twanabok grumbled, and returned to his worktable. "You are officially released, Captain. Now . . . go save the Commonwealth and be done with it."

They had gone only a few steps in the corridor when Triscoe's TC clicked on and his executive officer's voice sounded in his ear.

"Marteen," he said, skimming a sideways glance at his companion.

"Captain, Captain Finot has just informed me that Pedlam left the reception."

"Did Finot say why?"

"No sir."

"Keep your eye on the *Prodigy*, Aarkmin. I'm headed for the bridge, now. Marteen out." He frowned at Robet. "Pedlam's left the reception."

"Looks as if we've started something," Robet commented.

Triscoe clapped him on the shoulder. "Get yourself home and get your crew ready. This may rapidly evolve into a very unpleasant situation."

Nodding, Robet switched on his TC and said, "DeVark to *Prospectus*."

Triscoe didn't bother to say good-bye. He was too busy thinking about all the people on board the *Prodigy*. Too busy wondering about Rieka.

Rieka heard the sound of footsteps coming toward her from an intersecting corridor. She turned and entered her quarters, her mind on two distinct tasks. First, she needed to modify her TC signature in the communication grid so that her exact position could not be pinpointed by the central computer. She figured Triscoe could find her just about anywhere, no matter what; but Pedlam could only find her by tracing her TC.

The second thing she needed to do was arm herself. A maitu was a good idea, but too easily confiscated if she were to be surprised or overpowered. Unfortunately, aside from that, no one else carried a weapon, not even security people unless they were stationed somewhere.

She scanned the room quickly and found nothing that triggered her imagination. Disappointed, Rieka sat at the computer console and linked up with the base's communication grid. Thankfully, a tech-pro had enough clearance to do a signature modification request. She found three other signals nearly identical to hers, then piggybacked onto them. Smiling, she wondered what trouble the Procyons would run into when they went after a Human, a Vekyan, and an Oph.

When the instructions had been given and the

computer verified them, Rieka relaxed slightly. She picked up her stylus, the long three-sided pointer that went with her datapad, and drummed it on the desktop. It could be used as a weapon, she decided, as a last resort. The only other things she could think of would be a dinner knife or a chemical spray, but she wouldn't be able to locate such things until morning. And she still had to be present for the inspection with Commander Bohm.

Deciding she could think better with a decent night's sleep, Rieka grabbed the datapad, snapping the pointer into its place. Staying in her assigned quarters was too risky. She left the room and locked the door. The nursery probably stored cots for expectant parents. She'd try there, first.

Admiral Nason sat in the office he'd commandeered from a base architect, going over his plans for the day. The night had been a long one. He'd kept himself going with *colan,* knowing he couldn't rest until the dedication ceremony was over and the Procyons were all in custody.

At least Robet had been found and was back in command of his ship. Nason wasn't happy Degahv had acted alone and without permission. But, he thought wryly, the rescue had to have unsettled the alien who had taken the place of Captain Pedlam.

And now that the other Pedlam's suspicions were substantiated, he would be doing a lot of second-guessing. He'd be coming up with contingency plans. Escape routes. He'd be going over his crew list with a wary eye. And he'd be keeping tabs on who boarded or left the *Prodigy.*

Possibly, Nason decided, they could find a way to capitalize on that.

The door chimed, then opened, and he looked up to see Finot shuffle through the threshold.

"Anything happening?"

"Quieter than the black void."

"Good." He pushed his datapad out from under his nose and rubbed his bibbets. "Is the auditorium ready?"

Finot bobbed his huge head silently. "Commander Klin has made the arrangements. His percentages are not as I would equate, though. The systems are prepared as the slide."

Nason frowned. It wasn't like the captain to be anything but one hundred percent behind his people. "What is wrong with Klin's percentages?"

Finot waved a five-pointed paw. "His hatching is at hand. All he cogitates is bonding."

"Children bring out the soft spots in most species, Finot. Being Vekyan, Klin isn't immune. Neither are the Boo."

Black eyes double-blinked. "My young ones reached maturity over a century ago."

"I suppose longevity has some quite commendable strong points." He chuckled at the sound of Finot's kroi. "At least you've managed to see this project to its completion."

The kroi clicked again, but Finot said nothing. He sucked on his tube.

"What do you think Pedlam will do when I've announced the dedication ceremony has been relocated from the *Prodigy* to the Little One?"

"His logical progression would be to regroup with his Bittin, then take the ship like mimlet caught with the Skou on a tangent," Finot said, shuffling closer to the desk.

"I agree. If we can't contain them, we'll need to force a confrontation—before they're ready. *If* the big ship is as blind and dumb as it's supposed to be, there's a chance we can win her back."

"Karina of the Rock has done her job," Finot said. He blinked and undulated the fleshy patches over his eyes. "It is inequality for you bipeds to abuse the hearts of Humanity. Many of them have I supervised." He tipped his huge head to the side. "Will our Karina be given credit if today's equation achieves its balance?"

Nason was astounded by the speech. A Boo fond of a Human? "Yes," he said, finally. "I didn't realize she carried meaning for you."

The big sentient sucked some chlorine and blinked again. "This one equates," he said. "She has reached my *ckla*"—he touched his head—"and there is symmetry."

Not knowing quite how to react to this admission, Nason nodded. "I . . . think I understand." He took a moment to collect himself and glanced at his datapad. "I plan to make the announcement at zero-eight-hundred."

Finot's kroi clicked. "I will inform Klin to be ready. The duplicate factors should not be pleased."

Nason smiled. "That's what I'm counting on, Captain."

The main dining room in the Delta Dome bustled with activity. Rieka was silently glad of it. She hadn't been able to sleep well on the tiny cot in the nursery, especially with Klin hovering over his eggs, and wasn't in a mood for polite company. She figured the best place to hide would be a crowd and hoped she could find a big table with an empty seat. She tapped out her request for a pastry and a cup of *colan,* waited for it to emerge from the kitchen hatch, then hunted for a spot.

Three Ophs, a Vekyan, and two Centauris were in a heated debate over the number of sister ships the Fleet would create for the *Prodigy.* One of the Ophs growled something and left. Rieka slid into her chair, happy to eavesdrop on the conversation while she kept watch for anyone who might be searching for her.

She was halfway through her meal when the Vekyan lieutenant lurched out of her seat. "It's a safe bet, I say. The Fleet will have six more in space within a year."

"Not with the economy going the way it is," countered a Centauri. "You can't build ships without money."

"But you're forgetting the incident with the Procyons, Des," the other Centauri said. "No matter what they say Captain Degahv did, she was defending the Eta

Cass system. That was her job. With a Procyon threat, more like the *Prodigy* will come. The Procyons are the only reason the Fleet carries weapons—otherwise we'd still be the Transit Authority!"

Rieka liked her immediately. "I have to agree," she offered. "I heard a rumor that they're designing a dock for the assembly line."

"See, it's only a matter of time, Des," the other said.

They finished eating and stowed their trays. Rieka glanced around. Not finding anything suspicious about the crowd, she followed the group from her table out into the corridor, enjoying the company and animated debate. They were waiting for a Chute to take them to the equipment lockers when she felt something hard nudge her side.

She glanced to the right, smiled at a Centauri lieutenant who'd stepped too close, and eased left. When she bumped into the other Centauri, who had come out of nowhere to flank her, Rieka realized she was in trouble. The half-hidden maitus answered all her questions.

"You will come with us," the one on the right said softly, "or your friends die."

Rieka's half smile faded. It was two against one. The odds weren't that bad, but the weapons definitely prodded her to comply. Not for anything would she risk the others.

"Coming, Lieutenant?"

Her eyes snapped around to the Centauri called Des, who now stood in the open Chute door. "Uh, no, thanks. I've got to—uh . . . I just remembered something else I have to do."

He smiled at her. "See you around, Lieutenant."

As the door closed, Rieka felt her future sliding away with the car. The maitu nudged her in the side again. The two Procyons led her down the main hall to a small alcove.

She kept her shoulders back and stood straight, clutching her datapad and casually unclipping the stylus. Transferring the computer to the other hand,

Rieka slid the stylus up her sleeve, breathing a small sigh of relief that neither of her captors had noticed.

"This is Gilm," the man said, speaking to his TC. "We are ready to transport." He nodded and said something alien to his comrade.

Rieka found herself watching them with a mixture of curiosity and malice. Whatever was in store for her, she knew she could not show fear. The Procyons fed on fear like a hurricane fed on warm water.

"We're going to the *Prodigy,* right?"

"Affirmative."

"Well that works out perfectly," she said, smiling. "I've got an inspection with Commander Bohm in—a few minutes. It's flattering, but I really didn't need an escort."

"You will not see Bohm," the man replied.

Before she could come up with a suitable reply, the InterMAT effect began.

K'resh-va was neither awake nor asleep when the TC in his ear clicked. Cursing its designer to a slow and painful death, he accepted the signal. "What now?" he snapped, switching on the light over his bed.

O'don-la's voice spoke in his ear. "Your uninvited guest is aboard, Captain. Where would you like to interrogate her?"

All thoughts of the TC inventor's entrails left his mind. His men had apprehended Degahv. It was time to put his strategy to work. E'bid-va lived in a dreamworld where plans were never altered. K'resh-va wondered how the old man had gotten as far as he did. "Bring her to the conference room in quad B, level 2. Post guards at the door."

"At once, Captain."

Wanting to present a formidable impression on his captive, K'resh-va dressed in a fresh uniform, groomed the blond hair around his face straight back in his old, Procyon fashion, and left his rooms. A moment later, he was nodding at the pakits guarding Degahv.

"She offered no resistance, sir," one said.

"*You* found her?"

He nodded.

"And you left unseen?"

"Yes, sir."

"Excellent work. Make sure Commander Durak has your file updated."

The man stood straighter. "Thank you, sir."

He grunted, lifted his chin, and entered the chamber. O'don-la was seated at a long oval table. There were nine additional seats, but the room's other occupant had chosen to stand. She leaned toward him with a look on her face that professed a desire to kill.

"Captain Degahv," K'resh-va chimed, giving her cause to divide her attention. "I see you have met my second-in-command."

Rieka's expression melted into a false smile. She recognized the man who'd taken Pedlam's place even before she looked at him. With a glance at Durak that told him the conversation wasn't finished, she straightened to her full height.

"We've been debating the outcome of your plan to take over the Commonwealth," she said sweetly, shoving her fear aside. This shrewd Procyon would be judging her, calculating everything she did. Like any predator, he would know she was afraid—and base his opinion of her on how she reacted to it.

No fear, Rieka, she told herself. Think of the Heralds. Think of Finot. Of Triscoe and Robet. Klin and his eggs. No fear. She took a deep breath. "I'm sure you don't mind if my opinion differs from yours."

"Of course not," he agreed. "Opinions often have nothing to do with facts."

Cute, she thought, for a bastard. But how to handle him, even without fear? She held herself ready, waiting for some kind of clue as to how to proceed. He stood there, watchful, probably trying to unnerve her.

"Who told you who I was?" she asked.

"You did." He smiled wolfishly at her surprised reaction. "You left a bit of yourself on the console in detention."

She accepted that with a shrug. Having the console checked would have been on her list of things to do, too. Obviously, he knew his job. She'd have to be careful with what she told him. He'd be second-guessing everything she said.

He gestured her to sit. She did, selecting a chair far from Durak. The captain took a seat across from her, and they sized each other up for a long moment. He leaned over the table. She sat back and crossed her arms over her flat chest. Her fear was under control. But what about his?

What are you thinking, Procyon? she wanted to ask. *What are your plans?*

He watched her watching him, waiting for the bravado to crack. But this Human, even in the guise of a Centauri, had an alien quality he could not name. When she had merely been Mogin, she'd seemed complacent, even passive. Now, as Degahv, her whole appearance had changed—even though she still looked the same. He found the divergence remarkable. It intrigued him. K'resh-va found himself poised with anticipation.

"If all you wanted to do was look at me, I'd have sent you a hologram," she said.

"Oh, I plan to do much more than look, Captain," he replied softly. "At the moment, however, I am trying to decide whether to kill you now—or later. Or, I could keep you for . . . entertainment."

He had no intention of coupling with an inferior being, but research had provided him with certain aspects of Commonwealth culture. He hoped he could now capitalize on the information. Humans, especially, were unstrung by the thought of either torture or rape.

To his surprise, she laughed. "Oh, you're a charmer, aren't you?"

K'resh-va sat back, trying not to let his temper show.

He collected himself and changed tactics. "What have you done to my ship?"

"Technically," she corrected, "it isn't *your* ship."

"You have been aboard for days, Captain. I have seen you at work," he snapped.

"Have you?" she asked, her blue eyes issuing a tacit challenge. "Have you really seen me *do* anything to this ship? I've set up some test programs. You've probably already checked them out."

He nodded. "Of course." That had been the first order of business, E'bid-va be damned. His precious schedule meant nothing, now.

She leaned an elbow onto the arm of her chair. "I'm a Fleet captain—as you've so astutely deduced. What the hell would I know about panoply circuitry? Captain Finot briefed me on how to handle the equipment, and how to set up some preflight tests. Your instruments were installed to Fleet specs weeks ago."

"Then why were you aboard as a tech-pro?"

"Can't put anything past you, can I?" she said sarcastically. "You already know they put me here to find out how much of your crew is . . . not of Commonwealth descent." She casually glanced down the table at Durak. "That was all. I've done my job."

"And a bit more," he coaxed.

"Really?"

"I refer to that little incident with Captain DeVark."

"Oh." She waved that off. "That was nothing. He'd do the same for me."

"We shall see." He shifted in the chair. "Now, you will tell me just exactly what the Fleet knows."

She grinned at him. Time to play the game. She'd lied, telling him things he expected to hear—things he would believe. Now, she'd have to tell him something he wouldn't believe.

"We know everything, Pedlam—or whatever your name *really* is," she added with a small wave of her hand.

He growled, and it sounded like some kind of unintelligible word, probably a Procyon curse.

"What?"

"My name is unimportant. And I don't believe you, Captain. Your people cannot possibly know *any*thing, much less *every*thing."

She had him, now. He didn't believe her! Time for the most outrageous story to be told. Time for the truth.

"Oh, but we do," she returned, with another arrogant grin, hoping he'd believe the whole thing was an act. "*Every* last detail. From that fake Tohab who's stolen my ship, to the people that had their minds raped by the machine on Aurie—to the bunch of you who think they can get away with the *Prodigy*." She clucked her tongue, reminding herself of the Boos. "What do you think we are, a flock of sheep? Wake up, Captain, the panoply is fine-focusing—on you."

During her speech, K'resh-va found himself growing more and more irritated. She was in no position to try to harass him. Yet while she answered his questions, Degahv seemed to be slapping his face with them. Obviously, some kind of ploy. He growled. She didn't react. More bravado.

"How did you discover us?" he demanded.

"Why should I tell you?"

"To save your life."

She shrugged and said nothing. Apparently that was not the proper bait. "I still have Fleet personnel aboard," he said. "If your own life means nothing, what of your people?"

"You're lying. They're probably dead already."

"I assure you, they are happily working at their stations. Of course, once the Heralds arrive, the lives of the crew will have little value. But for the moment . . ."

She made a strange face at him and took a deep breath. If he read his aliens correctly, this meant she would tell him how they'd uncovered the deception. "I'm waiting, Captain."

"You didn't bother about the Boos," she said, finally.

"The Boos?" he repeated. A curious correlation.

"Your engineers. Those big blue beings that suck chlorine as an atmospheric additive. You know, the ones with three legs—that talk in images and—"

"Yes, I know who they are," he snapped. "What about them?"

"They're very good judges of character, Captain," she answered. "They saw through you like that." She snapped her fingers and leveled her gaze at him. "It really got funny when Finot kept calling you Pzekii—to your face."

"Pzekii?"

"Oh—so now you're curious?" She was silent for a moment. "Any Centauri captain would have studied the Boos and their language well enough to know who Pzekii was." She waited and watched while he remained silent. "A traitor. A sniveling, backstabbing, lying excuse for a Boo. That was Pzekii. They put him to death when they finally caught up with him. Slowly, of course." She smiled. "Flayed him alive, if I remember my history right. Suffice it to say, the term Pzekii isn't flattering."

He smiled at her attempt to irritate him. The Boos followed no one. They served the Commonwealth simply because their planet was located near the space-transit lanes. "Name-calling is a trait of inferior beings, Degahv. Even if all this is true, your Commonwealth is on the verge of a new future, and neither you nor your precious husband—or even the Boos can stop it."

Rieka ignored the threat. "Look," she began, sitting up straight. "I've been kidnapped by your people several times now, and it's lost all its charm. You want to interrogate me? I don't know much—just what I've been told. And for obvious reasons, it isn't enough to help you in any way."

He gritted his teeth at the retort. "What you do not seem to understand, Captain, is that your life—"

She threw up he hands. "You want to kill me? Then do it. You want to rape me? Fine. The outcome of that would leave one of us mortally wounded. Preferably you." She leaned, ever so slightly, over the table. "I'm tired to death of high-handed fatheaded types—in the Commonwealth or out of it. Do what you're going to do, and quit wasting my time."

She glared at him. What are you thinking now, Procyon? she wondered. Not sure about your plans anymore? Thinking about me, instead of your duty? Lost a touch of your confidence? Good.

K'resh-va found her gaze unnerving. That such an inferior creature could even attempt to intimidate him was a curious, unpleasant experience.

For some reason, though, he wanted to pursue it. But not now. Once declared a hero, he could spare the time to delve into his whims. His immediate concern involved the final preparations for the dedication ceremony in just over two hours.

Without taking his eyes from hers, K'resh-va spoke to O'don-la. "She will remain here, under guard. Feed her if she is hungry."

"Should we not put her in a detention cell?"

"The dignitaries will be arriving soon," he replied, this time looking at his second-in-command. "Some may wish a tour. We cannot risk her being seen."

"Understood, Captain."

K'resh-va rose and went to the door. She had asked him to kill her, more than once. Perhaps her wish would be granted, but not yet. "Welcome to the *Prodigy,* Captain Rieka Degahv," he said. "I'm sure we can find ways of making your stay here . . . interesting."

She continued to hold her ground. "No doubt."

He nodded to O'don-la, who rose and stood at his shoulder. They left the room together and headed for the bridge. "Remarkable Human," K'resh-va said, finally.

"The only one I've had more than a passing conversation with," O'don-la replied. "But, as you say, remarkable. None of our people would have spoken to you like that."

The captain smiled a lower-toothed Procyon smile. "She's desperate—and worried we will kill the Heralds once they're aboard. She knows this ship is invincible, and lashes out to make us reconsider our plans. An obvious ploy, O'don-la."

"Of course."

They entered the bridge together. K'resh-va took his seat while O'don-la checked the morning news on the information grid. A few moments of silence passed before the other man gasped and cursed.

"What is it?" K'resh-va demanded.

"It is in the Base announcements," O'don-la explained. "Admiral Nason has relocated the ceremony to an auditorium on the Little One."

"He *what?*" K'resh-va hauled himself from his chair and shoved O'don-la aside.

"It is here, Captain."

He scanned the communiqué. "Damn him to the Pillars of Teska," he muttered, gripping the console as he tried to make sense of what was happening. "I knew the incident with DeVark would be our undoing. Find E'bid-va. I will speak to him. He should have listened to me before," K'resh-va muttered. "He will now." The ceremony and the Heralds had slipped from his grasp, but at least he had the *Prodigy*. He looked at O'don-la. "Prepare the ship for departure."

"But, Captain, we have only just begun the preliminary checklist."

"I said we are leaving, Commander. As soon as possible. Have I made myself clear?"

Quickly, the other man nodded and stood straight. "I will commence with departure procedures immediately."

"And power up the weapons systems. Before we leave, I wish to bestow a gift upon Admiral Nason."

Twenty-one

Triscoe entered his bridge wearing a scowl. Technicians were still working on various consoles and exposed hardware, reminding him the *Providence* was not ready for battle yet. And they hadn't finished testing the new circuitry on the light-bending screens, either. Couldn't Nason have notified him of the change in plans before they had been posted with the morning bulletins? It seemed like everyone had conspired against him.

But his orders, now, were clear and concise: keep an eye on the *Prodigy*.

Was that some kind of a joke?

The big ship's dock orbited the Little One directly opposite the *Providence*. Without a direct line of sight, they were forced to use images provided by the base. The odd perspective made Triscoe anxious, though he wouldn't have been comfortable even if the image came from his own panoply.

The worst thing was they could not leave the docking platform. If they did, Pedlam would know immediately he'd been lied to about the status of the ship. By staying in the dock, though, the *Providence* would lose precious minutes should the *Prodigy* try to run, or attack.

"Update tactical, Aarkmin," he said while setting up his console for a running report of communications between Pedlam and the Little One.

"As we speak."

A glance at the DGI told him the admiral's announcement had rearranged more than just the Herald's plans. "She's leaving." He hit the intercom button. "*Providence* crew this is Captain Marteen. Condition red. All hands to your stations. This is not a drill. I repeat, this is not a drill." Then, to the technicians still working on the bridge equipment, he said, "Keep at it until you're done."

"We can't handle this alone, Captain," Aarkmin advised, her expression grim.

"I know. V'don, get me Admiral Nason." His crew had performed well in the skirmish with the *Venture*. But what would happen against the *Prodigy*, even with the *Prospectus*'s help? He could not allow himself to doubt. It would show, sealing their doom. "Lisk, prepare us for immediately departure," he said.

"I can't get a direct line to the admiral, sir," V'don said. He lifted his hands and shrugged. "His aide keeps telling me to stand by. He's giving the opening speech. I'll try Captain Finot—or would you rather I try the Prime Admiral?"

"Whoever will talk to you," he spit. "We need to coordinate, now."

Triscoe felt as though he were falling from a great height. "Open a channel to the *Prospectus*. Put it on one-third screen." He waited impatiently until Robet's face took up a section of the DGI.

"I'm here," he said.

"They're leaving," Triscoe began without preamble. "Nason's giving his opening speech and his aide won't allow a channel through. We went over this scenario last night. Let's assume the Procyon captain will not leave peacefully."

Robet sighed. "I hope they're ready down there. They have no experience protecting themselves."

Triscoe nodded. "The admiral's just nipped him where it hurt. It would be foolish to think he wouldn't snap back." Though designed to resist Eridani's occasional deadly radiation, the base's defense screens were not military-standard. Triscoe hoped they would provide some buffer against antimatter shells. "At least the auditorium is on a lower level. The Heralds are probably safe enough. It's the rest of the base I'm worried about. Right now, the best we can do is offer ourselves as alternative targets."

Robet nodded. "I'm ready."

"Nason's plan is to lure them away. Are we agreed on Jaxu? It isn't far and has several moons that aren't too close to be in the way."

Robet nodded. "Agreed. When do you want me to get his attention?"

"Now, but nothing overt, yet," Triscoe warned. He could feel Aarkmin wince. She, too, liked things to be plotted and arranged.

"You really think we can take him?"

"If Rieka has done her job, we have a chance."

The image of Robet was uncharacteristically sober. "Whatever happens here, I'll leave first. It'll look like we've gone off on different trajectories."

Triscoe nodded. "Keep the channel open."

"Absolutely."

Ignoring the camera, Robet carried on, and Triscoe ordered the DGI sound cut down to the minimum. He looked at his executive officer. "Take us out of port and into orbit, Aarkmin. I'll be in the Status Room working on tactical."

"Yes, sir." Glancing at Lisk with a trace of apprehension, she began issuing orders.

Admiral Nason had just finished his speech and taken an aisle seat. He tried to focus on Bik Honutik's address when he smelled chlorine. Finot stood less than a meter away, looking directly at him. He immediately forgot the Vekyan Herald, quietly left his chair, and caught up to Finot in the curved corridor beyond the last row of seats.

"Something has happened?" he whispered.

"Enough."

Nason followed Finot's gesture. Several places were

empty. Most were those reserved for people from the *Providence* and *Prospectus*. He had noticed it some time ago. Now, he realized Pedlam and Bittin were absent, not just running late.

"The big ship is leaving," Finot explained quietly.

Nason looked at him in disbelief. "What?" Marteen had express orders to report any odd behavior with regard to the *Prodigy*. Why hadn't he said something?

The Boo did not repeat himself. "It is a factor," he replied cryptically. "Perhaps the Procyons have seen Mohb beyond the decimal? We are like the Little One in the Light. Sometimes illuminated. Sometimes not."

"This is bad," Nason mumbled, not wanting to face the possibilities the captain implied. His primary plan had just been cast aside. Would the backup do the job? "But they can't mobilize the ship yet," he complained. "There isn't a full crew aboard."

Finot blinked. "Analysis of the assessment shows you are incorrect. Has our Karina reported many Centauri-not crew?"

Nason frowned. "Certainly," he said softly. "She estimated there were just over forty. That's not nearly enough to man a ship that size."

"You speculate like an Aurian, my admiral," Finot said.

A sobering concept. Nason stopped to consider it. He had been thinking as if he were the *Prodigy*'s captain. But would a Procyon think that way? Probably not. At least DeVark and Marteen had already planned a counterattack. It remained to be seen if that would do any good.

"We'll need to get these people to a better-protected area," he said quietly, gesturing toward the auditorium.

"Obviously."

Turning on his heel, Nason headed for the door. "And notify Klin to set the screens. It may already be too late."

With the Boo stumping alongside him, he left the auditorium. A small lobby separated it from the corridor. Blocking the door were two Centauri lieutenants. Nason saluted briefly. "At ease," he said.

The guards remained standing in the path to the exit, the salute unreturned. Maitus were strapped to their hips. The man on the right took up his and leveled it. The other followed his example. "No one is allowed to leave the ceremony."

Inwardly, Nason huffed. "By whose order, Lieutenant?"

"Captain Pedlam."

He glanced at Finot. The Boo clicked his kroi slowly. These men were Procyons. "I see," he said, addressing the guard. "Well, I'm Admiral Nason— Captain Pedlam's superior officer. Captain Finot, here, is commander of this base." He gestured toward the Boo. "We have urgent business to attend to at the mission center." He tried to step through the pair. They didn't budge.

Finot's kroi began to click strangely, as if the Boo had devised some kind of plan. Perhaps they could distract them, somehow, and overpower one or both.

He glanced at Finot and nodded. "Gentlemen, you don't seem to understand the gravity of the situation."

The guard on the left pulled himself a bit straighter. "It is you, Admiral, who fail to comprehend the situation. Our orders come directly from Admiral Bittin through the captain. No one leaves."

"Lieutenant, I shall personally see that you are—"

"Lieutenant," Finot interrupted, stepping between Nason and the guards, "is there no way to circumvent the orders? Perhaps, equate this through Admiral Bittin? Or additionally, the Prime Admiral is within." He gestured with a star-shaped hand toward the doors just behind Nason. "The word of the Fleet Chief Executive Officer would slide quickly over a mere admiral in charge of internal politics."

"No one is to leave," the man said implacably.

Nason wondered what Finot's plan might be. Crush the biped? Crude, but effective. The Boo stood in front of him, gesturing with his huge hand, and Nason got the idea he was being protected. Then, the odor of chlorine became very strong.

Perfect, Nason thought, grab the maitus while they're half-blind with tears.

But then a weapon discharged, and the huge Boo stumbled backward on his three legs, crashing into Nason, driving them both back through the auditorium doors.

The commotion will disrupt the ceremony, he thought perversely, as he tried to support Finot's massive bulk. A sharp knifelike pain shot through his chest as he went down under the captain. His awareness quickly shrank to a sticky black ooze on his hands, a crowd beginning to form, and the grisly crunch of snapping bone.

A moment later, or perhaps an hour, he struggled to open his eyes. The pain was intense, now, but he fought through it. Lives were at stake. What had happened to Finot? The *Prodigy*? The base? Had more people been hurt by the Procyons in the foyer? Or had they been overpowered?

Setana Marteen crouched over him, her face drawn with concern. "Merik, do you hear me?"

"Mmm." He wanted to say more but couldn't get his breath.

"Do not try to talk," she soothed. A small smile found its way to her face.

Relief, he thought. She's relieved I'm still alive. *But what's happened? Can you tell what I'm thinking, Setana?* he shouted in his mind. *What's happened?*

"I will tell you everything you need to know," she said, though he couldn't tell if she'd heard his plea. "You have been unconscious for less than five minutes. Ker and Cimpa pulled you out from under Captain Finot. He's been wounded by a maitu. We think he crushed one or more of your ribs. You may have a punctured air sack. Remain quiet. Security has been alerted and are on their way. Two guards are blocking the door and the Prime Admiral is furious." She gripped his hand. "It may be a little while before you can receive medical attention, Merik. There are three physicians here, but, without facilities, they are completely incapacitated."

Nason nodded that he understood and turned his head slightly, noticing Cimpa, the Oph Herald, and Ker Marteen standing over him. "Thank you, Merik," the tall Centauri said jauntily, though his eyes were bright with concern. "I would have started snoring soon, had it not been for you."

He managed a half smile and mouthed, "You're welcome." It felt like being singed by fire to breathe, but he kept the movements small and through his nose. Unable to see more than a few faces, the ceiling, and a knot of milling dignitaries, Nason wondered whether his people had the slightest chance of retaking the *Prodigy*.

Think positively, he told himself, trying to beat down the feeling of fire in his chest. He had to assume Marteen and DeVark had gone after it, as planned. At least there were two ships and their captains ready to do battle.

The pain in his chest, searing as it was, could not mask the growing sense of doom Nason felt. In a battle with the *Prodigy*, they might not make any difference at all.

He gripped Setana's hand and instantly her eyes were on his. "You must evacuate to the lower levels," he whispered hoarsely. "The *Prodigy* has left port."

Her expression turned steely and she squeezed his fingers. "I'll tell the Prime Admiral," she whispered. "And I'll see that we get you to a ward. Rest, Merik. You've done all you can do. It is up to the young ones, now."

He had no choice but to obey her as he lost touch with the pain. Unconsciousness wrapped itself around him like a welcome black shroud.

* * *

K'resh-va looked impatiently at O'don-la. "How many did we leave on the Little One?"

"Two. Just the ones that were sent a few minutes ago to stall the Fleet at the auditorium."

He grunted and kept his eyes trained on the DGI. It had taken them much longer than he'd hoped to be ready to leave. An analysis of all the systems Degahv had worked on was still in progress. Thus far, what she'd told him seemed to be true. Everything, including the DGI, worked perfectly.

But K'resh-va did not believe her. He told himself to be thankful that she hadn't gone near the defense or propulsion labs.

"Have you collected the rest of the Commonwealth people and locked them up?"

"That task should be complete momentarily," O'don-la said. "Many were already on the base."

"Captain." The communications officer jerked to attention. "I have a report from the guards at the auditorium. There has been a confrontation of some kind. At least two Fleet personnel are injured. They feel sure they will not hold their position."

"The job is done, that is all we need consider." Two less to man the ship would be felt, but he could not afford to waste time by retrieving them. The Little One's defense screen hadn't been activated. He needed to attack now. "Bring our orbit in to twenty thousand kilometers, C'res-la."

"Yes, Captain."

He waited impatiently while his orders were carried out. He would soon have the opportunity to test the huge ship under his feet. The *Prospectus* would come after him, of course. But he would crush DeVark in a matter of moments.

Prodigy, he thought. Even translated, it was a stimulating word.

Silently, K'resh-va reviewed the farsighted rationale of this plot. Nothing in the Commonwealth could take on this vessel. Even several of them together did not have the firepower the *Prodigy* had. With a Procyon smile, he took a great breath and expelled it slowly. Being the commander of an invincible ship was a feeling he had not been able to anticipate.

"Captain!" O'don-la exclaimed. K'resh-va's reverie came to a halt, and his eyes widened at the image on the DGI.

Space docks on the far side of the Little One were visible, two ships conspicuously missing. "Where are they?" he barked.

Frantically, both O'don-la and the communications officer, N'orb-ta, worked their consoles. "We've been off-line with the station," N'orb-ta explained. "They must have made their departure in the last few minutes."

"To where?" he shouted.

"Unknown," N'orb-ta said.

"Then get back on-line, double-check your panoply reports," K'resh-va barked. "They could be anywhere! And bring us to an optimum position to fire on the base's Delta Dome."

"Yes, sir."

"Where would they go?" he muttered to himself, trying to ignore the fact that Marteen had obviously lied about the *Providence*. It struck him, then, that Degahv might have actually been telling him the truth.

Until this moment, he had not believed a thing she'd said. Now, he saw the design of her cleverness. How long had the Fleet known? He found it incredible that they had let him carry on as if he were the real Pedlam. But if they had not been able to trust anyone, any scenario would have been difficult to predict.

Grudgingly, he had to admire Marteen for his control. He wondered how calm the Centauri would be, however, when Degahv's life dangled before him.

If it was their intent to challenge, K'resh-va decided, they would not travel far. They would want enough room to move without concerning themselves about engaging an enemy so close to the Little One, but not so far they might lose him. Nodding to himself, he called up the tactical display of the system in orbit around Forty Eridani.

Concentrating, K'resh-va studied the orbit of a gas giant whose present position was barely eighty million kilometers away. "There, O'don-la," he said, finally, pointing to the closer planet.

"Sir?"

"Jaxu. A planet in this system," he explained as if to a child. "The Fleet ships will most likely be waiting for us somewhere between here and there. Once we destroy the moon base, we'll follow them to seal their doom."

"Of course sir. Optimal striking distance—less than a minute."

K'resh-va glanced at the lieutenant in charge of weapons deployment. "Report."

"Systems are on-line, sir," he said.

"What kind of array can you arrange, M'arv-la?"

"Twenty-eight shells, Captain. Our maximum single volley."

"Prepare them. Launch in fifteen seconds."

"The *Providence* is coming around from the far side," O'don-la announced. "Its weapons are powered up."

"Shall I redirect our target, Captain?" M'arv-la asked.

"No. It is obviously a ploy to keep our attention from the primary target. We will deal with Marteen later. Our screens are up. Nothing is a threat to us. Fire at the base. I have a craving for destruction."

Rieka smiled at the guard. Maybe, she thought wryly, I should have been an actress. The interview with the captain had surprised her. In the face of losing it all, she'd found a talent she hadn't recognized before. Pedlam's irritation only served to fuel her resolve. She wondered how long she could keep up the act.

The Procyon called Gilm had posted himself inside

the door. She needed to use her TC. But in order to do that, she had to get rid of Gilm, first.

She circled the table, tapping a chair every now and then with her fingers. Rounding the last corner, she faced him. "Look, uh, whatever your name is . . ."

"Gilm."

She made a face at him. "I mean your real name."

"Pakit G'ilm-ta."

"Pack-it?"

"My rank."

She nodded. "Fine, Pack-it. I don't know about you Procyons, but we Humans have a thing called a digestive system. We eat. Our bodies process the raw materials into useful compounds, and then we have to eliminate the waste." She squinted at him. "Is any of this familiar to you?"

"You have need of the lavatory."

"On the first try!" She smiled. "I'm . . . it's kind of an emergency? Could we go now?"

He frowned as if trying to decide whether or not he needed to get permission first, then nodded and leveled his weapon at her. "I will escort you."

"Perfect."

She allowed him to gesture her out the door and ambled in front of him until they got to a lav station. The door opened when she pressed the entry switch. When she stepped inside the small room, he followed.

"Now, wait just a minute, Pack-it," she warned. The look she gave him would have withered an ordinary lieutenant, but the Procyon didn't seem to notice. "A Human female requires privacy."

"Captain K'resh-va's orders are that I must be with you at all times," he insisted.

She noted that tidbit of information and gestured to the small room behind her. "Where am I going to go?"

Gilm studied at her. Seconds passed while he made his decision. "I will wait outside this door," he said, gesturing to the stall containing the humanoid toilet. "You will expedite the process, or I will enter."

Rieka decided not to argue. He might decide to forget the excursion and go back to the meeting room. The moment the stall door closed, she flushed the toilet and clicked on her TC. "Link to the *Providence*. Mogin to Captain Marteen," she said softly.

The voice in her ear seemed both relieved and frantic, but it crackled with static. "Rieka, where are you?"

"You're not going to like it."

"The *Prodigy*?"

The water bubbled back up into the tiny commode, so she flushed it again, hoping the *pakit* wouldn't realize what she was doing. "Right. Two of Pedlam's men personally invited me. I couldn't resist."

"There's no easy way to say this, Rieka, and I don't know how much time I've got. He's left the dock and fired an entire volley at the base. Robet and I are going to try to—"

"Triscoe? Tris?" She clicked her TC again. It was still on. "Triscoe! Dammit." They'd been cut off. Rieka knew her modified signal could not have been traced in under a minute. That left only one other possibility— the base's comm grid had been hit. It wasn't unlikely, the static had been pretty bad to begin with.

She found herself breathing too fast. What had happened to the base? The Heralds? Was it completely gone, or had they managed to switch on the radiation screens? Would it have done any good?

She felt her stomach lurch. Admiral Nason's words echoed through her mind. Should the most undesirable situation take place—the *Prodigy*'s theft—she would be considered expendable.

Triscoe and Robet would attack, and she knew Pedlam would not give up, ever. To stop him, they would have to try to destroy the *Prodigy*—unless she could somehow immobilize it first. She peered over the partition walls, scanning the ceiling. Nothing but a vent panel, too small to crawl through.

Thankful she'd managed to palm the stylus from her

datapad before it had been confiscated, Rieka bent to pull it from her sock. She looked back up at the panel. It was hopeless. And she'd be better off if she had a real weapon. Gilm's maitu sprang to mind.

Smiling to herself, Rieka tugged off her tunic and removed the strip of material Twanabok had given her. Sliding back into her shirt, she wrapped one end of the binding around her hand. She could see Pack-it Gilm's boots under the door. He faced away from her.

Perfect.

Pushing the flush switch once more, Rieka quietly undid the latch. As far as anyone knew, Procyons were similar to Humans in the agility and strength departments. With the element of surprise, she figured she could take him. She had to.

Curling her shoulder to soften the blow, Rieka threw herself at the partition door. It flew open, crashing into Gilm. He stumbled forward. Then, growling from deep in his chest, he turned, aiming the maitu.

She recovered faster than he did and tried to knock the weapon from his hand. He staggered back, still facing her. If she couldn't disarm him, she needed to get behind him.

He wasn't cooperating.

Gilm brought his hand up. Before he could fire, Rieka launched herself, headlong, into his midsection. Gilm fell back against the partition between the Vekyan and humanoid toilets, then reeled from the impact. Rieka avoided the flailing arms, then slipped the binding over his head and tightened it around his throat.

The Procyon turned, trying to dislodge her. His fingers clawed at the binding. She twisted it tighter. He threw himself back against the wall, but Rieka hung on, knowing he'd black out soon. Still, he continued to use her for a battering ram. Three times. Four times. Her breath caught at the pain in her side. She lost count after the fifth impact.

When Rieka thought she could not take another jolt,

Gilm began to weaken. His face had turned an astonishing shade of orange. He staggered, fell to one knee,
and made strange hissing sounds. Then he suddenly
spun around, jerking her into one of the toilet's parti-
tions. The edge clipped her solidly behind the ear.

Both she and Gilm sank to the floor, unconscious.

Triscoe watched, horrified, as the *Prodigy*'s barrage
contacted the Little One's Delta Dome. Explosions
annihilated great chunks of it, leaving gaping holes all
the way through to the inhabited sections. The spheres
that missed the dome touched off smaller blasts on the
moon's surface, closing on the next nearest dome. He
felt his jaw clench with anger and inadequacy. The big
ship could destroy the entire base, given enough time.
He had to do something. Now.

"V'don, are you sure we've lost contact with
Admiral Nason?"

"Nothing's working, Captain," the communications
officer replied. "The grid's completely gone." The
worry in his voice was barely under control. "All
we've got is inter- and intraship."

He looked up at the DGI. Robet's bibbets were pink.
Keeping his own voice as even as he could, he said,
"We're on our own, Robet."

"You want to call this one?" he asked from his third
of the DGI.

"Yes," he said. "The Pzekii's screens are active, but
I want you attack from below his canopy, anyway. Aim
for the central pylon and the engineering pod. I'll work
on the panoply from above. Try to stay beyond his port
meridian. I'll keep to starboard."

He glanced at his helmsman. Lisk nodded and bent
to his console. They needed to keep Pzekii from firing
on the base again, perhaps draw him into a battle.
Seeing what had already been done to the Little One,
Triscoe knew they might very well lose.

Robet grinned at him. "I almost forgot how quick

you are, Tris. That cuts his counterassault on either one of us by half."

He nodded. It might help, but not much. The defensive strategies they'd all been forced to learn came back to him quickly, though he'd hoped he'd never have to use them. Triscoe detested violence, but the Procyons could be dealt with in no other way.

He frowned as the *Prodigy*'s image slid past a nearby docking station, blocking the big ship from view. They were too close to the base. There were things in orbit everywhere, both manned and unmanned.

"We need to draw him away from the Little One," he advised. "I can't keep him in view. And there's no room to maneuver here with all these support stations and docks."

"I'm with you," Robet said. "What about the base?"

Triscoe felt an ache in his fingers and looked down. His left hand was clenched to tightly he could not relax it. "Let's just think about one thing at a time," he replied, looking up into the bright eyes of his friend.

"Understood." Robet nodded, and glanced to his right. "We are coming up on minus forty-five degrees off the *Prodigy*'s port side."

"We'll be at positive forty-five degrees to her starboard," Lisk offered, "in . . . seven seconds."

"Fire when it suits you, Robet," Triscoe said. "The best we can do right now is avoid too many impacts. Don't use the new equipment until we've got some room."

"Absolutely." His attention left the DGI as he concentrated on his assault.

Triscoe glanced at Becker. "Aim a steady flow of maximum charged spheres at his upper sensory equipment. We need to weaken his screen."

"As we speak, sir," the Human said.

Before they could fire their first shell, the flash of incoming spheres lit the DGI. Triscoe sat forward and studied the tactical display on his console. Lisk automatically made an evasive maneuver, shifting their position away from the onslaught. Six of the spheres sailed past. The other eight made contact, but none simultaneously, which would have overloaded the system. With the sabotage Rieka had committed, the *Prodigy*'s aim was definitely off. He wondered how soon the Procyon would realize it.

Triscoe looked up at the DGI. "He's only making contact about 60 percent, Robet. We've got to get him away from the Little One. Areas without screens will be hit by stray shells."

"I'll pull away first," Robet offered. "We'll see if he follows."

Triscoe's attention returned to the tactical screen at his elbow. He watched as the small circle that represented the *Prospectus* moved off. The *Prodigy* followed but only enough to stay midway between the smaller ships.

"V'don," he said, "set up a comnet with that ship."

"Yes, sir."

The DGI's blank section flashed for a moment but stayed gray, indicating an incomplete circuit. He looked at V'don. The Aurie communications officer nodded that their end of the link was open.

"I know you can hear me," Triscoe taunted. "Are you too frightened to show your face?"

The image cleared instantly, revealing a not-quite-Centauri captain. He grinned in a way Triscoe found vulgar. "You are doomed, Marteen. This ship can take on a dozen of yours and prevail. I will crush—"

"Then why haven't you, already?"

The man's leer turned to outrage. "What?"

"You're producing spheres, but I'm still here," Triscoe advised. "What's the use of a sphere if you can't hit anything with it? Your people weren't trained properly. You won't win, Pzekii. You can try"—he smiled—"but you will *not* prevail."

The other squinted at him. "A commendable front, Marteen. But words only."

"You're telling me you're *not* trying to hit something?"

"I am telling you nothing!" he snapped. "Except, perhaps, that—"

Triscoe motioned V'don to cut the signal and the image instantly returned to the *Prodigy*'s curved exterior.

"Why did you do that?" Aarkmin asked.

"He was going to tell me Rieka's aboard. I know that already. But I don't want him to know it. Now, perhaps, he's done with the base and ready for a fight." He focused on Robet's image. "Did you hear that?"

"Loud and clear."

"Cover the base. Let's see just how badly he wants to prove his point. Lisk?"

"Sir?"

"Take us out to Jaxu on a propulsion curve that would suggest we're powering up to slide."

"As we speak," Lisk replied. He then relayed the order to Memta, in the engineering pod.

"What of Captain Degahv?" Aarkmin asked.

Triscoe frowned and looked at his executive officer. Then, not quite believing it, he repeated the words his mother had spoken last night. "Whatever is going to happen, will happen."

Twenty-two

K'resh-va scowled at the DGI's image, and muttered a curse under his breath. They'd left the base in ruin and followed the two Commonwealth ships for over an hour. But the sweet victory he'd anticipated still eluded him.

"The *Prospectus* is breaking off pursuit again, Captain," C'res-la reported in his habitual monotone, though it now carried a trace of fatigue. "It is twenty degrees to port and fifteen point three degrees negative planar at sixteen thousand kilometers. Twenty-three thousand. Twenty-eight thousand."

"Magnify the DGI," K'resh-va said. He watched the image waver until the blip appeared, a small glowing dot dwarfed by the huge arc of Jaxu's outer gaseous regions. Now, it seemed, DeVark wanted to hide behind a moon.

"Where is the other one?"

"The panoply is not picking up the *Providence* at this time," C'res-la said. "Tactical puts it on Jaxu's far side."

"They are toying with us," O'don-la spit.

K'resh-va smiled, thoroughly enjoying the long-awaited chase. "It is the ploy of an inferior mind." He looked at C'res-la. "Our new objective is the *Prospectus*."

"Yes, Captain."

"Shall I—" C'res-la began.

"How long until we encounter the ship?" K'resh-va asked.

"Sir? We can deploy at this distance. There is no need—"

"How long?" he repeated, glaring at his helmsman. "I

wish to witness the destruction, C'res-la. Not merely to be notified of it by some piece of electronic equipment."

Properly chastised, the *pakit* rounded his eyes. "Three minutes, Captain."

K'resh-va glanced at his console, noting all systems were reporting readiness. "Alert the crew," he announced to no one in particular. "We will engage the enemy in three minutes."

"Yes, Captain," said N'orb-ta. He bent to the grid and began speaking softly.

"Antimatter spheres ready to deploy," M'arv-la at the weapons console reported.

K'resh-va said nothing. He watched the *Prospectus* grow on the DGI. DeVark was a rash captain. He didn't contemplate the repercussions of his actions. But here, he waited near a moon. Had an ambush had been set up—by him and Marteen? K'resh-va stifled a laugh. Those two in their puny ships could not put a dent in his screening, much less damage the hull.

"We are being hailed," N'orb-ta said.

Not bothering to hide his delight, K'resh-va growled. "Let's speak to the Aurian."

DeVark's face appeared, his bibbets flushed, eyes wide. "You are hereby ordered to surrender, Pzekii," he said. "Do not jeopardize the lives of those aboard."

"Oh, be serious, Captain." K'resh-va leered at him, ignoring the now-obvious insult. "*Your* people are the only ones in jeopardy."

The Aurian shook his head. "I'm afraid I can't agree with you. Lower the screens and we can do this without destroying you."

"Your dreams are about to become a nightmare." K'resh-va smiled. He signaled M'arv-la, and a barrage of antimatter spheres spewed toward the smaller ship.

It maneuvered quickly but the screens were contacted a dozen times. "They can hold out indefinitely unless our spheres make simultaneous contact," C'res-la said.

K'resh-va nodded. "Swing us twenty-five degrees to his starboard side. Hit him again with a full barrage."

"Captain," O'don-la began, "I'm picking up the *Providence* again, thirty-six degrees negative planar, ninety-two port, by one hundred thousand kilometers."

"Fine," K'resh-va told him, waiting to see what would happen. Twenty-eight spheres erupted from the *Prodigy*'s canopy and sailed toward the *Prospectus*. He watched it dodge almost half of them.

"His screens are still intact," C'res-la said.

Nodding to himself, K'resh-va squinted, concentrating. They were talented at maneuvering, but more spheres should have made contact. It had been an unanswered question since their first barrage. "How?"

C'res-la said, "We have incoming spheres, Captain. Three in succession from the *Prospectus* and an additional three from the *Providence*."

"Where? Get me a tactical display." K'resh-va cursed at the new image. The second ship had come around Jaxu's south pole while his attention had been directed solely on the first. The *Prodigy*'s DGI image flashed as its screens engaged the assault.

"No damage," C'res-la said.

"Fire off a volley at Marteen," K'resh-va ordered. "And send another at DeVark."

"Yes, sir."

Both ships avoided most of the spheres. "Again, M'arv-la."

Another barrage sailed toward both ships but only 50 percent made contact. K'resh-va growled again, this time with frustration, as he watched the explosions touch themselves off, far from their intended targets. The distinctly Procyon sound came from deep in his chest. "O'don-la, check the panoply's efficiency again."

"Yes, Captain." O'don-la requested the information while K'resh-va concentrated on the battle. Both ships were striking his own repulsion screen with deadly accuracy. Possibly, they might eventually force it to overload.

K'resh-va waited, his impatience and temper growing. He ordered more weapons deployed. The results were, again, disappointing.

O'don-la hissed. "It is correct that we are not efficiently making contact with our target. But the panoply is not in error."

As the thought struck him, K'resh-va instantly knew the weapon-deployment master program had been tampered with. "Degahv!" he shouted, making it sound like an oath. "She ran an efficiency test in the weapons lab."

"But we have confirmed the system's integrity," O'don-la said.

"She's an expert—especially at lying," he snapped. "We have verified a bogus program."

"But how could a captain who knows merely something of every system on a ship become a master of such specific equipment?"

K'resh-va shook his head. "That does not matter. Our aim is off, O'don-la. How else can you explain it? Those ships should be reduced to atoms by now."

"Agreed," his first officer said. "What are your orders, sir?"

K'resh-va thought for a moment and came to a satisfying conclusion. He relaxed back into the contours of his chair and allowed himself to smile slightly. "Repairs could take hours. We shall keep firing at them. It will take longer this way. But the results will be the same, sooner or later."

"Yes, sir."

"Another round," K'resh-va said with a wave at M'arv-la. "Let's get on with it."

Rieka opened her eyes slowly and discovered the pale green underside of a ceramic toilet designed for Vekyans. She peered at it for a long moment before she remembered the battle with Gilm. Rolling quickly, she fought a wave of nausea and lost. Dry-retching into the toilet, she noticed Gilm beside her, still unconscious. She snatched up his maitu, rinsed her mouth with cold water at the sink, bound his hands with the material she'd used to choke him, and went to the door.

How long have I been out? she wondered.

Rieka!

Triscoe? I haven't used my TC. How can I—

The Singlemind. You've done it, he told her. His mind-voice clearly sounded impressed with her new ability, but she immediately recognized his concern.

How long? she repeated. Celebrations could wait.

Almost two hours. We've pulled him away from the Little One. We're at Jaxu, now. He isn't hitting much, Rieka. You did a good job.

That remains to be seen. I've got a maitu. I'll see what kind of damage I can do from here.

Rieka winced and rubbed the knot on her head. She went to the door and peered down the corridor. Empty. A good or bad sign? With the battle still in progress, all hands were probably busy, but she could still run into someone.

Silently cursing Vekyan toilets, she left the lav, walking purposefully away from the interrogation room.

A number of strategies came to her and were dismissed. She didn't have time to find her way to an InterMAT station and pull people off the bridge and into detention. Likewise, there was no time to set up a way to gas the Procyon captain and his cronies.

She had to plan an overt attack. It needed to be quick, simple, and clean. And, she decided fatalistically, it had to work even if the *Providence* and *Prospectus* weren't around to back her up. Triscoe could tell her one thing in his mind, but he couldn't hide how he felt. He was scared. A lot of people had probably died already. More could easily join them.

Planning her strategy in the corridor became too distracting, not to mention painful, since she kept turning her head to scan for Procyons. Rieka decided a Chute was a better hiding place, especially since it could take her wherever she wanted to go.

She stepped to the nearest door. It opened and she immediately regretted her decision. A Boo stood there, silent and huge. She didn't recognize it. There were

many on board, but somehow this encounter felt
planned. Like some kind of trap had been sprung.

She knew the Boo could not chase her if she ran. It
simply didn't move as fast as a human. Still, she stood
there, rooted to the deck, waiting in a kind of hypnotic
stupor, wondering what it would do.

It blinked at her and shuffled forward. Rieka stepped
back to give it space. A glance at its rank bar told her it
was a lieutenant, equal to the rank on her own sleeve.
She nodded and smiled up at it.

The door closed and she realized the Boo had become
a mobile blue wall between her and her objective.

"Excuse me. I need to get to the weapons lab."

"Negative," it rumbled.

She thought the sound from the voice box was
strange, especially since it hadn't been accompanied by
the usual click of kroi. Then, she pondered the
meaning. Negative. No, it wasn't going to let her go to
the lab? Or, no, that wasn't where she needed to be?

"Really, I need to get—" The Boo turned her then,
angling them both down the corridor. The Chute door
was behind him. Her. It. Whatever.

"Well . . . I could just use another one."

She turned and walked ahead of it, hoping she didn't
look as frantic as she felt. *Had* anyone ever asked a
Boo about loyalty? Just why *did* they decide to give
the Commonwealth the gift of their engineering
genius? Would they be just as happy to share it with
the Procyons?

The thoughts racing through her mind came to a
standstill as the next nearest Chute door opened and
another Boo emerged, blocking her path. She gasped.

Rieka, what's happening? Tell me!

It wasn't exactly what she needed at the moment, but
she welcomed Triscoe's voice. Apparently, he'd picked
up her anxiety. *Two Boos have me pinned in a corridor,*
she thought back to him.

Hostile?

I—I'm not sure.

I can't help you!

She felt his anguish. *I know. Get out of my head and let me think. Worry about the* Providence, *not me.*

I can't help it. And then he was gone.

They were closing in on her from both sides. She had the maitu but wondered how much damage it might do to a Boo. Possibly not enough. On the other hand, shooting them would be better than being asphyxiated by chlorine or flattened like a bug. There were no doors to use as an escape route, giving her cause to wonder how well they had this planned. She was considering her chances of slipping past either of them without being crushed into a bulkhead, when the first one spoke again.

"You are Mogin?"

Deny it or not? she wondered. There wasn't time to ponder the choice, so she went with her instinct.

"Yes. Mogin," she answered not wanting to give too much away by saying more. Most junior officers had little contact with Boos. Few had studied the history of their terms well enough to communicate. Maybe, if she left the Lieutenant Mogin facade in place, they would leave her alone. Casually, her palm tightened around the maitu.

"Also the reciprocal, Degahv?"

She watched it blink and her eyes stung with the odor of chlorine. Not knowing whether she wanted to admit that, yet, Rieka asked, "Who wishes to know this?"

"Lieutenant Keldan."

"Why is it so important a thing to know?"

"I am ordered to seek the reciprocal Human," it said.

"By whom?"

The wait seemed to go on forever. The Boo behind her made small noises with its kroi but said nothing through the translator. At the point Rieka thought she was about to hear that Captain Pzekii had sent it, the Boo simply blinked at her and twitched the fold of skin over its eye.

"Bohm."

She felt almost light-headed with relief. "And why does she wish this? Are you to take me to her?"

"Negative. Bohm rests in the pod of gravitational birth. Communication request is desired without searching from the bridge."

A secret communication? This sounded better all the time. Rieka nodded up at Keldan. "I'm Degahv. Let's get out of the corridor. Are you supposed to act as an intermediary? A bridge over the Driel toward an accurate response?"

Now, the kroi clicked in a cadence she recognized. "Correct to the equation." The Boo turned and retraced its steps. They passed the Chute and lav, and went in the interrogation room, now empty.

Keldan immediately began speaking in what she recognized as the Boo's native language. A moment later the voice from the box on its chest said, "Who speaks?"

"Degahv. I go by many names. Captain Finot called me Karina of the Rock, Commander," Rieka replied, wondering how they'd managed to hook up the voice box with the ship's TC grid. "I have spoken to you in the corridor."

"It is negative for you to be here, Karina-Degahv. I am Bohm."

"Yes. Bohm." The female, she reminded herself, rubbing the lump on her head. It still hurt, and she couldn't ignore it. "Do you look for Varannah from the Procyons, Bohm?" she asked, staring up into the shiny, vacant black eyes of Keldan.

"It matters not," she said. "I am as the stars. Not aligned."

She had wondered about that. But if she wasn't loyal to the Commonwealth, then why go to all the trouble of arranging this private conversation? Could it be because she wanted a push?

"Then think of this, Bohm of Boo. Will you raise your mimlets and their mimlets in a place where no one seeks to know you? Where you are alone as if on your own world? Where for your effort, nothing equates?"

"It would be illogical to choose inequality," the voice said after a moment.

"The universe is like pi to the Procyons," Rieka continued. "It does not end. Not the destruction. Not the consumption. They just continue to feed—and give nothing back."

After another long silence, kroi clicked slowly. "What is your equation, Karina of the Rock?"

She smiled. She had her. And perhaps, the other Boos on board. "The battle continues. And who shall prevail?"

"We are engaged with the *Prospectus* and *Providence* at point two AU from the planet, Jaxu of Forty Eridani. We are unable to function a victory."

Rieka felt a wave of relief. If it hadn't been impossible, she would have ordered Keldan to take her to the pod so she could kiss the big blue engineer. Instead, she clasped her hands and nodded. "Then, you must shut down the main power supply, Bohm. The Centauri-not captain is Pzekii reborn. We must work together to silence him."

Kroi sounded again. "The ship will function on reserve for twenty-two," she said.

Could Triscoe and Robet hold on for almost half an hour? "I understand. But we must try. Will you do this? Will the other Boos?"

"Positive, Karina. I have no mimlets. But Finot placed you high as a factor. And he is one who we all look on as *Shree*. It is my comprehension into the heart of Mohn. My people follow me. I will follow you, to Varannah."

"Thank you, Bohm," she said softly. "You will not regret your choice."

The *Providence* danced around the shower of antimatter spheres like an inebriated ballerina. It spiraled and pivoted in a valiant attempt to keep from getting hit. Triscoe had called the course adjustments at first but decided to rely on Lisk's navigational talent. Since then they'd had far fewer contacts to the screen. Robet followed suit, and the three vessels cavorted in the space near Jaxu like fairies in the night.

Robet rubbed his bibbets and spoke. "My people are tiring, Tris. If they slow down, even a little, my screens will overload."

Triscoe nodded. He glanced at the time. Lisk had to be tiring, too. They couldn't take the chance of losing either the *Providence* or the *Prospectus,* but he didn't want to gamble with Rieka's life, either. "Rieka says Bohm has taken the pod off-line. Pzekii's running down the storage batteries."

"How soon until he runs dry?"

"Hopefully, soon enough. If either of us loses repulsion capability, the decision will be out of our hands. We'll have to stop stalling and actually try to destroy the *Prodigy.*"

Robet's bibbets darkened. "Let's not even talk about that," he said. "I'm ready to disappear. What do you think?"

As far as Triscoe was concerned, there wasn't much to consider. Rieka's best had to be good enough. He did not want to destroy the *Prodigy.*

"I'm willing to give it a try, Robet. Make a run for it. I'll draw Pzekii's attention. Try a spin around the closer moon."

Robet smiled. "I'll be waiting."

While Triscoe watched, the *Prospectus* vanished. He smiled. "Marvelous. I can't imagine what Pzekii thinks of that."

"Plenty, sir," Lisk said. "He's firing everything at the *Prospectus*'s last position."

"Stupid," Triscoe commented. "Robet's long gone from there. Get ready to move quickly, Lisk. We'll head toward Jaxu's equatorial area, then pull out around Rijo."

"Yes, sir."

"And double-check our new equipment."

"It's on-line and ready, Captain."

They led the massive ship near the planet and its inner moon. On the far side of Rijo, they pulled ahead of the *Prodigy* by a few thousand kilometers.

"Now, Lisk," Triscoe said. The light-bender was activated and the DGI went blank. "Alter course positive forty degrees planar."

"As we speak."

Triscoe watched his console, amazed that the computer could calculate their position in space without the aid of sensory equipment. His only disappointment was that he couldn't watch as their attacker foundered aimlessly, looking for a target.

"Swing around now," he said, studying his own console as it tracked their position. Once safely behind Rijo, Triscoe heaved a sigh of relief. "Turn it off, Lisk."

The DGI came to life and the *Prospectus* appeared as an enhanced blip, near the moon called Meili. The *Prodigy* turned and assailed it, and Triscoe allowed himself to laugh. It was suddenly like a game of Rhondeem.

Rieka.

I'm here.

Something felt wrong. He sensed a color washing over her thoughts. A sallow yellow. *How much longer?*

Bohm says not very. But we don't know what Kretchva will do once he figures it out. He may try to self-destruct.

Kretchva?

It's what one of his men called him. Captain Kretchva.

Forget him. I'll send a security team to the bridge as soon as the Prodigy's *screen loses power,* he told her.

I'm going to try something in the meantime, she said, a hopeful note in her thought voice.

He didn't like the sound of it at all. The yellow deepened and softened toward orange. *Stay where you are!* The laugh caressed his mind, even as he willed her to keep away from the bridge.

                      *   *   *

Rieka stood outside the bridge door. Bohm had told her there were five Procyons inside. She figured she could use her maitu on two of them before receiving any return fire. The positions she needed to hit first were navigation and weapons control. In all probability, the remaining three Procyons couldn't work those consoles with any degree of expertise.

Rieka waited, solidifying her plan and bolstering her confidence. All she knew, despite the perversity of what she was going to do, was that she had to stop K'resh-va, no matter what.

She afforded herself the luxury of a broad grin. Both Nason and Triscoe would be beside themselves.

Taking a deep breath, she entered the bridge with her weapon drawn and took down the two men and the crucial stations. The Procyon, Durak, was as fast as she'd imagined and returned fire before she could take aim again. Diving for cover, she was aghast to see a smoking hole in the wall. Rather than frighten her, the stench made her angry. Even if the Procyons didn't value life, it seemed incredibly stupid to destroy the ship while trying to get rid of her.

She heard the one called K'resh-va shout, "Who was that?"

"Degahv," Durak replied. "She must have gotten away from Gilm."

"Obviously, fool," the first man's voice chided. "Tone down that weapon or there will be nothing left of this ship to steal."

Predicting it would take Durak a moment to decide to obey his captain, Rieka timed herself to spring when his attention would be on his maitu. She managed to cut him down, but caught the edge of a beam of return fire from K'resh-va himself. With a groan, she slid back behind her cover. Her shoulder felt like it was being assailed by a thousand hot needles, but Rieka gritted her teeth, refusing to make another sound.

The Procyon at the comm console took aim, but she

was either faster to the trigger, or surprised him by staring him in the eye. Either way, he went down before she ducked back behind the singed console.

"I guess that leaves the two of us, Captain," she called.

She waited a long moment but nothing happened. Was he silent because he wanted to bait her, or because she'd clipped him when she'd hit Durak, and that last shot of his came before he lost consciousness? Rieka didn't know, but she couldn't afford the time to try to deduce an answer.

The DGI showed both the *Providence* and *Prospectus* closing the distance. The space around Robet's ship flickered, as if his repulsion screens were ready to fold. The *Prodigy* continued to spew antimatter shells at an incredible rate. If she didn't shut it down soon, both ships could be destroyed.

Wait, Tris. I'm on the bridge.

You're hurt!

I'll survive. Give me a minute to shut things down.

She rolled again, not quite able to ignore her shoulder, and used the weapons console for cover. K'resh-va did not fire.

Cautiously, she peered over the potent computer. Both the captain and his EO were slumped over their chairs. Still holding her maitu with her thumb on the trigger, Rieka leaned over the Procyon's body and deactivated both the repulsion field and firing sequence. She went to the communications board and signaled the *Providence*.

"This is Captain Marteen. What—" Triscoe's face and voice reacted almost immediately. "Rieka! Are you all right?"

"Reasonably," she answered still breathing hard, as she moved to the navigation console. She tapped commands to save what little reserve power was left in the engines before shutting them down, leaving the ship to coast slowly along its current trajectory.

"What's the status?" he asked.

"The bridge crew is unconscious. The rest of them

don't know what's happened. I'm shutting down the major systems, now." She clicked on her TC. "Karina to Bohm."

"Yes?"

"The situation is positive now, my friend. Thank you for your help."

"I did nothing," she answered, her kroi clicking.

"If that is what you wish to think." She closed the channel and looked at the DGI. "How is everything with you?"

Robet's face appeared, splitting the screen as he tapped into the channel. "So the war's over?"

"Not hardly," she answered, smiling. "But this battle is. Any damage?"

"Nothing significant," Triscoe said. "I'll send a security team to you immediately to clean up that mess on the bridge."

"I'd appreciate it."

"That wasn't so hard, really," Robet offered. His bibbets were pink and looked swollen. Rieka found herself smiling at his animation. "My ship didn't even sustain a direct hit."

"Yes, but this ship wasn't up to full firepower," she reminded him, not bothering to mention that his repulsion screen nearly buckled.

"Twenty-eight shells at a time isn't full—?"

"You're forgetting the IRB units haven't been installed yet, Robet." She frowned curiously as Triscoe's image disappeared, but kept her attention on her Aurian friend. "And, you're forgetting I did a decent job sabotaging the weapons systems. I wouldn't start bragging yet. The Procyons won't be happy that their scheme didn't pan out."

Robet nodded. "They did steal the *Venture*."

"That's another problem. Right now we have to deal with *these* Procyons."

"Correct," said a new voice from behind her.

Rieka recognized it and knew Robet would, too.

Apparently, he had only faked unconsciousness. Slowly, she turned. "Why, Captain Kretchva—"

He grimaced. "The name is K'resh-va," he corrected. "I realize inferiors find it hard to pronounce. But that does not—"

"Surrender now, K'resh-va, before you do something you'll regret," Robet warned helplessly from his bridge.

The Procyon kept his gaze on Rieka. "I should have killed him when I had the chance."

"Stay out of this, Robet," she said. "I'll handle the captain. I owe him that much."

"Really?"

"Really." She shrugged and changed the subject. "I thought you were sleeping like a baby."

"Hardly," he replied. "The Commander of Radjie does not allow any situation to get beyond his grasp. My task is to spearhead the downfall of your precious Commonwealth. It will be done."

He stepped away from his chair and lifted his hand. In it, he had a charged maitu. "Drop your weapon, Captain."

In her head, she heard Triscoe's voice. *Bluff.*

What?

You heard me. Keep his attention.

How did you know?

I saw him move.

"Your weapon, Captain," K'resh-va prodded.

Rieka looked down and realized she still held her maitu. Glancing casually at Robet's worried expression, she set it carefully on the communications console. "So, what do you expect to do now?" she asked. "The Boo that you cared nothing for has shut down your power supply. Energy for anything but life support is virtually used up. Captain Marteen is already collecting and detaining the rest of your people." She looked at his maitu, then at him. "Not very good odds if you're after a victory."

To his credit, K'resh-va smiled wolfishly. "But your

husband will grant any request I make," he leered. "I
have you as my hostage."

"I wouldn't count on it. My life has no value—
compared to the Commonwealth."

"This is what I was told," he agreed, nodding. "However, I have recently come to a different conclusion.
You are something of a prize, Captain. And I am sure
your husband is well aware of that fact." He watched
her for a long moment. "But, of course, it really does
not make much difference in the final outcome."

"Doesn't it?"

"No. Even as we speak, a large party of ships from
our present home planet will be invading one of your
member star systems. We will have the Commonwealth. We always get what we want. What we *need*."

He moved toward her, coming almost within arm's
reach.

Rieka watched him close the distance, frowning
slightly but with no other hint of concern for herself.
Then, she shook her head and sighed through her nose.
"You people really give me heartburn," she said, crossing her arms over her chest. "Not even children are
allowed to take things that don't belong to them. And
now here you come—winging in to a thriving civilization, expecting us to roll over on our backs like a
cowering puppy and—"

"Silence."

"How long does it take for you to see the obvious,
Procyon?" she laughed, poking a finger at him.

"Stop that!"

"Really, Pzekii, you do have quite a talent for it."

He lifted a pale brow. Rieka forced herself to keep
her eyes fixed on him rather than the man behind him.
In another heartbeat, K'resh-va was turning, shifting
his attention from her to Triscoe.

She took advantage of the opportunity, kicking
the weapon from his hand. He reeled back, grunting,
and lunged, knocking her off-balance. Together, they
crashed to the floor.

K'resh-va went for her throat, tumbling and twisting them among the bodies and rubble littering the deck. Rieka knew he was doing it to make sure Triscoe could not get a clear shot. She fought furiously, trying to both push him off her and jab him in a sensitive spot like an eye or ear. With his face close to hers, she could see the hateful gleam in his eye that was obviously not Centauri.

Unable to loosen his grip, Rieka felt the rage in her grow. She grabbed his ear and pulled hard, wanting to distract him, wanting it to come off in her hand. K'resh-va howled and punched her. Instantly, she tasted blood and spit in his face.

Rieka felt the pointy stylus slip from her pant leg as they wrestled, and let go of him with one hand while the other searched for it. Out of the corner of her eye, she saw Triscoe hovering above them, but then the Procyon turned her again. As he did, she felt the welcome smoothness of cold metal.

Gaining a better grip on her weapon, Rieka raised her arm to strike. K'resh-va flipped her onto the floor, a weak position, but it didn't stop her from trying to stab him.

Then, suddenly, she saw the ceiling.

She watched, aghast, as Triscoe picked the Procyon off her with one hand, threw him aside, and stunned him.

She stayed where she was, wide-eyed and breathing hard, waiting for his face to lose the contemptible expression, hoping it wasn't directed at her. "Tris? Are you all right?"

He nodded.

"I've never seen anyone pick up a person with one hand before," she offered, trying to catch her breath as she rolled onto her elbow. "I didn't think you were that strong."

"I didn't think so, either," he admitted, relaxing the grimace as he looked down at her. "But I couldn't let you kill him."

"With this?" She sat up, hefting the stylus. Her neck

felt as if it had been twisted completely around. A couple of teeth were loose. Her tongue touched her swelling lip. The bleeding might stop on its own, but she'd sooner bleed to death than have anyone on the *Prodigy* treat it. "I was just trying to get his attention."

He shook his head. Obviously, Triscoe didn't believe her.

When she stood up, Rieka looked at the stylus, then at him. "Maybe I was after blood," she admitted, tasting her own. "But it was self-defense."

He said nothing more, and she knew he was right. She had wanted to kill. K'resh-va represented a lot more than just an enemy Procyon. She'd wanted revenge. For her. For Midrin. For Humankind.

Triscoe clipped his weapon to his thigh and held out both hands. "I swear I wasn't trying to take care of you, Rieka. But if you had killed him . . . I couldn't let you do that to yourself. To us." He offered her a bleak smile.

"To us?"

"We *are* married now—in the Centauri sense," he reminded her. "Single heart. Single mind."

She began to understand the blessings and burdens of such a union. They would share everything now. Even feelings and thoughts.

Rieka felt a wave of panic at that revelation, but Triscoe's quiet chuckle curbed it. "Don't look so frightened. I'll be good—as long as you are."

She couldn't be angry at that hopeful face. "What am I going to do with you?" she muttered, stepping over K'resh-va's body to survey what was left of the bridge.

"Several things come to mind."

An erotic image swept across her consciousness and Rieka turned abruptly to look at him. The dimple had appeared, right next to an almost-conceited smirk. "Something to look forward to," she commented, not wanting to encourage him.

"It seems we keep having to postpone things."

"A captain's life, I'm afraid," she said dryly. "There are just never enough hours in a day."

Twenty-three

Two hours later, Rieka watched, transfixed, as the Little One appeared on the *Prodigy*'s DGI. The moon, pale gray in the light of 40 Eridani, looked like a huge exhausted spore. New craters were everywhere, some of them kilometers across. Out of the base's seven domes, four had been hit. The three that had escaped damage were presently on the dark side. Rieka figured they'd simply been lucky.

Triscoe, seated at the helm, guided the big ship among the low-orbit stations and docking pylons. Rieka focused the DGI on the nearest domes. Air still seeped from cracks, ornamenting them in wisps of precious gases, now useless to the inhabitants. She watched a shuttle skim along the closer dome's surface, probably assessing the damage.

As they rounded the Little One's far side, light from Dani cast an eerie glow on the carnage. Whole sections of two domes had been blown away. Debris tumbled like jagged splinters, ready to wreak further havoc on unprotected spacecraft. She wondered if any bodies were floating out here, or if everyone had managed to get to the underground levels before the attack. Silently, she hoped that K'resh-va and the forty other Procyons in custody would meet an end just as grisly.

Trying to shake that thought from her mind, she muttered, "They'll be picking this stuff up for weeks."

Triscoe nodded silently.

The big ship approached the space dock, and she continued to assess the damage. A significant portion of three space ports were unscathed. Apparently the screens had done the job. Nason had probably kept Commander Kiln on continual watch, ready to switch on the defense network at the first sign of trouble.

"Think we'd better get down there right away?"

"We need to report to Nason," he agreed.

She tried to open communications. "The grid is still off-line, Tris."

"I think we're close enough," he offered. "Let me see if I can reach Mother."

She watched him as he carried on the conversation in his head. No wonder the Centauri were the ones who'd developed the TC, she thought. To them, it must have seemed like the rest of the Commonwealth walked around with a severe handicap.

He turned to her, face grim. "We need to transport to Delta Dome immediately. Admiral Nason and Captain Finot have been injured."

A tingle of apprehension went through her. She took a breath to get past it and nodded. She switched on ship-to-ship communications. The screen split to reveal the stern faces of Commander Aarkmin and Robet.

"Triscoe and I are headed for Delta Dome," she told them. "Medical section. We're to report to Nason, there."

"I'll come, too," Robet offered.

"Continue to see to the repairs, Aarkmin," Triscoe ordered as he pushed himself from his seat. "I should be back within an hour."

"Yes, Captain," his executive officer said.

Delta Dome had the appearance of normalcy, with the exception of being overcrowded with refugees. Crowds clogged the corridor as they made their way from the InterMAT to the medical ward. All faces, no matter the race, were sober. Rieka sensed they were still in shock. Sandwiched between her two companions, she wondered how long it would take for any of them to feel safe again.

Three guards stood outside the door to Nason's

ward. Since she was still wearing lieutenant stripes, she let Triscoe and Robet handle them.

"No one is allowed admittance," the Human guard replied to Triscoe's request to pass.

"You don't seem to understand," Robet offered, letting his bibbets flush to a deep mauve, "we must see the admiral, immediately."

The guard looked pointedly at the bibbets, then at Robet's face. "No one," he repeated.

Rieka had to smile at that. For once, Robet wasn't going to threaten his way through a guard. "Are you sure?" she asked.

For a moment he seemed confused, as if wondering why he should explain himself to a person of his own rank. "There are—"

He was saved his explanation when the door opened and Setana Marteen appeared behind him. "There you are," she said to Triscoe. "Merik's been waiting, most unhappily I should add." She looked directly at the guard. "Of course these officers may enter, Lieutenant. And you're doing a wonderful job. The admiral truly appreciates the quiet he's gotten since your arrival."

Confused, the young man nodded. "Thank you, Herald." He stepped aside and Rieka smiled to herself as she passed him. Setana Marteen had it down to a science.

Nason, as Rieka had expected, was fuming. The damage to his rib cage and air sacks had been repaired, but he could not leave his bed. His expression changed when they entered the ward. He clasped their hands warmly, advising them about what had happened on the base in their absence.

When Triscoe had briefed him on the battle at Jaxu, the admiral's frown lifted a bit. "Well-done," he said, his bibbets in a rare dark phase, his voice trembling slightly.

Rieka nodded. "Except for that threat K'resh-va made about an invasion," she amended. "I suppose, once you've crewed the *Prodigy*, that can be taken care of."

"That situation is under control," he replied. "I got a little forewarning from Perata. Five cruisers were waiting for the Procyons at Medoura. Captain Goresch may have already sent a communiqué."

"Perata?" Triscoe asked.

The admiral nodded. "I pressed your mother for information—and she got it for me. A remarkable woman."

"Why thank you, Merik," she said, coming into the room. "You are fortunate to have fared better than the poor captain. He may not be with us much longer."

Nason's face fell. "A great loss," he said softly.

"Finot?" Rieka asked, feeling her heart lurch.

"The surgeons did what they could, but the damage was extensive," Setana said softly. "He is in a pressure chamber, now."

"This place won't be the same without him," Robet murmured.

"Can we see him?" Rieka asked.

The Herald looked at her, and she knew the other woman could feel what she felt. "Not right now, dear," she said softly. "His family is with him."

Rieka said nothing and cast her eyes at the foot of Nason's bed. The base had taken a bad pounding, true, and a dozen people had been killed when the Kela Dome burst. But it could have been much worse. That Finot, the indestructible Boo, could have been hit point-blank and survived, even for an hour, was truly remarkable. And yet, the thought of him dying gave Rieka a hollowness in the pit of her stomach.

As if on cue, Triscoe put an arm around her shoulders. "Don't worry, I'm sure Mother will get you in to see him," he whispered.

"I've explained a few things to the Prime Admiral," Nason said, looking directly at Rieka. "He'll probably want to do something about your present status, Captain. Personally, I will not feel comfortable until the charges against you are dropped and you have your command again." He paused. "I trust you'll be available?"

Rieka suddenly felt humbled in an odd, unexplainable way. They were going to recognize her for a job well-done. In the face of total disaster, maybe Humans counted for something, after all. She straightened her shoulders and nodded smartly. "Yes, sir."

A nurse entered and informed Nason he should be resting. He started to give her an argument, but the Herald lifted a warning hand. "Do as you are told, Merik. Perhaps the doctor will release you tomorrow."

"Wishful thinking," he groused, but dutifully slid back beneath the covers.

"Be that as it may," Setana said, "my family has a long-overdue discussion to attend to, and we might as well get on with it."

They said good-bye to Robet, then collected Triscoe's father in the waiting area. No one spoke on the way to the InterMAT station. Rieka noticed that Prefect Marteen wore that curious expression of nausea she remembered so vividly from their last encounter. He recoiled perversely when she accidentally touched him in the crowded hallway. Feeling cantankerous herself, Rieka felt her hand itching to slap him.

After Triscoe led them to Rieka's old guest suite, Setana allowed her poise to metamorphose into an attitude of matriarchal authority. She gestured them to sit as she eased into a chair in the small salon area.

Before the Herald spoke, she glanced at Rieka with a soft expression and winked. Rieka pondered the gesture, sure she must have imagined it, but Setana gave her a little nod and directed her attention toward the prefect.

"Allow me first to apologize to you, Ker," she began. "Certain information has been kept from you. It was not vital to your health or well-being—and it may, unfortunately, have had an undesirable effect on your, shall we say, aggressive attitude."

Ker nodded. Apparently, he'd guessed as much.

"What sort of information, Setana?" he asked, sounding annoyed.

"Nothing critical, I assure you. And it has not presented itself as an issue until now." She lifted a slim hand from her lap and gestured toward Rieka. "It has to do with your daughter-in-law, of course."

"I might have guessed," he grumbled, not looking at Rieka. "I have already told you, clearly, that I will not—"

"And Triscoe," Setana added.

This was enough of a goad to bring Ker's curiosity to the fore. He sat up straighter and glared at her. "Am I deemed qualified to hear it now?" he inquired sarcastically.

"Of course," she replied, oblivious to his tone. "I always planned to tell you, Ker, dear. The question was just a matter of when. Now that they are married, I think explanations are due. But I must ask, are you ready to listen?" She sat back, shoulders erect.

Ker sighed in a way that made Rieka think he'd gone through this ceremony before. "I believe so."

"Good."

Setana took up the conversation as if she felt no tension. Rieka, on the other hand, gripped Triscoe's fingers. Though the Herald had taken charge, her heart felt leaden. She knew she could live quite happily without the prefect's acceptance, but it might have a terrible effect on Triscoe. She wondered how he would deal with his family if his father actually refused to listen.

"Let us begin twenty-three years ago, then," Setana said softly. "Triscoe was a schoolboy, unable to attain any of the goals you set for him." She looked at her son fondly. "The summer he was sixteen was when I discovered he had the *quantivasta*-gift."

"He—what?" The prefect gaped. "He has it? That is the most ridiculous thing I have ever heard. And you let him waste his Gift on *her*?"

Rieka vividly recalled that combustible look, but his wife continued, nonplussed.

"Yes, the Gift," she said, ignoring his accusation. "I

said Triscoe has it. He had just turned seventeen when my mother died. You remember that, Ker. I went to Perata to look after her things."

"I remember. And I suppose I should ask—do the other children have it, too?"

"No," she replied. "Only Triscoe. But I'm digressing. On Perata, I learned a most astonishing fact. Several facts, really. That the individual known as the Oracle actually existed—and that, through my mother, I was one of his descendants."

The prefect stiffened, and his jaw clenched. He glared at Rieka, and, for a moment, she though he'd leap across the small space between them to attack her. But his wife casually got up and brought him a glass of water. "It's a shock, I know, Ker. And there is a great deal more."

He sipped the water, and she continued. "Yillon wished to meet Triscoe. He had begun seeing Triscoe's future and recorded the visions in a book. He wanted to meet the boy. Soon after that—his plans for Triscoe began to clash with yours."

Marteen nodded but said nothing. Setana smiled at him. "I made excuses whenever possible for Triscoe, because I understood the long-range planning involved. You argued and fumed and made our lives quite miserable, I must admit. But Yillon had asked that I not reveal his role in our lives to you. I was obliged to meet that request. So was Tris." She looked at her son, and he nodded once.

"In point of fact, Ker, his relationship with Rieka has been directed by Yillon. They performed more than one Singlemind session four years ago, while attending the training course that transformed the Transit Authority into the Commonwealth Fleet. Yillon knew of her role in today's turn of events. He knew that Triscoe's presence was equally important. All of this, in fact, had been documented years ago."

"Then why leave me in the dark?" he demanded. "If

this Human was so important, then there could have been no reasonable purpose—"

"You see," she interrupted, "this is exactly why. You think of her, even speak of her as—a Human. Nothing more. But she is infinitely more, Ker. Do you begin to understand? Had you known what was happening, your attitude—what you might have done—could have changed history.

"She saved your life today. Many lives, in fact. Do you think for one moment I would have jeopardized that—just to keep you informed?" When he looked properly confused, she smiled softly.

"Captain Degahv will have a respected place in our family," Setana announced. "And you will treat her as you would a Centauri." He began to balk, but she cut him off with a raised hand. "No. You will, Ker. Because every time you speak to her, or of her with disrespect, I shall remind you that I am not a widow, nor you a widower. Am I understood?"

"Perfectly, Setana," he grumbled. "But this does not change my—attitude." Casting a look at Rieka, he said, "For a moment, this afternoon, I did not recognize you. When I realized Merik and the rest of them had allowed you such immense responsibility, I understood something of a nature of Triscoe's choice. And now, this . . ." He shook his head, overwhelmed.

Rieka nearly believed what he said. But something about him that told her this was a well-polished act. Despite what he'd been told, he would never trust or accept her. For now, she decided to go along with the charade.

"Thank you," she managed after Triscoe gave her a small nudge.

"Perhaps knowing the inner person is something I have neglected," he admitted. "You have stood up to me even when I've growled my loudest. I will endeavor to think better of you, Captain." He glanced at Setana. "And in time, perhaps, look forward to your visits—though you would be wise to keep them short."

"Triscoe said you were happiest when you were arguing with someone," Rieka quipped.

"Then we shall have many joyous occasions together, I'm sure," he answered, a strange look on his face. "I moved the Rembrandt, by the way. I won't admit to its improving the display. But it *is* different."

"There," Setana said evenly, looking at her son. "We have both defeated the Procyons, and gotten your father to speak to your wife without raising his voice. I think that is quite an accomplishment."

"Definitely a first," Triscoe agreed.

Rieka hated the feel of her palms sweating. She always had. But the Prime Admiral had sent for her and, nervous or not, she needed to see him. With her career on the line, he held her future. And, because of the state of emergency on the base, he didn't need the trappings of a special court. Three flag officers in agreement was all it took.

Thankful that Triscoe had been asked to come with her, she took a breath, stepped through the door to Finot's office, and saluted.

"Captain Rieka Degahv, reporting as ordered, Admiral."

"Captain Degahv," Hursh greeted her from behind the Boo's podium-desk. He, and the two admirals with him, returned her salute, and Triscoe's.

"Sit down." He gestured her to a chair and she took it. "Captain Marteen, you will observe this meeting as is your right—as next of kin."

Triscoe remained behind her, near the door, and she all but forgot him. The two admirals seated to Hursh's right looked grim. She reminded herself that Frotii tended to look that way, despite his easygoing disposition.

"Good evening, sirs," she offered. Frotii nodded, as did the admiral she hadn't met before—Hinvok, a Vekyan.

"Shall we get to it?" Hursh began, his beaklike

features taking on an even more pinched look. "Now, to begin with, Captain, I have been kept abreast of matters by Admiral Nason."

Rieka nodded. She didn't quite know what to expect, but three sober admirals gave her the impression of a court-martial. "Sir?"

"Nason forwarded to me all pertinent data he collected with regard to your case. I have had access to your attorney's files, as well. Your plea of innocence due to outside influence is justified." He looked at the other admirals. "Are we in agreement?" Frotii and Hinvok nodded. "Let the record show that the initial charge of treason has been dropped by order of this council."

Hinvok tapped something into a datapad on the table before him. "So noted," he said.

Rieka nodded, but she didn't allow herself a sigh of relief, yet. Hursh looked as though he had a great deal more to say.

"There were additional charges against you, Captain. Those involving ejecting your crew and firing upon a friendly ship. Thanks to statements made by Nason and Captain Marteen, those are hereby dismissed. I see no need to waste the court's time on this matter of your moral integrity."

"Thank you, Admiral," she managed. She nodded at him this time, but still held herself tightly, as if getting the things she'd wanted most was as implausible as a dream.

Is this really happening? she asked.

Yes, Triscoe answered. *Believe it, Rieka. A Human is getting official credit for having moral integrity.*

"Now, as to the *Venture* . . ." Hursh looked down at the podium to study something before glancing back at her. "I received this communiqué only a few moments ago, which is why I summoned you, both." He looked past her and nodded at Triscoe. "It came from Captain Goresch of the *Merger*. He and four other ships engaged the *Venture* and a large number of small Procyon vessels—similar in design to the *Vendikon,* near Eta Cass. After a short skirmish, both the Procyons and the *Venture* left the system. Two of our vessels sustained damage."

Rieka felt her heart in her throat. The *Venture* was now, officially, an enemy vessel. She had never lost a ship before. As far as she knew, neither had any other Fleet captain.

"My crew?" she asked. "Do you know . . . ?"

"Captain Goresch informs me here that they are dead. The Procyon in command of the *Venture* claims to have killed them. The five Boo engineers apparently remained aboard to oversee the gravitation pod—though no mention was made of them."

Rieka tried not to let the news impact her. With so much destruction around them, they needed to concentrate on action, not reaction. "Does that mean they must be considered enemies?" she asked.

The Prime Admiral frowned. "Not all of them, I should think," he replied. "Though they don't lie, one must ask direct questions in order to get direct answers. We'll be doing just that—to every Boo citizen in the very near future. Fleet personnel, first."

This time she did smile, a little. "Thank you for telling me, Admiral," she said.

"Yes. Well," he harrumphed, "I suppose that's a courtesy due you, Captain."

She said nothing. He looked as though he were about to continue, and she didn't want to interrupt him.

"Now," Hursh looked at the other admirals to his right, "we would like to address your present status."

She sat straighter. "Sir."

"Because the charges have been dropped, you are to assume your proper rank," he began, gesturing to the lieutenant's tunic she still wore. "And when the treatments wear off, you are to assume your proper Human countenance, as well. You will be recognized as yourself, Captain. A Human, not a Centauri."

"Dr. Twanabok informed me the reversal treatment would take some time, sir," she offered.

"Mmm. So be it, then." He looked at Triscoe, then at Frotii. "This panel and I have discussed our present dilemma, Captains. Until the entire plot is unearthed, we are left to assume that those who were 'influenced' must be identified and reconditioned. Identities of *all* Fleet personnel will be verified, I assure you. And extensive searches will be conducted for those of us who are missing . . . such as Admiral Bittin and Captain Pedlam. I fear, however, that they may not be recovered."

He looked at his podium again, then back to Rieka. "We have a captain without a ship and a ship without a captain. It is the ruling of this council that you assume temporary command of the *Prodigy,* Captain Degahv. And, in the event that the *Venture* has suffered damage beyond repair, I am recommending that the placement be permanent."

"Admiral," she whispered, unable to make herself utter more.

"I am well aware of criticism—throughout all the Commonwealth—with regard to Humans, Captain Degahv. The Fleet must remain above such petty grievances. Earth, when it has recovered from its cataclysm, will, so I am told, outproduce Aurie in agricultural commodities. Your people have a unique role to play in our future, and I see no reason why you should have to wait. Your actions today should prove something to the skeptics. Let us hope they reserve judgment long enough so that our decision will prove the correct one."

"I . . . I—don't know what to say, Admiral," Rieka stammered. "I'm honored."

He made a strange sound through his nose. "Mmm. Yes. Well, Captain . . . the assignment has been recorded. Nason is happy. The Heralds are happy. But we still have this business at Eta Cass.

"You will proceed to the system and rendezvous with the *Merger.* The *Providence* and *Prospectus* will accompany you. Your orders are the same as Captain

Goresch's. Stop the Procyons. Turn them back, destroy them, do whatever it takes to keep them out of the Commonwealth, for good."

"Understood, Admiral," she said.

"I expect your first order of business will be to bring your ship up to full capacity."

"Yes, sir," she replied, smiling. "I'll check everything, myself."

"To be sure. If that is all then, you are dismissed."

"Thank you again, Admiral. Admirals." Rieka stood and saluted each, individually. "I appreciate your confidence. I'll do my best." After they'd returned her salutes, she pivoted smartly and headed for the door.

Triscoe was at her shoulder, and as soon as the door closed behind them, he faced her. "Congratulations," he whispered, his face beaming. She didn't need the Gift to sense the pride he felt.

She couldn't stop herself from grinning. "I feel like I'm floating, Tris. Everything that's happened in the past month has been like some . . . warped reality."

"I told you when we first met—you could do anything," he reminded her.

She shrugged. "People say things like that all the time."

"Not Indrans with the Gift."

She nodded, but as a new thought struck her, her face fell. "I've got to see Finot. I've got to tell him the *Prodigy*'s all right." She looked up at him, knowing he would understand. "I'll get a crew together as soon as possible after that—but I've got to see him, before—"

"Go," he said, nodding. "I'll tell Robet the good news."

Rieka found she couldn't smile at that just now. She squeezed his hand, then headed for the medical unit.

Finot lay encased in a clear pressure cylinder in a small room. A nurse had directed her to the door, then left her alone. A chair sat against the wall, but Rieka didn't use it. She stood, watching him, and felt death close in.

The slate blue surface of his midsection was now
concave. His lower body had been covered, but the
damaged area remained exposed. Jagged lines ran
across the large indentation, marking the places where
he had been put together during surgery. His eyes were
closed. The translator box had been disconnected. She
figured it would be worthless in the pressure chamber,
anyway. His torso moved slightly, giving small evidence of life.

Why, she wondered, when I lose someone, does it
always take me back to when Dad died? The hollowness she felt at that time returned like a painful echo.
She'd come to terms with her father's death, and knew
she'd do the same for Finot. Maybe it was death itself
that held her in its grip, giving her a shake now and
then, as a reminder of her own mortality.

"I'll miss you, you big blue monolith," she whispered. "And as long as I live, I won't forget you."

The door slid open behind her and Rieka heard the
distinct shuffling of Boo feet. "He will pass," the translated voice said.

"Into the night—like the stars over Varannah," she
finished, then turned. "Bohm, I didn't expect to see
you, here."

A cleft of skin wiggled over her right eye as the kroi
clicked slowly. "I am his *bilgish*, of feminine descent.
You would call me his granddaughter."

She recognized the slight dappling over the left
shoulder. "Of course. I have no wish to intrude. He has
been my friend. I feel, negative—that he will no longer
factor."

Bohm blinked. "There is no intrusion. He will
equate. He will factor. His existence simply slides from
our view, not our heart."

Rieka said nothing. She turned back to look at him,
jaw clenched.

Kroi clicked a strange cadence. "You were exponen-
tial to him, Karina of the Rock. You equated to his *ckla*
and stood in the light."

Her throat was burning, but she said, "I wanted to tell him that . . . the *Prodigy*'s all right. Prime Admiral Hursh has put me in command of her." Rieka dabbed at her nose with the back of her hand. "I wanted to tell him . . . he was right. There *is* a Procyon base. We're to join Captain Goresch on the *Merger* and get rid of them for good."

"I am your engineer, Captain. We will find the fulcrum. All will equate."

Rieka took a ragged breath and nodded. She didn't know whether to be infuriated or embarrassed that she was on the verge of tears, while Finot's own granddaughter stood there like a giant blue piece of stone.

Bohm shuffled closer. "Why sorrow, Captain?"

She thought for a moment, trying to put words to the emotions she felt. "He gave his existence for Nason's life. Humans value life over everything. Even knowledge. It—sits like pi in my mind that he should be robbed of it."

"He gave life, Captain," Bohm observed. "Many times, many places. He equates this. All the factors will equate. That is the way of the Universe."

She wanted to bite her lip to keep from crying, but it was still too tender from contact with K'resh-va's fist. Her throat burned. She sniffed again.

Inside the chamber, Finot had stopped moving. They watched him silently for a long moment, then Rieka sighed. "I wanted to tell him . . . he touched me, too, like the sun over Varannah. I wanted to tell him so much."

Bohm made a soft sound with her kroi. "He knows, Captain. He knows."

Wearing her proper uniform, Rieka returned to the *Prodigy*'s bridge a few minutes later. It took her a moment to grasp the changes that had taken place in her absence. Every position was manned, each officer concentrating so hard they didn't even notice her.

As she stood there, watching the activity, the thin

Centauri in the EO's seat turned, then stood. The gleam
in Midrin's brown eyes spoke more than any words
could say. She cleared her throat and announced, "Captain on the bridge."

All faces turned toward Rieka. As one, the crew stood
and saluted her. "Welcome to the *Prodigy*," she offered,
returning the salute. "I'm Captain Degahv. I'm sure
we'll get to know one another soon enough. But right
now I'd appreciate it if you ignored me and got back to
work. We've got a very big ship in need of repair."

There were smiles and nods all around. Rieka
returned them, looking finally at her second-
in-command. She hadn't dared to hope Nason would
team them again.

"Midrin," she said cordially, wanting to hug the breath
out of her. "Were have you been hiding yourself?"

"Admiral Nason brought me along," she explained.
"I've been, in his words, 'sequestered for my own good.'
But I'm fit for duty, now. He's assigned me to you."

"I wouldn't have it any other way," Rieka replied.
"I'm going to need the best to get the job done the way
Admiral Hursh expects. Welcome aboard."

"Thank you." Midrin looked embarrassed at the compliment, then said, "Gorah is here, too. She was on her
way back to Oph, but stopped at Dani for the dedication
ceremony. When everything started to happen, she
spoke to Herald Cimpa about postponing her matrimonial—because of the crisis. He granted a short reprieve."

"I'm glad to have her aboard," Rieka said. "As soon
as I have a minute, I'll be sure to tell her that." She
glanced down at the floor, noticing small splatters of
brown. Her blood. She ran her tongue over the sore
spot on the inside of her lip. Eventually, she'd have the
stain removed. For now, it reminded her of how the
battle might have ended.

"Have all the Procyons in custody been transferred
to the base?"

"Yes," Midrin replied, leading her toward the half-
meter hole in the wall left by Durak's maitu. "As you

can see, the damage to the ventilation conduit is rather extensive. Since the system is functioning and the repairs are mostly cosmetic, the estimate for the entire job is a day. And due to the fact there aren't any spare parts for the *Prodigy,* yet, it will be a while before we have anything other than a stock wall panel to hide it."

"I'm afraid we're going to have to put up with a whole lot more than that, Midrin," she said, wryly.

"Of course."

Rieka had to laugh at her stern expression. "Don't worry, we'll manage. We've got a thirty-one-hour slide to make before we have to deal with any opposition. Everything should be functioning by then."

"Should be," Midrin echoed.

Rieka looked past her EO at the crews repairing or checking the equipment. "I'll need a printout of all the results of test programs run on systems undergoing reconstruction or replacement—and the names of the people working on them."

"Yes, Captain."

"And, I'll need a complete crew roster, if we have one." Midrin nodded. "And schedule a meeting with all the department superintendents for two hours from now. That'll be 16:50 hours."

"Location?"

Rieka rubbed the knot at the back of her head. It was still tender enough to make her wince. "In the meeting room, quad B, level 2." She sighed and looked around. "How long for that printout?"

"A few minutes."

"What about the weapons systems?"

"Nearly everything you did to disrupt aiming accuracy has already been corrected. It was easy, since we knew exactly what had been done. I believe Finot planned it that way," Midrin said. "Final checks are scheduled to be made while we're in transit."

She nodded once. "Fine. Bring me that printout as soon as you get it. I'll be in the medical suite."

Twenty-four

Thirteen hours of the thirty-one-hour slide had already passed, though it seemed like far less than half a day to Triscoe. He sat in his quarters going over the latest weapons-team drill results, wondering if he could adequately prepare his people without working them to exhaustion.

Rieka, he knew, had the more difficult task of melding an untried crew. The vital positions, formerly held by Procyons, had been given to whoever was available. He wondered how they managed to function at all.

Despite the handicap, he knew Rieka would not allow them to lose sight of their goal. He would have liked to help her, but that wasn't physically possible. The InterMAT did not function during a slide.

Triscoe switched off his datapad and raked his hand through his hair. The weapons-teams' results could have been better, but not by much. He shouldn't be too concerned—they had more battle experience than any other ship in the fleet. For some reason, that distinction didn't make him feel much better.

Rieka.

Hope you didn't plan on catching me when I had time to spare, her mind-voice replied, unmistakably weary, as the thought popped into his head. He could sense her watching other people nearby.

He ignored the comment. They were both tired. *Did you find anything in K'resh-va's quarters?*

A sense of bitterness preceded the reply. *Hell, no. The place was clean. He probably destroyed every-*

thing that might be found and used against him and committed the essentials to memory. Too bad we couldn't keep him aboard. I might have enjoyed extracting a little information.

A sense of evil accompanied that thought, encased in the color green. *You don't mean that.*

Don't tell me what I do or do not mean, Triscoe. Twenty percent of my crew have no defense training at all. They're Scientists. *That's with a capital S. The* Prodigy *was supposed to be a research vessel, too, remember?*

Of course.

Well, now, they've been ordered to learn how to do things beyond their wildest dreams. Actual Labor. *Capital L. You'd think I was ordering them to eat anti-matter. I've got them to train, plus put the ship back together—plus wonder what we're going to find at Eta Cass. Don't give me any Centauri criticism, dear. I wouldn't want to put a strain on our relationship.*

How could he even begin to reassure her, when he felt so disconcerted himself? Maybe changing the subject would help. *How is Midrin?*

Nice try, she replied, echoing his thought. *She's doing great. I swear the woman's a phenomenon. I have yet to see her tire. Or lose her patience. I've already hit that wall myself. Twice in the last two days since Hursh put me in command.*

Triscoe could tell she left him for a moment while concentrating on what she said to a crewman. *But you're feeling better now.* It was a statement. Almost.

The bump has gone down and the lip is almost healed, if that's what you mean.

Not exactly, but Triscoe didn't feel like debating the point. He felt her attention slide away, as she spoke to someone else. At least the person received praise. Things couldn't be as bad as she made them seem.

When her attention returned, he told her, *I want you to go to your quarters in three hours.*

Why?

Because you need to rest.

Big surprise, there. Got any more?

I think so. And the surprise will be on you if you're not alone in your room.

He could feel her curiosity begin to build. *I'm intrigued.*

You'll be more than that, Rieka. I'll talk to you again in three hours.

He sat back, smiling. They both needed a break. What he had in mind wouldn't be much; certain limitations governed his Gift. They would have to make do.

Nason sat at the desk in Finot's old office. The Fleet logo blinked incessantly at him from the small DGI near the door, indicating the end of the communiqué. His attention, though, was far away. Numb, he rubbed his bibbets and stared at the wall.

He didn't know how long he'd sat there before the door chime brought him out of his stupor.

"Come," he said, trying to pull himself straighter in the chair.

Setana Marteen entered, a worried look on her face. "Merik I—endless heavens!" she gasped after looking at him. "What's happened?"

Her sudden reaction made him realize his bibbets felt cool. He tried to bring them to a normal flesh tone, hoping the lie would reassure her.

It didn't work. She hurried to the desk and stared down at him. "It can't be Triscoe, or I would have felt it. Merik, please—"

"Sit down," he said softly, gesturing to the chair. She perched there, looking as apprehensive as he'd ever seen her. Unsettled. Almost out of control. "What's the matter, Setana?"

"Nothing, really," she replied, casting a suspicious look at him. "We've got to evacuate another section of Kela Dome so repairs can be made. Three more people were hurt when a scaffolding collapsed." She stopped herself and sighed. "Now, you tell me what is wrong."

He shook his head. How could he say this? How could he break the news to this woman? He looked at her face and knew she would accept no sweetened truth. She wanted it all. Now.

"I'm sorry, Setana. I've sent them . . ." He sighed heavily, trying to find words to explain the lack of choices he had. "There's almost no chance for our people. I just received a second, more detailed communiqué from Eta Cass. The estimate is that the Procyons have well over one hundred of those small ships there, similar in design to the *Vendikon*, with maser weaponry *and* light-bending screens. Captain Goresch has been engaged long enough to deduce that the as-yet-undiscovered 'base station' is capable of refueling them indefinitely. Of the five ships I sent last week, the *Collateral* is now useless and the *Stipend*'s maneuvering thrusters aren't functioning." He stopped, then looked away from her before he could continue.

"From the description I've received, they'll be in bad shape before the *Prodigy* gets there. Although, I'm . . . sure they'll do their best."

"Oh, Merik . . ." Setana whispered. Her face had gone pale, even for a Centauri. He wondered at the reaction. As a Herald, she'd experienced unpleasantness before. She would never allow herself an outward reaction to bad news, especially in public. He'd done the same, plenty of times, himself. Still, he had to admit that the past economic catastrophes the Commonwealth had weathered couldn't compete when you were talking about the survival of a civilization.

"Over a hundred ships," he repeated, his voice bitter with defeat. "Who could have imagined?"

"Don't say that, Merik," she told him. "Remember that you, too, have done your best. It is all anyone can ask. Don't blame yourself."

He heard her. The words sounded correct. The meaning behind them, sincere. But that didn't help. He was the Fleet admiral in charge of transit scheduling and military exercises. Until now, they'd never had an

enemy to fight. Ordering people to their deaths had
never seemed like a possibility. No Aurian had been in
his position for hundreds of years. No wonder he
wasn't prepared for it.

He took a deep breath and pulled himself back to the
present. "I'll have to confer with Prime Admiral Hursh
on this. I have the authority to declare a Fleet emergency. That means I can pull every ship out of its
schedule and sent it to Eta Cass. It will disrupt commerce and travel everywhere, but we may not have any
choice."

"I'm sure you know what is best," she said, wood-
enly. "You should speak to the Prime Admiral
immediately."

"Yes. Yes, I will." He pushed himself to his feet,
then looked at her, recalling she'd already been concerned about something when she'd walked in the
door. "You—looked upset when you came to see me,
Setana. I apologize for not giving you a chance to talk
about it. If you're concerned I'm overworking myself,
I assure you. I feel fine. Only a twinge of pain now and
then."

"It wasn't that."

"Then, what?"

He watched as she wrung her hands in her lap and
gnawed lightly at her lip. He had never seen her this
agitated before. Or hesitant. Slowly, Nason sank back
in his chair. He leaned toward her, wishing he had the
Centauri Gift, so that she would not have to put her
fears into words.

"Setana?"

"It's Ker," she said, finally.

"What about him?"

"He's—gone."

"Gone? What do you mean?" Just the look on her
face made his bibbets flush with apprehension. He
fought to control them, hoping she wouldn't pick up on
his fear. Worrying wouldn't help anything.

"I think . . ." She sighed. "I was so busy, you know,

with the other Heralds and helping the injured, trying
to keep everyone calm. He told me he planned to have
lunch with Rieka's brother, Paden Degahv. After that, I
lost track of him."

"When was this?"

"The day before yesterday."

"What are you telling me, Setana? That Administrator Degahv might have done something to Ker?"

"I don't know. Ker dislikes Humans—but he seemed
to have accepted Rieka. I thought his appointment with
Degahv was about that. But now I don't know." She
paused for a short moment. "You were watching Paden,
weren't you? He had been to Aurie. He *was* one of a
number of people that could have been under Procyon
influence. Isn't that right?"

"Absolutely," he agreed. "But his actions were not
suspect regarding his sister's disappearance on Yadra.
He notified Admiral Bittin, and his people helped in
the search. Other than that he hasn't done a thing out
of the ordinary. No odd communications. No unnecessary travel. Nothing."

"Yes. But he might have been influenced to do a specific thing, don't you see? No one suspected Rieka
because she did nothing out of character. The same
thing might have happened to her brother."

Nason frowned, thinking to himself that she'd never
come to him with a problem like this in all the years
he'd known her. "What do *you* think has happened?"
he asked, finally.

"There is no trace of either of them on the Little One. I
see no reason for them to have gone off on a shuttle—and
I would sense it if Ker were still that close. I think . . .
No. I know—they've gone—somewhere. There is no
record of them leaving on any ship that has departed in
the last three days. They could not have secured rooms
on those ships without being placed on the passenger
manifest. That leaves only one other possibility. They are
on either the *Prospectus,* the *Providence* or the *Prodigy.*"

"Why would they do that?"

She shrugged ever so slightly. "If Paden Degahv has been programmed to do some kind of dirty work for the Procyons, any number of things are possible. He may have been told to sabotage a ship. Even if he's aboard the *Prodigy,* one less ship will hardly make that much difference."

He sighed. "I'm afraid there's more to it than that."

She shook her head. "I don't understand."

Nason dropped his eyes to the desk, embarrassed, knowing his bibbets were turning dark. But there wasn't any point in trying to hide his fear. Setana would probably pick up on it, anyway. He braced himself, then looked her in the eye.

"If he's aboard and acting for the Procyons, he doesn't need to get to Eta Cass to do their dirty work. An antimatter explosion during a quantum slide would be enough to collapse the wormhole. They're traveling in formation. It would destroy all three ships."

Vaguely, Rieka felt the pillow's coolness beneath her head. She rolled and let her eyes open slowly. How long have I been asleep? she wondered groggily. So much to do, yet. We'll never be ready.

She focused on the wall chrono and grimaced. She hadn't been on deck in almost eight hours. There were only six hours left before they arrived at Eta Cass.

She sat up, rubbed her face, and was surprised to find she still had on her uniform. She distinctly remembered Triscoe undoing the rank bar and tugging her tunic off. Where was he? Confused, she got to her feet and went to the lav to wash.

Slowly, her mind cleared. She'd ignored the three-hour time limit he'd given her and was in engineering, talking to Bohm, when the first wave of heat hit. Standing there in her uniform, she'd felt Triscoe's fingers caress her neck and wander down her back. The Boo must have thought she'd lost her mind when she made a stupid excuse and practically ran from the room.

You promised to be good! she'd complained.

Only if you were, he reminded her. *You're wearing yourself out, Rieka. You'll collapse by the time you have to engage the Procyons.*

No, I won't.

A gallon of colan *might keep you awake, but you won't be thinking straight.*

Triscoe!

Trust me. It will only be for a few minutes. Go. Now.

And then, there were no more words. He'd used only the projection of his thoughts and imagination to make love to her from kilometers away, through a quantum unreality even a TC could not penetrate.

He'd let her get to her room, at least, before removing her clothes. She could recall almost every detail as if he'd been present. The odd, almost-real sensation when he'd loosened her rank bar. Her tunic sliding off. The soft coolness of his fingers, again, as they caressed her.

Once she'd overcome the shock of this nonphysical contact, Rieka decided she could reciprocate. She tried to imagine Triscoe's clothing as it came off, though it didn't work out the way she'd planned. The tunic bunched and got caught on his wrists. It made her especially angry when he laughed.

I'm not laughing at you, love, he assured her.

Then, what?

You've only known what it's like to Singlemind for three days. I've had the Gift all my life. It takes time to teach your mind how to do things. Let me do this.

So she did. And it was as good as if he'd actually been there. Better, because he'd been in her mind, knowing what she thought and felt. And she'd been in his, too. There were no assumptions. It was real. Immediate. And surprisingly satisfying.

And she'd slept for seven hours.

Shoving the memories aside, Rieka surveyed herself in the mirror. Other than the obvious things, like her face being washed and hair combed, she did actually *look* better. She was rested, now, and more relaxed.

Deciding she had a lot to learn about the Singlemind, Rieka left her quarters and went to the bridge, ready to catch up on what had been done in her absence.

The moment they'd emerged into real space, the *Prodigy* received a communication signal. Rieka knew the crew thought she had everything under control and ready for whatever might come. She and Midrin had tried hard to project that image. She only wished she could be as confident.

"Open the channel, Lenge," she told him.

"Robet wants in, too," Triscoe said without preamble. "I think we should have a short conference before we tell the Fleet we're here."

She nodded. "Open communications with the *Prospectus,* Lenge."

"As we speak, Captain," the post-Advanced Oph replied.

Robet's animated face appeared on the screen. Rieka looked from one man to the other. "You go first, Triscoe."

"We should split up," he said.

Robet frowned. "We'll be a bigger help to the cause if we head for the battle zone together. I make it about twelve million kilometers inside the orbit of Groot, thirteen degrees off our starboard. Are we agreed on that?"

Rieka checked the navigator's board. A definite energy disturbance resonated in the area he'd described. "Confirmed," she said, then looked up at Triscoe. "Why shouldn't we all go?"

"The Procyons may be expecting the *Prodigy,*" Triscoe replied. "We don't know what K'resh-va's plans were, but it seems reasonable to assume he'd come here as soon as the ship was his. Yillon saw no other area involved in a battle."

"Yillon?" Robet frowned strangely, and his bibbets darkened slightly.

Rieka smiled at him. "Yes, Yillon. But let's not get into that now, Robet. Just accept what Triscoe's saying. We'll brief you later."

He huffed. "I'm sure you will."

Rieka focused on Triscoe's section of the DGI. "So you think K'resh-va might have been expected to rendezvous—where?"

"At the mysterious base we've all decided exists somewhere," he answered. "His superiors would be aboard the base, not on a ship involved in combat. With the transit time lag, we don't even know if the battle is already over. It could be. We need to send off a communiqué right away—to Goresch on the *Merger*. But I think the *Prodigy* should attempt to find the base. If anything, K'resh-va would have orders to report as soon as he arrived. You can use that to your advantage."

"It makes sense," Rieka said with a shrug. "And once I find it, I suppose I should try to destroy it."

"The *Prodigy* is the only ship that can handle such a big job. But, let's wait and see what Goresch tells us. We have no information about what's happened here during the past four days. Our decisions have to be based upon facts."

"Agreed," Robet said.

"We should have some sort of news in a few hours."

"Then we wait," Rieka said. "Maybe he's already located the base. Maybe they've already got everything under control."

Three hours later, Rieka sat at the *Prospectus*'s conference table, kicking herself for being naive and hopelessly optimistic. The news had been so bad, Triscoe wouldn't even discuss anything over the DGI.

"Do you think Nason or Prime Admiral Hursh has declared an emergency and sent us some help, at least?" she asked.

"We can hope," Robet offered. "Captain Goresch dispatched his last communiqué before we left Dani. It arrived while we were still in transit. If the Prime Admiral declared a crisis, he would have alerted the entire Fleet. They could start arriving as early as tomorrow."

"To find what?" she wondered aloud. "Let me play the devil's advocate here for a minute. By the time help arrives, all of us could be dead—and the Procyons swarming all over Medoura."

"You didn't get command of the *Prodigy* with that kind of attitude, Rieka," Triscoe chided. "You've just got to—"

"No, you, Triscoe. *You* take a good look at reality!" she snapped. "We might be able to put up a good front on our own bridges, but out there"—she pointed in the direction of Medoura—"are 118 Procyon ships—out of a battalion of 140!

"Goresch has told us every one of them can disappear from DGI sensors the same way we can—just like the ship that set me up. Our people have been fighting for over four days and have only destroyed 22 ships. The Procyons are supported by an obviously immense base station that has also remained invisible, so far."

She shook her head and continued. "What do you expect me to say, Triscoe? 'Gee, that's not so bad. With the *Collateral* and *Stipend* out of commission, that leaves just 17 Procyon ships left for each Fleet ship. What *ever* shall I do after lunch?' "

"Sarcasm won't help."

"You're right. If you want me to take the *Prodigy* out of the fight, then you've got to wait until reinforcements arrive."

"We've got to stop the Procyons, *now*," insisted Robet.

Rieka looked at him. He'd said it with such confidence, she knew he wasn't kidding. "How, Robet?"

"They're chewing up Goresch and the others, piece by piece. Rieka, these ships are small," he began, using his hands to animate his words. "They must use a tremendous amount of energy when they create that light-bending field—just like our ships do. But by doing that, they can avoid our spheres. So, the obvious thing to do is quit feeding them."

"How?" Triscoe echoed.

"Take out the base station. If the little ships can't refuel, they'll go easy on power consumption. They'll *have* to travel visibly. Then, at least, we'll have something to aim at."

"That sounds good, in theory," Rieka agreed. "But Goresch has been here almost a week. He hasn't found the base. If it's invisible, too—"

"I don't think it is," Triscoe said, leaning forward. "They're supporting a huge number of ships in battle. They wouldn't dare expend the extra energy. I'll bet that Goresch hasn't found the base because he's been too busy to look for it."

Rieka digested the idea with a sigh. "Which is all the more reason I should take the *Prodigy* and go off after it," she grumbled. "I don't relish the thought of leaving the six of you to handle that many Procyons— especially when I can offer so much support."

"No one else could possibly get near the base," Triscoe said softly. "No other ship can do the necessary damage."

"You hope."

"Neither of us can go with you, or the Procyons will suspect something is not right," he added. "The decision to go is yours."

Rieka knew he was trying to take the pressure off. But it didn't work. The Procyons and Admiral Hursh had already made all the decisions. Nothing more remained, except for her to do her duty. She could see how the future wove itself from the past, and didn't envy Yillon his gift. It was a double-edged sword.

"What did you tell Captain Goresch?" she asked.

"Just that we'd arrived. I didn't say who, specifically, if you're wondering whether the Procyons are eavesdropping and might have guessed the *Prodigy* is no longer under K'resh-va's command. Swing out over, or under the solar plane—and I'll bet you find them."

Rieka looked him in the eye. She glanced at Robet, whose expectant expression made her want to smile. But when she returned her gaze to her husband, she knew there was no questioning what she had to do.

"I bet I will, too," she echoed. "But tell me one thing, Triscoe. This business about killing and the Singlemind—I don't follow it. You let K'resh-va off with a stun. But now, you expect me to destroy the base."

He raised a hand. "K'resh-va was personal, Rieka," he said, "This is a matter of survival for our entire civilization. Impersonal. There is a difference between defending yourself and murder. The Singlemind's influence is that we would both bear the guilt. Good or bad, we share everything."

She nodded, understanding. The desire to kill K'resh-va came out of anger and hate, not duty. Not because she'd promised to protect the rights of innocent citizens. But still, dead was dead, no matter which way you looked at it.

"All right. I'll take the *Prodigy* and hunt for the base. I'm not sure we can destroy it, but we'll do the best we can." She offered both of them a half smile to cover her uneasiness. Other than the relatively simple job of having to locate it, Rieka wondered what she would find once she did. What kind of defensive weapons did it have? Or did it need any? Considering the hundred-plus ships it sustained, most of which had the capacity to travel unseen, she could be walking into a massacre.

She felt Triscoe's eyes on her and glanced up. His strange, closed expression even without the Singlemind told her he was thinking the same thing.

Twenty-five

Triscoe watched, already knowing the futility of his optimism, as the antimatter shell sailed across the DGI. A few seconds later, no longer visible because of the distance, the magnetic shell decayed and the trace of antimatter contacted atoms floating in real space. The explosion only served to remind him he was wasting ammunition.

Every training exercise he'd had, every war game he'd fought, every drill he'd been put through, involved an enemy you could see. But the Procyon ships buzzed about like invisible insects. The panoply could not locate something unless it produced some form of energy. With a light-bender screen active, the ships emitted nothing. They appeared only long enough to fire a weapon. Then they vanished again, into the void of space.

Frustrated, Triscoe wondered how Goresch and his crew had tolerated such an onslaught for nearly a week. The Oph captain had explained his strategy of continual random movement in his first two-way communication. He'd set the *Merger* on a series of unpredictable course adjustments. As a moving target, he'd avoided being seriously damaged. Conversely, he'd been responsible for destroying only five Procyon ships in all that time. Triscoe had been at it for four hours himself, and felt the chaos of this strange standoff wearing on his nerves. It came down to little more than a battle of wills. Sooner or later, something would have to reverse the impasse.

He thumbed the intercom switch. "Commander Aarkmin, report."

The small screen on his console immediately lit with her pale face, the lines of concentration having deepened in the last hours. "We are still working, Captain," she said.

He stopped himself from snapping at her, and instead offered, "Why don't you brief me on the progress, so far?"

"Of course," she replied, nodding. "When Lieutenant Roddik proposed altering existing equipment to pick up high-gravity non-energy-producing bodies, we generated several theoretical schematics. The first seventeen of these were deemed unusable. We have begun an eighteenth—which appears to be a suitable candidate for our first working model."

"Excellent," Triscoe said. "I'm glad to hear we've got more than a theory. How long before we can test something?"

"Roddik estimates at least a day."

"A day," Triscoe repeated. "Can we cut the time?" He glanced up to see a small wedge-shaped vessel appear on the DGI and release a bolt of maser energy. Becker responded almost instantly, but by the time the sphere had been discharged, the little ship had already vanished. "How about having teams work in tandem?"

Aarkmin glanced away, then back to him. "The lieutenant's estimate is based on six teams working simultaneously, Captain. A day is the minimum—for preliminary testing. We don't even know if it will work."

He sighed. "Then let's get started on it, Aarkmin," he said.

"As we speak." She paused for a moment, then said, "Captain?"

"Yes."

"We could use the light-bender unit ourselves, and buy some time."

Triscoe nodded. "True, but then they'd simply concentrate their attack on the other ships. This way we're drawing fire away from the *Collateral, Merger,* and the others. That equipment also eats a lot of energy. We don't know how long we'll be here."

"Of course." She cut the communication and Triscoe looked at the Human manning the defense console. "Becker, let's try the IRB again."

The *Prodigy* had been en route to an anomalous energy source, her only lead in the search for the Procyon base, for two hours before the communication signal came in. As she and Midrin had planned, in the event this should happen, Rieka left the command chair, making sure to keep herself beyond the holo-camera's range.

From her place at the first officer's position, Midrin stood.

"Acknowledge it," Rieka said to Lenge. The Oph nodded and the DGI instantly lit with a Procyon high commander in full, shell-studded regalia. His wispy black hair had been combed straight back from a broad, bronze forehead. The slanted brow ridge overhung round, deep-set eyes and a thin, almost delicate nose. Several vertical nostril slits descended from the bridge to the upper lip, revealing the upper jaw's bumpy bone structure and stubby teeth. The lower jaw was wide across the base, giving him a triangle-shaped appearance. This was mirrored by the decorated shell design on the front of his black uniform.

Midrin glanced at her, and Rieka offered a nod of confidence. They had to get through this dialogue and that depended on Midrin being taken for her look-alike Procyon.

"Captain L'gith-la," the man said with a growl, "what are you doing aboard the *Prodigy*? Where is K'resh-va?"

The first hurdle cleared, Rieka watched as Midrin jutted out her chin and replied, "K'resh-va is below. There is some difficulty with the prisoners. When I offered the use of several of my crew to augment his, he suggested I return to the base on the *Prodigy,* as new plans may be in the making. Shall I call him to the bridge?"

"I will see him soon enough."

"Of course."

"Where is E'bid-va?"

"Attending the Heralds as well, sir," she answered.

Knowing Midrin hated falsehood, Rieka wondered how she managed to come up with a decent reply. She watched, fascinated, as Midrin said, "In his guise, it is easier to placate them."

The Procyon nodded. "Your estimated arrival time is thirty-one *reks.* I will meet with you both in the Hal Denk. K'din-va out."

The DGI's image returned to blackness dotted with stars, and Midrin sank into her chair, heaving a long sigh. Rieka couldn't help smiling. It had gone better than she'd hoped. The man, K'din-va, hadn't even asked anything specific. On the other hand, he'd been so agreeable, Rieka wondered if he might have already guessed things had not gone as planned.

"Good job, Midrin," she offered, keeping her concerns to herself. "He bought everything you told him."

"Impossible to tell, Captain," Midrin replied, throwing her a skeptical glance. "These people are clever."

Rieka took her seat. "Doesn't matter anyway. We'll be there in another twenty minutes. Clever or not, they're due for a dose of nonverbal communication." She switched on her console and called up spot reports from the engineering labs. "Let's do another systems check. I want to be sure our aim is perfect."

"Of course."

While Midrin spoke to the engineer in the weapons lab, Rieka looked at her bridge officer in charge of deploying them. He was a big Human with skin dark enough to remind her of her father. "Benala," she began, then waited for his broad face to turn to her, "let's just keep it loose and relaxed this time. I'll call the attack, you send the relay to deploy."

"Yes, Captain," he replied, the whites of his eyes nearly glowing against his dark cheeks.

"Lieutenant, I trust you to do your job. What I need from you is a little faith in my judgment."

He nodded, and she saw his shoulders relax. "I will do my best, ma'am."

He swiveled back to his board and she watched the tension return slowly. "Benala," she said softly, forcing him to look at her again. "I know you've never been in battle before. Not many officers have. That's what our training is for. It'll be all right. Your job is to give me your personal best—not some illusive idea of perfection. Let the Boos struggle with that; they're good at it."

She made him smile, then, and knew she'd struck a soft spot. "Yes, Captain," he said, "they sure are."

"Then all you have to remember is that this ship is the best thing they've ever produced."

"I will," he promised.

"They're ready in engineering," Midrin told her.

"Then let's get started. This is our dress rehearsal, everyone. Any bugs we come across now will have to be corrected by show time."

She looked at her navigator, a Vekyan named Hipidok. "Go ahead and give us the simulation again, Lieutenant. Benala, be ready to fire a volley of antimatter spheres at every target I call. When they're taken care of, you may have to use the IRB."

"I'm ready, ma'am," he said.

"Time, time, time," she muttered, looking at the chrono on the wall. The attack simulation had been completed five minutes ago. Everyone had performed fairly well, but she'd come down to the weapons lab, anyway. A backup firing unit panel had been burned and the board singed. Gorah stood by while she inspected the damage.

"Any trace of what might have done this?" she asked.

The Oph was agitated enough for the hair to stand up across both shoulders. She shook her head. The new jewelry in her ear tinkled pleasantly. "None, Captain. I checked this room just before the last simulation. Everything was in order then."

Rieka ground her teeth. This wasn't what they needed less than ten minutes before contact with an enemy of unknown strength. She sighed. "All right, Gorah, let's get someone down here to do a scan of what's left of this deck mount. If they come up with anything, let me know right away. Have someone stand by with a replacement for the backup unit. I want it installed as soon as that scan is done."

"I'll get on it immediately, Captain."

She nodded and let Gorah get to work. The Chute ride, although only seconds long, pushed her anxiety another notch farther. It gave her time to consider sabotage. Had they missed someone back at Dani? Was as Procyon still aboard, trying to take them apart any way they could? Or had the unit simply been defective and overheated on its own?

She didn't know. And it would only serve to destroy her concentration if she dwelled on it. The status of a backup system wouldn't affect their performance, and she couldn't let one burned-out piece of nonessential equipment bother her. If more systems were damaged, they would order an intruder search and have the medical super, Darid, scan everyone aboard. But for the moment, she did not want to jump to conclusions. Not now. Not yet.

The door to the bridge slid open, and Midrin's head snapped around. "It's incredible, Rieka," she said.

Her eyes swept to the DGI. "Good God, that's it?" she gasped, not bothering to wonder why Midrin had used her first name. The answer was in front of her, displayed in three dimensions. "It's—" She choked back the word "immense," and sputtered, "It's . . .

unbelievable. An asteroid with some kind of propulsion unit built into it. A helluva piece of engineering." Still thousands of kilometers away, the panoply had been able to magnify the structure enough to make out horizontal rows of lights running from end to end. She looked at her communications officer. "Lenge, get me Bohm."

"Right away."

By the time she got to her seat, the Boo had responded. "Captain?"

"Look at your DGI, Commander, panoply's main visible sensor."

"The base?" Bohm asked.

"Right. We're looking at"—she glanced at a screen she'd called up on her console—"your average asteroid. Looks like a conglomerate—made up of nickel-iron fragments and general rubble. Oblong. Six point three kilometers in length, two point eight-four in height. The maximum diameter is . . . near the center, at one point three kilometers. She's big."

"Yes," Bohm agreed. "But a conglomerate structure should simplify the equation. I will analyze the minimum impacts required for separation."

"You think we can break it up?"

"The factors are present."

"Let me know the minute you have something. Are we talking IRB?"

"To the crest of the hill, Captain," Bohm replied. "The Resonant Beam will weaken the network and factor the asteroid."

"That's what we're after," Rieka said with a smile. If Bohm could give her the exact spots to shoot at, and the IRB worked, the whole asteroid would crumble. The entire plan revolved around the word "if," but she refused to consider failure. "I'll need the points plotted and sent up here to Benala as soon as you get them figured."

"Affirmative."

When Bohm cut the communication to follow her

orders, Rieka called up another screen on her console. "Is this the panoply report on their defensive weaponry?"

Midrin nodded. "Even for an estimate, based upon what we can see from here, it seems like a lot," she said. "But adjusted for size, the numbers are really quite average."

They were now close enough for individual lights to be picked out along the asteroid's dark silhouette. Running lights from dozens of hangars revealed them to be about one-fourth capacity, based on the section she could see.

"Let's give them a show, Hipidok," she told the navigator. "We'll pretend K'resh-va wants to impress his superiors. There isn't a dock to fit a ship this size, anyway."

"Yes, Captain," the Vekyan said, clicking his talons twice.

"Circle us around to the far side—so the panoply can get a good look at what's over there, then swing back to the center point on this side, and match their speed and heading. We'll hold that position for thirty seconds."

She watched while he preprogrammed his console, then adjusted her attention to Benala. "At that time, Lieutenant, you will start your first volley of antimatter shells. I make seventeen ships in port on this side. Target the maser cannons along the top ridge with the other eleven shells. Got that?"

"Yes, ma'am."

By the time he'd answered her, Rieka sensed the DGI's shift as Hipidok angled them toward the asteroid's far side. Another set of space docks became visible, about a fourth of them occupied.

"Those ships will come after us almost immediately," she said, knowing the thought was echoing in every other crewman's head. "Be ready."

"We're being hailed, Captain," Lenge said.

"Ignore it for now," she told him, betting that

K'resh-va would want to make a grand entrance. The one called K'din-va would probably be more annoyed with them, rather than suspicious, at least for the moment.

The *Prodigy* circled aft, and Rieka saw Benala's board come to life with green lights. The entire volley of spheres was ready to deploy. He began feeding updates to the targeting computer as they slowed their relative speed and closed on the center area.

She leaned forward, gripping the arms of her seat, watching the DGI as Hipidok continued to reverse their forward speed. Individual lights appeared out of long, blurry streaks. After a moment, they could be tracked across the screen.

As they eased off to little more than a drift, Lenge said, "They're hailing again, Captain."

"Fire the entire volley, Benala. Now."

She saw his finger move to meet her order. "Firing all spheres, Captain," he said.

"Pull us out, Hipidok. Twenty thousand kilometers. As soon as you can make it."

"As we speak," he said.

She watched the antimatter touch off the almost-simultaneous explosions at the docks where ships twin to the *Vendikon* were berthed. Eight bolts of maser light erupted from the asteroid, even as they backed away.

"Screens on," she said. "Call up another complement of spheres. We'll be needing them in a few seconds."

"Second volley is ready, Captain," Benala replied.

Rieka glanced at him and smiled. He'd correctly second-guessed her next order. All he needed was something to concentrate on, other than his fear, and he'd be fine. Her attention slid back to the screen. "Why aren't they launching the other ships, Midrin? Have we caught them off guard?"

"Unknown, Captain. But it is possible they are not visible."

"Damn." Rieka slapped the arm of her chair. "I should have been ready for—"

She didn't get to finish her criticism. The DGI suddenly picked up six small ships off the starboard bow. A glance at the extended readout put eight more behind them. "Evasive maneuver, now Hipidok," she spit.

Their position, relative to the smaller ships, immediately shifted down. But the Procyon weapons had already been deployed. The insulation screen lit with a simultaneous overload and began to shimmer.

"Down to 30 percent effectiveness, Captain," Midrin told her. "One more attack like that and we're defenseless."

"Mmm." The Procyon ships were gone, probably regrouping for another coordinated attack. She had to do something to make them less vulnerable. But what? In space, they could be completely surrounded. There was nothing to hide behind, like the goal in zero-G speed volley. She could probably outrun the little ships, but that wouldn't serve any purpose.

The speed volley image bounced back in her mind. Yes! The two circumstances were similar, except that this was no game. "Retreat to the asteroid, Hipidok. Take us right in, as close as you can get. Benala, on the way in, I want you to knock off as many maser cannons as you can. We'll worry about those little mosquitoes once we only have to guard half the space around us."

"Mosquitoes, Captain?" Midrin asked.

"Pesky little bloodsucking insects, native to Earth," she said. "They make an irritating buzzing sound, but you really can't see them until they've landed on your skin."

Midrin nodded, but said nothing. The asteroid took up more and more of the DGI until the space around it disappeared. Rieka could see the fires burning in the holes left by the first series of antimatter spheres. She wondered if they were being fueled by the oxygen in the docks, or if the interior had been breached. Then they closed in so tightly nearly everything was beyond the DGI's perimeter.

"How many more cannons did you get?" she asked Benala.

"Another eight, Captain," he replied. "There may be one or two left, but I can't be sure."

"That'll do for now," she said. "Bulk up the screens on our vulnerable side. Ready all shells and pop them off as soon as those ships become visible. We might not hit anything, but we're damn sure going to try."

"Yes, ma'am," he said, then bent to his board to program her command.

She thumbed a toggle. "Bohm, have you got those coordinates yet?"

"Not all," the Boo voice replied.

"We need to get started, Commander. And double the backup power to the screens on the starboard side. We're going to need it."

She watched again, as the small ships appeared, and bolts of maser energy spewed from them. Benala sent spheres at them all. Only one made contact.

"Nice going, Lieutenant," she told him as their repulsion screen flickered but held. "Those things are like phantoms. I still can't figure how they do that. We've only just developed the light-bending technology."

"They have been in the Commonwealth before, Captain," Bohm's voice reverberated at her elbow.

"Yes. Five years ago. What do you imply? I'm not following your horizon," she replied.

"The Boo do not devise their technologies to the Nth in short factors."

Rieka felt her jaw drop at the idea some Boos must have joined the Procyon cause during or after the war. She snapped it shut before anyone could notice. "But . . . that's incredibly paradoxical to the inclination of Varannah."

"This is true," Bohm admitted. "Those without the flow have distorted the equation."

"Jeez," she muttered, swiping a glance at Midrin. Then another thought hit. "Tyrinne on the *Venture* picked up 'strange particles' near Aurie. She reported them to Captain Finot, and he tried to let on they were important. He was concerned about them, but couldn't say anything."

"You speak of particles from light-bender screens," Bohm gold her. "Yes. The factors dictate a new Pzekii. One who gave such information to the Procyon equation. Perhaps they needed this to move like the *vel* in the night."

Rieka raked her hand through her hair, not wanting to hear any more. Too much was happening too quickly to get a decent grip on anything. No wonder the Procyons figured they could take on the Commonwealth. She couldn't guess what it would take to bribe a Boo. With no clue as to when that happened, or how many were involved, she figured the Procyons must have thought *all* Boos would decide to join them.

Fortunately, though, from what Bohm had said, most of them thought the Commonwealth was the closest thing to reaching Varannah.

Rieka rubbed her face, filing that thought away for later analysis. She had to concentrate on the moment. Anything other than their need for survival and to take the base apart would have to wait.

"Bohm's sent up four fissure points, Captain," Midrin said. "We can strike only two of them from this side of the asteroid."

"Hipidok," she said.

He turned slightly, so that she could see almost half of his leathery face. "Captain?"

"Can you keep us this close to the asteroid, and simply slide us forward and back, up and down, along its face."

"It could be difficult—if the fires are still burning in the docks we hit."

She nodded and pulled herself straighter. "Granted. Then this is what we're going to do. You get us to the coordinates I'll relay from Bohm. Benala will keep the mosquitoes at bay."

Both he and the dark-skinned lieutenant at the weapons console nodded.

Rieka shifted her attention to the woman at her side. "Midrin, pulled the IRB up on your console and do the honors. They are *not* going to get the best of us. Not if we work as a team."

Ker Marteen paced the floor of an executive guest suite. He turned when he reached the door to the sleeping room and looked at the figure huddled over the computer desk.

"What are we doing, now?"

"She's engaged the Procyon base," Degahv answered, not looking up. "It's huge, Ker. She's insane to try to defeat it."

Irritably, Ker went to the desk and peered over his shoulder. He found it odd beyond belief that he'd believed the Human's brother, back at the ruined depot at Dani. "We've got to keep an eye on her," he'd said. "She's been influenced by the Procyons. If the Fleet allows her to command the *Prodigy,* unsupervised, it may be the end of the Commonwealth."

Ker knew he'd been receptive to Paden's suggestion simply because he didn't like his daughter-in-law. The *Prodigy* was an awesome ship. To let her go into battle without insurance that she wouldn't turn on her own people again seemed foolish. But, Ker realized, the way Setana had described the machine on Aurie, every person's integrity could be questioned.

Now he could not tell if his irritation was the result of his own bad judgment, or the fact that Paden Degahv, a Human, had orchestrated it. He did not belong here, outside the Medouran system. He did not belong on the *Prodigy.* And he certainly had no place in a battle with Procyons.

The computer screen revealed an asteroid studded with great rows of metal housing that looked like a

combination of shipping docks and habitats. Sections
of them were lit by flames, now flickering out as their
source of oxygen waned. He watched, entranced, as
they moved very close to the huge body of rock.

How could she do this? he wondered. She'll kill us
all. And for what purpose?

"Shouldn't we let them know we're aboard, now?"
he asked. "If, as you say, we need both to observe and
judge her behavior, it seems to me—"

"No, no," the Human interrupted. "They've been too
busy to realize we're here, Ker. That has been to our
advantage. We can't let them know yet. We have to
catch her doing something wrong. Then we'll step in as
authority figures."

Step in—and do what? Ker wanted to ask. But the
odd look the Human gave him prompted only a nod of
agreement. Damn him, this was no game. To give her
the chance to "do something wrong" might mean bil-
lions of lives.

He shook his head, realizing he'd been a fool to trust
this Human, and walked away. Perhaps he could just
leave. Go up to the bridge and announce himself. He
didn't see what good it would do, but at least it meant
being honest. The skulking about he'd done for the past
several days didn't sit well.

Perhaps Setana had been right, he thought, grudgingly reminding himself her ability at such things had
yet to be surpassed. She told him he had a role to play
in the future. All he could do was hope he'd cast himself correctly.

"Incredible," Paden said, bringing his attention back
to the present. "My sister is using a speed volley ploy. I
taught her that when she was eight years old."

Ker did some quick calculating and decided that
lying came easy to this man. When Rieka was eight, he
would have been close to twenty. Setana told him
Paden had spent much of his youth with his mother,
and Rieka with her father. What he said might be possible, but given their unhealthy relationship now, Ker

didn't think brother and sister had ever played speed volley, much less traded strategies.

That left him to wonder the same thing he had considered a thousand times since they'd left Dani—why had they really come?

"*Barnel* to the *Providence*," an impassioned voice rang out. "We require immediate assistance. Our screens have collapsed. Repeat. Immediate assistance."

"Tell them we're on our way, V'don," Triscoe said smoothly. "Lisk, set the course, maximum available speed."

Lisk nodded. "I make it four minutes to intercept, Captain," he said.

"Relay that, V'don. Request they have their people standing by to evacuate."

"As we speak," the lieutenant replied.

Triscoe hit the switch to signal the InterMAT chief and had to smile as Becker got off another three shots with the IRB. A valiant, if futile, attempt.

"Kyliss," the voice from the speaker announced.

"We've got incoming, Lieutenant," Triscoe said. "The *Barnel* is in trouble. Get your people ready to man all stations. We probably won't have to pull off the whole crew, but if no other ship is close enough, I won't be willing to wait."

"Understood, Captain," Kyliss said. "We'll be ready."

Triscoe rested his chin in his hand and looked down into the dregs of the latest cup of colan he'd consumed. How much longer could any of them hold out? Seven ships had now been whittled down to four. And of those four only the *Providence* and *Prospectus* were still in decent shape. If it hadn't been for the light-bender screens keeping the Procyons guessing, he wondered if they wouldn't now be faring as well as the *Barnel*.

The biggest shock, though, had been the ability of the tiny Procyon ships to appear invisible. He'd been prepared for it by Captain Goresch's communiqué, but actually to see them wink in and out was disconcerting at the very least. Their power consumption had to be enormous. He wondered how often they needed to refuel.

And the *Prodigy*? Had Rieka managed to find the base? If not, how long would she search for it before coming to the battle, herself? She was too far away for him to reach her mentally, and he did not have the time to set up a long-distance grid link. But the questions burned there, in the back of his mind. Unanswered.

"Coming up on the *Barnel,* Captain," Lisk announced.

Triscoe looked at the DGI in horror. The little Procyon ships were cutting into her hull as though they were slicing a dessert. "Becker, all twelve spheres, now!"

The Procyons did not have time to disappear before the onslaught. Nine were contacted by antimatter and disappeared, this time, for good. The other three broke off their attack and spun around. Becker picked off two of them. The third sailed safely past his last attempt with the IRB and disappeared as they watched.

Triscoe wanted to congratulate him. It was the finest piece of offense Becker had managed thus far. And the fact that he'd destroyed eleven ships in a few seconds, compared to one in the last seven hours, required celebration. But people were dying on the *Barnel*. They were close enough, now, to see the atmosphere escaping through the punctures in her hull.

"Kyliss, begin transporting. Get everyone off that ship as soon as possible."

He didn't wait for a reply, but flipped the switch to signal Dr. Twanabok.

"Medical," the Vekyan's voice replied.

"The *Barnel* has had its hull compromised, Vort. You may have a lot of incoming casualties. Get a team to each station."

"We're on our way," the doctor told him. Triscoe

could hear voices and the movement of equipment in the background before the signal cut.

He turned to Becker, who was busy watching his screen for Procyons. "Good job, Lieutenant," Triscoe said. "I suppose the trick is to catch them off guard."

"Well, sir," the Human replied, never taking his eyes off his console, "you might say that. But eleven of theirs for one of ours doesn't do much for my ego."

"Ego?" Triscoe repeated. "I don't recall ever hearing the term."

"That's a Human word—for our sense of self. Our value as a person, in our own mind."

"Hmm." Triscoe thought it over for a moment, then said, "Well, your ego for the crew of both the *Providence* and *Barnel* could not be greater at the moment, Becker. I wouldn't mind at all if you can do it again."

The lieutenant turned toward him, for just a second, looking confused. Then, the expression changed until he was wearing a broad grin. "I wouldn't mind that, either, Captain."

Kyliss's voice came through the speaker. "Sixty percent aboard, Captain Marteen. They're all in pretty good shape, so far. I'll let you know when Captain Velgo transports."

"Thank you, Kyliss." Triscoe left the channel open and leaned back in his chair. Now that he could afford a moment to reflect, he didn't want to. Rieka's determined face kept surfacing in his mind, and he couldn't suppress a disturbing sense that something had gone terribly wrong.

Twenty-six

"Are you sure this will work, Bohm?" Rieka asked. She watched as the IRB's bright blue beam cut into the asteroid. "This is the third one we've done. We're not picking up a thing. No movement, no increased internal heat from friction, nothing."

"Patience, Captain," the Boo advised from her post in the engineering pod. "The factors are present, the place of some things takes time. It is like Mohb when one tries to slide in a matrix. I have no wish to die, yet."

Rieka knew what she meant. They had discovered the energy source the Procyons used—a fission reactor housed within the asteroid's nickel-iron section. That chunk would have to come off whole, or there would be an explosion big enough to be seen, someday, by telescopes on Yadra.

"We don't have that kind of time," Rieka muttered. She could already see the influx of Procyon ships in her mind. They'd all be coming to protect the base. K'din-va had to have called for help. Estimating the amount of time it would take, given the distance between the asteroid and the rest of the Fleet, Rieka figured they had another half hour or so before reinforcements arrived.

As they stood now, things weren't too bad. The little Procyon ships risked hitting the base and doing further damage, if they attacked the *Prodigy*.

At least that strategy had worked.

"Let's try raising K'din-va again, Lenge," Rieka said to her communications officer.

She watched Lenge shrug to himself, and had to agree with his reluctance. They'd already tried three times.

"Nothing, Captain," he said. "They don't want to communicate."

She thought for a moment, then looked at Midrin. "Scaring them doesn't work," she began. "How about goading them?"

"It's worth a try," Midrin said.

She looked at Lenge, again. "Hail them and—let me make the overture, Lieutenant."

"Yes, ma'am."

He signaled her the channel was open. Rieka looked at the holocamera and smiled. "K'din-va, I'm Captain Rieka Degahv, the officer who destroyed the *Vendikon* not far from here a few weeks ago. To my left, you might recognize Commander Midrin Tohab. She was replaced by—L'gith-la, I believe—as my executive officer. Your operatives most likely reported to you that we were dead."

Lenge shook his head that the receiving end had not tried to complete the circuit, so she shifted to a more comfortable position in her chair and looked at the camera with amusement. "Well, you can see that the report was premature. Not only are we among the living, we command the *Prodigy*. Let me assure you, this ship is capable of all that you had hoped for." She paused, letting him absorb that little dig, then changed tactics.

"I'm Human, and therefore capable of showing mercy," she told the blank screen. "If you would like to plead for the lives of your people . . . I'm willing to listen."

She glanced at Lenge and nodded. He cut the signal. "We'll give him a few minutes to chew on that. Hipidok, if the asteroid is as ready to fall apart as Bohm thinks, I want an emergency retreat sequence plugged in and ready to go." She swiveled slightly. "And how are we doing with the repulsion screens, Benala?"

"Commander Bohm's still working on it, Captain.

But, doubled up, it's only 52 percent on the starboard side," he replied. "Backup system's up to 83, though."

"Good."

"Captain."

Rieka turned to Midrin, already disliking her tone. "What?" she asked softly.

"Lieutenant Gorah is reporting damage to the panoply backup array."

She sighed and called up the video intercom on her console. Gorah's black lips were curled in a curious frown. "Report, Lieutenant."

"This time there is no mistaking it, Captain," the Oph engineer told her. "I had a scan done immediately."

"And?"

"Circuits have been cut, panels melted. Looks like some kind of surgical tool was used. I've asked Dr. Darid to inventory her equipment. We should know something soon."

Rieka called up her mental image of Darid, the Oph who had been chosen as her medical superintendent. Dark coat and eyes, and a lavish ear jewel that had been studded with two diamonds indicating her children.

Darid had done a remarkable job on her split lip. With a staff of thirty in the Medical Arts Department, Rieka wondered if the Oph had managed to get to know many of them well in the last several days—well enough to determine if they were candidates for Procyon influence. There could be no other answer. Sabotage. Someone aboard must have slipped past their security checks.

She waited for what seemed like a long time, then her small screen split as the physician tapped into the channel.

"Captain," Darid began. "I was asked to inventory my surgical tools. Because Lieutenant Gorah requested it, I performed this task myself."

Rieka wanted to shake her and demand she get to the

point. But an Oph had to be handled a certain way. "And your findings, Doctor?"

"Two robotic arms have been dismantled, and the scalpels and energy packs removed," she replied. "They were full surgery units, capable of handling all body tissues, including bone."

Rieka held back an unhappy sigh. "Two of them. You're sure?"

"Affirmative, Captain. Everything else has been accounted for."

"Thank you, Darid," she said. "That's all for now." The screen cut back to Gorah, alone. "Midrin, send two non-Centauri security people to the medical suite. I want them posted at the door. No equipment is to leave for any reason unless authorized by the bridge."

"Yes, Captain."

To Gorah, Rieka said, "Can we repair the damage, Lieutenant?"

The Oph's ears flipped up, then down. "We aren't carrying many replacement parts. But we can patch most of it."

"Do that. In the meantime, I'll notify Kellik in security that you have authority to post his people to guard any other vulnerable equipment. Don't go overboard, Lieutenant."

"I understand," she replied with a nod.

Rieka flipped a toggle and Kellik's blue Boolian face appeared. "Kellik here, Captain."

"We may have a security problem," she told him, trying not to sound paranoid. "Gorah is going to need some of your people. Make sure none are Centauri and are sent in teams of two."

"I understand." His face dipped from the screen. "Security out."

When the screen went blank, Rieka rubbed her face, hoping to massage away the tension that had settled there like a painful mask. She sighed heavily, feeling the weight of the last hours like a tangible thing. "I'll never understand how these people—"

A shudder under her feet interrupted the thought, and Rieka's head snapped up. "What was that?"

Benala spoke up. "There are Procyon ships everywhere, Captain. Dozens of them! And they're all firing at us!"

"Return fire," she snapped. "All antimatter shells. Midrin, man the IRB." The DGI showed that all the ships were staying visible, a good sign, despite the number of them. There looked to be several dozen, the number growing by the minute. Obviously the reinforcements had orders to destroy the big ship despite the additional damage to the base. Rieka watched as the *Prodigy* returned fire and felt the odd shudder pass through the ship again.

"What *is* that?" she demanded.

"Debris from the asteroid is hitting our hull," Hipidok answered. "It's breaking up under all that incoming fire. They're cutting it apart!"

"Get us out of here, Lieutenant. Emergency retreat sequence, now." She'd underestimated the Procyons again. They were committing suicide to avoid admitting defeat.

"But the incoming fire," Benala insisted, "our screens can't handle—"

"Forget the screens," she said, trying to keep her voice even. "If the asteroid blows, the *Prodigy* goes with it."

Relaxed, eyes closed in the quiet room, Triscoe felt his head roll to the side. He snapped it back. He inhaled, eyes still closed, and shifted, pushing himself higher against the cushion. That nudged him a little farther toward consciousness. He raked his fingers through his hair and took another deep breath. A noise in his ear called to him.

He had been dreaming about a fight, one that he could not win, and, as he tried to open his eyes, Triscoe realized it had stayed with him as he woke. His body demanded sleep, while his mind insisted on being alert.

He yawned and stretched. The TC signal sounded in his ear, again.

"Marteen," he muttered. Tired eyes blinked, searching his quarters as to why he'd fallen asleep in a chair. He recalled taking a shower and having some food delivered to him. On the table were the remnants of a meal. He'd never made it to bed.

"Have you seen it?" Robet's voice asked.

Unable to fathom how his Aurian friend could still be alert after nearly thirty hours in the command chair, Triscoe pulled himself straighter, rubbing the stiffness from his neck. "Seen what, Robet?"

"Look at the closest DGI, and tell me what you think."

Triscoe swiveled in his seat. The unit in his quarters displayed the current image from the bridge. A bright spot blotted out the distant starfield.

"Have we got a spectral analysis, yet? A position?"

"Position looks to be about one point eight-five million kilometers above the solar plane, here, in the Eta Cass system. Spectral analysis is showing—"

"Never mind, you know what it is."

"It *was* the Procyon base," Robet corrected. "Have you heard from Rieka?"

Triscoe felt an unwelcome surge of panic and quickly sank back into the chair. The sudden Procyon retreat, an hour ago, had been the source of a lot of speculation. The general consensus was they'd gone off to refuel. He had hoped Rieka would have defeated the base by then. Now, staring at the immense explosion, he realized all he had left was hope.

"No," he said stupidly. She was too far away for the Singlemind. "I was trying to get some sleep. You're the first person to—how long has that thing been out there?"

"Only a couple of minutes," Robet offered. "But, she's all right, right? You'd know if something happened, wouldn't you?"

Stunned, Triscoe answered without thinking. "Yes."

"Well, at least that's something. And since we've got a reprieve from all the Procyons, for the moment, anyway, Goresch suggested we regroup on the *Merger* and do an inventory."

"Fine. I'll get back up to the bridge right away and contact him."

"See you in a bit, Tris." Robet's voice rang with a note of delight. "This is great. We're going to make it."

Triscoe wished he could absorb some of Robet's enthusiasm, but his thoughts centered around Rieka. Could she be dead? Yillon had only told him so much. He'd never linked with anyone other than his old mentor and Rieka. Communicating with his mother did not actually involve a true Singlemind. He had never known what to expect.

Still, he felt in his mind and his heart that she lived. The need to know, for sure, drove him to push his feet into his shoes and hurry to the bridge.

Captain Goresch, his coat turning a dusty color with age, licked his dark lips in a typical Oph gesture of satisfaction and looked across the table at Triscoe. "The *Prodigy* has done better than anticipated, Marteen," he began. "It was wise of you to suggest Degahv take on the base."

"Thank you." Triscoe nodded, accepting the captain's recognition. He glanced at Robet, then at Velgo from the now useless *Barnel,* and Tolidok from the likewise disabled *Collateral.* The *Stipend* still managed to stay in the fight, even with limited mobility. Her captain, Shreen, looked as tired as Triscoe felt. Bedish, of the *Wayfarer,* like Goresch, had managed to keep her ship in fair shape after five hellish days. Triscoe was convinced it had to do with the Ophs' incredible endurance.

"Moments ago, I received word from the *Prodigy,*" Goresch continued.

The captains, including Triscoe, perked up. "What did Rieka say?" Robet asked.

"Degahv expects to rendezvous within the hour," Goresch replied. "The report will be sent to each of you for study. To summarize, the Procyons used an asteroid, instead of constructing a vessel large enough to dock their fleet. The *Prodigy* had been in the process of carving up this asteroid when approximately three dozen ships appeared and attacked. Degahv barely reached a safe proximity when the fission reactor within the asteroid breached. The result is that explosion we've all seen."

"Then only the small ships are left," Robet noted happily. "They'll be visible and conserving power now that the base is gone."

Goresch raised a paw. "That is not a given, Captain DeVark," he said.

"What are you implying?" Triscoe asked.

"The evidence we have is that the Procyons will destroy a thing, rather than have it captured."

"You're saying they blew up the base on purpose? Rieka didn't destroy it?"

"Precisely," Goresch replied. "We need to speak to Captain Degahv directly. Even then, our questions may not be answered."

Bedish from the *Wayfarer* spoke up. "Then you are telling us that these Procyons on the small ships would be willing to destroy themselves in an effort to destroy us?"

"That is possible."

"In other words, we will not be taking prisoners," Triscoe offered. "The only question is—how will they do it? Ram us? Close in, invisibly, and perform some kind of self-destruct, hoping to rip a Fleet ship apart?"

"Something like that, I'd expect," Goresch answered. "We will know more when the *Prodigy* arrives. There is one other thing I would like to caution you about."

"What's that?" Robet wondered.

"Do not let your crews rejoice in this temporary suspension of battle. We may not have seen the worst of things, yet."

* * *

Rieka felt as though she were sitting on a wobbly fence. On the one hand, with the screens completely off-line, Bohm had managed to repair them to an efficiency rating of 82 percent. By the time Rieka needed them again, they could be almost as good as new.

On the other hand, a search for intruders continued. In the meantime, two guards had been ambushed, and the lines for antimatter-sphere production cut for an entire quadrant. The repair crew's report looked encouraging, though it would take hours to fix. She was certain, now. The intruders were Procyons who had somehow managed to evade the sweep at Dani.

Her TC clicked. "Degahv," she said, tapping her datapad while trying to eat a sandwich at her desk.

"Ensign Kona, Captain," the woman's voice began. "We've discovered evidence of someone living in the guest quarters."

"Evidence? Like what?"

"Personal items, clothing, beds that have been slept in."

"Which suite?"

"Executive, number six."

"Don't touch anything. I'll be right there." Shoving a final bit into her mouth, Rieka shut down her datapad and headed for the door.

Kona's description had been accurate. The personal items, toiletries, were evidence of male inhabitants—simple combs and no heavy cosmetics. The clothing in the closets were of two sizes. Again, presumably masculine garments. She didn't see any evidence of a large amount of body hair, and so assumed neither of them was Oph.

"Get a tech-pro with a DNA scanner in here right away," she told Kona, then clicked her TC and requested the chief of security.

"Kellik," the Boo voice translation reverberated in her head.

"We've discovered some evidence, Lieutenant. Notify your teams that we're looking for a pair of bipeds.

Probably Centauri, Human, or Aurian. One is tall, almost two meters, I'd estimate. The other is shorter. Apparently both male. I've got a tech-pro on the way, but knowing who these intruders are is not necessarily going to help us find them."

"Understood. The factors will be touched."

"I'll let you know the minute I have more," she said, hoping his people could understand the Boo well enough to follow his orders. They had been hard-pressed to pull together a new crew in a short period of time and she hadn't bothered worrying about her senior security officer. Now, Rieka wondered what other details she'd overlooked in her haste to leave Dani.

The tech-pro arrived and had begun to scan the lav area when Rieka's TC clicked again. "Degahv," she said.

"Ensign Eld, Captain," the voice said. "Lieutenant Kellik asked me to report to you. I'm in the corridor, lower level, quad C, engineering. There's an argument going on in the weapons lab. I don't know what to make of it."

Rieka frowned. "An argument? Who's on duty down there? Can you tell what it's about? How many people are involved?"

"The voices are muffled by the door," he answered. "But it's not a simple disagreement. It sounds like these people are going to kill each other."

"Stand by, Eld." The tech-pro was still working. Rieka wished she'd hurry. "Got everything you need, Ensign?" When the young woman nodded, Rieka touched her arm. "Then come with me."

With Kona bringing up the rear, Rieka spoke again to Eld. "Stay where you are, Ensign. Don't go in. We're on our way." She signaled her companions to follow her into the corridor and toward the nearest Chute.

After relaying the information to Kellik who dispatched an armed team, Rieka heard the scanner beep, signaling the conclusion of its DNA search. Standing before the open Chute door, she looked at the tech-pro. "Do we have an identification?"

"Sorry, Captain," the woman said, shaking her head. She turned the scanner for Rieka to see. It read: No match in Fleet personnel records. Two individuals. Male. Species identification: Centauri-Indran and Human.

"Damn," she muttered. The thought of a Human spy made her wince inwardly, but she kept her expression casual. "Good work, Ensign. Go back to the suite and try the living area, this time. Be sure to report to me or Commander Tohab when you get the results."

"Of course."

Rieka nodded at her, then stepped into the waiting Chute. She wasn't surprised when Kona followed. She'd always shown a lot of initiative.

As Rieka ordered the car to the lower engineering section, she said, "I didn't ask you to come, Kona. This could be dangerous."

"That's exactly why I'm here, Captain." Kona's eyes glittered jauntily. "We Humans certainly do have spunk, don't we?"

The Chute door opened. "Maybe just bad judgment," Rieka agreed quietly.

The security team arrived in the corridor, maitus in hand, and Rieka found herself gratified she was no longer on the receiving end of one. The voices were still audible beyond the door, but not as deafening as Eld had implied.

"They've stopped a couple of times," he offered. "I think there are four of them in there. One is very loud."

"You've done your job, Eld," she told him. "Now let the security people handle it." He nodded and stood back with Kona while she briefed the Oph team as to what she wanted them to do.

"Weapons ready, minimum stun. Don't fire unless they fire first—or unless I signal you. Then dose them all, no matter how many we find."

When they'd all nodded their understanding, Rieka set herself for the possibilities within the room. The weapons lab housed essential equipment, but lives were more important than circuitry. She clicked on her TC. "Degahv to Tohab."

"Yes, Captain," Midrin's voice answered.

"I'm at the weapons lab, the situation inside is unknown. Monitor my TC. If it looks like we're in trouble, do something."

"What?"

Rieka glanced at Eld. "I don't know, Midrin. Use your imagination." Leaving the channel open, she signaled the team leader. The squad entered quickly and took their places, fanning out behind anything that could serve as cover.

Aghast at the sight she saw through the moving bodies in front of her, Rieka stepped through the threshold. Three Centauris and a Human were in the room's far corner. Two of them, she recognized immediately.

Ker Marteen and her brother, Paden.

The prefect had been beaten and was on his knees, leaning against the wall. Paden stood over him, almost protectively, and she could see a bruise beginning to swell on his face. The two others, Centauris dressed in Fleet uniforms, had maitus. Their attention, now divided by their prisoners and the security squad, made Rieka think they were running scared. That made them more dangerous, but they might also be looking for options. With hostages involved, she knew her own choices were few.

One of them focused on her, but kept his aim on Paden. She saw him glance at her sleeve before staring her in the eye.

"You will do as I say, Captain, or these men die."

She instinctively knew he wasn't bluffing. The image of hate in K'resh-va's face echoed from his. The man was undoubtedly no more Centauri than she. Still, what could he possibly want? With the base destroyed, the Procyons could never conquer the Commonwealth. If he'd wanted his life spared, he could have played the part of a Centauri for a long, long time, with no one the wiser.

Paden's presence only created more questions. That bruise might have been put there for her benefit, Rieka decided cynically. Had he really been taken prisoner? When? And how had he and Ker Marteen gotten on the *Prodigy* in the first place?

The Procyon shifted his weight impatiently, aiming his maitu at Paden's chest.

"I will take no orders from you," Rieka told him evenly. "Nor will you, or your companion, there, harm either of those men."

"I hold the weapon, here, Captain," the man told her.

Rieka nodded. "True. But if you're counting, I've got you outgunned."

"You will not have me take a life," he answered.

Nodding, Rieka said, "You're right, of course." Always agree with the madman, she thought. It keeps him guessing. It keeps him from making decisions. "So, why don't you tell me what it is you want?"

"Hostages. These two will serve me."

"Not for very long." She pointed at Ker. His head hung from his shoulders, and his breathing seemed labored. "The Centauri needs medical attention. He won't last long enough to be of any use."

"He is the mate of the Indran Herald. She will pay anything," the Procyon told her.

Rieka took that to be a universal misunderstanding about Centauris. While they were generally known as intellects and pacifists, they weren't like any other bipeds in the Commonwealth when it came to things like perceiving deception. Setana, especially, could probably see a lie coming before it could be verbalized. That uniqueness had made them masters of the business world. And it stood to Marteen's advantage, now.

"I wouldn't be so sure," Rieka said, relaxing her stance. "The Herald can touch minds with her mate. She'd know if he was dead or not—even from a distance. And it probably wouldn't matter much, either way. Centauris are matriarchal. He's already given her the children she wanted. There's not much value to his life now."

Ker looked at her sharply, even through his pain, but she ignored him. Paden, she noticed, was gaping. She thought she might like a hologram of him wearing that expression, so he'd never be able to forget this moment.

The Procyon's tone took on a confused rhythm. "If that—is the case—his life has value—only to you. Is that not—correct?"

As long as she could keep him off-balance, Rieka figured she controlled the situation. If she could get close enough, she might even manage to disarm him. The security team could easily take care of his companion.

She eased forward a step. "Well, I'd sure be unhappy with you, if you killed him on my ship," she agreed. "But let's not worry about my problems. You're after hostages."

Another small step.

"That is correct."

Another inch forward.

He tensed. "Stop where you are—or I will kill him."

Rieka nodded and raised her hands. "Fine. No problem. I'm just trying to solve this dilemma to everyone's satisfaction."

The second Procyon said something, and the first barked a reply to him. Rieka knew if she could get them thinking independently, it would serve to her advantage.

"Look, uh,—" she said, taking another small step in his direction, "are you a *pakit*? I'd like to know who I'm talking to. It might make things easier."

"No." He pulled himself straighter and jutted out his lower jaw. She couldn't tell what he meant by that, until he said, "I am a triple-ranked *tilk* of the First Invasion Force. Tilk E'ton-la."

"I'll assume that's a higher rank than *pakit*."

"This is correct."

She nodded and eased forward, again. "I recognized that aura of authority, immediately, Tilk E'ton-la," she told him. "You remind me a great deal of K'resh-va."

Another small step.

His chin jutted further. The weapon was aimed at her. The second man's weapon wavered, as if he could not decide on a target.

Paden fidgeted. "Rieka, what are you doing?"

The second man's maitu locked on Paden, and he said something Rieka couldn't understand.

"Shut up, Paden," she warned. "You're on my ship now, and these men want to kill you. Let's try to keep you alive long enough to determine whether you're a traitor or not."

He huffed, but clamped his mouth shut.

"You know this one?" E'ton-la asked.

"Well enough," Rieka said, not wanting him to realize an advantage. She guessed the *tilk* was still a good three meters from her. Too far, if she wanted to disarm him without taking a big risk he'd shoot her.

He growled, brandishing the maitu at her. She raised a hand, again.

"I was just thinking, E'ton-la, that maybe you'd take me—in exchange for the Herald's mate. I think I'd have some value—to the Fleet, at least."

"Why would you do this?" he asked.

"I am Human," she explained with a shrug. "We don't like seeing people killed. It upsets us. When we're upset . . . we act irrationally." With her face purposely sober, she could only wonder what E'ton-la might be thinking. "I'm sure you wouldn't want to—upset me, Tilk E'ton-la. Would you?"

He watched her for a long moment. "I will accept this trade," he said finally.

"Good." Carefully, she walked around him to where her brother stood over Ker Marteen. Paden, glaring at her, stepped aside. She ignored him and knelt.

"Are you all right?"

Ker nodded. "I think I'll live," he whispered.

"Can you stand? I'll have the medical superintendent send someone down to pick you up, if you like."

"No." He put out his hand and she took it, bracing him as he pushed himself to his feet. She put one arm around his waist and turned them.

E'ton-la touched his maitu to her back.

"I will see him safely to one of my people, *Tilk,*" Rieka said.

"This is a ploy," the other Procyon growled. "Humans are notorious in the use of ploys."

"I will decide that," E'ton-la snapped.

Marteen leaned heavily on her. Rieka thought he might topple them both. Not bothering to wait for the Procyons to finish arguing, she helped him step forward. Kona, who had been standing beyond the open doorway, rushed to help. When she had a decent grip on Ker, Rieka let go. "Get him to the corridor and have medical come to pick him up."

Kona nodded, leading Ker away. He looked over his shoulder at Rieka, then left with the ensign.

Rieka turned and walked to Paden's side. She could tell she'd confused E'ton-la. He made strange movements with his jaw. His partner had begun to grumble. She looked past them to her security team leader, still waiting for her signal, and nodded. "Now that wasn't so hard, was it?"

With both Procyons' attention on her, the Oph across the room raised his maitu. At that moment, Paden shouted and shoved her hard, knocking her to the floor. Startled, the Procyons turned their weapons on him, but they were already going down, stunned.

E'ton-la's maitu discharged as he fell, hitting Paden in the side.

Rieka scrambled to her feet, trying to determine what had happened in the split second she'd lost her balance. Both Procyons and her brother were on the floor.

"Paden!"

The security squad rushed forward. They quickly

collected the discarded maitus and took the Procyons into custody.

"Paden!" She shook him. Unconscious, he felt like deadweight. "Lieutenant, how high was that maitu set?"

"Setting three, Captain."

She looked up at him. Setting three might not have been enough of a jolt to kill. But then, in some cases, it could do just that. "Take them to detention," she ordered, putting her fingers against Paden's neck, checking for a pulse. "Midrin, are you still with me?" she asked.

"Here, Captain," came the voice from her TC.

"Medical emergency in the weapons lab."

"Already on their way."

Had they tried to kill him to shut him up, she wondered, or had he not been part of their plot? Either way, he didn't deserve this. Triscoe had been right. Killing people was no answer.

Kneeling on the floor next to him, Rieka studied his face. It was like a stranger's. She had never known him, really. Certainly never loved him. But he had been her brother, and his death would be a loss. Perversely, she didn't think she'd miss him. She'd never really missed her mother, either, after the divorce. With a sigh, she remembered how Candace had promised Paden he'd one day fill his father's shoes as Earth Herald.

Rieka stood as the medical team arrived. An ensign scanned him, then looked at her. "Nothing we can do, Captain," she said. "Sorry."

Rieka nodded. Looking down at his face, she saw it had relaxed into a soft expression, far from the sneer he'd always used on her. "Good-bye, Paden," she said softly, then turned and walked away.

Twenty-seven

Rieka sat numbly at the foot of her bed. She'd just sent off a communiqué to Admiral Nason, updating him on the event at the base and what had happened on the trip to rejoin the Fleet. She wondered how he would take it, how the Commonwealth would react. But at the moment, it seemed removed. Unimportant. Right now, she only felt guilty because Paden's death might have been prevented.

The computer on her desk beeped, indicating Midrin needed her. She pushed herself up and walked to the other room. Flipping the toggle, she said, "Degahv."

The screen lit with Triscoe's face. "Rieka, what's happened?"

She froze for a second, startled that they'd already gotten close enough to the battle area for two-way communication. Triscoe's expression seemed strange, too. He looked both confused and sympathetic. Belatedly, she realized she couldn't sense him. Maybe they weren't near enough for that, yet.

"Paden's dead," she blurted. "He stowed away with your father. Two Procyons were aboard, too. They were trying to sabotage the *Prodigy*." She stopped, unsure of what she'd just said. "I confronted them and a Procyon shot him with a maitu. My medical super says the stun disrupted his neurological system. She couldn't do anything." When Triscoe said nothing, she offered, "I know I'm not making much sense . . . it's just such so absurd . . ."

His face had furled into a painful frown. "I'm sorry, love."

"Your father's all right," she said, trying to reassure him. "They'd beaten him, but no serious injuries. He's been asking to speak to you as soon as possible."

"I'll have him transported to the *Providence,* if you like."

"He's fine where he is, Tris," she said with a little shrug. "The experience seems to have taken the edge off his negative opinion of Humans."

His eyes seemed dark with worry. "I'd feel better if he were here."

She had to smile at that. He wanted to protect her from something that didn't exist anymore. After the ordeal he'd just been put through, Ker Marteen had lost a lot of his abrasiveness. "Whatever," she agreed quietly. "Maybe you should ask him what he wants to do."

"I will," Triscoe promised. "Captain Goresch is calling another conference as soon as you're within InterMAT range." He said nothing for a moment, then blurted. "Rieka, are you all right?"

"You can't tell?"

Triscoe offered her a sad smile. "You're like a blank wall. I'm feeling nothing from you. I wasn't even sure you were alive."

She shook her head. "I don't know how I feel," she admitted. "Paden's dead, and all I can think about is whether or not he'd been working for the Procyons. He was my *brother,* Triscoe. I don't even feel . . . like I've lost someone. I mean—with my father, my ship, Finot . . . every time something's been taken away forever, I've felt an emptiness. But with Paden—there's nothing."

He smiled, but it carried an edge of pain. "Perhaps you're still in shock. That would explain why I can't sense you."

"Maybe," she agreed, shifting uncomfortably in her chair. "I hope I get over it, soon."

He nodded, then gently asked, "So, you saw the *Venture* destroyed, too? How awful. I'm sorry."

Rieka frowned. She felt goose bumps on her arms, and knew something was not right. "No. I meant that figuratively." She shook her head. "I thought the Fleet must have—dealt with her."

The expression on Triscoe's face changed. She thought she picked up twinges of apprehension. "The *Venture* hasn't been seen since just after Robet and I arrived at the battle zone. I assumed it had returned to the base."

Reading the worry in his eyes, Rieka felt her muscles tense and a familiar pressure in her chest. "I don't think this is over yet, Triscoe."

"Coming through now, Captain Marteen," Kyliss told him.

Triscoe waited nervously outside the chamber in Station One, unsure of how to deal with his father. Rieka had said his ordeal had changed him, but Triscoe couldn't allow himself to accept that. He wasn't all that sure he wanted to see it for himself, either.

The chamber activated. He heard the soft pop that accompanied the travelers, and felt his jaw clench. Rieka smiled. Triscoe noted the bruise on his father's temple, as well as the odd gesture for her to exit first. She did, but went only to the doorway.

"Request permission to come aboard," she said formally.

He caught her eye. *And for much more than that,* he told her.

Verbally, she insisted.

Her look warned him to be serious. Unfortunately, he realized he was. "Granted," he answered, then stepped past Kyliss to perform the open-palmed Indran welcome on first Rieka, then his father.

"Are you all right?" he asked.

"I'll survive," Ker said stoically. "I've seen things I would never have believed, Triscoe. What Rieka did—"

430 Jan Clark

"Can we go somewhere and talk privately?" she asked.

"Of course." Triscoe looked at her again and realized she felt uncomfortable at the recognition his father had been about to bestow. He led them out of the station and back to his rooms. When they arrived, Ker immediately sat in a cushioned chair and heaved a long sigh.

"Darid warned you the InterMAT would be tiring, Ker," she said.

"Yes, I know," he grumbled. "Damned Oph doctor's always right."

Rieka laughed and shook her head.

Triscoe watched the exchange, fascinated. They'd both used one another's given names in companionable conversation. And Ker hadn't made a derogatory remark about Humans since he'd arrived. Remarkably, Triscoe realized he felt different, too. He didn't feel less than himself. They were simply three compatible adults.

Grabbing Rieka's hand, he led her to the sofa, then pulled her down with him, to sit. "Something profound has happened between you. I want to know."

He watched as Rieka looked at his father. Then, shrugging, she said, "I told you. We had a problem with Procyons. Ker was involved. Everything's fine."

"And you expect me to accept the abridged version?" he asked her. "There's no animosity in this room. That in itself requires an explanation."

Before Rieka could answer, his father raised a hand. "All right. Let's not have the two of you arguing."

Triscoe looked at him, and for the first time in as long as he could remember, his father's face was relaxed. He seemed to be in the midst of an inner peace. The fire in his eye was contentment, the spark in his voice, pleasure. "Then you tell me, Father."

Ker looked toward the DGI and his expression took on a faraway look. "Back at the Little One, I allowed your mother to believe I'd accepted Rieka. But I hadn't. Just before you shipped out, Paden Degahv paid me a visit. He wanted my help, he said. He convinced me that Rieka could still turn on the Commonwealth—it didn't take much persuasion, I'm now sorry to say. He felt that between the two of us, we could manage to force her to step down from command—if anything happened.

"The first few days, nothing. Then the *Prodigy*'s vital systems started going down. A backup unit burned out. Antimatter-sphere production was cut in an entire quadrant. Paden figured Rieka had done that. We'd decided to contact Tohab, when he suddenly got this strange notion to go down to the engineering labs. I didn't know why, but I went with him." He shrugged and ran his fingers across his forehead.

"I didn't realize who or what the Procyons were when they took us hostage. They were going to kill me, I'm sure," he said. "Just when I thought they'd actually do it, Rieka showed up with a security squad. She convinced them I had no value, dead, and traded herself—for me. After that . . . they killed Paden." He stopped and looked down at his lap. "The man only wanted what was best for the Commonwealth," he added quietly.

Triscoe looked at Rieka. Her face had gotten stony, as if she couldn't bear to hear the incident recounted. Sadness for her welled up and became a lump in his throat. Ker would be telling this tale for a long time to come. "How did you . . . get aboard the *Prodigy*, Father?" he asked, gently squeezing Rieka's hand.

"Paden sneaked us in with a group of suppliers a few hours before you left Dani. We didn't even know if there'd be a place to stay. Fortunately, on the *Prodigy* there are many places to go—if you don't want to be found."

"I've learned that the hard way," she mumbled.

Ker then looked up at her with such respect, Triscoe didn't know what to think. "She deserves every bit of trust the Prime Admiral has in her, son," he continued softly. "I suppose, once you've seen death at the hand of a true enemy, you begin to see things clearly."

"Everything will be fine, now," Rieka told them both. "We'll get Ker back to Indra as soon as possible. I've sent word to Setana to meet us there."

Triscoe sat back, watching them, not knowing what to think of the evolution of his family. They had both changed a great deal in the last few days, Rieka perhaps even more than his father.

He looked into eyes so like his own, and for the first time in as long as he could remember, did not cringe. "Would you mind if I spoke to Rieka, Father?"

"Of course not. I'll just—"

"You're fine, there," Triscoe said quickly, when Ker shifted his weight as if to get up. "We'll go in the other room." The older man relaxed into the cushions and waved them off.

As soon as the sleeping room door closed, she turned. "So, no one has seen the *Venture* for what— nearly two days?"

He nodded, wanting to do far more than simply caress her jaw. "Goresch's conference starts in a few minutes. I thought you might leave my father here, and we can go to the *Merger* together."

"That's fine," she answered. He didn't get the idea that she was ignoring him, so much as concentrating on something else.

"What are you thinking, Rieka?" he asked softly. "The *Venture* is not a threat. More Fleet ships should arrive in the next few hours."

"I know, Tris," she said, offering him a reluctant smile. "But something just doesn't feel right."

"You're still thinking about Paden."

"True, but I'm not obsessing over him. I'll never know for sure why he did what he did. I have to accept that." She caught his eye then, and Triscoe felt her tension like a jolt of electricity. "But the *Venture* is gone. That's a fact. The question is, where did she go? And why?"

* * *

Rieka soon found herself repeating her questions to the ten other captains seated around Goresch's conference table on the *Merger*.

A long silence followed, after which her Oph host offered, "Unknown. Why is this of such importance, Captain?"

"Think of it this way," she began, gesturing vaguely with a hand. "The Procyons had a huge number of ships. These ships were equipped with light-bender devices like the *Providence* and *Prospectus*. We know this because we've seen them wink in and out, and the enhanced fields left particle trails.

"Obviously, they've had contact with Boos. There is no mistaking the origins of this technology. Even my chief engineer has suggested as much. But when it comes down to it, they were just ships—all small. All alike. Anonymous."

She stopped and looked around at the faces of her comrades. There wasn't another Human among them, but they all listened to her, respecting her knowledge and her instinct. Something had changed, subtly, and for a moment, Rieka wondered whether it had happened to them, or to her.

"The asteroid supported about a hundred ships. Between our efforts and the base's destruction, there should be at least thirty ships left—depending upon whose numbers you use. They aren't on their way back across the void. We know that because they can't slide for great lengths of time, and even in a wormhole, it would take weeks to get to the nearest Procyon star. They didn't carry the power necessary for such voyages.

"We also know the *Venture* must be with them. No one's seen her in days. Have they regrouped somewhere? Gone off to plan an attack on Medoura or Groot—whose people might not be able to call for help until it's too late? Or is there another base out there?

One capable of supporting at least half the number of ships the first one did?"

She shook her head. "I don't know. But I do know that as long as the *Venture* is unaccounted for, this party isn't over."

Goresch nodded slowly. "I have many questions, myself, Captain," he agreed. "Are there any suggestions as to how we handle this situation?"

Bilik, a Vekyan in command of the *Currency,* said, "We came across the solar plane about two AUs from Eta Cass. My navigator made note of an anomaly, but we were too concerned about getting here to take the time to find out what it was."

"What kind of an anomaly?" Goresch asked.

"Heat energy."

"Heat energy," Rieka repeated. A strange feeling came over her, something indistinct, though familiar. A piece to the Procyon puzzle. She just needed to identify it, and figure out where it fit. "Where was this?"

Bilik shrugged, his chest heaving out, then in. "Between Groot and Medoura, I'm not sure of the exact position."

"Moving?" she asked.

"Yes, toward Eta Cass."

Rieka squinted her eyes shut. She slid her lip between her teeth and opened her mind to all possibilities. An anomaly, an asteroid, the Procyons, she thought to herself. Something is here, and it's so obvious I can't see it. And then, everything suddenly fell into place.

"Oh, no," she whispered. "Oh, God, we should have guessed." A tightness constricted her entire body. It seemed too impossible to believe. Quickly, she took herself through Commonwealth history to see if her theory made any sense.

The alliance had formed 204 years ago for economic purposes, but there had been other motivating forces involved. The Procyons had attacked a distant Centauri outpost on Marma, orbiting Delta Pavo. The Centauris, outraged at their loss, instigated the formation of a union among all the planets with whom they had commercial accounts. The five original planets, known as the Commonwealth, pooled their resources. The Boos then designed the Transit Fleet, enabling goods and news to travel quickly and efficiently.

Apparently, everyone assumed the Procyons were intimidated by a multiplanet alliance. And, since no one had direct contact with them until five years ago, it looked as if there were enough unpopulated planets beyond the Commonwealth to keep them happy.

But maybe they weren't happy. Maybe, they realized they were up against something too big to handle, all at once. What if they'd wanted to upset the balance of things?

The asteroid was the key.

Triscoe, seated next to her, touched her arm. "What are you thinking?"

"The asteroid. Maybe it wasn't an accident."

"Of course not," Goresch countered. "You said, yourself, the Procyons carved it up until the reactor—"

"No, I'm not talking about *that* asteroid. I mean the one that hit the Earth 188 years ago. Of course, Human technology was nothing much back then, but they called the asteroid—*an anomaly*. And it unbalanced the Commonwealth because the Centauris insisted on rendering aid—even though Earth had never made contact with extraterrestrials and had nothing to offer, commerce-wise."

"You're thinking the Procyons tried to take over the Earth by striking it with an asteroid?"

Triscoe's voice sounded incredulous, and she couldn't blame him. "Not take it over," she corrected. "Just unbalance the Commonwealth. Make them come to the aid of a helpless civilization—one that couldn't pay back the debt anytime soon. And it worked, but not exactly the way they anticipated.

"Anyway, that doesn't matter now," she said, looking first at him, then Goresch. "What matters is if they try it again. If that 'thing' Bilik's navigator found is really another Procyon asteroid on a collision course with Medoura, every being on that planet is at risk."

"Are you recommending we investigate?" Goresch asked.

Rieka looked at him, knowing the Oph would take her word on what they should do. "There certainly isn't any point waiting for them to come back here. We've got too many ships now. Why bother with a suicide mission that won't accomplish anything—when you have the option of one that does?"

Seated in the command chair, Rieka sipped her *colan* and stared at the DGI, willing the ship to go faster. The notion was little more than fantasy, the laws of the universe could not be altered in real space. But she sat there wishing it anyway, knowing they might already be too late.

Bohm had conferred with the other engineers and decided that, if the telemetry the *Currency* had picked up was accurate, the asteroid would hit Medoura. If it made a few minor course adjustments in another hour or so, it could easily target a major metropolis.

Though it loomed in the forefront of her mind, Rieka couldn't accept the fact the Fleet might be too late. Goresch had already send word to Medoura, warning them of the impending disaster. Maybe, she thought, that would be something. But, if an asteroid is about to crash into your world, where do you hide? Where do you run?

The DGI blurred as Lenge accepted an incoming transmission. Goresch's furry gray face appeared. "It looks as though your theory is correct, Captain," he said. "I am eight minutes ahead of you, and my panoply is now picking up evidence of life on the asteroid, as well as particle emissions in its wake."

She nodded. "And the *Venture*?"

"Gone, apparently. Perhaps it returned to the Pro-

cyon star. It was the only ship in their possession that
could make the trip."

She'd already thought of that. Another loose end.
Paden, and the *Venture*. They were like black holes in
her mind, sucking away all her attention, the answers
never to be known. She told herself to be glad of what
she'd gained in the last few weeks. Things could have
been a lot worse.

"My position in the assault has been plotted," she
told him. "I'll be ready when you give the word."

"Keep your screens up at all times," he warned. "The
smaller ships may be nearby."

Rieka smiled. "Thank you for the warning, Goresch.
Even the *Prodigy* is susceptible. We've already learned
that lesson."

The Oph snorted, and the DGI returned to the
starfield beyond Eta Cass. Medoura and the asteroid
were not yet visible. Neither was any other Fleet ship.

"Benala, keep your eye out for the Procyons.
They've probably drained every bit of power from the
second base to try to strike at us one last time."

"Screens are ready," he replied. "Shells are ready.
IRB is available on both Commander Tohab's and my
board."

"Good." She smiled at his back, then glanced sideways at Midrin. Her executive officer nodded, indicating that she'd also seen the improvements in his
demeanor. A little experience had forged him into a
valuable bridge officer. Surviving an ordeal together
had molded them into a coherent unit.

Restlessly, she drummed her fingers on the arm of
her chair. "How much longer before we catch up to it,
Hipidok?"

"Just under an hour, Captain," the helmsman replied.

Rieka called up Bohm's engineering report and read
through it twice. She then requested panoply records
for the last ninety minutes, and frowned at how big a
lead the asteroid still had. Fortunately, though, they
had begun to receive the same information Goresch

had already given her. At least they'd gained a few
minutes on the thing.

With an impatient sigh, she turned to Midrin. "Page
me if I'm needed. I'll be in my quarters."

"Yes, Captain," Midrin replied, giving her a curious look.

The Chute brought her within a few steps of her
door. She entered the living area and sank into the
chair at the computer desk. Activating her datapad,
Rieka took herself back through Earth history, trying to
pinpoint how the Collision had been recorded—and
how the asteroid had been discovered.

Nothing seemed to make any sense. According to
astronomers of the time, the thing hadn't come from
the asteroid belt. Those same experts had agreed that it
wasn't one of several large bodies known to cross
Earth's orbit. It wasn't a comet, or comet fragment.
They'd called it a mystery, an anomaly—a huge chunk
of rock that had come out of nowhere.

And now another one, though no longer mysterious
but equally lethal, headed straight for Medoura. Coincidence? She didn't think so. But if the Procyons had
used Earth as a lever to weaken the Commonwealth all
those years ago, it could never be proved.

She had to smile at their oversight and the fact that
history could repeat itself. The one thing the Procyons
hadn't counted on, had never been able to understand,
was the tenacity of the Human spirit.

She remembered reading the letter her great-
great-grandfather had written to the Centauris once
they had made themselves and the Commonwealth
known to Earth. An astronomer, and one of the first
Humans to be in contact with a sentient race, Peter
Degahv had made history. He'd requested aid without
begging and promised that Earth, if it ever recovered
from the Collision, would pay back the favor. Little did
he know that guarantee would be upheld by his own
progeny.

Rieka turned and looked at her DGI. The Earth

rotated slowly against a sea of stars. Traditionally, the position of Earth Herald was handed down within the family. With old Peter taking the initial job, it had been an honored responsibility along his bloodline for nearly two centuries. If the existing Herald died or chose to retire, as Uncle Alexi had, an election was held among those eligible for the post. Paden, she knew, had planned to claim what he called "his birthright." He'd already begun to campaign for next year's election. Fortunately, several cousins were available to challenge him. Now the ballot would not carry his name.

She thought of her father. He'd trained for the Herald's seat all his life but occupied it only ten years. How sad he never got to see the Earth as it was today, ready to be rededicated to the Commonwealth. Able to support a civilization and enter the interplanetary marketplace. He would be so proud, she thought. He would show everyone the honor it is to be Human.

Frowning, Rieka sighed. It would be the hardest thing she'd ever had to do.

Rieka? Is something wrong?

She felt the warmth of Triscoe's nonexistent greeting, and smiled. *No, I've been thinking.*

About what?

Duty. Responsibility. She smiled her herself. *The usual.*

A sense of Triscoe's compassion preceded his next thought. *You've already accomplished a great deal. I should think you would be ready to take some time off. I'm sure Admiral Nason would be willing to grant you leave.*

She raked a hand through her hair, unsure if she wanted to tell him in Singlemind, or in person. *It's more than that, Tris. I think . . . think I have to resign from the Fleet.*

What? The question surged at her with confusion, shock, and bewilderment. She thought she even felt a color, bright pink.

And . . . something else, too. Rieka hesitated only a moment. She knew now what had to be done. As long as Triscoe stood by her, she could accomplish anything. The hard part would be convincing him that her decision was for the best. Maybe, once they got back to Indra, Yillon could help.

I . . . want to have a baby.

She could almost feel him flinch. *You know we can't,* he countered. There was an undercurrent of pain associated with the thought, and the sense of color deepened. *We've already talked about this, Rieka.*

I know. We *can't,* she agreed, keeping her thoughts gentle. *That doesn't mean I can't. We will just have to work it out, somehow.*

And you've decided all of this in the last two hours? he asked, still incredulous.

Actually, in the last five minutes.

Confused, he said nothing for a long moment. *What's happened? What is wrong?*

Nothing. I've just realized— Her TC clicked on. "Degahv."

"You're needed on the bridge, Captain," Midrin told her.

"On my way." *We'll talk about this later, Tris,* she offered, heading for the door.

We will, he promised. *We most certainly will.*

The bridge buzzed with quiet activity as her crew prepared themselves for the coming event. The asteroid, still invisible in the darkness, continued to surge toward Medoura, now a tiny dark dot against the growing light of Eta Cass. She took her seat and called up a tactical screen on her console.

"We're in line with it at the moment," Midrin advised her. "Goresch will signal us to move into position."

"Are we ready, Hipidok?" she asked.

"Yes, Captain. The course is plotted and on standby."

Rieka tensed, hoping no one would pick up on it. They

were about to do more than save a world, here. They were also about to annihilate quite probably hundreds of Procyons. Provoked or not. Noble cause or not. Living beings were about to die—despite the fact they chose to commit suicide by impacting Medoura. She didn't know if she could feel good about that.

Then, the first Procyon ship appeared out of nowhere.

"Screens," she ordered. "Fire off a sphere."

"Activated," Midrin said.

"I'm on it," Benala told her.

The sphere deployed before he finished speaking. They watched the little ship fire and wink out before it could be hit.

"A single maser strike," Hipidok reported. "Screens are undamaged and functioning at 91 percent repulsion."

Rieka watched her tactical display and frowned. "Desperation leads people to do extreme things. Things no rational individual would do," she murmured. Then, she told them all, "Be ready for anything."

Lenge sat straighter. "We're receiving the signal from the *Merger,* Captain. All ships to their positions."

"Then let's do it. Hipidok, punch in that course."

"As we speak," he replied.

"Lenge, let Goresch know we've been attacked."

"Yes, ma'am."

The starfield changed subtly and soon the dark spot against the light of Eta Cass could no longer be seen.

"We should be coming up on the asteroid in five minutes, forty-two seconds, mark," Hipidok announced.

Rieka sat forward in her seat. "Be ready for more incoming fire," she warned. "The Procyons have decided they want to die—they'll take as many of us with them as they can."

"Understood," Benala replied. Rieka watched as he reset his firing sequence. She marveled at the rate at which his defense expertise had evolved. It would be difficult to leave all this, she knew. But then, nothing ever stayed the same.

"Two more, Captain," Benala announced.

"Fire spheres," she said, then pounded the arm of her chair when the Procyons disappeared. "Damn, they're fast."

Hipidok made a strange noise of discontent, something like a grunt, but not quite. "They managed a simultaneous hit," he said. "Our repulsion effect is down 28 percent."

Rieka's jaw tightened as she flipped the toggle on her console. "Bohm?"

"Here, Captain."

"Can we do anything about boosting the screen?"

"The factors are damaged," the Boo announced. "We can do nothing while they are in use."

Rieka already knew that, but it unsettled her to have it confirmed. "Ready your people for a hull breach," she said as matter-of-factly as she could. In her mind's eye, she saw the little ships punching holes in the *Prodigy*'s hull. She'd have to think of something to keep them at bay.

"Captain?"

"You heard me. Degahv, out."

"A hull breach?" Midrin repeated. "But our screens are only down 20—"

"Procyons dead ahead," Benala said.

"Fire, Lieutenant."

Again, it did no good. They disappeared before the sphere could make contact. "Let's try the IRB next time," she advised Midrin, after checking that the screen's effectiveness had been reduced another 8 percent.

"Two more minutes before we reach optimum position to strike the asteroid," Hipidok said. "The other Fleet ships are nearing their designated coordinates as well."

"Good. Go ahead and preprogram an emergency retreat again, Lieutenant. I don't want to be caught anywhere near an explosion like the last one."

"As we speak," he said.

The asteroid could not be seen on the DGI. Rieka tapped the controls and set them for infrared detection. Immediately, a white dot appeared between them and the large, cool object designated as Medoura. Her breath caught. It was far too close to the planet. They couldn't just break it up. Antimatter annihilation was the only answer.

"There they are," she announced, as two more hot spots appeared. "Procyon vessels. Line them up and fire."

The IRB made contact, but they couldn't tell if any damage had been done before it disappeared. Their own screens were down another 12 percent. Rieka drummed her fingers. There had to be something they could do to improve the dwindling odds.

"Benala, are the appearances of those ships in any way predictable?"

"Um," he began, tapping the keypads of his console, "not quite. Less than one minute apart."

She frowned. "Too big a margin for an anticipated counterattack."

"Coming up on a minute to—Captain!" Midrin exclaimed.

Rieka saw it, and the shock only spurred her to react faster. A Procyon ship had appeared within their insulation screen. "Now, Midrin," she shouted, even as her first officer punched at the controls. Benala prudently kept his hands off the deploy switch. An antimatter explosion within the screen would destroy the *Prodigy* in less than a heartbeat.

The IRB sliced through the Procyon ship's hull. A split second later, it was too close for the DGI to pick up. And a moment after that they were flung from their seats by the impact.

Rieka scrambled back into the command chair, barely watching what went on around her. Her fingers danced over her console, calling up damage reports from various levels. Those that were conspicuously absent were the ones that worried her.

"We're in position now," Hipidok reported. "Holding at 150,000 kilometers from the asteroid."

Rieka looked up and saw it as a huge white blur on the DGI. People were dying on the decks below, and she couldn't do much to help them until Medoura was safe.

Gnawing her lip, she quickly reset the controls for visible light. The rock before them looked remarkably like the one they'd seen destroyed only a few AUs away. The planet beyond took up nearly all the remaining screen. Were they too late?

"Tell Goresch we've arrived, Lieutenant," she told Lenge. "Have damage control teams sent to deck three, quadrants one and four.

"Message sent," he answered. "Damage control teams are on their way." A moment later, he said, "We have a go in eight seconds."

"Ready a full volley," she told Benala. "Take aim on any fissure you can find. Hipidok, keep your claw on that button. We won't leave until we know she's going to blow."

"Understood," he said. "And . . . four . . . three . . . two . . . one."

"Deploy all spheres."

"They're away, Captain."

Bohm's voice came through the speaker near her arm. "We must remain still in the light, Captain."

The air caught in her throat. Remain still? "Why?"

"There is extensive damage to the support grid. The little ship has been caught in our gravity well."

Rieka held back a gasp. "We can't, Bohm. The asteroid's about to blow. Our screens aren't going to protect us. We *have* to move. Get your people up to the main hull, immediately."

The Boo made a strange noise with her kroi. "I will see the darkness before Varannah," she said cryptically, then cut the link.

Rieka looked at Hipidok. "Retreat sequence now,

Lieutenant. If we start vibrating, slow us down. But we've got to get away from the blast zone."

"As we speak," the Vekyan replied. The image on the DGI altered immediately. Eta Cass slid quickly from view.

Rieka called up the aft picture. "Give me a distance every hundred thousand kilometers."

"We're coming up on two hundred, now," Hipidok reported. "I'm slowing our forward speed. Bohm is reporting excessive vibration."

She tensed but said nothing. At least there were no more Procyon ships in their path. She wondered how Triscoe and the others had fared. She could sense him faintly, both nervous and excited.

And then the bridge was bathed in white light. Rieka covered her eyes, knowing the DGI's safeguards would shut it down before an overload. A moment later, she looked up to see the image had automatically gone back to the forward view.

"Position, Hipidok?"

"Two hundred thirty-six thousand kilometers from the asteroid's last location." He leaned to check something on his board. "It's gone, Captain," he said. "Medoura might have to deal with a few outer atmosphere problems for a while. But no major impacts."

"We'll need to make orbit around Medoura, Lieutenant," she told him, consciously ignoring the sense of euphoria that filled the bridge.

"Yes, ma'am."

"Lenge, get me the *Providence*."

"As we speak," he replied. "Captain Goresch is sending a congratulatory message and requests status reports from all ships."

"Comply with that, and request immediate assistance from anyone near us," she ordered, knowing Triscoe would come, no matter how far.

She was surprised as Robet's image sprang from the DGI. "Congratulations! We did it!" Then, after he'd gotten a good look at her, he asked, "What happened? Is anyone hurt?"

"Yes," she answered stoically, not wanting her crew to know how awful she felt. "We've suffered a severe impact. What's your ETA to our position?"

Robet's expression sobered. His bibbets darkened slightly. "Four minutes," he said. "We're on our way."

"Thank you, Robet."

"No need. I owe you a lot more than that. Everyone does." Then the screen abruptly went blank.

While she tried to fathom Robet's comment, Triscoe's face appeared. Instantly, Rieka knew he'd been spared from an attack by the Procyons. There must not have been enough of them left to strike at every Fleet ship. A small consolation.

She nodded a greeting, unable at the moment, to produce a smile. "No one ever bothered to consider that the *Prodigy* is big enough for a Procyon ship to materialize *inside* her screen," she said, hoping her voice didn't betray her worst fears. "We've got major structural damage. I'm going down to survey it, now." She pushed herself out of the command chair. "If you're close, I could use a hand."

"We're already en route," he told her. "I'm sure you'll have everything under control when we arrive."

She had crossed in front of Midrin, but turned at his remark. Wearing a faint smile, Rieka lifted her brows, surprised at both the admission, and the fact that it came out sounding like a compliment.

She looked directly into his eyes. *Thank you, Triscoe.* "I'll expect you soon. *Prodigy* out."

She turned to Midrin. "Make sure Hipidok doesn't shake us apart, and keep me updated on the casualties. We'll probably need to take gravity off-line before this is over."

"Yes, Captain."

Rieka stopped at the door. As she stood quietly, surveying her comrades, an unbidden sense of pride nearly overwhelmed her. "You're the best crew I've ever had," she told them. "Good job."

One by one, they looked at her. She smiled, saluted them, then said, "Back to work."

As she strode to the Chute, Rieka heard a soft pop and turned to see Triscoe standing behind her. "Permission to come aboard, Captain?" he asked.

The dimple was there, flaunting itself on his left cheek. "Granted. So long as you're here to help me, not distract me. Did you get a look at the pod?"

"It's still intact," he replied, sobering. "And Robet's only a minute or two away."

He stepped up to her shoulder, and they turned to enter the Chute. Rieka ordered it to the lower level. "Good, then get your people coordinated and we'll start evacuating the injured."

"I left Aarkmin in charge of that," he answered. "Right now, I want an explanation."

"For what?"

"You don't remember our earlier conversation? Your resignation? Motherhood?"

"Oh, that." She smiled crookedly. "Hasn't Yillon already predicted it?"

"Possibly. I don't know."

The door opened to the pungent smell of chlorine and smoke. Rieka shrugged and stepped into the chaos. "Sorry, Tris. That conversation will just have to wait."